DRIVE TIME

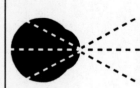

This Large Print Book carries the
Seal of Approval of N.A.V.H.

A CHARLOTTE McNALLY MYSTERY

DRIVE TIME

HANK PHILLIPPI RYAN

KENNEBEC LARGE PRINT
A part of Gale, Cengage Learning

GALE
CENGAGE Learning

Detroit • New York • San Francisco • New Haven, Conn • Waterville, Maine • London

GALE
CENGAGE Learning

Copyright © 2010 by Hank Phillippi Ryan.
Kennebec Large Print, a part of Gale, Cengage Learning.

Kennebec Large Print® Superior Collection.
The text of this Large Print edition is unabridged.
Other aspects of the book may vary from the original edition.
Set in 16 pt. Plantin.

LIBRARY OF CONGRESS CATALOGING-IN-PUBLICATION DATA

Ryan, Hank Phillippi.
   Drive time : a Charlotte McNally novel / by Hank Phillippi Ryan.
     p. cm. — (Kennebec Large Print superior collection)
     ISBN-13: 978-1-4104-3020-5 (paperback)
     ISBN-10: 1-4104-3020-0 (paperback)
     1. McNally, Charlotte (Fictitious character)—Fiction. 2. Women television journalists—Fiction. 3. Investigative reporting—Fiction. 4. Secrecy—Fiction. 5. Extortion—Fiction. 6. Large type books. I. Title.
PS3618.Y333D75 2011
813'.6—dc22   2010040064

Published in 2011 by arrangement with Harlequin Books S.A.

"Only enemies speak the truth;
friends and lovers lie endlessly,
caught in the web of duty."
— Stephen King

CHAPTER ONE

I can't wait to tell our secret. And I'll get to do it if we're not all killed first.

We're ten minutes away from Channel 3 when suddenly the Boston skyline disappears. Murky slush splatters across our windshield, kicked up from the tires of the rattletrap big rig that just swerved in front of us on the snow-slick highway. Eighteen wheels of obstacle, stubbornly obeying the Massachusetts Turnpike speed limit.

I brace myself once again. During this afternoon's teeth-clenching, bone-rattling, knuckle-whitening drive, I've learned how J.T. feels about speed limits.

"Fifty-five is for cowards!" he mutters. My new photographer powers our unmarked car into the passing lane, sloshing what's left of my coffee and almost throwing me across the backseat. Franklin, seemingly oblivious to our icy peril, is in the front seat clicking on his newest phone gizmo. As usual these days, my producer's deep into texting.

"Thanks, I'm fine back here," I call out, blotting the milky spill from my just dry-cleaned black coat. I don't even attempt to keep the sarcasm out of my voice. J.T. Shaw may be a hotshot when it comes to news video, but he apparently learned his driving skills chasing headlines in the network's Middle East Bureau. Now, even though he's back stateside shooting my investigative stories, he still thinks he's driving in Beirut. Where they don't have ice. Or speed limits.

Eight minutes away from Channel 3. Eight minutes away from the rest of my life. I hope I make it.

I look at the still-unfamiliar emerald-cut diamond on my third finger, left hand. Even in the fading winter light, it glistens, catching the January sunset, fire in the center. I'm strapped into the backseat of a death-trap news car, but memories still spark the beginnings of a smile. Josh handing me the heart-stoppingly iconic robin's-egg-blue box. The creak of the tiny hinges as I opened it. The twinkle, the love, the passion in his hazel eyes as Josh slipped the glittering surprise onto my finger. Charlotte McNally, soon-to-be married lady. *The family of investigative reporter Charlotte Ann Mc-*

8

Nally, age forty-seven, of Boston, announces her engagement to Bexter Academy professor Joshua Ives Gelston, fifty-two, of Brookline . . .

"Charlotte! Get the license number!"

Snapped out of my bliss by the squeal of brakes, I look up to see Franklin twisted over the front seat, pointing out the back window. And then I hear a skid. Metal on metal. A horn blaring. Then another one. Then silence.

"It looks like a — blue? Black? What kind of car?" Franklin's squinting through his newest pair of eyeglasses, these rimless, almost invisible. He's jabbing a finger toward the highway behind us. We're going at least seventy now, speeding away from whatever he's looking at. "Over there, across the Pike. Right lane."

I follow his finger, unsnapping my seat belt and yanking my coat so I can face backward on the seat, knees tucked under me. My turn to squint. "The guy in the — ? I think it's blue. Some sort of sports car? Going too fast — he's crazy. All I can see is taillights. What happened?"

Then I see what's on the side of the road. The puzzle pieces snap together. And the big picture means J.T.'s Indiana Jones driving ability may come in handy. Problem is, we're going in the wrong direction.

"J.T.! Check it out in your rearview." Using one finger, I poke him in the shoulder. "Behind us. Other side of the Pike. Looks like a hit-and-run. A car ran into the guardrail. Any way to get us there? Like, right now?"

I grab the leather strap above my seat, preparing for the inevitable g-force. Traffic accident? Definitely. News story? Maybe. But I'm a reporter and it's my responsibility to find out.

Keeping my eyes on the accident scene, I use my free hand to grope through my bottomless black leather tote bag for my phone. I know it's in there somewhere, but I can't take my eyes off the crash to look for it. Why are we still speeding away?

"J.T.? Listen, we've got to turn around somehow. Come on, just do it! Franko, you call 911, okay? My phone is —"

"Hang on!"

With a blare of the horn, J.T. swerves us across two lanes, skidding briefly in the slush and splattering ice pellets across our windows. I'm thrown across the seat again, grabbing to get my seat belt back on before I'm the next casualty. So much for getting to the station on time. And this was my idea.

J.T. checks his rearview, his expression hidden behind his oversize sunglasses, then jounces us across an emergency lane in a who-cares-it's-illegal U-turn. With a two-handed twist of the steering wheel, he bangs the gas to speed us in the opposite direction.

"We're approaching mile marker 121," Franklin is saying into his phone. He's braced for the ride, one hand clamped on the dashboard, and his voice is terse. "Mass Pike. Westbound. Car in the ditch."

We're almost there. Off the road, skewed and tilted at an angle that telegraphs disaster, there's a set of taillights that's not moving. The trunk of the blocky sedan is open. I can't see the front of the car. And I can't see anyone getting out.

"Tell them the guy who caused it left the scene," I instruct. My fingers touch my own phone. "Tell them — blue or black. Sports car. Headed west. Fast. And no movement at the crash site. And no fire. Yet. I'll call the assignment desk. Let them know we're on the scene." And we'll be late getting back, I don't say.

Josh should be used to it by this time. And he — generally — understands a reporter can't control breaking news. Thing is, being late today has some extra baggage. In two hours we're supposed to be breaking our own news: telling Penny she's getting a new

11

stepmother. Me.

The nine-year-old was at Walt Disney World with her mother and stepfather when Josh and I got engaged. This week, still on school vacation, Penny's back with Josh. Now it seems like our news, Reality World, will have to stay secret a bit longer. My mother knows, of course. And Franklin. He and I have no secrets. Working as a team, sharing an office, there's no way.

Franklin and I usually handle the blockbuster stories, long-term investigations, Emmy caliber. Two months ago, we pulled off a showstopper, revealing international counterfeiting and FBI corruption. But after twenty-plus years in the biz, I know local news demands local news. And a hit-and-run tragedy could lead the show. I punch 33 on my cell phone's speed dial.

Clamping the phone to my ear with my shoulder, I rip off my black suede heels and yank on the flat snow boots I always carry this time of year in a red nylon Channel 3 pouch. Yes, I'm a pack mule. But I can't be worrying about slush on suede. Or cold feet.

Notebook. Pencil. And finally, the assignment desk picks up.

"Channel 3 News . . ."

"Hold some time on the six," I interrupt. "It's Charlie McNally. Got a pen? Tell the producer. Spot news on the Mass Pike. Hit-and-run. Car in a ditch. Casualties unknown. Franklin Parrish is with me. J.T.'s shooting. More to come. Got it?" I flip the phone closed in the middle of "Okay" and open the car door.

We're there.

A blast of January hits me, and I scramble to keep my balance in the frozen slush of the rutted roadside. A quick check of my trademark red lipstick in the car's side mirror also reminds me my hair's brownish roots are invading their painstakingly blonded camouflage. Flipping open my spiral notebook and edging across the breakdown lane, I look over my shoulder to make sure J.T. has his camera out and rolling.

"Right behind you, Charlie," J.T. says. He slams the trunk closed with one hand, and aims the camera at a pile of still-white snow, hitting the white-balance button to make sure our video is set to the right color. His leather gloves have the fingers cut off, allowing him to make the tiniest adjustments in video and sound.

"You got your external audio potted up?" Franklin asks.

I can't believe the boys are bickering again. J.T., battered leather jacket and broken-in jeans, foreign-correspondent cool and with a network résumé, is my age, but he's still the new guy at Channel 3. Franklin, pressed and preppy in Burberry camel hair, is ten years J.T.'s junior, but still holds station seniority. Picking my way toward the car, I turn to watch, half amused, half annoyed, as they continue their battle for turf. Can't we all just get along? *Men.*

J.T., aviator sunglasses now perched in his sandy hair, throws Franko an are-you-kidding look, but gives the camera's built-in microphone a tap just the same. He checks to make sure the needle on the audio meter is moving. "Rolling with sound, Charlie," he announces.

Franklin waves him off. "Just doing my job, pal."

"Me too, brotha," J.T. says.

Franklin hates when a white person calls him "brother." And J.T. knows it.

"Guys?" I interrupt the escalation of World War III. "The car? Someone's inside?"

We all head in the direction of the still-silent accident scene. All I can hear are our footsteps and the hissing splatter of cars streaking by on the crowded highway. Then I see the whole picture. The mangled car, its front end tangled in a now-twisted metal guardrail, is perched precariously over a shallow embankment. The hood of the dark red sedan is tented, crumpled, a discarded tin can. Tires in shreds. Something hot is hissing onto the snow beneath the chassis. I know the longer nothing moves, the more likely the news inside is bad. "Come on," I say softly. "Get out of the car."

And then, a quiet sound. Like a — cry. A baby. Crying.

"Guys?" I stop. Listening. But all is silent again. "Did you hear that?"

And then, the car's front door creaks open. Driver's side. Slowly. The car shifts, briefly, then settles back. No one gets out.

I flash a look at J.T.

J.T. holds up a reassuring hand, his eye pressed to the viewfinder. "Rolling," he mouths.

Franklin points to me, then J.T., then to the car. He raises one eyebrow. We don't want to say anything out loud — it'll be recorded on the tape.

The crying starts again. Getting louder. Where's the ambulance? And then I see what J.T. is capturing on camera. A man hauls himself, hand over hand, out of the front seat. He leans against the open door, parka to window, and presses one gloved hand to his bleeding forehead. He's thirtyish, suburban. His pale blue puffy jacket, striped muffler and jeans are spattered with blood. "Gabe," he says. "Sophie."

He gestures toward the car, then crumples onto the front seat, planting his salt-stained Timberland boots in the snow. Red drops plunk onto the white, then one splats onto his tan boot. "I'm okay," he insists, waving a hand. "Just dizzy. Head on the steering wheel. Please. Gabe and Sophie."

"Sir?" Franklin says, stepping closer. "We called 911 and . . ."

I'm already yanking open the passenger-side rear door. A boy, five years old maybe, in chunky mittens and red parka, is still in his booster seat, seat belt on. His cheeks are wet. His eyes are wide. The crying is coming from beside him. There, an unhappy toddler in a pink hat, squirming in her flowered sweater and matching snow pants, is strapped into a padded baby seat.

"Are you the doctor?" the boy asks me. "Daddy said you would come."

"Hi, Gabe. I'm Charlie," I say. Am I supposed to move him? I glance at the driver's seat. In a newish car like this, I would have expected air bags in the front. "Everything is going to be all right, sweetheart. The doctor will be here in one second to get you out. Is that your sister? Do you hurt anywhere?"

"I was in a crash, so I cried a little," Gabe says. He's earnest, his brown eyes trusting. "But I'm a big boy. And I always wear my seat belt. So I don't hurt. Is my daddy hurt? Sophie is crying. She always cries. She's only one years old."

"Your dad is fine, that's a good boy," I reassure him. Little Sophie begins to wail full blast. Her blanket is on the floor of the car. I can't leave her there. Where is the ambulance? What makes a car blow up?

"Gabe? If I unhook your seat belt, can you get out? I'm going to get your sister, and then we'll all walk away from the car. Can you do that?"

If I move the kids, am I going to make this worse? Neither seems really hurt. And the ambulance must be on the way. And except maybe for the hit-and-run element, this is not much of a story. Luckily for all involved. But we have to wait for the EMTs, at least. And maybe the cops, too, since, technically, we're witnesses.

"I want out." Gabe, his face suddenly racked with uncertainty, elongates the final word into a mournful plea.

I reach over, unclick four pink webbed straps from around the now-quieting Sophie and ease her out of the baby seat, grabbing

17

the yellow chenille blanket from the floor and wrapping it around her as I back out the door. Sophie sniffles, once, then I feel her little body burrow into my shoulder. On the other side of the car, her father is standing again. Where's the ambulance?

"The kids are fine," I call to him across the car. "We'll come to you."

The sky is steel and ice, promising another bitter night. I tuck the blanket closer around Sophie, and wiggle my fingers toward Gabe. "Take my hand, honey. Can you get down?"

Gabe slides off the seat and grabs my hand. His lower lip gives the beginnings of a quiver. "I want to see my daddy," he says, looking at me.

"Absolutely," I say. "And we can tell him how brave you are."

This has got to be the strangest interview I've ever done. The EMTs finally arrived, pleading "wicked traffic" and "buncha jerk" drivers. They checked the kids, plastered Declan Ross's forehead with a gauze-and-tape bandage, pronounced everyone fine and took off. Now Sophie's nestled peacefully over my shoulder, her little breath sounds snuffling into my ear. Franklin and Gabe, holding hands, are watching as I use my non-Sophie hand to hold the Channel 3 microphone, its chunky logo red, white and blue against the gray slush. I know we probably won't use my interview with Declan Ross, or even the video J.T. shot of the victims' car — Franklin's already informed the assignment desk it's too minor to make air.

And I'm yearning to leave, meet up with Josh, share our celebratory dinner. Take a step closer to becoming Penny's mom. But we're here, and my years of experience dictate it's easier to erase an interview than regret not doing it. Better to be safe than scooped. Your job could depend on it.

"So just to be clear," I say, bringing the microphone back in my direction, "this car is rented because yours is in the shop?" I flip the mic back to Ross.

"Yes, ours was recalled. Just a day ago. For bad brakes," Ross says. His eyes are clear again, and he's the picture of a middle-class dad with kids. And a bandage. "We got a, well, somewhat frightening letter from the manufacturer, indicating we should bring it in to have the brakes looked at. So, of course, we did. My wife dropped it off yesterday, got this rental. Gabe and Sophie, we're certainly not going to risk —"

He breaks off, looking at his son. I can see his eyes welling. His yuppie-casual clothes are still ominously smeared with browning red. No question this family had a narrow escape. "Gabie, you okay?"

"You're on TV, Daddy," Gabe says. "And Franklin says I get to see a tow truck. And a police."

"So what happened?" I continue, getting him back on track. My calculation, we've got only a few minutes of daylight left. And according to the EMTs, the state police should arrive any second.

"A car — switched lanes. Cutting me off. Nothing I could do. I saw him barreling toward the tollbooth. Boston drivers . . ." He pauses, and I can see his hands clench into fists.

Sirens approach. The cops.

"Did you get any identification? Of the car?" I ask. Just making sure. "License plate? Make? Color?"

"No," Ross begins, "I —"

"It was a blue car."

Gabe, still holding Franklin's hand, is standing on one foot, then the other. "Like my Matchbox car, Daddy," he says. "I saw it."

Two state troopers are out of their cruiser, doors slamming, almost before the gray and black Crown Vic comes to a halt. Hulks in stiff steel-blue uniforms, opaque sunglasses, massive leather belts armored with weapons, high-polish boots, they stride toward us, shoulder radios squawking static.

Gabe takes a step back, mouth open, then runs to his father, his little arms circling one blue-jeaned leg in a death grip, his face buried in his father's thigh.

"Everyone all right here?" One trooper's embossed metal nametag says Scott Maguire.

Maguire, I say to myself, remembering it. Again, better to be safe.

"We're fine, Officer. We just need a tow truck." Ross says, smoothing Gabe's hair. He smiles at me, then points. "And I need my daughter back."

"It's for your own good, I promise you." I'm on the floor, on all fours, pleading. "No, not you, Franko. I'm talking to Botox."

I'm finally back at my apartment. As I predicted, the producers spiked the hit-and-run story, so we dutifully stashed the accident video in our archives and split. Two hours of overtime pay for J.T., two hours of unrecoverable Josh-time for me. But on the way home, in one of those everything-happens-for-a-reason kind of moments, the whole crash thing gave me a potentially brilliant idea. Now, with the phone clamped

21

between my shoulder and my cheek, I'm trying to explain my brainstorm to Franklin and coax Botox into the cat carrier at the same time. She made herself heavy when I picked her up, then twisted out of my arms and is now glaring at me from under my dining room table. She's bitter. Slashing her calico tail. Daring me to make a move to grab her.

"Hang on, Franklin, I never should have hauled out the cat carrier. She despises it." I pause, clamber to my feet and peer at her, glaring back. "I'm going to leave you, you know. And you'll hate that even more. No, not you, Franko. The stupid cat."

Franklin is already home, probably already cuddling with his adorable Stephen. But me? I'll never get to Josh's house. And though Josh is used to my excuses for being late, "the cat was hiding," though true, is not the most compelling.

And I still have to tell Franklin my idea.

"So here's the scoop," I say. "And maybe we can pull it off in time for the February ratings book."

Before I can begin, Franklin interrupts to tell me what I already know. We're working a solid lead on phony organic food.

"And Charlotte," he says. His leftover Mississippi drawl always makes my name sound charmingly like Shaw-lit. He's the only one, besides my mother, who never calls me Charlie. "February is looming, less than a month away. You want to switch gears now? What if it falls through?"

"Yeah, yeah, I know," I reply. He's such a Boy Scout when it comes to rules and schedules. "But this could be big. Listen. Spend one hour thinking about it. I vote — let's risk one day on it. Maybe two. Hear me out. Just briefly."

"It's your funeral," Franklin says.

I stick my tongue out at the still-unreachable Botox, head down the hall to my bedroom and begin throwing clothes into a suitcase. "You know Declan Ross's car? It was recalled, right? And he got it fixed. But how many people just ignore those recall notices? Don't bother to take their cars to be repaired? And how many of those cars are still on the road? They're like — time bombs, you know?"

I scout my closet, listening while Franklin, reluctantly at first, agrees I might be on to something.

"And you know, I see what you mean, Charlotte. All we need is a few victims," he says. "People who bought used cars with open recalls. And what if they got hurt?"

"Uh-huh," I say. Part of my mind is in the

closet. Black suit for work tomorrow. Sweat-pants for tonight. Sweatpants? On the other hand — I dig into my dresser and find a gauzy black nightgown, still wrapped in hot-pink tissue paper. If not tonight, when? Into the suitcase. Now for my perfect jeans. I scrounge into the closet, dragging clear plastic hangers across the metal rod, one after the other. The jeans are not there. I scrape through the hangers again. Nothing.

Are my jeans at Josh's? Half my stuff has already migrated to his house in Brookline. Half my stuff is still here in my condo on Beacon Hill. I just don't know which is where. I have two toothbrushes. Two com-plete sets of contact-lens solutions. Two hair dryers. Leading a double life is increasingly complicated. And expensive.

Franklin continues, having snapped up my story bait so completely he's now content with my scattered *uh-huhs.* "If we search through the files at the National Highway Transportation Safety Administration and demand records and documentation . . ."

"Uh-huh."

He's hot on the trail. But I'm suddenly distracted by my third finger, left hand. For better or for worse, my life is about to change.

I plop onto the bed, listening to Franklin

with half an ear, awash with uncertainty. We may finally have a good story for the February ratings: how many dangerous recalled cars are still on the road? But for the first time since I can't remember when, I've realized our sweeps story is not my top priority.

What if that's a life-wrecking mistake?

Fifty percent of marriages end in divorce. It already happened to me once. And once to Josh. What if I'm panicking now, freaking out at age forty-seven? What if I'm tossing away twenty years of television? Sometimes when you try for everything, you wind up with nothing. But if you don't try, you could also end up with nothing.

In the news business. And in real life.

"Okay, Franko, glad you think it'll work," I say. "We can hit Kevin with the idea first thing tomorrow. And maybe wind up doing some good. Give my love to your adorable Stephen."

I click off the phone. With a snap of the locks, I pack my fears away, slam my suitcase closed and head down the hall to give Botox another chance. This will work. I can make it work. A job. And a husband. Watch this, statistics guys. I'm going to have it all.

CHAPTER TWO

"Clink me again, Daddo. Clink me again, Charlie Mac." Penny's crystal glass is full of ginger ale, ours of champagne. My giggling stepdaughter-to-be is more interested in toasting than taking a sip.

Not me. I'm on my second fizzy glass of Veuve Clicquot and I'm delighted there's more where that came from. It's not every day you have to inform an unpredictably prickly preteen you're going to be her stepmother, move into her house and sleep with her father.

We didn't actually go into that much detail. And we still haven't set the date. But Penny — nine going on sixteen — knows the score. She came back from Walt Disney World with cropped hair, pierced ears and a vocabulary that includes incomprehensible abbreviations and unknown (to me at least) pop music stars.

Happily, she says she's "cool" about our

plans. She tried on my ring, performed a spot-on walking-down-the-aisle imitation, then ran off to call her new after-school babysitter and instant role model, Annie Vilardi. Annie's a Bexter senior, and suddenly her word is inviolable. Now Pen's back clinking faux champagne. Anniefied, she's part little girl, part prom queen.

"So, pumpkin, you think you'd like to be in a wedding? The flower girl? You think you and Charlie Mac might be able to shop for a dress?" Josh scrabbles Penny's spiky new do and smiles at me over his glass.

He and his daughter have on matching Bexter Academy sweatshirts, Penny's inside out, and plaid flannel pants. His salt-and-pepper hair, more pepper, is rumpled as usual. Tortoiseshell glasses. Even after more than a year together, I still think "Gregory Peck as Atticus Finch" every time I see him. And now, his verging-on-smoldering expression makes me pleased I packed the slinky nightgown.

"I knew you were getting married," Penny says, swatting her father's hand away. "That's no biggie of a secret. Charlie Mac had a toothbrush at our house. Annie says when there's a toothbrush, that's serious. My mother had a toothbrush at Elliot's house before they got married. I saw it. An-

27

nie says —"

"Was it your mother who agreed to the pierced ears?" Josh interrupts. Teasing. "I thought you two agreed to wait until you were sixteen."

Penny puts down her glass and crosses her spindly arms in front of her, still brown and freckled from the Florida sun. She rolls her eyes, impatient, then settles her face into a parent-weary look. "Daddo, you know about Bexter. When Mom told me about that, *that's* when she told me I could get pierced ears. Annie says pierced ears are cool. Charlie Mac, you know about it, right?"

Yes. I do. And that's my own Reality World. Penny's doctor-mom, Victoria, and her doctor-husband Elliott snagged some high-security medical center research grant in Los Angeles. Just for "a while," she told her ex-husband, it was no kids allowed. As a result, Josh is getting a full-time daughter. For "a while" at least, Penny lives with her dad and goes to Bexter. Entering midterm, and, courtesy of her professor-father, tuition free.

"Of course, honey," I reply. "And Bexter is —"

But Penny's not listening.

"I'm not gonna die from one little taste,"

she says, hoisting the green champagne bottle, dripping with melted ice, out of the silver bucket. "Annie says she had champagne when her brother graduated Bexter. The real stuff. And so did all the kids at the party. She says everyone's parents let them do it."

"If Annie says you should jump off a bridge, would you also do that?" Josh guides the bottle back into the bucket. "How about . . ."

Taking a sip from my own glass, I watch their playful battle, and mull over our looming future. Sooner or later, we'll set a date. Sooner or later, I'll sell my condo. We'll decide whose coffeemaker we keep, whose set of silverware, whose toaster oven. Divide the closets and the medicine cabinets. Learn to schedule shower times. I'll be a full-time reporter, full-time professor's wife and full-time stepmother.

A yowl arises from near the living room couch. A wail, laden with despair. Botox refused to exit her once-loathed cat carrier when I opened the latticed door, and has now plastered her body to the back wall of the plastic box. Apparently this is an announcement that she's going to stay inside it. Forever. Botox hates transition.

"What's wrong with Botox?" Penny asks.

Her face twists with concern. Champagne wars forgotten, she runs to the carrier, crouching in front of it, peering inside.

I link my fingers through Josh's, leaning into his shoulder, and raise a headache-risking third glass of Veuve. My ring reflects the candlelight, and in the tiny glittering flash I'm hit with my new reality.

"Your new family," I say. I hear my own voice turn husky. It's not from the champagne. "You like it?"

"I do," Josh replies. He looks down at me, then squares my shoulders and stares into my eyes.

"Sweetheart?" He looks perplexed. "Are you crying?"

The nightgown was a major success. But I still can't sleep. Brookline's old-fashioned streetlights weave crisscross patterns on Josh's bedroom ceiling, stripes of shadow across the stark white. They're now as familiar as my own ceiling design, Beacon Hill's gas-lit yellow cast across the pale blue I painted myself. It's been home for a long time. Now I sleep here as much as there. And I'm feeling just as comfortable. Almost. After so many years on my own, what will it be like to share everything?

I wrap Josh's burgundy-striped down

comforter closer and struggle to quiet my thoughts. I can make out the silver-framed photos and diplomas on the walls, key rings and loose change on Josh's imposing walnut dresser. I like his dresser better than mine. Will I get half the drawers? His books and old skiing trophies already crowd the built-in shelves. Will there be room for my books? *Go to sleep,* I silently chant. *Go to sleep.* Tomorrow, actually today, is a work-day. And Franklin and I have to get started on the car-recall investigation. Lots to do. Too much to do. I close my eyes.

"Sweets?" Josh whispers. "You asleep?"

"Not one bit," I say. "I'm trying, but not terribly successfully. My brain won't turn off. Nor will the rest of me, thanks to you."

I move to face him, eyes open again, smiling with possibility, glad for a good excuse to be awake. I'll just be tired tomorrow — today. It's happened before. And it's not every night your engagement goes public. I expect Josh to reach out for me, but his expression is — concerned? And why are his glasses back on? My Josh-radar pings into the red.

"What?" I ask. "What's wrong?"

"Can you keep a secret?" he says. He's still on his back, hands clasped over his chest, head turned to watch me.

31

I sit up, yanking the comforter over me, and twist around to look down on him, assessing. I hate secrets. The reporter half of my brain is pitching out disaster scenarios faster than I can bat them away.

Can I keep a secret? What kind of a question is that?

"Um, keeping a secret, that's the reporter's credo, right?" I smile, trying for adorable-cheerful. Maybe I've misread his mood. I squint at the digital alarm clock. It's hard to be perceptive at 3:34 a.m. "Confidential sources stay confidential? And hey, I didn't call Maysie to tell her about the engagement, how about that? If I can keep our news from my own best friend?"

Josh isn't laughing. He scoots up, back to headboard, grabbing his half of the comforter. "It's Bexter," he says. He leans over, gives me a quick kiss. "I'm sorry, sweets, to be distracted. Tonight, especially. But you know Dorothy Wirt? The Head's assistant?"

I nod. Josh tells me she's such a snoop, he secretly calls her Miss Marple. Gray hair, cardigans with brooch. A mental pack rat. Organized as a dictionary.

"Well, the Head and I found her at her desk a few days ago. Crying." He blinks, remembering.

"She was in tears. Inconsolable. It took a

lot of convincing, but she finally told us she's been getting some pretty disturbing phone calls. She didn't want to tell, she insisted, didn't want to 'alarm' the Head. I mean, I think it's more alarming that she tried to keep it to herself."

Josh holds up a hand. Stopping his own story.

"She may have a point," he says, sighing. "It could be the first of this year's Bexter senior pranks. But Dorothy told us someone called Bexter and, using an obviously disguised voice, asked, 'Do you know where your children are?' That must be a student. It's so ridiculous. Clichéd. Right from some made-for-TV movie. Maybe it's nothing."

"I don't know, Josh," I say, mulling it over. My sleep-deprived brain is beginning to churn. It's clearly not nothing. "All those Bexter students with rich and famous parents. Doesn't Headmaster Forrestal want to call in the police? Even the FBI? Isn't there caller ID? A pattern to the calls? To the timing? What about the parents?"

Now I'm wide-awake. Penny. Bexter. "And hey — I'm a parent. Or will be, soon. And you are, too."

"Nope. Nothing." His hands smooth the comforter in front of him. Again. And again.

I'm confused. "Nothing what?"

33

"No pattern. No caller ID. Sometimes there's no one on the line at all, Dorothy says. The number is blocked so it doesn't come up on caller ID. And no to the cops, too. The Head is insisting. He says, since there are no specifics, there's nothing to investigate. 'It's not like it's a bomb threat.' In that voice of his." He raises his eyebrows, miming an aloof demeanor.

" 'We cannot overreact,' " Josh says, mimicking an almost-British accent. " 'What if our students are involved? We need to deal with this within the Bexter family. Moreover, *we must not tell the parents.* Otherwise, it would be impossible to keep out the —" He stops.

"Media," I finish, nodding.

"Correct," Josh says. "That's exactly what he said. I don't agree with him, but he's the boss. And that's why I asked you about keeping a secret. You can, right?"

Silence has never been so noisy. How do I answer that? For the past twenty years, my loyalties have been only to journalism. My position never compromised. My goals clear. I stare at my ring again. Somehow, now, the glitter contains a bit of a taunt. I take a tentative step onto the tightrope, struggling for balance. Who'd have imagined a continental divide in the middle of a king-size mattress?

Pulling myself as close as I can, I link my arm through Josh's, tucking my head against his shoulder. Trying to close the gap.

"I'm thinking," I say. "If there's a possible danger to the kids, including Penny? There may be a greater good here, more important than 'keeping the media away from Bexter.' Doing that could be something you all bitterly regret. I've seen it so often, the tragic results when people try to cover up a problem or pretend a threat doesn't exist. And it's my responsibility as a journalist to investigate what people are trying to hide. Right?"

I look up at him, waiting. "Right?"

Josh's turn on the tightrope. Are his loyalties to me? To the Bexter kids? To his boss? This is a discussion we've never needed to have. Now we're having it in the middle of the night, naked, when I kind of have to go to the bathroom.

"Wrong," Josh says.

I shiver, though it's not cold. I need to let him continue. I need to hear this.

"Wrong," he says again. "Because it's your job to — to wait. Until you have all the facts. And we don't have any facts. I told you something in confidence."

He turns to me, face softening, then picks

up my hand, twisting the diamond on my finger. "We're not source and reporter here, sweets. We're almost husband and wife."

He's right. And I'm right. Is there a right?

Josh, wearing full Bexter regalia, navy houndstooth jacket, striped tie, corduroy slacks, appears at the kitchen door. He spins a finger by his head, making an exaggerated show of being confused.

"Weren't we — talking?"

"We were indeed," I say. I hold out his mug of coffee, hesitant to say more. I'm a little bit cranky over last night's debate. I don't tell him how to do *his* job, right? Plus, my brain is so fried, I can't even tell if Josh is being sarcastic. When I got back from the bathroom last night, he was dead asleep. I'd carefully removed his glasses, and at the time, was relieved. Now it feels as if our conversation is uncomfortably dangling. I've confronted corrupt politicians and chased down criminals, all in a day's work. Nevertheless. Sussing out my husband-to-be suddenly seems more complicated.

Franklin's waiting at Channel 3. I'm in my own work regalia, black suit and possibly too-high black suede pumps. But Josh and I have unfinished business here. He's stirring milk into his coffee as if it requires

36

every bit of his concentration.

"Listen," I begin. Might as well get this wrapped up. Penny will be down soon.

"Charlie," Josh says. His spoon leaves a milky ring on the granite countertop.

"Go ahead," I say.

"Go ahead," he says at the same time.

I love this man. We're going to be married. And we haven't touched each other yet this morning.

Josh sips his coffee, raising an eyebrow. Meaning I'm supposed to talk?

"Okay, here's what I think," I say, treading carefully. I pull a wicker-seated stool up to the counter, its cast-iron legs skreeking on the tiled floor, and try to sit on it without snagging my panty hose.

"I had wondered whether, maybe, if you knew something confidential — like the Bexter situation — it would be better if you didn't tell me. Then there would be nothing to decide. You know my job, what it entails. If you thought there would be a conflict, we could avoid it."

Josh begins to shake his head, dismissing, but I raise a hand to stop him.

"But then I thought, you know, 'don't ask, don't tell' doesn't work for a marriage. A relationship can't grow if there are secrets."

Josh pauses, then gives a quick nod.

"Exactly. Avoiding a problem is never the answer."

He's just given me a huge chunk of ammunition, but I tuck it away for later. I hop down from the stool, trying to feel connected.

"Right. So here's a solution. I'm a reporter. And I'm going to be Penny's stepmother. Instead of making that a conflict, why don't we take advantage of it? What if I do some digging? Off the record. Behind the scenes. I could —"

"Absolutely not," Josh interrupts. "If you start asking questions, it will be obvious to everyone that the information came from me. And that's the end of my career at Bexter." He puts his coffee on the speckled-marble countertop, the ceramic mug clattering on the stone. It nudges the spoon, which falls to the floor.

We both reach for it. Both pull back. Look into each other's eyes.

I don't want an impasse. I want a solution. But I also want some answers. How would reporter-me handle this? She's got more experience than fiancée-me. If Josh were a reluctant source, I'd pull back and push forward at the same time.

"Look, sweetheart, I absolutely promise I won't do anything without letting you know." That's a promise I can keep. I hope. I pick up the spoon, put it in the sink. I can feel Josh relax.

Now the push forward. His job is important, too, of course, and I won't do anything to jeopardize it. I also can't do anything to jeopardize mine. Until now, our skirmishes have been brief and simple and social. Low-caliber. A big story conflicting with a Bexter dinner party. But we've never had our personal life present a professional conflict of interest.

Used to be, my only interest was the truth. Now I'm also interested in the rest of my life. This is what they don't teach you in journalism school.

"Just tell me this, though." I fire the first shot. "Who knows about the calls? And what, if anything, are they doing about them?"

Josh pours another cup of coffee from the glass carafe, then leans against the counter, holding the steaming mug with both hands.

"Dorothy Wirt knows, of course. What's she doing? Losing sleep, is what she says. Though she'd probably kill without a flinch if she thought one of her Bexter kids was in danger. Stab someone with her letter opener." He smiles, looking up briefly, indicating that's a joke.

39

I nod, silently acknowledging I get it.

"The Head," he continues his list, "he's doing nothing, far as I know. Waiting. The bursar came in while Dorothy was telling us the story. So he's aware. And maybe Dean Espinosa. She's Dorothy's best friend. Maybe Dorothy told her. But maybe not."

"Some secret," I say, making a skeptical face. "That's three, four people right there. Not counting you. And who knows who else each of them 'confided' in."

I have another thought. "Does Penny know?"

"Do I know what?" Penny's flip-flops slap onto the linoleum. She's clutching Botox, who with one suicidal look at me writhes out of her arms and scampers away. Penny's wearing red drawstring pajama bottoms printed with what look like Scottie dogs, a ruffled pink camisole and a sideways Red Sox cap. Still deciding on her image.

"Shoes?" Josh says. He reaches for her hat and Penny ducks out of his way. "It's the bleak midwinter, pumpkin girl. School vacation doesn't mean —"

"My feet aren't even cold," Penny retorts. "It's inside. There's heat, you know? And Annie wears flip-flops in winter. Her parents let her. She'll be here soon and I bet she'll have flip-flops. You'll see. Charlie Mac, when can we pick out my junior-bridesmaid dress?"

"Nice try on changing the subject, kiddo," I say. I love my nickname. Penny came up with it; Charlie Mac evolving as her eventual compromise between her initial choice, "Um," and the already-taken "Mom." It took a year of negotiation and territory marking, but now we're pals. I'd rather not let her know there's a tiny bit of tension between her dad and me this morning. She's resilient, but she's already handled enough with her parents splitting. And now her new school. New home. And me.

"Go get shoes, as your dad said. Then we'll discuss shopping for your dress. We'll need to get your Bexter uniform, too."

Penny hesitates just long enough to prove she's not instantly obeying me. "Annie wears clogs sometimes, too," she says. Then she flip-flops out of the room.

"Good one, 'Charlie Mac,' " Josh says. He takes a step toward me and I meet him halfway. His arm circles my shoulders, mine slides around his waist. I smell lime and cedar and coffee. "You're going to be a very successful mom," he whispers. He kisses my hair with the briefest of touches and the oxygen is back in the room.

"Though somehow our Penny has pro-

41

moted herself from flower girl to 'junior bridesmaid,' " I reply. "Very smooth."

"Annie's idea, most likely. As always."

We made it. We're back. I can do this.

Penny sticks her head around the corner, her body still in the dining room, her feet out of sight. "Hey. I forgot. Do I know — what? What were you talking about?"

"Shoes," Josh says. He points her away, then turns to me as we hear Penny's footsteps heading upstairs. "Bexter's not open for student orientation until next week. There's time. And we'll have to wait and see. But no secrets. Not for either of us. Agreed?"

Ah. That doesn't mean I can't investigate what may be happening at Bexter Academy. It just means I'll have to tell Josh when I do.

"No secrets," I say. I know I can make this work.

CHAPTER THREE

"Tough morning, Charlotte?" Franklin turns his head like an owl and keeps one hand on his mouse, clicking his monitor screen closed. He peers at me from under his glasses, then gestures at the battered wood-framed mirror we've got pushpinned to the office wall. "Unless you were actually going for the wet-poodle look. In which case, congrats."

"It's snowing, Franko," I say, checking the mirror. He's right. I deposit my waterlogged latte on my desk, then yank open my metal desk drawer.

Franklin's file drawer contains files. Mine has a 1600-watt hair dryer, a round hairbrush, hair spray, nail-polish remover, black panty hose, a backup pair of black panty hose, nude panty hose, a backup pair of nude panty hose, contact-lens solution, a bag of almonds, a tin of tea bags, a thing of Tums and several thousand Advil. I pull out the dryer.

"Take off your coat, then I'll tell you the news," Franklin says.

"What news? Good news?" I ask, peeling off my soggy coat. "Progress on the car thing? Emmy in our future? Story for the February ratings sweeps? We keep our jobs and everyone lives happily ever after?"

I stash my wet boots under my desk and unzip my black pumps from my tote bag. At least they stayed dry. Now Franklin needs payback for the unnecessary poodle remark. "Oh, I get it. You're stalling. Because you can't find anything."

With a snap, Franklin swivels back to his computer, clicks his mouse and then taps his keyboard while he talks. "Yes, Charlotte, you're so very perceptive. But before you find yourself a better producer, feast your eyes on this. May I present to you —" he pauses, apparently savoring his big reveal, "— the good news. The Web site of the National Highway Transportation Safety Administration."

"NHTSA." I say. *Nitsa.* "It's all there? All we need? Right on the Web site?"

Franklin taps a finger to his lips. "Well, yes and no. Yes, I suppose, but in a rather needle-in-a-haystack kind of way."

Franklin clicks me through the Web site,

me leaning over his shoulder as he mouses through the pages of red, white and blue drop-down menus and links. "Here's the bottom line," he says. "The NHTSA site does contain every vehicle carmakers have admitted is defective and have been forced to recall. That's what I mean by the haystack."

"Does it tell how many of the recalled cars have actually been fixed? And which ones?" I turn to Franklin, hopeful for the second time today. What he's telling me is possibly great news. "Fabulous. Then we can find the ones that're not repaired. The ones that are still potentially dangerous."

"Well, that's the needle, Charlotte, finding the individual cars," Franklin says. He's moving his cursor across the screen. "See? This Web site only shows which makes and models have been recalled. Not what happened after that."

"Really? That's absurd," I say. I turn away from the monitor and perch on Franklin's black metal file cabinet. "Car owners get notices when their cars are recalled, right?"

Franklin nods. "It's all on computer. Manufacturers find the car owners by looking up the unique Vehicle Identification Number of each car. And after the owners take them to the dealer to be repaired, the dealer checks it off as done, and puts the VIN into the same computer network."

"Exactly my point," I say. "So the feds absolutely know which cars have been repaired and which ones haven't."

And that makes me angry. I wave toward Franklin's monitor. "So why isn't all of it public information? The feds regulate all those recall notices, right? I think it's their responsibility to keep track of who's still driving a dangerous car. They know it, but they're not telling? Ridiculous. Who knows how many accidents those cars have already caused? And how many are to come?"

The system is broken. Maybe we can fix it. This is what keeps me going. I point to the phone. "Call them, Franko. Try it the nice way at first. Maybe they'll just hand the documents over. And tell them —"

Franklin's holding up a hand to shush me. He's already dialed, and wonder of wonders, apparently a real person has actually answered the phone. Score one for our tax dollars.

"This is Franklin Parrish, at Channel 3 News in Boston?" Franklin says. He's using his most polite voice, and a remnant of his mostly erased southern accent. "I need to talk with someone about recalls, please."

I can't stand it. I scrawl instructions on

my reporter's notebook and hold it up. "Pssst," I say, waving the page. *Tell them we got a call from one viewer, no biggie.*

Franklin looks over, reads it, and nods.

"We're just researching a little consumer-education story," Franklin says, his voice still mild and nonthreatening. "We got a call from a viewer, you know? And he just wondered how to find out whether his car has ever been recalled."

I nod, this is good. Be polite. Ask an easy question first, and one we already know the answer to. I go back to my notebook while Franklin continues.

"Oh," he says, all innocent. "You can look it up online? Terrific."

"Pssst," I say again. I hold up the notebook. *Can the viewer find out if it's been fixed?*

Franklin looks over again. This time, reading my note, he makes a torqued-up expression implying: Duh.

"That's interesting," Franklin says. "But, hey, quick question. If it has been recalled, can our viewer find out if it's been repaired?" As if the thought just entered his mind. Franklin's a pro.

"Pssst." *Say he's thinking of buying it in a used-car lot.*

This time Franklin's look verges on exasperated. Then as he reads the note, he gives me a thumbs-up.

"Yes, he's shopping for cars, you know. Sorry if I wasn't clear." Franklin puts a hand to his throat, mimes gagging. This part of journalism often includes a bit of theater. It's worth it for a good story.

And this might be a great one. There could be millions of unrepaired recalls in used-car lots. Like I said, time bombs, waiting to endanger unwitting drivers and their families. We have to find those cars. Warn people.

Get specifics, I write.

"You know what," Franklin says, sitting up a little straighter. I can hear his voice hardening. "You must have records of this, I'm sure. Instead of spending time looking for my viewer's request, why don't you send us the records for the past three years. All the cars that have been recalled but not repaired. By date, by manufacturer and by model type and year. We'd prefer to have the data sent electronically, not on paper."

This should all be public information. I hold it up, and then put it down. *It's outrageous!* I scrawl in double-size letters. I hold up my instructions again. "Pssst."

Franklin's glare could curl my hair, if it weren't already ridiculously curly. He swiv-

48

els his chair away, all drama, putting his back to me and covering his ear with his free hand.

An e-mail pings into view. It's from Kevin O'Bannon. Cue the suspense music.

Come to my office. ASAP. Confidential.

Music up full. I glance at Franklin, who's still deep into negotiations.

A summons to the news director's office. A summons I'm not supposed to discuss. And what could be confidential? In an instant, my brain catalogs my recent actions. Do they think I'm taking too many pencils from the mail room? Have they found all the department store orders on my computer? Long-distance calls to my mother in Chicago? E-mails from wedding caterers? Maybe I won't have to worry about balancing job and Bexter intrigue. Maybe I won't have a job.

"Pssst."

Franklin turns, wary, narrowing his eyes.

I give him my brightest smile and point down the hall toward the bathroom.

He flutters a wave and turns back to his call. I head into territory unknown.

"Have a seat," Kevin says, waving me to his

navy-and-burgundy tweed couch. He crosses to the office door. And closes it.

I sit. I worry. Something major is about to happen. Kevin's door always stays open.

Half of the news director's attention is always tuned to the clamor of pagers, beepers, Nextels and police radios buzzing and squawking at the four-person assignment desk just outside his office. If Kevin closes his door, he closes out the rest of the world. And news directors can't afford to do that. Unless it's something really — I don't have words for how big it has to be.

Kevin sits down beside me. Unheard of. The walls close in as I struggle to predict the future. Whatever he's going to tell me has got to be life changing. For someone. But what if it's not me? What if it's Kevin's life that's changing? Maybe he's dying?

No.

Maybe he's quitting.

My fear evaporates as my instinct kicks in. Sometimes I just know things. And I've learned to trust those times.

Kevin is quitting. It's not my job at Channel 3 that's ending. It's his.

Maybe.

I shift around to face him, trying to organize my legs and choose an expression.

Kevin adjusts his sleek tie of the day, this

one covered with the tiniest of greyhounds, nose to tail. The greyhounds match his perfectly tailored gray pin-striped suit. Which matches his graying but salon-sleek buzz cut.

"Let's cut to the chase, Charlie." Kevin stops. Clears his throat. "Bottom line. Big picture. I've been offered a new job. In market one. New York."

I flutter a hand to my chest, then reach out to touch his arm. He's quitting. I knew it. "Well, that's — congratulations, Kev —"

"And that's not all," Kevin continues, ignoring my reaction. "I'll be helming the news division of a new cable network. It'll be the antithesis of everything that's now on local TV. It'll be all journalism, all the time. The depth of public TV, the production values of MTV, the nose for news of Murrow. No cute titles. No more pandering feature stories about puppies and pandas."

"News nirvana, sounds like," I say, smiling. "Really, Kevin, congratulations. We'll miss you. I haven't heard of this, though. What's it called?"

"No name yet. Rollout's not till May. This point, it's all confidential." Kevin raises an eyebrow, conspiratorial. "I trust you, Charlie, as always, to protect your source. And keep this news to yourself. Don't tell anyone."

"Oh, of course, I — of course." My brain is churning, projecting my own future. The average life span of a local news director is about eighteen months. Kevin lasted a bit longer than most. Who'll be my new boss? A man? A woman? Someone better? Worse? I'll certainly have to prove myself all over again. And that makes me suddenly weary of the endless game. Maybe I should quit, too. Be a wife and a mother. Be my own boss. I steal a comforting glance at my ring, twist the stone to the back so Kevin doesn't notice it yet. Maybe this is a sign. No more TV news for me. Maybe it is my life that's changing.

Kevin's up from the couch, headed back to his desk. He turns, leaning against the blond wood.

In the silence, I hear the electronic hum from the bank of television monitors flickering silently on his floor-to-ceiling shelves. The muted buzz of the newsroom.

"Charlie? I want you to come with me. Move to the Big Apple. Be my senior investigative reporter. It's the big dance, kiddo. And I'm your ticket to the job of a lifetime."

New York. Network television. Senior investigative reporter. As good as it gets.

The diamond ring on my finger suddenly weighs a million pounds.

I trudge up the two flights of stairs leading back to my office. My dreams have just come true. Journalism prayers answered. And yet, it would all be so much easier if I could go hide under my desk. Job of a lifetime, huh? Just when I thought I had my lifetime in order.

I promised Kevin I would give him my answer as soon as the February book is over. Yes. Or no. Stay. Or go.

I trudge a few more steps, regretting my cantilevered heels, yearning for coffee. I can't discuss this with Franklin, since I've been ordered not to tell him about it. And that's not really fair, since if I move to New York, his job will also change. And he should have some time to plan his own future.

I also can't tell Franklin about the Bexter phone calls. I can't tell Kevin, either. And that's not really fair, since kids might be in danger.

How many secrets can one person have?

I shake my head, focusing. I don't have to decide anything right now. Franklin will think I was in the bathroom and won't ask any questions. Tonight at dinner, I can pump Josh for more information about Bexter.

When I tell Josh about the New York offer, he'll —

I stop, hand clutching the banister, three steps from the top.

Kevin ordered me not to tell anyone. And I agreed. Does "anyone" mean Josh?

"You've got to love valet parking," I say, sliding out into the snowy night. A navy-jacketed doorman, umbrella popped, is waiting to shelter us to the entrance of the Paramount Hotel. Huge marble lions, sphinxlike, stand sentinel in front of cut-glass and polished-brass revolving doors. Inside is old-world Boston — chandeliers and brocade settees and gold braid and burnished oak paneling, budget-shattering bouquets towering on curvy antique tables. The city's most elegant place for a wedding. I'd confided the possibility to my mother, who, for perhaps the first time in our lives, agreed I might have a good idea.

"How long will you be?" A twenty-something in a navy slicker slides past Josh into the driver's seat. The back of his jacket says Beacon Valet. He slams the door, rolls down the window and clicks down the gearshift. "Overnight? Or just dinner?"

"Dinner," Josh replies. He barely gets the words out before the valet steers the blue sedan into Boston's Back Bay murk.

The maître d' of the Brasserie flickers recognition as we approach her desk. Elegant in a navy suit, an updo and pearls, she says something into a silver-and-white phone before turning to greet us.

"Miss McNally, the Brasserie is delighted to welcome you." There's a trace of the Caribbean in her voice. Her name tag says LaVinia. She gestures us to follow her through the crowded restaurant, winding our way past white tablecloths, crystal decanters of wine and shimmering candelabra. "Your table is ready, of course. And Miss Tolliver is on her way."

A silver bucket of champagne, dripping with condensation, is displayed on an ornate pewter stand next to our table. I look at Josh, surprised. I'd made the reservations for our tomorrow-our-engagement-goes-public dinner, but I did not order champagne. And who is Miss Tolliver?

Josh pulls out my chair. I'd specified dinner for two. But this is a table for four.

I'm juggling the unexpected champagne, the hovering maître d' and the mysterious Miss Tolliver when another glossy navy-suited woman arrives. She's carrying a sleek briefcase and holding a bulging Filofax and hefty expensive-looking pen.

"Renata Tolliver, the Paramount's wedding consultant." LaVinia performs the introductions, then returns to her post.

I look at Josh, questioning, but he's shaking hands with the newcomer.

The consultant smiles at him, then me, then Josh again. She's my mother's age, just as well preserved and even more professional. Chunky gold earrings, conservative pearls. Her platinum hair is snipped into a flawless bob, which swings effortlessly as she motions to a nearby waiter. She points him to the champagne. Instant hostess. Instantly in charge.

"Champagne with the hotel's compliments, Miss McNally," she says. "Your fiancé called me, thinking you might be interested in having a brief chat before dinner. As I'm certain you know, Paramount weddings are the crème de la crème."

We're each handed a crystal flute, and Miss Tolliver raises hers in our direction. "To your own wonderful ceremony. We would be delighted to arrange the most perfect Paramount event for the two of you."

I'm still flummoxed. My Josh? Made an appointment with a wedding consultant? I take a wary sip. I'm so not buying that.

"Your mother called. I happened to mention our dinner here tonight. The rest is history," Josh says. He touches a quick kiss to the top of my head, then pulls out his own chair. "She who must be obeyed."

Twenty minutes later, champagne half-gone and Josh still looking amused, Miss Tolliver is winding up the sales pitch for her vision of our wedding: the Paramount Platinum Package. My first wedding, twenty-five years ago, was the City Hall Package: fluorescent lighting and flowers from the vendor outside the Government Center subway stop. Sweet Baby James and I didn't last a year. Now, I'm struggling to stay skeptical, but every luscious photograph of pink-peony garlands and intricate buttercream frosting exposes some long-forgotten, deep-seated wedding fantasy. I know I should want to elope or do something simple. But I feel more like simply signing on the dotted line.

Miss Tolliver pulls a glossy white folder from her briefcase, points her pen to the embossed Paramount lion on the cover.

"My card is enclosed. Here are suggested menus. Flower arrangements. Tablecloth swatches. Photographs of cakes. The Platinum Package, as your mother suggests. And she says to tell you —" Miss Tolliver pauses, purses her lips "— well, I don't understand it, but she says to do this."

She holds up two fingers in the peace sign. "Is that right?" she asks.

"Mother is pulling out all the stops," I say. Even long-distance, she can never quite let go. "That's our sign that means 'the two of us, in it together.' "

"She seems to love you very much," Miss Tolliver says. She hands me the folder and stands to leave.

"She loves that I'm getting married," I reply.

"So do I," Josh says. He holds up his glass, saluting me.

So do I, I think. So do I.

"I can't believe she gave us samples of wedding cake to take home." I'm clutching my white wedding folder and two beribboned boxes of cake and psyching myself up for the big moment. And it's not just about our wedding.

"I can. The woman's a wedding machine and your mother is relentless," Josh says, teasing. "Much as we love her."

We peer through the front doors of the hotel, waiting for the parking valet to return. Josh had nothing new to report about Bexter, no more menacing phone calls. No matter how creatively I inquired, it seemed as if he's really told me everything he knows. Which gets me nowhere.

There was no time during dinner when it felt right to bring up New York. We promised each other no secrets. I'm determined to keep my promise, but I refuse to pull another all-nighter discussing our future. So during the car ride home it is. Fifteen minutes, Boston to Brookline, and I'm dropping the bombshell. Life is suddenly very complicated.

"There's the valet with our car." Josh points outside. "Finally."

We race through the snow, past the marble lions and into the car. The doors slam.

Here we go.

"So I have news," I say as we pull away from the hotel. Trying to keep my tone light. "Guess what Kevin told me today?"

"He's quitting," Josh says. He punches a few buttons on the dashboard radio, tuning it away from raucously grating sports talk. "Who changed the station? Anyway, I predict he's giving up TV to become a used-car salesman. Why not use his skills where he can really —"

"Yeah, well, funny. But yes, Mr. Clairvoyant. He's quitting." I adjust the boxes in my lap, hoping it won't be the only time I get wedding cake, and turn to Josh. I hadn't planned to say it this way, but it's kind of ironically sweet. "Can you keep a secret?"

It took five minutes to tell Josh about my New York offer. And almost every minute after that, he's been silent.

"Let me think" was his only reaction. In TV news, we often have to make split-second decisions. And when it's not necessary to decide instantly, we debate the pros and cons until the very last minute. With Josh, I'm still trying to learn his rhythm and not be afraid of quiet. The comfortable jazz from the radio disappears. Chatty voices from some talk show now make his silence more profound. But I can wait. And it won't be long. We're almost there.

We turn onto Bexter Academy Drive. Penny will be asleep, Annie waiting up for us. Josh will leave to drive her home. Here we go.

The porch light is on as we pull up to the curb. Josh turns the key and unbuckles his seat belt. As I'm trying to read his expression, the ceiling lights click off. We're in the darkness, snowfall ending, a few final flakes disappearing as they hit the hood of the car.

"Victoria left Penny and me because of her job." Josh is staring out the windshield. "Is that what you're going to do?"

I grab his hand. One box of wedding cake tumbles to the floor. "No. No. No, no, no. We just need to talk about it. I don't even know what I want to do. It's just — sudden. And big. And I wasn't supposed to tell you. And maybe I shouldn't have."

My chest tightens. This is new territory for me. Am I already lost?

"Maybe I should have worked it all out by myself," I continue. "But we promised, right? No secrets?"

"Sweetheart, I can't ask you to give up your dreams. You've wanted this for your entire career." Josh looks at me, as if he's trying to smile. Then he shakes his head. "I adore you. You know that. But you know Penny and I can't move to New York."

Okay, statistics guys. Maybe you're on to something. But I'm not going down without giving it my best shot. And maybe my dreams are changing.

"Drive time to New York is only about three hours," I say, testing this prospect. I'm still clutching Josh's hand. "If I drive fast. And you know I do. I could commute, live here on weekends, New York during the week. When school's back in session, your schedule is just as crazy as mine. It would hardly be different from the way it is now."

Josh picks up the box of cake from the

floor and hands it to me. "We'd better go in," he says.

The bluestone walkway to the front door is lined with graying piles of shoveled snow. We leave footprints in the newly fallen white. Through the front curtains, I see Annie's gauzy image and the flicker of the television.

"It's more like four hours of drive time," Josh says. "But we'll do what we have to do."

"Honey, I —" I see something. A piece of paper taped to the glass of the storm door.

Josh gets there first. In two more steps, I see the message, too.

I recognize Penny's artwork. Nine-year-old primitive, but instantly understandable. A bride, billowing veil and extravagant skirt. She's holding hands with the top-hatted groom. Next to the Crayola couple, a beaming flower girl (or maybe junior bridesmaid), enormous pink dress, masses of curlicues around her skirt. And scattered across the page, dozens of red hearts, flying through the awkward drawing like happy butterflies.

"Looks like the votes are in," Josh says. He snaps down the drawing with one hand and reaches toward the doorknob with the other. "From Penny, at least."

And from me, too, I want to say. I know

our future is together. I'm just not sure how. Everything good is happening at the same time.

One hand still on the knob, Josh turns to me, his face softening as he holds up the drawing. "She's never been so happy. I've never been so happy. So, there's a bump in the road. And I'm sure there'll be more. But we'll ride them out, sweetheart. Together."

I hold up the boxes. "Piece of cake," I say.

I hope I'm right.

CHAPTER FOUR

"If he's such a hotshot, why isn't he still in Beirut, or wherever he was? Whoa, look at me. Even after Max and Molly, I still can't believe this. This is like — three basketballs' worth of baby."

Maysie takes a sip of her morning tea, standing sideways in front of the mirror of the fourth-floor ladies' room. She's scrutinizing her alarmingly pregnant profile and chattering nonstop, as usual. Just back late last night from covering Super Bowl preparations in Dallas and soon to give birth to her third child, she's the only woman who works in Channel 3's all-sports radio station, so she's been able to commandeer the fourth-floor ladies' room as her exclusive salon. It's also a private spot where we can share our scoops without fear of interruption. And this morning I've got the biggest one yet.

"Mays?"

"And you're going out on these under-cover shoots with him? Are you sure you can trust him? I mean, like, do you know whether he got fired? Or flipped out? Or some unimaginably hideous other thing that he's keeping a big secret? Somehow? On the other hand, he's truly hot. Those cheek-bones alone . . ." She eyes me appraisingly. "Think he's single?"

I'm standing with my hands behind my back, leaning against the door, carefully hiding my ring. Maysie and Matthew Green are Mr. and Mrs. Suburban Married Bliss, and for years, Mays has indefatigably analyzed every available single man for what she calls his "Charlie potential." Margaret Isobel DeRosiers Green has been my cheerleader and confidante through a succession of unsuitable suitors who turned out to be either too attracted to my success or too intimidated by it. When *Bride's Magazine* started appearing in my mail a few months ago, it could only have come from Mom or Maysie. Maysie confessed. She's a top-notch reporter, tough and knowledgeable as any guy in the sports trenches. But I'm about to spring some real breaking news. As soon as she stops talking.

"Mays?"

"Still, why would he give up the network

to come to Boston and work with you?" She's tucking her brown hair into the usual ponytail and yanking on a Celtics cap. "No offense, Brenda, but I mean, who wouldn't want to work at the network if they could? And hey, you're still guest-hosting my Wixie show, right?"

Brenda Starr, the glam comic-strip reporter who never gets old. The nickname always bugs me, since I'm a real-life reporter whose aging is all too apparent. Still, Mays is just being affectionate. I wonder what she'd say about Kevin's network offer. I wish I could ask her.

"Mays," I say, stepping into the room. "We've gotta go on this shoot in about three minutes. I have no idea about J.T. Shaw. Maybe he's secretly some kind of ax murderer, okay? I'll keep a lookout for an ax. Yes, I'm doing your radio show. Josh had WWXI on in the car just the other night. But listen —"

"Gotta love radio," she says. "Don't even have to comb your hair and lipstick is optional. And I told you they're paying, right? Not much, though, kiddo. Probably enough for a new pair of shoes, the way they're chintzing out these days. But thanks, Brenda. Soon as little Maddee or Malcolm arrives, you take over the microphone."

Time's up. Franklin and J.T. are waiting. I've never kept a secret from Maysie before.

I hold out my left hand.

And I don't say a word.

Her scream echoes down the hall as I head out the door.

"Can you hear me now?" Franklin's voice is muffled. He's walking across Route 1, the so-called Auto Mile, headed for one of the many car dealers lining this section of the highway. We're talking by cell phone, making sure we're connected.

My laptop and I are stashed in the way-back of our "undercover car," the unmarked black SUV we use for stakeouts and surveillance. The one-way windows are tinted as dark as they can be and still pass state inspection. I can see out perfectly from my vantage point in the McDonald's parking lot, but no one can see in.

This is the annoying part about being recognizable. I can barely go undercover anymore, around Boston at least, unless I'm deeply in disguise. So we've devised a scheme where I can stay hidden while Franklin and J.T. act as my eyes and ears.

"Ten-four, gotcha. I hear you loud and clear." Phone clamped to my shoulder, I twist out of my hunter-green down vest and fold it against the back of the front seat as a makeshift headrest. No telling how long this is going to take. My boots are off, too, and my legs are stretched out the length of the back compartment, my black wool pants already attracting a coating of carpet lint. I'll have to change clothes before the Bexter party tonight. But now I've got my computer on my lap. Latte in the cupholder. A pretty good view out the back window.

Red-white-and-blue-striped banners flutter across a block-long used-car lot. The mammoth sign on the flat-roofed showroom behind them proclaims Miracle Motors. Lines of glossy vehicles with grease-pencil prices scrawled on the windows glisten in multicolored rows. Towering above, on a two-story metal contraption, a bright yellow minivan rotates like the car lot's own moon. On its windshield: Take me Home — I'm Your New Honey.

Just as Franklin walks onto the lot, J.T. pulls in, driving his dark blue Audi. Right on schedule. J.T. emerges in a burnished leather jacket, black jeans and black turtleneck. He looks like a walking American Express gold card. Franklin, sacrificing style for the benefit of the story, wears a too-big Celtics hoodie he snagged from the sports department and some garish basketball shoes.

Let's hear it for stereotypes. The salespeople lock their sights on conspicuous consumer J.T. Franklin is just a guy in a sweatshirt with a Bluetooth earpiece. Again, our plan works.

While Franklin heads for the back of the lot, J.T. tries to engage as many of the salespeople as possible. I burst out laughing as J.T. takes out a pocket-size digital camera and gets the slavering employees to snap his photo with car after car. Our cover story is that he wants the photos to show his wife her new-car choices. The snapshots will prove dangerous cars are for sale. If we can find any. And I'm betting my job we can.

"Try to find a 2006 Cambria," I remind Franklin. I tap the keyboard, check that my battery level is nice and plump and click open my notes. "They've been recalled for transmission failures. Look for the first character in the Vehicle Identification Number to be a one. A two means the car was made in Canada and we don't want those."

All the way across the street, I see Franklin gesture to wave me off. He knows. The seventeen-digit VINs on each car are the key to this story. They're like a car's social security number. Its unique fingerprint.

Once we grab the VIN, we can look up the car's repair history.

"Here's a pale blue Cambria, 2006," Franklin says, opening the driver's-side door to see the metal plate on the inside of the doorjamb, one of the places where the VIN is always stamped. "Yes, one is the first number here. And now, confirming that the tenth character is six for made in 2006. Yes. Ready, Charlotte?"

Franklin reads me a string of letters and numbers. I type it into the computer database we're creating. He moves down the row to the next Cambria, and then the next and the next. It's time-consuming and there's absolutely no room for mistakes. If I type even one digit incorrectly, we'll be looking up the wrong car and our story will crash and burn.

Franklin moves away from the line of Cambrias. I see J.T. leading his entourage to get the same cars on camera. Little do they know.

I get a little flare of goose bumps. And it's not because the heat in the car is off. We're a great team. And this is a great story.

"Franklin, you there?" I say into the phone.

I just had two more ideas about how we can make our story even better.

70

■ ■ ■ ■

I flip open my reporter's notebook. Although we're verging on late for the Bexter party, my eye-wearying day of transcribing VINs is not over yet. Josh is still inside changing, so there's just enough time.

"Just read me the numbers and letters, okay?" It's probably the last thing Annie Vilardi expected me to say about the new — well, new to her — Ombra sedan her parents just gave her. She's helping to make payments with the money she earns sitting with Penny. Now the two of them, wearing identical Bexter jackets and tasseled ski caps, are delightedly demonstrating every gadget and gizmo on the white four-door. It's the automotive version of a refrigerator, safe and boxy. But my research is about to prove even cars like this could have unrepaired recalls. So practicing what I preach, I'd better check out Annie's car.

"Look through the windshield, on the dashboard. Nope, tucked in farther. The numbers are on a little metal placard."

"Oh, yeah, I see it!" Annie says. She calls out the rest of the VIN as Josh trots down the front steps, checking his watch.

"Keep the porch lights on," he says.

"Don't let anyone in. You have our cell numbers. And turn off the oven after you take out the pizza."

"Of course, Professor Gelston," Annie says.

"Duh," Penny says.

One Bexter Academy Drive, the most prestigious address in Bexter faculty housing, is just five houses away from Josh's number six, though we can't see it through the neighborhood's stand of evergreens. Tonight is Headmaster Byron Forrestal's annual open house, a command performance for Bexter faculty and staff, as well as parents of new students.

And it's my first appearance as a parent. At least, stepparent-to-be. I link my fingers through Josh's as we approach the Head's ornately carved oak front door and ring the bell. It feels as if I'm stepping into a new life. It's also my first real opportunity to sniff out the truth about those phone calls. If I'm a parent, I don't want my daughter to be in danger.

"Sweets?" I say. "They all know we're getting married, right?"

Before Josh can answer, the door sweeps open and a cultured voice comes from behind it.

"Indeed. It's our Josh and his beautiful

Ms. McNally. Welcome, welcome. And my most sincere congratulations to the happy couple."

The Head himself has answered, looking as stereotypically predictable in his prep-school mode as Franklin and J.T. did in their undercover outfits this afternoon. Our coats are whisked away. The Head is clipped and almost military, compact and square shouldered in his double-breasted blue blazer and yellow Bexter tie. Gray slacks match his gray temples.

As the Head leads us into a cozy living room, all firelight and candles and buzzing with low-key chat, it looks as if every other man is dressed almost identically. What's more, someone must have sent the women a twin-set-and-pearls e-mail. I adjust the collar of my black turtleneck dress. Close enough.

"Biscuits and brandy, of course, for you both. Our little tradition." The Head gestures to a gleaming array of silver trays and cut-glass decanters matching crystal glasses. "Then do look around the cottage, my dear."

Very lord of the manor. I don't sense any hesitation or nervousness. I guess he assumes Josh didn't tell me the Bexter secret. He's quite an actor.

"You'll see I'm a history buff. As your Josh will explain. Our meeting starts in just a few moments."

The Head strides away, leaving the faintest scent of — scotch? Josh pours brandy. Which I couldn't possibly drink at this hour.

" 'Cottage,' did he say? History buff?" I ask softly, close to Josh's ear. His living room is twice as big as what I'd consider a cottage, and twice as elaborate. Handsomely patterned rugs. Majestic fireplace. Mahogany paneling. Elaborate ship models, sails full. Swords, be-tasseled and polished. Glowing sconces. I steal a close-up look at a framed parchment document, elaborate and unreadable, then at a stand holding an open leather-bound book, pages yellowing and brown edged. "Looks like a Revolutionary War museum in here. How does he afford all this valuable stuff on a school administrator's salary? Or is that a lot higher than I'd imagined?"

A tweedy couple, her scarf recognizably expensive and his tie yellow, both holding brandy glasses in hand, pass by us with polite party smiles. I see the woman do a fleeting double take. I've seen that look many times before. She's realized who I am.

"One Bexter Academy Drive is endowed, so it's rent free," Josh whispers after they're

74

out of earshot. "Plus, he's single. Uses all his salary on his colonial history obsession. That book on the stand is his latest treasure, scuttlebutt is he outbid some museum for it. But there's nothing old-fashioned about his alarm system. He showed me once. It's state of the art."

"Who's that? In the Hermès scarf?" I ask. I tuck myself behind Josh, scanning the room. I hide my brandy snifter behind a massive white poinsettia. "Dorothy Wirt is here, right? Where? Who's the guy with the —"

Someone claps for attention, instantly silencing the cocktail-time chatter and the beginnings of my detective work.

Josh shoots me a "you're not fooling me" look. "Tell you later," he says.

The Head is the center of attention.

"Welcome all, to our annual gathering. New parents, tonight we'll discuss rules and regulations. Responsibilities. And of course, my favorite topic and yours, fundraising."

My brain clicks off a bit, scanning faces in the crowd, as the Head natters on in the plummy voice Josh imitated so perfectly. Luckily, I manage to hear my name and look attentive again before it's too late.

". . . and we'd like to extend a true Bexter welcome as she enters our little community.

Now we have our own in-house investigative reporter." He raises a glass in my direction.

Dear Miss Manners.

"Always looking for a good story, Headmaster," I say. My most congenial. I went to Chicago's Public School 11, and I may not ever be comfortable calling someone "Headmaster," but here I am in Rome.

There's a smattering of applause as the formal part of the evening ends. I grab Josh's arm, pull him to a corner. "Show me everyone," I demand.

Josh looks perplexed. "Everyone who?"

"You know. The people you said know about the calls."

Josh's arm stiffens. I watch his expression change.

"I just want to know," I say, attempting to cut off his inevitable protest. "I just want to see them. I promise I won't say anything."

Josh sighs, then looks down at me skeptically.

I try for earnest. "Soul of discretion."

Josh points across the room, defeated. "You see Dorothy? Just coming out of the other room. Holding what looks like scotch. That's Alethia Espinosa with her. Dean of girls."

"Are they sisters?" I ask. "They're like

fluttery little wrens."

"Hardly. Like I said, don't get in their way," Josh replies. He puts down his brandy. "And Dorothy has a real sister, who lives with her."

I feel a touch on my elbow.

"Miss McNally, I have some members of our Bexter family you must meet." The Head has two more men in copycat blazers in his wake, both half a step behind him. Their posture verges on obsequious.

"May I present Harrison Ebling, our new development consultant, and our bursar, Aaron Pratt."

The moneymen. The fundraisers. I almost smile. They think I'm making the big reporter bucks and are gunning to put the hit on me for a donation. But this may be a plus. Josh had told me the bursar knew about the calls. Maybe this development person does, too. I plot strategy, wishing for my notebook.

"How nice to meet you," I say. "We're so eager for Penny to start next semester. How long have each of you been with Bexter?"

Josh's foot goes on top of mine. And it's not a mistake.

I move my boot away, resisting the urge to add a tiny kick indicating I'm just delicately probing, and keep my eyes charmingly fixed on the two newcomers. "And do tell me what you're each working on. I'm so eager to learn everything about my new Bexter family."

It's a private school. But I bet nothing stays private for long.

CHAPTER FIVE

"Just look at me, not at the camera." I smile encouragingly at Declan Ross. We're in his living room, sitting knee to knee on the spindle-backed chairs Franklin and I moved out of the dining room and placed in front of the fireplace.

I knew today's interview would make our story. Put a real face on the problem. When I called from Channel 3 earlier this morning, giving the accident victim the tried-and-true "it could help other people" tactic, he'd agreed. Happily, this time it's actually true.

"Rolling," J.T. says. "I have speed."

Franklin, notebook in hand and sitting out of camera range on a flame-stitch sectional couch, performs an overdramatic cough, complete with eye-rolling. "I have speed" is movie jargon, because film cameras have to rev up before you can start shooting. Our video camera is at the proper speed instantly. J.T. just says it to sound hip and Hollywood. Franklin isn't going to let him get away with it.

I throw him a cool-it look and turn to Declan Ross.

"So, Mr. Ross," I begin. I adjust the skirt of my new and somewhat risky aubergine wool suit. "How did you feel when you got the recall letter, saying your car's brakes could fail, and that most likely, a failure would happen at high speed?"

"How can carmakers get away with it?" Ross says. He holds out both hands, supplicant, illustrating the depth of his concern. "They manufactured vehicles that were defective. Thousands of them. They should never have left the factory. I could have been killed. My family could have been killed. It's a nightmare, not just for me, but for every driver on the road. I'm enraged."

I pause for a beat or two. Truth is, we're done. In thirty seconds, Mr. Ross has given me all we need: anger, disdain, fear for his own family and outrage for others. We could take down all our equipment and walk out of here right now. I glance at Franklin again. We don't need to exchange a word. He shrugs, smiling, then rolls a finger, pantomiming, "It's a wrap."

But suddenly I'm not sure.

"Couple more questions," I say. It's rude to take your sound bites and run. Plus, I just thought of something. "Back to the accident. When you were driving the rental car. The air bag on your side didn't go off, did it? Did you ever find out why? Did the police ask about that?"

"Hardly." Declan Ross is dismissive. He pushes up the sleeves of his navy turtleneck and blinks, briefly, after looking directly at the megawatt light pointed at his face. People only do that once.

"The cops couldn't get out of there fast enough as soon as they saw we were all okay. Once they realized I hadn't gotten the license plate — how could I? They were like, 'Well, we'll be in touch.'"

"Have they been?"

"Nope. And they sure didn't seem too optimistic about finding the guy. Now I check out every car that goes by, trying to find him myself. Bastar— I mean — oh, I shouldn't say —" Ross, suddenly flustered, looks at me.

"It's just tape," I say, waving off his embarrassment. "Not live television. You can start over, no problem. And I understand you're upset."

"Upset that we'll never find who did this," Ross continues. "Cops don't seem to care."

"Well, it's an unfortunate reality," I say. "If no one was hurt, it may not be worth their time to charge someone with driving to endanger. A trial could be tough. Because the other driver, forgive me, could say it was your fault. Or that it happened because of the icy road."

Declan Ross shakes his head. "It's just not fair. It was a rental car. And I didn't get the extra insurance. So now, I take the hit. And my insurance premium does, too. Someone should find that car, you know? Find that damn driver and take his license. Force him to pay. He could have killed my children."

I pause, leaving a beat of silence so that juicy sound bite is easy to edit. And he's right. Someone should find that driver. Maybe Franklin and me. Maybe there's a bigger story we're missing.

"Mr. Ross?" Franklin's voice. "Sorry to interrupt. You said you 'check out every car that goes by.' So did you see something recognizable? Even just the color of the car might prove helpful."

"Daddy?" a voice comes from somewhere behind me, then the squeak of rubber on hardwood floor. Gabriel, in gigantic rubber-soled running shoes, runs to his father's knee. "Can I be on TV?"

Ross wraps one arm around Gabriel, then

in one motion lifts him up and deposits him on his lap. In his floppy New England Patriots T-shirt, all ankles and knees and ears, the little boy looks a lot less scared than he did by the side of the road.

I decide to play along. After all, we have all we need. "So, Gabriel, who's your favorite football player?"

Gabe looks dubious. Football is not why he's here.

"It's was like I told you. Like I told Daddy," he says, stolid and serious as only a five-year-old can be. "It looked like my blue Matchbox car."

I'm silent. Franklin is silent. Behind me, almost in a whisper, J.T. says, "Still rolling."

"What kind of a car is that? Do you know?" I ask. I'm interviewing a five-year-old. How reliable can he be? Can I even use this on the air? But he's on his father's lap and his father isn't stopping me. I keep my voice gentle.

"Did you see the car go through the toll booth on the highway? You know the toll booths?"

"Yes. I saw it going. It went fast. Then our car went bang." His lower lip begins to pooch out, his long eyelashes cobwebbing with tears. "And Sophie was really crying. And Daddy wasn't talking."

Forget the camera. In one motion, I'm off my chair and crouched in front of him, eye to eye.

"Gabe? Can you go get your Matchbox car for me?"

The uniformed factotum at the guards' desk is barricaded behind a chin-level Formica fortress strewn with black vinyl ring binders I know are sign-in sheets. His back is to an array of tiny TV monitors, some flickering grainy black-and-white video of unrecognizably blurry figures waiting at elevators and walking down the institutional hallways of the Park Plaza state office building. As the three of us approach, the guard reluctantly puts down the greasy-looking paperback he's reading. He's curled the cover around to the back to hide the title.

"We're going to the Mass Pike offices, room 1504," I say, filling my voice with confidence. I don't tell him we have an appointment with Massachusetts Turnpike mogul David Chernin. Because that's not true. We have no appointment at all. We're just attempting to insinuate ourselves upstairs. If we fail, we'll be escorted to the down escalator and out into the overpriced food court.

An hour ago, Gabe showed us a tiny blue

Mustang. Here's where we might track down the real one. We've got to at least try.

"Synneer," the guard says. His plastic name tag says Bill Bevan. With a stubby finger, Bevan spins one of the notebooks in our general direction. "Idees."

"Sure, of course." I give the guys a surreptitious thumbs-up, and flash my driver's license instead of my station ID. If this guy is the slacker he seems, we may be able to keep people from confirming we were here. I sign on the next available line, although I write Tina Marie Turner instead of my real name. Franklin, nodding his understanding, signs Don Ameche. J.T. signs an illegible scrawl, keeping his camera low and out of sight.

Bevan "analyzes" our signatures without a blink. So much for security.

Just as I'm certain we're in the clear, the guard, whose pinkish scalp is attempting to burst through his invisible hair and whose neck flab is encroaching on the collar of his blue uniform, narrows his eyes at me. Unfortunately, I then get to see his teeth.

"You that TV girl," Bevan says. The smile evaporates and he begins to reach for an enormous phone console covered with push buttons. "Maybe I should call."

"Hey, man, cool setup," J.T. interrupts.

85

He unzips his black parka, hoists his camera onto the desk, then points toward the monitors. "You got surveillance video there? You got tape, or digital? How many eyes? Is it a VTR-54B? How do you recon the scenes?"

Apparently, the security guard isn't much of a multi-tasker. He abandons the phone and focuses on J.T. My photographer, I'm willing to bet, is talking complete nonsense.

But J.T.'s suddenly a team player.

"Show me your setup, dude," J.T. says. As the guard turns back to his monitors, J.T. cocks his head at us. In the direction of the elevators. "Go," he mouths.

David Chernin owes me big and he knows it. When he and his wife got some horrible stomach bug on their tenth-anniversary cruise a few years ago, he called me to do a refund battle with their uncooperative travel agency. Companies get very nervous when they hear "This is Charlie McNally from Channel 3." I managed to get all their money back. Although I never expect a quid pro quo for just doing my job, that fact places Franklin and me in a very nice negotiating position.

When he's not on a cruise, Chernin is the computer guru of the Mass Turnpike's toll enforcement division. After we promised not to tell where we got the info, he agreed to show us photos he probably shouldn't.

"Nope," Chernin says, pointing. "Nope. Nope."

We're watching black-and-white images flicker by on Chernin's flat-screen monitor. We're hoping to see a Mustang, just like the Matchbox car Gabriel Ross showed us, though of course we won't be able to tell if it's blue. Each photo, snapped automatically by the surveillance cameras mounted at all three tollbooths, displays the license plate of a car that blew through the tolls without paying around the time of the accident. If the driver we're looking for paid the toll, in cash or with an electronic transponder, there won't be a picture. But I'm predicting he was too freaked out and driving too fast to pay cash.

"Nope. Nope. Nope."

Each car is on-screen a fraction of a second, just long enough for the three of us to assess whether it's a Mustang or not. Dozens have gone by. So far, no Mustangs. But to me, each no means a yes is even closer. And I keep wondering. Why aren't the police using this technology to enforce the law? How many bad guys are out there, caught on camera but not caught by the cops?

"I understand you're not going to throw me under the bus here," Chernin says. His eyes never leave the screen as his right hand clicks the mouse on the Next button. One after another, the photos continue to appear, and his voice goes quiet. "You know as well as I do — this meeting never happened. So how are you going to explain how you found this car? Without implicating me?"

"*If* we find the car," Franklin says. He's also staring at the screen.

"When we find the car," I say. "And when we do, I'm sure we can figure out a way to protect you."

Chernin turns away from the screen, stashing his wire-rimmed glasses on the top of his head. He runs triathlons and has that gaunt malnourished look some runners cultivate. Cheekbones. Shortest possible hair. He tightens his tie, shoots the cuffs of his shirt. His face is hardening.

"Charlie," he begins.

We may be in trouble.

"There's one." Franklin had picked up the mouse and continued clicking through the photos himself. He points to the screen. "Look. Clearly a Mustang."

Chernin whirls back and we all lean in closer, focused on the fuzzy but recognizable image. Franklin's right. And the time stamp says 4:26. Perfect.

"We done now?" Chernin asks.

"You can print a copy for us, right?" I say. My fists clench and I feel my got-a-good-story shivers beginning. I always know. I also know it's a risk to get too excited too soon. I turn to Chernin, aware we're on thin ice. My fists become crossed fingers.

"And can we keep looking, please, just briefly? There could have been more than one Mustang."

Chernin tilts his head, considering. He's increasingly unhappy with this. And it is probably a job-threatening breach of something. He looks at the chunky black watch strapped to his emaciated wrist. "Ten minutes. At the most."

"Thank you so much," I say. We know the accident was over by then anyway. "We'll never ask for anything again."

"You got that right," Chernin mutters. He goes back to the mouse, clicking faster and faster as the image parade continues. Whatever is going to happen better happen fast.

By the time the time stamp says 4:36 p.m. we've seen no more Mustangs. Chernin clicks the screen to black. "Time," he says.

Franklin and I exchange glances. No question the whole thing is iffy. If little Gabe is right. If this car is blue. And even if so, if this is the right Mustang.

Still. It's more than we had when we came in. And we may have found the driver who caused the accident. And caused so much expense and fear in the Ross household.

"Again, you're the best. This could really help us," I say. "Can you hit Print? And we'll be out of your life."

Mission accomplished. I hope. I put on my black overcoat, wrap and tie the belt, and scramble through my cordovan tote bag for my gloves. We hear the photo of the Mustang whir out of the printer. Chernin pulls it from the tray. I hold out my hand, smiling. J.T. is probably waiting for us in the food court. He'll be psyched that his tactic worked.

"Thanks, David," Franklin says, zipping on his khaki parka. He takes his carefully folded black gloves out of a side pocket. "Obviously this is just for research. We won't use this photo in our story."

Chernin is holding the printed picture in both hands. Then, with one swift motion, he crumples it, shaking his head. He crams the wad of paper into his pants pocket.

"No," he says. "I can't let you have it."

"Seven, four, two, F, Y, six," I say as the

90

elevator doors close behind us. I dig for my notebook. Of course I memorized the license number. I'm sure Franklin did, too. "Regular Massachusetts passenger plate. With a sticker saying he's due for a new one next July. Is that what you got, too, Franko?"

"Yes, exactly." Franklin hits the button for lobby. "And there was a decal for Hallinan Motors. That car dealer. Guess your Mr. Chernin got cold feet."

"Or maybe he simply figured we'd remember the plate and make a public-records request for it. He knows the number's all we really need. Now he can deny he gave it to us. Plus, no one can make what's already happened *un*happen. That's a secret no one can keep. Toll violations are clearly public record. And we're the public. It's all good."

I tuck my notebook and pen away as the elevator door opens and deposits us in the food court. J.T. is at a corner table. Happily, he's alone.

My cell phone suddenly trills the voice mail–message signal. I flip open the phone, tap in my code. Message from Josh that must have come in while we were upstairs. This office building is a notorious dead zone.

"Franko, go tell J.T. the scoop, okay? And if you get lunch, will you order me a salad?

No onions and no croutons. It's already three. I'm starving. And maybe call the registry and ask for records of that Mustang violation. I've gotta call Josh, but we might as well get the show on the road. And we've got to follow up on the recalled cars."

Pushing through the revolving door out of the food court, I stand in the cold vestibule of the building, looking past the doors onto the darkening afternoon. Tremont Street bustles with swaddled pedestrians. A double-long city bus wheezes up to the curb. Snow-booted workers stretch over a gray pool of curbside slush to clamber inside. A man in a Yankees cap hops on just as the bus lumbers away.

New York. The words are a taunting mental billboard. Ten years ago, five, I'd have moved to the big time in a heartbeat. Now, I admit, I'm avoiding the decision.

"Sweetheart?" I say as Josh finally answers the phone. The signal is crackly, but I'll persevere. I feel my eyes narrow, blocking out everything but my fiancé's voice. Winter-wrapped downtown Boston fades as I listen through the static, intent. I'm surprised beyond surprise.

"She's — what?"

CHAPTER SIX

The plastic crime-scene tape loops around the three old maple trees in front of Dorothy Wirt's home, garish black and yellow fluttering in the afternoon chill. Two Brookline police cars, front wheels on the curb and rear wheels on the street, cordon off the sidewalk. Their sirens are silent, but spinning blue lights reflect, harsh and unnatural, on the snow. Four black-jacketed officers stand sentinel, blowing into their hands, their breath puffing white. An ambulance, rear doors toward the garage and a uniformed EMT beside it, blocks the driveway. The garage door is closed. The front door is closed. No one is hurrying. But me.

I trot toward the murmuring knot of onlookers, my mind racing for explanations, scanning for a familiar navy wool overcoat. Josh turns, sees me, just as I get close enough. A blue light flashes across his face.

"So it's true. Is it true? I got here fast as I

could," I whisper, tucking both arms through the crook of his elbow. I look around. "Penny?"

"She's home with Annie. The kids don't know yet."

"Who's here?"

"The Head's inside, so's Dorothy's younger sister, Millie. She's just back from a business trip. What a horrible — they live together. Lived."

His face is red from the cold. His eyes are also red. He stops, shakes his head.

"Anyway, Alethia found her. Espinosa, the dean of girls? Remember? In the garage. In her car. When Dorothy didn't arrive for work at Bexter this morning, we all thought maybe she'd had too much to drink at the Head's last night."

I wrap myself more tightly against him, fitting myself behind him, my face buried in his back, my eyes peering over his shoulder, watching the house.

"So then?" My voice is muffled in his navy overcoat.

The sound of metal on metal. Every head in the crowd turns, transfixed, as behind the ambulance, Dorothy's old-fashioned wooden garage door creaks open, inch by inch. The EMT leaves his post at the ambulance and ducks underneath as the door gets waist high.

The door slams back to the ground. I flinch as it hits. I feel Josh flinch, too.

"She's inside?" It still feels better to whisper.

"They think it's carbon monoxide, that's what the Head told me," Josh replies. "An accident. Maybe she did have too much brandy. Made it home safely, then fell asleep with that old car of hers still running and the radio on. Maybe she was listening to something. Who knows."

Part of me, the wife-to-be, wants to take Josh home and comfort him. Explain to Penny, somehow, that sometimes life brings sorrow and sad surprises. And these are times that remind us to cherish those we love.

The other part of me, the reporter, wants to whip out my press card, get past that yellow tape and see if I can wrangle some answers.

The reporter part emerges, carefully. All the local cops here are in uniform. Certainly, in a death like this, state police homicide detectives must be on the way. And we know something the police don't know.

"Sweetheart? Did anyone ever report those 'do you know where your children are?' calls to the police?"

"I know where you're going," Josh says, shaking his head. "No."

One more step. Carefully.

"Maybe the caller wasn't targeting the school. Maybe whoever it was — was targeting Dorothy. Personally."

Silence from Josh.

"The Head said police think it was an accident," he finally answers.

"We'll see, I guess." I close my eyes, resting my forehead against Josh's back. "We'll see."

It's a good thing my cell phone is on Vibrate. Through Dorothy Wirt's entire memorial service, it buzzes my thigh through the side of my purse. During the minister's somber introduction; through the Bexter choir's *Ode to St. Cecilia,* sweet and sorrowfully sung by mournful teenagers; during the heartbreakingly tender eulogies from Millie, her old friend the bursar, and confidante Alethia; during the stiff-upper-lip benediction from the Headmaster. I know it's Franklin who's covering for me back at the station this morning. But I don't understand why he keeps calling. At least no one can hear it.

The tolling bells in the historic Bexter Carillon signal the end of the ceremony. A muted organ begins an unadorned version of "Danny Boy." Millie, clutching the Head-master's arm, steps from the maroon-carpeted dais, past masses of pink-and-white lilies, down the carpeted aisle past carved wooden pews of mourners. Parents, teachers, administrators, some local semi-celebrity faces familiar from newspapers and television. A few, mostly students, reach out a hand to touch her arm.

"You okay, sweetheart?" I whisper to Josh. We're edging out of our pew, waiting as students and parents, teachers and adminis-trators silently take their leave, row by row. Some of the mourners I recognize from the Head's party. The last time Dorothy was alive.

Josh just smiles, a sorrow-tinged expres-sion I've grown used to over the past twenty-four hours. We told Penny what happened. Our first experience, Dad and almost-Mom, explaining the unexplainable. Penny didn't know Dorothy, of course. But she's uncom-fortable when people — as she puts it — "go away." Divorce is never easy. Leaves a mark.

My phone is vibrating again. I let it go to voice mail again as we file outside toward the receiving line forming in the entryway. It'll be Millie. Alethia. Bursar Pratt. Minister Ashworth. The Head.

"Josh?" A voice behind us. "A moment, please?"

The Head, acknowledging me with a nod, draws Josh aside, across the nave and into a tapestried corner. Josh turns, briefly waving me outside. "One minute," he mouths, holding up a finger.

Now I'll be able to check my voice mail.

One hand is already in my tote bag, searching blindly for my cell as I follow the congregation out the massive oak-and-stained-glass double doors and onto the steep stone steps of Bexter Chapel. Got it.

"Charlotte McNally?"

My hand comes out of my purse as I turn, facing back now toward the chapel doors. On the step above me stands an elegant gentleman in a charcoal coat, one gloved hand on the railing. Perfectly tailored alpaca sets off his snow-white temples and clipped beard. A paisley silk-and-wool muffler is knotted around his neck. I recognize him from pictures in the newspaper.

"Mr. Fielder?" I'm surprised. Loudon Fielder, the owner of WWXI radio, has children at Bexter? More likely to be grandchildren.

I reach out to shake his offered hand. "So sad about Dorothy."

"A very special person. Always remembered everyone's name," he replies. He looks down the steps, apparently recognizing someone. "Ah, my apologies. Someone I need to speak to. But I am looking forward to your fill-in appearances on Wixie. Lovely to have you on our air while our Maysie is tending to her baby. Perhaps radio will become your second career."

"Thank you, that would be —"

And he's gone. I shrug. I suppose he was just being polite. Time to check my voice mail.

"Sweetheart. I have news." Josh is behind me, his voice is close to my ear. "Let's walk, and I'll fill you in."

My phone goes back into my purse.

"The Head says it was an accident," Josh tells me, keeping his voice low as we walk, arm in arm, down the church steps. "She had too much brandy, or whatever she was drinking, maybe fell asleep with the car running. Way too much carbon monoxide in her blood. The medical examiner is going to sign the death certificate. Accident."

"So that's that," I say. We come to the bottom and stand on the Chapel Road sidewalk, looking out over the Bexter Common. The organ has changed to Bach. Milky sunshine glints off the snow still sticking to the lofty evergreens.

"Yes," Josh replies. "That's that."

"How many times did you have to call? I probably lost weight in my left thigh from all that vibration."

"I only called you twice. Maybe three times," Franklin replies. "Anyway —"

"Never mind," I interrupt. Maybe it was only three times. I called him back without even checking messages. I'm huddled, facing the wall, in a corner of the lobby of Landman Hall. It's called Main since it's Bexter's main building. Long tables, covered with damask cloths and the lilies from the chapel, offer tiny lemon cookies and delicate quarter-cut sandwiches. Everyone from the memorial service is here. I'm feeling guilty. I should be at work. "What's up?"

"Michael Borum." Franklin savors the syllables, drawing them out, as if saying the name is a pleasure. "B-o-r-u-m. Mr. Blue Mustang. The owner. The registry came through. It's a real break for us. J.T. and I are headed to his house in the South End right now. So. Can you meet us there?"

Now what am I supposed to do? I have to be here, for Josh's sake. I have to be with Franklin, for our story's sake. I lean my forehead against the dark paneling, trying to make an impossible decision. How can I be two places at once?

I delegate. "You guys go. Check it out, see if the car's there. Get some shots of it. And get the VIN if you can. Don't trespass. Too much. Then let me know."

"Will you answer your phone when I call next time?"

"If you're lucky." I glance toward the room behind me. Josh is waiting, alone, over by the silver tea samovars. He catches my eye and signals, *hurry up.*

"What if Borum comes out?" Franklin persists. "What if he wants to talk? Or what if he gets angry, yells at us? It would be terrific video. And so much more compelling if you were in it."

Like I don't know this. Why is Franklin pressuring me now of all times?

"What's more, we've got to be at the rental-car place by two. The health unit is demanding the hidden camera, they need it by five. For some story on deadly hot dogs." Franklin's voice is a sneer. "Big journalists, those health people."

Josh. Dorothy Wirt. Threatening phone calls. Mr. Blue Mustang. Our story. Our wedding. New York. The rental-car investigation. VIN numbers. Dangerous cars. New York. Deadly hot dogs?

I'm just about in over my head. I struggle

to stay afloat.

"Franklin. Just go, okay? Then call me. I'll meet you at Rental Car King in plenty of time. It'll work. All of it. One thing at a time."

"I certainly hope so," Franklin says. The phone goes dead.

Josh is heading toward me. Thumbs flying across my cell phone's keypad, I open the text messages to erase all of Franklin's calls. And see if there were really only three.

Ha. I was right. There were four. But I was wrong. One wasn't Franklin. It was Maysie.

New baby arriving. Tonight? Cross fingers.

"You there, Franko? I can see you guys perfectly." My laptop, my cell phone and I are once again stationed in the back of the surveillance car. I'm in a strip-mall parking lot and this time I've got binoculars. Last time it drove me crazy to be so far away.

Score one for me and for delegating tasks. Michael Borum wasn't home. And his car wasn't there. Therefore, I didn't miss anything. As I said to Franklin, Borum's probably hiding himself and his car from the police. We can try again later and hope we find him before the law does. Odds are in our favor, since we know the law isn't looking.

Now we're back to our recall story.

"Charlotte? Can you hear me?" Franklin's voice bristles through my cell phone. Acting like pals who want to rent a car, he and J.T. are heading across the street. J.T.'s job is to go to the main office of the rental-car agency, where he's supposed to distract the clerk. I'm hoping the clerk is female. J.T. will be in his James Dean element.

"Loud and clear," I say.

Meanwhile, Franklin will stay in the parking lot with a tiny hidden camera lens sticking out of what looks like an ordinary black nylon shoulder bag. The camera guts are inside the bag. His job is to pretend he's just waiting around, casually checking out the rental cars.

Thinking about Declan Ross's accident, I'd wondered if rental cars also had unrepaired recalls. So this afternoon, after my quick change into jeans and a black turtleneck, we're hitting the budget-priced agency where Ross rented his car. It's a franchise preposterously named Rental Car King.

"Ready, Charlotte?"

"Absolutely," I say.

No one watching would ever know. But Franklin's getting video of each car. And of their VINs.

"One, FTRX, 18W, 17, CA, zero, 1212," Franklin says as he peers through the windshield of a sporty red convertible. He takes a step or two back, obviously getting a wider shot of the car. "So when is Maysie's baby arriving? Is she okay?"

I flop against the seat, exasperated. I just forgot half the numbers.

"Don't wreck my train of thought. I told you, Maddee or Malcolm is probably coming tonight. Crossing fingers. Maysie's fine, in the hospital, Matthew's with her, kids have a babysitter, she's going to call. Okay? Now read me that number again. We don't have much time here."

I type the VIN into our database, then grab my binoculars as Franklin moves to the next car. If we find a car that has an open recall, we'll come back tomorrow and rent it. Rental Car King is mostly a car lot, with a squat yellow faux-brick office building planted in the middle. I focus my binocs through its plate-glass front windows, trying for a glimpse of J.T. and his quarry.

Frowning, I focus again. I can see J.T. pretty well, the back of his leather bomber jacket. And a fuzzy-faced but clearly female figure behind a long counter. But I can also see . . . ? I squint, trying to read the blocky words on the poster. It says Rental Car King. But even squinting, I can't make out the face beside them.

Franklin's Bluetooth voice squawks through my phone. "Here's another one. Ready?"

I put down the binoculars and type in the next VIN. We manage to get at least a dozen more before J.T. and a big-haired clerk in an unfortunate polyester tunic, complete with a king's crown on the back, come strolling out the door.

"It's all fine and we're coming back here tomorrow," J.T. says to Franklin. "Kelsey says we can choose any car we want."

I love technology. I can hear everything.

J.T. turns to the clerk, gesturing toward Franklin. "Told you he's fussy about cars. But tomorrow, when we pick up our rental? I'm bringing my older sister."

By the time the boys get back to the car, I've moved the front seat up so far it's impossible for them to squeeze in. At such short notice, it's the only way I could think of to pay J.T. back for the older-sister crack.

"Funny girl," J.T. says. He scoots the driver's seat back into place. "And after I risked my life doing all that dangerous reconnaissance."

"Some danger," I say. "Maybe from hairspray inhalation. Young Kelsey starting a fan club?"

"She's the owner's niece, I'll have you know. And Miss Kelsey Kindell knows her cars. When your uncle is Randall C. Kindell, the Rental Car King, you've got to —"

The picture on the poster. Now I recognize it. And that's a problem. "Randall Kindell?"

"He's the owner, Charlotte," Franklin chimes in. "Owns a string of RCK franchises. Didn't you read the e-mails I sent you this morning? It's all in there."

Franklin twists around and glares at me over the back of the seat. Frowning. "Can't know it if you don't read it."

It was much easier when my job was my whole life. I was lonely sometimes. But I never missed an e-mail.

"The memorial service," I explain. Lame excuse. But thinking again, maybe it was lucky I was there. Kind of. I mentally review the faces of the mourners. "Thing is, I'm sure I saw him this morning. Randall Kindell. He was at the service, too."

We pull out of our parking place, J.T. heading us back to Channel 3. I was hoping we'd be able to prove rental cars from RCK were unrepaired, and potentially dangerous. But now, it seems, if we wind up going on

106

the air with that, we may face an unexpected roadblock.

"Really? Does Kindell have a kid at Bexter?" Franklin asks.

"Wouldn't that be something?" I say.

"Well, you can't let that stand in your way," Franklin replies. "And clearly, if we think a Bexter bigwig is renting dangerous cars, you certainly can't warn anyone there about what we discovered. And by anyone, I mean Josh. We have to follow the story, no matter where it goes."

He's lecturing me about journalism ethics? I'm instantly seething.

I've never yelled at Franklin. Not even close. And wouldn't consider it, much less with J.T. in the car. As I do a calming mental count to ten, I sinkingly realize that part of my anger is directed at myself. Feeling guilty for missing the Borum reconnaissance. Guilty for not reading my e-mail. Guilty because it crossed my mind that maybe — if Randall Kindell is a Bexter bigwig — we could leave him out of our story. And that is unacceptable. There are no divided loyalties in TV.

"Lighten up, Franko," I say, making my voice cheery. "Think I'd let anything get between me and our next Emmy? No way."

I hope I'm telling the truth.

CHAPTER SEVEN

"You're on the air in three, two . . ." Saskia Kaye, her beaded mass of braids swinging with the motion, points a showtime finger at me from behind the Plexiglas that divides the producer's booth at WWXI radio from the on-the-air talent in the studio.

Tonight, I'm the talent.

"This is Charlie McNally from Channel 3 News, sitting in this Friday night for Maysie Green, thank you so much for inviting me! And tonight — a change in the conversation." I'm acting like someone else is in the glass-walled WWXI studio with me, but really I'm just talking to the thousands of listeners who tuned in for Maysie's weekly half-hour sports talk show. They're gonna be disappointed if they want me to talk about sports, unless it's Ralph Lauren's spring sportswear line. But I figure anyone who likes sports likes cars.

"New mother-to-be Maysie's off tonight,

and if she's listening, we wish her well. Can't wait to see the baby, Mays," I say. I'm going for breezy radio voice and channeling the seventies, when I had a part-time job in a Chicago suburb as a radio reporter. Until the news director found someone who had already graduated from college. I did farm news, mostly. But experience is experience.

I check through the Plexiglas as I continue my opening patter, raising a "how am I doing?" eyebrow. Saskia smiles back, her dark eyes twinkling, and gives me a thumbs-up. Okay, then. I'm back on the radio. And I've decided to use this gig to troll for some info for our TV story.

"Tonight, I'll be taking calls about your cars. Anyone get a recall notice? Did you do the repairs? Love to hear about it."

In an instant, the lighted buttons on the phone console of front of me begin to flash red. One, then another, and another.

"Good girl. You've got callers." Saskia flips a toggle switch so I can hear her voice through my headphones. She punches a button on her phone console. "Transferring caller number one. Here comes Edward from Saugus."

"Hey, Edward," I say. I know Saskia writes down the names and e-mail addresses of all the callers for the station's mailing list before she switches their calls to me. I hear their voices and mine in my headphones, and lean closer to the silver mesh of the football-size microphone. "Tell me about your recall."

Two flashing bright green readouts on the digital clocks in front of me tick off the seconds, one showing how much time I have left, the other showing the actual time of day. The calls never stop. As the back-timer approaches zero-zero-zero, my radio re-debut winds down without a hitch. And, bonus, in my thirty minutes of airtime I may have found several possible victims for our story. People who bought used cars, not knowing they had unrepaired recalls. I'll get their e-mail from Saskia. Suddenly she's giving me the one-finger "wrap it up" signal.

"And that's all the time we have for tonight," I say. Saskia holds up a piece of poster board with big block-printed letters. I get it. Radio's version of a prompter. No problem. "Keep your dial on Wixie for all the news, sports and weather. Stay tuned for *Taylor and Tyler's Drive Time,* coming up in just three minutes. Got a car for sale? Tell 'em all about it. And we'll see you back here real soon."

"And you're clear." Saskia slashes a finger across her neck. She punches a couple of buttons and the red On the Air light above my console fades to black. I take off my headphones, hoping my hair isn't hopelessly dented. Josh is waiting for me. If Maysie was right, we might be heading to the hospital.

Two lanky, identical-looking men, twenty-somethings in tucked-out plaid shirts and jeans are now lounging in Saskia's booth. They're poking at each other with the pointed metal plugs dangling from the curly cords of the padded-ear headphones they're wearing.

The heavy glass door to the studio clicks open as they saunter into my studio. They're obviously next on the air.

"I'm Taylor," one says.

"I'm Tyler," says the other.

"Two minutes, guys," Saskia yells as the studio door closes behind them. Time for me to go.

"What I heard, not a bad show," one of them says, looking me up and down.

The other one nods. "Ever thought of going into broadcasting?"

"We're not going to crash, that'd be way too much irony." I open the driver's-side

111

door of the black Vallero hatchback J.T. and I just rented from the Rental Car King and slide into the driver's seat. No news from Maysie yet. It's Saturday morning. There are no weekends in TV.

"Take as long as you want, McNally. Listen, I'll shoot you driving from the backseat. Then I'll hang the camera out the window — get us some hot on-the-road video. We did it at the network. It'll rock."

"Just get a few shots of me driving from inside the car," I say. I don't want to squash his enthusiasm, but I'm not so happy behind the wheel of a car the feds say needs to be repaired. It's only ten-thirty or so, but the morning's electric-blue sky has dulled to gray and white. And it's starting to snow.

"Then I'll pull over, you hop out, and you can get some footage of me driving by. We just need about a minute of usable video. Four or five good shots, okay? Franklin will meet us at the mechanic's."

What's more, technically, I shouldn't be doing this. Only J.T.'s name is on the rental agreement as a driver, since it's too risky for me even to show my face inside RCK. But local news is all about "reporter involvement," so if I'm doing a story about driving recalled rented cars, I've got to be driving a recalled rented car.

Yes, it makes no sense. Yes, I have no choice.

J.T. clambers into the backseat, struggling to fit his camera onto his shoulder without the light bracketed to the top smashing into the fabric-covered roof.

"When I was with the network in the Mideast, we were lucky to have a car at all, let alone with power steering. One that's recalled, who cares, right? Piece of cake." J.T. flips on his battery-powered camera light, glaring it briefly in my rearview, then adjusts it so I can see again. "Okay, McNally. I'm rolling. Hit it."

Flicking on the windshield wipers to battle the intensifying snow, I slowly back out of our parking spot, then turn into the shopping-mall lot. The power steering seems to be fine.

"These recalls are precautionary, anyway," I say, reassuring myself as much as him. I maneuver around a few shoppers and head for the exit to the highway. "But if the power steering goes, make sure you get the whole thing on camera at least. Ha-ha."

"Ha-ha," from the backseat. "You can get your Emmy posthumously. They can roll my spectacular video of the fiery crash at the awards ceremony. Very network."

"Just get the shots and then we can get

this baby's rotary valve fixed," I say. "Whatever a rotary valve is."

At least I understand the accelerator. Easing it down, I guide the hatchback up the ramp onto I-93 North. Our destination is the Power House, the state-of-the-art garage run by the top-notch mechanic who takes care of Franklin's silver Passat and the adorable Stephen's red Miata. Apparently the two of them take their cars in for service together, just like they do everything together. Somehow, Franklin never worries about his job distracting from his love life. Somehow, that relationship works perfectly. Of course, they live in the same city.

"A rotary valve is the thing that gauges how hard you're turning the steering wheel," J.T. says. "I had to deal with all our cars at the network. Check it out. You'd have big trouble turning a two-thousand-pound car. So the rotary valve is what makes the power steering —"

I glance into the rearview. J.T.'s still shooting. And talking. And talking. And, though it's not his fault, he's annoying. Every time he says *network* it reminds me of Kevin's offer. And that reminds me of Josh. And that reminds me I've got a decision to make. An impossible decision. Unless I can clone myself.

"Let's make sure the audio is clean, okay?" I say, trying to come up with a reasonable reason to keep him quiet. "Tell me all that later. We need the sounds of the highway. Without anyone's voice."

"You're the boss," J.T. says. "It's your funeral."

I wish people would stop saying that.

I see it almost in slow motion. Coming right at us. A rickety dump truck has been an annoying obstacle ever since the Neponset Road exit. Every time I try to pass the thing, some jerk driver, who for some reason needs to stay one second ahead of us, refuses to get out of the way. Other drivers, panicked by the increasing snow and squalling wind, decide creeping along at thirty miles an hour is somehow safer. Trapped, J.T. and I stay in the center lane.

Now something big is flying out of the back of the truck. A — bat? Part of my brain struggles to name it, while the rest of me, focused, calculates the best way to avoid it. A huge piece of — paper? It's metal. Metal. Metal. A huge scrap of metal, caught by the increasing wind, is flying toward us. We're caught. Hemmed in. I have no place to go. Teeth gritting, I steer straight ahead, hoping it won't slam into our windshield.

"Holy —" J.T. leans forward, clamping both hands on the seat in front of him. "Look out, Charlie! Floor it! Or get out of the —"

The hunk of debris misses, flying over us. Behind me, brakes squeal, horns blare, tires skid on the slickening highway. Both my hands clutch the steering wheel. Every part of me is clenching.

"That was close," I say. My heart is thudding, relief making my voice shaky and thin. Danger never feels real when you're shooting a story. Fires, floods, tornadoes. You're just doing your job. I hadn't really thought about the stupid power steering thing. Now I do.

"Yeah," J.T. replies. "Should we call the police?"

And then another flash of solid black escapes from under the fluttering green tarpaulin in front of us. Another shard, the size of a newspaper, careening across the highway, cutting through the snow. The driver — hauling scrap metal — must be oblivious. His wooden-sided panel truck picks up speed in the center lane. He thunders across a massive pothole, the truck lurching, and then the entire tarp comes loose, unleashing from its moorings, ropes flailing, plastic flapping.

It's a barrage of metal, piece after piece. All sizes, weird shapes, scattering in the wind, picked up by gusts and flying, like demented crows. Random. Wild. Terrifying. And inescapable.

On either side, other drivers, each attempting the same impossible calculations, are slowing. Dodging. Speeding. Swerving. Slowing. Switching lanes. And everyone honking. I'm as frightened of getting too close to the cars around me as I am of being battered by the slicing shower of metal. Which would be worse, to plow into another car? Or to get slammed by a knifing scrap of jagged-edged —

And then I can't avoid it. I see it, black metal, broad and flat, twisting across the snowy pavement and sliding to a stop. Right in front of us.

If I slam on the brakes, we'll skid. I glance to each side. I can't steer to avoid it. No room.

"McNally! Watch out for the —" J.T.'s voice is tense.

"I see it!"

Our wheels clatter over the bent and battered fragment, jouncing us out of our seats. J.T. yells something from the backseat. Whatever he says is drowned out by my own cry of dismay.

The truck, tarp now attached by just one corner and billowing like the cape of some comic-book supervillain, turns off the exit. I feel our right front tire make an unmistakable and stomach-churning rumble.

The rear of the car swings wide. Cars fly by us, but my view through the windshield is no longer forward. I'm seeing the side of the highway flash by. And we're spinning.

"We're skidding!" J.T. yells. "Steer in the —"

"Shut up!" I reach down for the stick shift, then remember I'm not in my Jeep.

"Quickly align your tires with the direction of your intended travel." It takes me half a second to recognize the voice of Mr. Grosskopf, my grouchy but effective drivers'-ed teacher at Anthony Wayne High School. We practiced exactly this in a slippery A & P parking lot. I take my foot off the brake, and quickly turn the wheel back the way I want to go. As soon as I see "ahead," the car starts skidding in the other direction.

Yes. I turn the wheel back the other way, straightening us out again. Back and forth, smaller and smaller turns. And finally it's clear road in front of us. And we're going — more like klunking — in the right direction.

I check the rearview. Nothing.

"I'm pulling over into the breakdown lane," I say, barely recognizing my own voice. "You okay, J.T.? We have a flat."

Once we stop the car and get out, J.T. starts unsnapping straps from the floor of the trunk. He's searching for a jack and spare tire that had better be there. Being stranded on the interstate was not in our plan. "What if the power steering had —"

"It didn't," I say. My heart rate is back to normal. My voice is, too. My knees, not quite yet. "I must admit, though, the words *defective rotary valve* did cross my mind."

The narrow, rutted breakdown lane of I-93 is never the safest place. Now, huddled behind our rental car, Saturday at noon, in freezing, bleak January with snow swirling and cars streaming by and a slashed-to-rubber-ribbons flat tire lying dead at my feet, I wonder, briefly, about my years-ago flirtation with law school. Choices then, choices now. I pull my wide plaid shawl up over my head, wrap it tighter and try to keep the glass half-full. "What they don't teach you in journalism school, right?"

J.T.'s hair is frosted with the falling snow, his sandy curls damp, cheeks ruddy. With one quick motion, he hoists the spare tire from deep within the trunk. Thankfully, it bounces on the pavement. At least the spare tires haven't been recalled.

He balances the tire with one gloved hand, pushes his sunglasses up onto his head with the other. He looks at me. Up and down.

"All in a day's work," he says. "But you know, McNally, you pretty much rocked back there. That was some smart driving. Most women would have —"

"Most women?" Ignoring his scrutiny, which is almost unacceptably unprofessional, I open my mouth to inquire what "most women" is supposed to mean. J.T. holds up a hand, stopping me.

"Hey, I take it back. I just meant you did a great job. Driving. And this is a hell of a story, too. You're all business, McNally. I can see why you've lasted this long in TV. Most women your age are —"

"Most women my age?" I try, again, to come up with some sort of retort, even though the ground he's treading here is actually a bit more solid. Fortysomething women in television are as rare as shoulder pads and leg warmers. I know my own style is destined to go out of style. You're only as good as your last story — or the whim of a new boss.

J.T. gives me an anchorman-worthy smile, all teeth and cheekbones. Crackling blue eyes. Major-league shoulders. He could easily be on camera, maybe in someplace like Santa Fe, or Cheyenne, where those super-tight jeans, leather jacket and kick-ass boots would wow the female eighteen-to-forty-nine demos. Which, of course, I'm still in.

"It's what they call a compliment, McNally," he says. "You've still got it goin' on, as they say." Tipping the tire against the car, he cranks the black metal jack one notch higher. With a few quick motions, he lifts the tire into place and slams on a wrench to tighten the lug nuts.

"You ever think of going network? Maybe some all-news operation? Can't imagine why they wouldn't be after you. Emmys, all that. You're too big for Boston, I'd say."

Keeping both hands on the wrench, he stops midmotion. He looks up at me, suddenly serious. "I mean it. They ever call you?"

A wave of suspicion flares, disturbingly, through my mind. Can he possibly know about Kevin's job offer? He can't. Kevin told me no one knows. What's more, that "still got it goin' on" remark is, again, uncomfortably close to the line. Or maybe I'm too sensitive. I mean, I was thinking about his jeans, right? But the observation was just clinical. I would never consider saying it out loud.

I wave a leather glove in his direction, trying to diffuse the moment. We just had a pretty narrow escape. It's cold. We have work to do. Franklin's waiting. The mechanic is waiting. And there must be a glass of wine and Josh's fireplace in my future.

"Hey, Boston's market five," I say. "How's that tire coming?"

"Changing the subject. Got it." With a nod and an overbroad wink, J.T. returns to work.

He's not even attempting to hide his smile.

The Power House Garage in Boston's South End reeks of oil and gas and rubber. Drills and power tools whine. Engines rev, ignitions churn. I'm sure the whole place is full of carbon monoxide. Which reminds me, for a melancholy moment, of Dorothy Wirt. A twist of concern, unwelcome and unpleasant, begins an uncomfortable spiral. How am I going to make all of this work?

Reining myself back into the moment, I put my other life on hold. Behind the massive glass doors of the garage, we're warm and finally dry. I'll think about the rest of it later.

Our rented black hatchback is high on a mechanical lift, its spare tire a glaringly obvious mismatch. Franklin, J.T. and mechanic Frick Jones, all wearing thick plastic safety goggles held on by orange plastic straps, are conferring underneath the chassis, heads tilted back, looking up at something. I know my limitations. I wouldn't recognize a broken rotary valve if I saw one, but I'll learn about it soon enough. We didn't tell Frick about the recall. We want to see what, if anything, he finds on his own.

I take a sip of the first chamomile tea I've ever had in a garage and wait for the verdict on our rental car. As so often happens in journalism, bad news would be good news.

"Here's your problem, Charlie." Frick Jones, who looks more like my ninth-grade chemistry teacher than an auto mechanic, selects a pencil-thin flashlight from a wide tool belt and shines it at the car's undercarriage. "You can see it right here. The torsion bar on the rotary valve is cracked. Actually, it's almost cracked through."

Score one for us. With Frick's pronouncement, we have our story confirmed.

I glance at Franklin, who's giving me a low-key thumbs-up at the good-bad news. He says something to J.T., pointing. The photographer takes off his goggles and picks up his camera from a sleek black Formica counter, adjusting the viewfinder. Franklin clicks open the tripod, a not-so-subtle suggestion to J.T. that he expects rock-steady shots of the broken rotary valve.

Frick's still talking, playing the light beam back and forth between the two front tires. "Good thing you brought it to us when you did, in fact. Couple more yanks on the steering wheel and you might have lost your control. You say you had a flat tire on the way here? In the snow?"

He emerges from under the car, slowly shaking his head. He points the flashlight at my chest. "Lucky you."

My knees, almost recovered, suffer a brief relapse. I know my smile is weak. "You can fix it, right?"

"One more thing," Frick says, pushing a red button on a gizmo hanging from the ceiling. The lift begins to lower. With a puff of hydraulics, then a soft clank, the car hits bottom. Frick clicks open the hood and points to what even I know is the battery.

"Look here. This black wire. One battery lead is loose. Look."

He reaches forward, and with two fingers, wiggles a thin black cable. Then he tightens the nut that's attaching the cable to a stubby metal post on the battery.

"Sometimes the cable works itself loose. Especially on newer cars. Easy enough to fix. But if that had come off while you were driving, you'd have lost power. Car wouldn't have started again."

Through his goggles, I can read Frick's troubled expression.

"You don't want the battery lead to come off." He gives me the flashlight in the chest again. "Like I said. Lucky you."

"I'm set to roll, McNally." J.T.'s voice interrupts the cataloging of our near disaster. "Whenever you say, I'll —"

"Can you put the lift up again, Frick? First we'll need you showing the problem to Charlotte," Franklin interrupts J.T., yanking back the alpha-dog position. He's put his goggles on top of his head and now looks like a prepped-out biker. "She'll need goggles. And then we'll need to show you repairing it."

J.T. is ignoring the tripod and ignoring Franklin. "I'll shoot off the shoulder. So it matches the other stuff we have. You know. The accident."

The accident. Gabe and Sophie. Declan Ross. Car smashed into the guardrail. A rented car. As I watch J.T. roll off a few shots of Frick puttering with the engine, I realize what's haunting me.

"Frick, can you check one more thing?" I put down my paper cup of tea and point to the black car. A dark hunch is percolating. "We didn't tell you about this initially, but can you check to see if this car has air bags?"

"See if it has air bags?" Frick looks puzzled. He hands me a pair of goofy-looking clear plastic goggles. "Of course it does."

"It's a 2006," Franklin puts in. "It's the law. They all have air bags."

"They're supposed to," I say.

"No air bags in our car," I say, shaking my head. "Can you believe it? And what if there were no air bags in the Ross car? And that's why they didn't inflate?" Frick's confirmation of my hunch haunts me as we leave the garage. I click open the passenger door of our news car, waving Franklin into the driver's seat. "You drive, okay? I've had enough for one day."

J.T. is returning the now-repaired hatchback to RCK. We got all the video we need. The defective torsion bar — now wrapped in tissue paper in my briefcase — we kept for evidence. Franklin and I are heading back to the station to drop off our tapes. We have a potentially blockbuster story. And a potentially blockbuster dilemma.

"What made you think of the air bags?" Franklin says, steering us out of our parking space and toward Huntington Street. "I'll never understand how your brain works, Charlotte. It's a beautiful thing. Strange, but beautiful."

"Yeah, well. Declan's didn't go off, remember? And that's been bugging me. It didn't make sense. They should have. And I read someplace, air bags are the hot new item to steal. Bad guys rip them out, replace the covers, then resell the air bags on the black market. Who'd know? Until there's an accident, of course."

I shudder. Most people are so trusting. And others are so cynically money hungry. That's a dangerous combination. I pause, considering.

"If other RCK cars have no air bags, does Randall Kindell know about it? Is he supplying stolen air bags for the black market? If so, we should get the story on TV right now. Soon as we can. Maybe even before the ratings start. The next crash could be fatal, you know. Lives are at stake."

"Charlotte, the February book is only three weeks away." He's shaking his head. "I think we can wait. And then put together two stories. We'll do unrepaired recalls first, then hit them with the big air-bag scoop. Even better, here's what I'm thinking. What if Kindell's doing it across the country? In all the RCK franchises?"

Franklin pantomimes basketball. "Slam dunk. A national story."

We stop at a red light. I reach over and touch Franklin's arm. I need him to look at me for a moment.

"But, Franko? What if Kindell doesn't know? What if someone is renting cars and then ripping out air bags? Then it's not just about RCK, but could be happening at every rental-car place. Don't you feel some obligation to tell the police? Warn Kindell? Warn the public? Right now?"

"Are you losing it, girlfriend? Where's the ratings-hungry Charlotte I signed up to work with? You know it's all about big results. And big numbers."

The light turns green. Franklin shifts gears into Drive, puffing incredulously as he turns left onto Charles Street.

"You can't win the sweeps if your story's on too early. And we're in it to win it."

Franklin and I are partners. But, more and more, it seems like we're not on the same team.

I've always thought my job as an investigative reporter meant helping people, warning them of danger, keeping them from harm. And exposing the bad guys. It always worked. I treasure every Emmy, but the need to consider schedule before substance seems so cynical. Am I still a good guy if I keep a secret just to boost the ratings?

Why haven't I thought of this before? Who's suddenly out of balance? Franklin? Or me?

"Franko? J.T. and I could have been killed this afternoon. We were driving a dangerous car. Unrepaired recall, no air bags. Yes, we got the video. Yes, it all worked out in the end. But Frick said it — we were lucky. I say we talk to Kevin. Monday, first thing. Tell him what we know. And I bet he'll want to get this on the air. Sooner rather than later."

Franklin waves me off, shrugging. "Bet he won't. I bet he'll grab the fifth-floor graphics gang and whip up some hot 'Charlie Mc-Nally Investigates' promo spots. For February. Bet you ten thousand dollars."

"You're on," I say. But I'm not exactly sure who's going to win that imaginary bet. On the other hand, truth be told, we don't really have a story. Just suspicions. We certainly don't have enough nailed down to go on the air. What if we sent viewers into a panic over missing air bags and it turned out to be a coincidence? Or a one-time-only event? Putting that on television would do far more harm than good. I struggle to regain my news equilibrium. Maybe I'm suffering PTSD from this afternoon.

I rest my chin on one hand, elbow on the armrest, watching bag-laden shoppers and camera-toting tourists swirl through the darkening afternoon. A woman in a sleekly tailored camel's-hair coat throws her arm across a little girl's shoulders — she's about Penny's age — bending briefly to kiss her hair. They're wearing matching plaid mufflers and carrying glossy bright red shopping bags. A thirtysomething man in a tasseled ski cap and puffy black parka peeks at a tiny passenger in an expensive stroller, then pushes it across the white-striped crosswalk. How many of them might be renting a car someday? Driving blissfully along, husbands and wives and their children, unaware of the danger?

How many families will be on the road before we air our story?

CHAPTER EIGHT

The glossy deep-brown front door opens with a twist of its old-fashioned wooden knob. Inside the warm vestibule another ornately carved door is latched tight. A harsh buzz sounds when I push the middle button on the ultramodern electronic keypad.

Michael Borum's condominium is one of three in a postwar brownstone in the South End. Post Spanish-American War. Built in boom times of a golden age, these elegant three-story buildings were battered and disdained through Boston's turbulent 1960s. Now they're the city's most desirable housing: bohemian, artsy and urban. Borum's place is right on the edge of safe, with aching poverty just a few blocks away. The Power House Garage is down the road in the other direction. Wonder if Michael takes his blue Mustang there. Wonder where he parks it. Maybe there's a lot out back? I don't see it on the street. Probably a sports-car thing.

No answer to my buzz. I know this is dicey territory. Close enough to noon on a Sunday morning not to be completely socially objectionable, but still pushing it.

Franklin left several messages for Michael Borum, but no reply. I called. No reply. Borum seems to be avoiding us. Of course he could be out of town. Or sick. Or dead. Since he's incommunicado, there's only one way to find out.

I push the buzzer again.

So it's Sunday. We're local television. We have no manners. Now I hear footsteps. And then the glass door flies open.

"It's about time. If the damn newspaper is late once more, we're going to cancel our subscription and call the publisher."

If this is Michael Borum, he hasn't bothered to add a shirt to his attire this cold January morning. Or maybe he's waiting for the photographer from *Bodybuilder Magazine* to show up. His licorice-dark hair is slicked back, maybe from the shower. His drawstring sweatpants are fighting a losing battle with gravity. I calculate zero body fat. Wreathed around his remarkable biceps are intricately complicated monochromatic tattoos, spiky-leafed vines and ivy. One throbs dramatically as his fist-clenched tirade continues.

"This is the third Sunday that you guys have —"

"Mr. Borum?" I hold out both hands, empty, attempting to illustrate that I'm not here to provide newspapers. If he's this angry over missing the *Boston Globe,* I wouldn't want to be in his way when he's angry about something big. Which means perhaps I should have continued to try to reach him on the phone.

"I'm, um, not from the *Globe*? Are you Michael Borum?"

"Yes, I'm Michael Borum." He narrows his eyes at me, dark eyebrows knitting across his broad forehead, then moves forward. His brawn occupies the open front door, preventing me from seeing what's inside.

"And you're Charlie McNally. Channel 3. Why in hell are you hounding me? Have you television people lost your minds?"

A question I get more often than I care to admit. And one I still haven't figured out exactly how to answer. I ignore it as politely as I can.

"Thanks so much for coming to the door, Mr. Borum." I hold out a hand, smiling as if we've just been introduced. Old trick. If they agree to shake hands, in that moment they've relinquished their power.

Borum's glance is withering. One of his hands stays clamped onto the doorjamb, the other on his hip.

"Thanks so much for your patience, yes, we've been trying to get in touch with you for almost a week now," I continue, lowering my own hand and pretending the handshake thing never happened. I glance around, as if checking for privacy. "We'd like to chat with you, briefly, about an incident on the Mass Pike the other day. Monday, late afternoon, as we said in our phone messages. Is this a good place?"

Borum crosses those arms in front of his imposing, distractingly naked chest. Frowns. And doesn't budge.

"You've got five seconds to tell me what this is about. It better be good. Because I wasn't on the Mass Pike Monday afternoon. Or any time Monday."

Which I know is not true. But of course, right now I don't have the photo to prove it. But of course, he doesn't know that.

I scratch my head, feigning confusion. I pause, deliberately using up two of my five seconds. I move in for the kill. Again, oh, so politely.

"Well, Mr. Borum, we know you were. Maybe you forgot you were there? We have a photograph of you in your blue Mustang driving through the Fast Lane Monday. Around four-thirty. There was an accident about that time . . ."

I stop. Shift tactics. This is hardly the time to accuse him of being a criminal. I smile, conciliatory.

"And we're just searching for people who might have witnessed it. There was a family whose car was wrecked, the father hurt. Do you remember that? I mean, did you see anything?"

"Let's see the photo." Borum, challenging, is obviously not enchanted by my little performance. And is neatly calling my bluff. "Let's see that photo you say you have of me driving on Monday."

"I . . ." I think fast. I pat my purse, as if the photo's inside, then shake my head. As if I'm making a decision. I pull out a business card. "Here's my card, with my work and home phone numbers on it. Call me if you think of anything. I'll be happy to show the photo to you, at some point. But —"

"You know what, Miss McNally?" he interrupts, holding up a palm. "Forget it. You go ahead, put your photo on television. See what happens. See how fast a subpoena arrives at your general manager's door. I was not on the Mass Pike Monday, at four-thirty, or any other time. I was having drinks with friends at Bistro Zelda. You've got the wrong time. Or the wrong day. Or the wrong car. Or all three. Put that photo on your news? Say it's me driving? Do it. I mean it. Do it. Then let me warn you, Miss McNally. I'll own Channel 3."

Borum backs into the dimly lit hallway behind him. He stops, his narrow smile radiating contempt as he slowly pulls the door closed.

"Do your homework," he says. "Or I'll see you in court."

"He didn't say he didn't *own* a blue Mustang," I say. "I take that as a good sign. And I guess he got all our phone calls, he was just ignoring us. That makes him guilty, too."

Juggling an elaborate bouquet of pink roses and a beribboned stack of my favorite kids' books, I jab the up button on the Mass General Hospital elevator.

Franklin is carrying a huge, ungainly, black-and-white stuffed panda. Puffed out arms and legs dangle as Franklin shifts the bear from one position to another. Button eyes now stare at the floor.

Sunday visiting hours are two to four. Josh and Penny are on the way. We're all going to meet brand-new baby Maddee. She was a little late. But fine.

"So that's the good news." I press the button again. Then one more time.

"We've been over this before, Charlotte. The elevator does not come any more quickly if you —" Franklin sighs. Then gives up.

"Can we just agree to disagree on that?" I ask as the door opens. I dramatically gesture Franklin inside.

"The bad news is, Borum insists he wasn't there. And he offered an easily traced alibi. Something is very wrong. We've seen the photo. Borum can't be in two places at one time."

The elevator pings. Doors slide open onto the pastel wonderland of Maternity. Floor-to-ceiling murals, ice pink and soft blue and buttery yellow, show smiley-faced suns, lush fields of impossible daffodils and every cute baby animal imaginable. Some carry balloons and cotton candy in their paws or webbed feet. All are clearly blissed out.

"Remember that pink lotion?" I close my eyes and sniff at the familiar fragrance, swept back into some fuzzy half-memory. "It smells like baby in here, doesn't it? In a good way?"

But I'm talking to no one. Franklin and

his stuffed companion are conferring with a ponytailed nurse in a Pooh-covered tunic. She points him down to the end of the hall.

And there's Maysie. My dear best friend. With a tiny yellow-swaddled bundle in her lap. Three pink helium balloons are tied to the back of Maysie's wheelchair. This far away, it's difficult to tell who has the bigger smile — the new mom or the new dad, Matthew, who's pushing their newest family member toward us. Talk about blissed out.

For a briefly disquieting second, I can hardly look at them. I remember the moment, almost the exact moment, when I knew my biological clock had ticked its last. At birthday thirty, I did my first calculation. Fifteen more years. It seemed like forever. At birthday forty, I counted. Five more years. Plenty of time. At birthday forty-five, I began my birthday-math ritual. And stopped. I blew out the candles, smiled at my birthday-party pals, and said a silent goodbye. Goodbye, little whoever. You are not to be.

I look down at my rainbow-wrapped parcels. *Pat the Bunny. Goodnight Moon. Many Moons.* And, for later, Maddee's first Nancy Drew. I'd have been a good mother.

"Baby Maddee's too young to be in our wedding." My favorite voice.

I turn to see Josh, smiling, emerging from the elevator. I see Penny peeking out from behind him. "And you know Penny would never stand for it," he continues.

I try to untangle my unexpected rush of emotions. Love. Hope. And time. There's time.

Penny races down the hall as Josh kisses the top of my head. He's carrying a cellophane-wrapped bouquet of plump white roses. Twisty fuchsia ribbons trail from around the stems. He pulls one flower from the center and hands it to me.

"Congratulations, Auntie Charlie," he whispers, leaning close. "You're my baby, you know."

He lifts my chin, locking my eyes with his. This time, his kiss lingers, tender. For that moment, only the two of us exist.

"I know," I finally manage to say.

"Come look at her toes, Charlie Mac, they're the littlest of littles." Penny has already scampered back, and grabs the belt of my coat, pulling me away from Josh and toward the baby parade. Franklin's perched the panda on the back of the wheelchair, paws sticking straight out, balloons bouncing against its floppy black ears.

"Would you like to give these to Maysie for us, sweetheart?" I say, holding out my bouquet.

"And these, too, kiddo," Josh adds, giving her the rest of the white roses. "Maybe give them to Matthew, since Maysie's arms are full of baby."

Penny carefully wraps her arms around the two bouquets, then, with a brief furrow of her little forehead adjusts the satin ribbons so they fall just so. "I'm practicing for the wedding," she announces, her voice brimming with pride. "Watch this, Charlie Mac."

Penny walks in bridal procession touch-steps up to Maysie and Matthew and solemnly presents her bouquet. Then, placing one snow-booted toe carefully behind her, she performs a deep and perfect curtsy.

Our laughter fills the hallway as the Maysie entourage draws closer. Matthew's face is almost covered by the masses of flowers he's wound up carrying. Franklin's taken Panda from his perch and is carrying him again. Maysie looks ecstatic but exhausted. No makeup, hair slicked back, wearing a pink-striped hospital gown, hospital-issue pale blue slipper socks and a plastic hospital name bracelet around her wrist. A crocheted yellow blanket is tucked across her legs.

"You okay, Mays?" I lean down and kiss her hair, then hand the books to Matthew.

"You look fantastic."

"I'm fine, perfect, wonderful," she says. Her voice is thick with emotion. "Meet baby Maddee."

Maysie carefully slides her right hand underneath the swaddled bundle on her lap, then cradles Maddee's tiny head with the left. Smiling, she lifts her new daughter, sleeping and unaware, and hands her to me. "Maddee, meet your Auntie Charlie. And your Uncle Josh."

Penny, hanging on to Josh's sleeve, on tiptoe for a better view, watches intently as the newborn passes across from mother to best friend.

"And me, Cousin Penny!" she adds. She frowns, perplexed. "Aren't I a cousin?"

Maddee's heavier than I expected. Solid. Her tiny chest rises, falls, rises again. With one tentative finger, I smooth the almost-invisible silky fuzz across the top of her head, then bend, briefly, to inhale the unmistakable scent. Her eyes flutter open, just a fraction. I glimpse a flash of blue.

"Welcome to the world, Maddee girl," I whisper.

"Want to walk with me back to the station?" Franklin pulls on his gloves, then ties the belt of his navy coat in a knot, the two loose ends exactly the same length. "Talk with Kevin about what Borum said? He's probably working today, this close to the beginning of sweeps. Then I can collect my ten thousand dollars."

Franklin and I are in the two-story glass-walled entry hall of Mass General, waiting for Josh and Penny to bring the car from the parking lot. We're planning a Sunday evening — a family evening — of carryout barbecue from the Blue Ribbon, followed by a G-rated Netflix. I'm hoping for an R-rating, or even X, after Penny goes up to bed. And I don't mean in a movie.

"Oh, right, Franko. Just what I wanted to do on a Sunday night. Work. You're kidding me, right?"

Franklin is not amused. "We need to screen the undercover video of the rental company. Transcribe the Ross interview. Finish looking up the VIN numbers we pulled from RCK and Miracle Motors. Find more unrepaired recalls. There's a lot to do, Charlotte. And not long to get it all accomplished."

A bevy of coats and hats and umbrellas passes us, visitors, patients, doctors, pushing through the heavy front doors and into the waning afternoon. Four o'clock. It's already getting dark. Why is Franklin suddenly so eager to spend all his time at the station? Maybe the better question is — why am I suddenly so not?

"Let's give ourselves a little break," I say, keeping my voice light. "I got Borum this morning, but we can't do more on that until tomorrow. And tomorrow, I'll come in early. Look up VINs. Talk to Kevin. Bet I get started before you do. It'll all work."

"Your call," he says. "It's your face that's on the air, not mine. Your name on the story. If there is a story." Franklin unwraps his herringbone muffler, then reties it with what seems like unnecessary drama. A honk beeps from outside. Josh's Volvo. Penny's hanging out the passenger window, waving.

Franklin's poised, his glove on one curved metal handle of the revolving door. He cocks his head toward the car. "You coming with me? Or going with them?"

I love my work. I love my new family. I can't be two places at once.

It's Sunday night. Family night. I take a deep breath and step into a new world. "Going."

I hope it's the right decision.

CHAPTER NINE

"No. Not later. Now."

My hand tightens around my cell phone as the unfamiliar voice persists. Wenholm Dulles, who says he's a Bexter parent, called me on my private line just after Franklin went to Buzz World to get us some late-afternoon caffeine. Franklin seems to be over his work panic. This Monday, feeling like a team again, we've already plowed through most of our video and targeted some potentially unrepaired recalls. Some are used cars still for sale and some are rental cars. It's taken all day, but our story seems to be working. Cross fingers. Now we have to find those cars and check for air bags.

This unexpected phone call has screeched my momentum to a halt.

"Mr. Dulles, I'm afraid I don't remember you from the Head's party, forgive me. And —"

"It's critically important," Dulles interrupts. "As I said, about something that may
be happening at Bexter. The Head said we
should call you. And now, we're just down
the street. In the Parker House café. It'll
take fifteen minutes of your time. Ten. But
again, Miss McNally. This must be a secret."

Of course. What else is new.

"Hold on," I say. I clamp the phone
against my shoulder, grab a pen and scrawl
on a yellow sticky pad. What I write is a lie.

Dentist. Forgot. Back soon. C.

I stick the note to Franklin's monitor. I
know he'll believe me. We've never deceived
each other. We've never kept secrets. But
first there was New York. And now Bexter.
And now an imaginary dentist.

Bexter. I yank myself out of guilt and back
to reality. Has there been another phone
call? Or is it something about Dorothy Wirt?
Josh? Penny? Something is truly wrong
there.

"Mr. Dulles? I'm on the way," I say, struggling to talk and button my coat as I hurry
down the hall. "But can you tell me more?
On the phone? I truly have to get back to
the —"

"I have two children, both attend Bexter,"

145

he says, cutting me off again. "Lexie's a freshman, Tal's a senior. About to graduate. All these years, we've insisted on only the best for them, and —"

Silence.

"Mr. Dulles?" I clatter around the final landing of the back stairwell and out toward the side door. "Mr. Dulles?"

I check the cell-phone screen. Green letters pop into view. *Dropped call.*

When I reach the Parker House, I instantly spot Wenholm Dulles, wearing a double-Windsor rep tie, button-down white oxford shirt and expansive demeanor. He takes up most of the room on his side of the plush taupe suede booth. More a salon than a café, Parker's has a subdued exclusive air that keeps tourists away and conversations private. Big menus. Big prices. Big business.

Dulles has his camel's-hair overcoat folded plumply, russet satin lining showing, on the seat beside him. That obviously means "this seat taken." I guess I'm supposed to sit next to the woman across the table.

"Miss McNally. Wen Dulles." Dulles rises, much as he can. His navy-blazered bulk snags the tablecloth, gold buttons catching on the linen as he leans toward me. I get a solid handshake. Dulles smoothes his striped tie back into place, then gestures.

146

"My wife, Fiona."

Leaving my own coat on to telegraph my intentions, I ease into the booth. My back is to the restaurant. I can see my own reflection in the hazy mirror that stretches the length of the filigree-papered wall. I can also see the weary face of Fiona Dulles. Carefully ash blond, flawless eyebrows, pale skin stretched tight across patrician cheekbones. She's one second away from tears. She hasn't spoken a word.

"Call us Wen and Fee, Charlie," Dulles instructs.

Fee, who must weigh less than a hundred pounds, is wrapped in a Burberry shawl. The fringed plaid is draped over her boiled-wool jacket, its tiny buttons embossed with an elaborate design. Her leather gloves, caramel and creamy as expensive chocolate, are on the table in front of her, one laid carefully on top of the other. Fee Dulles drops her eyes, and begins to stroke the gloves with a manicured hand.

Now I remember. This is the woman in the Hermès scarf who recognized me at the Head's party.

"Lost connection earlier," Wen Dulles continues. His voice, gruff-edged, seems impatient with the apology. "Damn phones."

"Wen," his wife says. Her voice barely

registers above a whisper. "Please. This isn't necessary."

A waitress arrives at our table. With one silent glance, Wen instructs her to leave.

"Mr. Dulles?" I begin. I can feel the clock ticking. Franklin will be back any moment. My brain begins to concoct dentist stories. I have to hurry. But I'm so curious. "You said it was about Bexter?"

Dulles splays both hands on the white tablecloth, showing manicured fingernails, a chunky class ring with a deep amethyst stone.

"Fee went to Bexter. We both did. It's a fine school. Old school. Got the right stuff. We've donated a pile of money, I don't mind telling you. To keep it that way." He leans toward me, sizing me up. "But now we've gotten phone calls. Two of them. Nasty stuff. Nasty. My wife doesn't think we should involve you. But I want you to find out who's behind those calls."

"I can't —" I pause, stopping myself mid-refusal. I didn't contact Wen and Fee Dulles. They contacted me. This is inarguably a green light for me to investigate the Bexter phone calls without it being linked to Josh. And that's what I'm going to do. "Can you tell me more? When did the calls come in? At your home? Who answered?

What did the caller say?"

Fee looks at me and opens her mouth to say something.

"Our home. Our private number." Wen raises a hand to stop her. "Fee answered the calls. Same person. Same message. But this remains confidential. Agreed?"

"A man or a woman?" I nod, directing my questions to Fee. I need this information. "What did they say?"

Wen nods, apparently giving his wife permission to continue. Or maybe, ordering her to.

"I couldn't distinguish, male or female," she begins. She puts a hand to her throat, pursing her lips. Shakes her head. "No. I just answered, as I usually do, and the voice said . . ."

She pauses, looking at her husband. He tips his head, go on.

"The voice said, 'Do you know where your children are?' And hung up. Have you ever heard of such a thing? That silly slogan from television. I thought it must be the prank. Senior prank at Bexter, you've heard of it?"

"I have. Heard of the prank, I mean." But I'm thinking that's not what this is.

"But I was so . . . unnerved, I called Bexter to check on Lexie and Tal. Dorothy — poor Dorothy — said they were fine."

"The second call was no prank." Wen's voice is judgmental. "Last Wednesday. The same caller. This time, asked for money. Go on, Fee."

"You're aware of what happened at Milton Academy? The scandal? The sex? The voice told me Bexter was in the same situation." Fee's hushed voice catches, and those tears seem imminent. With two long fingers she begins to worry a votive candleholder, the flame flickering as she twists the crystal cylinder.

"Not sex, though. It was drugs. Pills. All kinds. That our son, Talbott, was deeply involved in it somehow. The police were closing in. They said if we sent a money order for nine thousand dollars, Tal's name would be kept out of it. If we didn't, everyone would know."

"We mailed a check to the post-office box," Wen says. "Yesterday. With Tal's college applications pending, we couldn't risk it."

"Oh, Mr. and Mrs. Dulles, this is a matter for the police." So much for my big Bexter story. This is far beyond anything I can handle. I put up both palms, stopping any further discussion. "It's extortion. Blackmail. You must report this. You couldn't be the only ones getting calls. And drugs being sold? To students? And you know blackmailers never stop. They always want more."

"I understand. However —" Wen Dulles makes a flat dismissive gesture "— I'm certain Tal has done nothing wrong. But it's imperative that our son goes to college with the spotless record we've all worked so diligently to keep. We'll pay whatever we need to make that happen."

"But this is just the beginning." Why doesn't he grasp the big picture? "It's not going to end. And we only investigate what may be possible stories for the news. That publicity is exactly what you say you don't want. You want the police. You really do."

Fiona's tears have won their battle. She's dabbing her face with a delicate handkerchief.

"You have an inside track at Bexter, do you not?" Wen Dulles gathers his coat, his voice carefully polite. "And you solve problems. Solve this one. And keep our children out of it."

I watch the couple leave the restaurant, Wen striding ahead, his wife behind. And I'm left alone. With another secret.

So much for teamwork. Although it's my fault. Back at the station, Franklin had left a sticky note of his own on my computer monitor. It said: *Tomorrow.* Not even signed. In just that one word, I can feel the tension.

But, fine. Tomorrow it is. And at least I didn't have to lie about seeing Wen and Fee Dulles.

Tonight, Josh is working late, Penny's having dinner with Annie. I'm at home, my Beacon Hill home, in sweatpants and a vintage Beatles sweatshirt, having a glass of wine and nibbling ancient but vacuum-sealed string cheese from my neglected refrigerator. Prime-time CNN mumbles in the background. I'm on a ruthless mission. Suddenly, there's too much stuff in my apartment. It's all got to go.

I've already yanked three of the four drawers from my dresser, dumping more T-shirts and scarves and forgotten sweaters than anyone could possibly own onto my bed. That way I can't go to sleep until it's all divvied up. Three big green plastic bags await my decisions. Keep. Throw. Charity.

With a sigh, I put my wine on the nightstand and sit cross-legged on the floor. Selecting a never-worn and perfectly good turquoise wool hoodie, another failed attempt to break out of always wearing black, I fold it into the charity bag. But I'm thinking more about Wen and Fiona Dulles than my fashion mistakes. Organizing my

152

thoughts along with the sweaters.

Kids using drugs at Bexter? They probably do, like everywhere, but Josh never mentioned anything remotely like that. And he certainly wouldn't put Penny in danger. But maybe he doesn't know. On the other hand, it doesn't need to be true. The caller could have made it up. It would be simple enough to concoct a believable and devastating scenario as a way to scam money from wealthy parents. Risky, though.

I shake my head, selecting a chunky cabled cardigan with regrettable buttons for the donation pile. Dorothy told Josh and the Head she'd gotten exactly the same kind of sinister phone call. But Dorothy's calls occurred more than a week before Fee's.

And now Dorothy is dead. She always knew everything going on at Bexter. Did she try to track down the caller? And whoever it was killed her in retaliation? Does that mean Wen and Fee are in danger?

I stop, midfold, trying to retrieve an escaping idea. What did I just think?

Dorothy always knew everything that was going on at Bexter.

Maybe — maybe she was the blackmailer.

I put my head down on the stack of sweaters and stretch out my legs, just for a moment, to think about whether my idea could work. Dorothy, knower of all Bexter knowledge and with access to every personal file and phone number in the place, gets wind of a drug ring? Students selling drugs? Or more likely, someone from outside. Dorothy's lonely. She's trapped in a menial secretarial job on a modest salary. Frustrated, bitter, having to cater to wealthy parents and pampered students. She can't take it anymore and starts her blackmailing scheme. To draw suspicion away from herself, she pretends to get a semi-threatening but possibly prank phone call of her own.

When actually, she's the one making the calls.

What if a parent who discovered her extortion scheme killed her? Even Wen and Fee? Well, okay, not them. But what if whoever is actually selling the drugs found out? And he killed her?

If Dorothy was the blackmailer and she's dead, the envelope with the Dulleses' check is still in the post-office box. And maybe there are others.

"Josh? Is something wrong?" I guess I fell asleep in my sweater pile. Squinting at my nightstand clock, I realize it's after midnight. Why is Josh calling? What's the noise in the background? I press the phone closer to my ear and remove a piece of fuzz from my lip. "Honey? Are you home? Sorry, I fell asleep and I just —"

"I'm still at Bexter," Josh interrupts. Hs voice is tense. Guarded. This is no late-night cuddle call. "Can you hear me?"

"Yes, what's going on? It sounds like sirens. Are you okay?" A dozen disasters instantly present themselves, ugly little life-changing possibilities. Outside my window, white flakes glisten through the streetlights. It's snowing again. "Are you okay?" I repeat. "Is Penny?"

"We're fine. She's home. Hold on."

Muffled voices on the other end. Josh is talking to someone else. I close my eyes, straining, unsuccessfully, to hear what they're saying. Whoever it is.

"You there, Charlie?"

"Yes, yes, of course. But hey, you're scaring me. What's . . . ?"

"Alethia Espinosa. Dean of girls? Fell down the steps outside Garrison Hall."

I picture Garrison, one of the newer classroom buildings, a three-story redbrick designed to look authentically colonial. The building houses mostly midlevel administrative offices. The steps are stone. And steep.

"Is she — ? How did — ?" My hand grips

the phone, clamping it to my ear so I don't miss anything. I hear cars, people talking, another siren. Josh is obviously outside.

"I don't know," Josh says. "We don't know. It's snowing again, the steps might have been slick. We suppose she was working late and fell as she was going home. She was out cold when the Head found her. Lucky he was there. Otherwise, I don't know. She might have been there until morning. The EMTs are working on her now. And, Charlie? The Head also told me — Hang on, okay? Sorry."

Am I too suspicious? I flop back onto my clothing-strewn bed, considering. That's two "accidents" in less than two weeks. Dorothy. And now Alethia. Her best friend. And the Head found her? Why was he in Garrison? His office is in Main. The steps couldn't be that icy. Yes, it's starting to snow now. But barely. And the Bexter people are scrupulous about shoveling.

"Charlie?"

I sit up. "Yeah?"

"I had to go around the corner. Listen, sweetheart, there's more. The Head told me there was apparently another phone call. Like the one Dorothy told us about."

I start to tell him about Wen and Fiona, who must have taken my advice and reported their call. Then I decide — no. Let him tell me about it. Then I can tell him I already know. "Really? Who answered it?"

"Alethia."

I made it to Bexter in record time. And I'll be fine as long as no one makes me take off the ankle-length parka and substantial muffler that are hiding my sweatshirt and sweatpants. A stretchy wool cap camouflages my yanked-back hair. When Josh told me Alethia got a "Do you know where your children are?" phone call, I almost lost it. I insisted he tell the police, no matter what the Bexter hierarchy said.

Turned out, they'd already done that. And now the police are demanding everyone stay at Bexter for questioning, even though it's the middle of the night. It's frustrating that I can't tell the police about the Dulleses' call, but no way I'm staying home. Annie agreed to stay overnight with Penny. At least I can sit with Josh until it's his turn. If police are investigating, maybe this will all be solved.

We'd walked arm in arm down the echoing paneled hallway, deciding to wait for the police in Josh's office. I can tell Josh is running on adrenaline. He tosses his parka on the couch, yanks open his tie, and for the

157

millionth time, runs a hand though his still snow-damp hair. His jeans are soggy from the slush. He told me the dean of boys, Kent Bishop, is in the conference room already. Then they're calling the new development consultant, Harrison something. Hope they won't mind I'm here. But it's too late if they do.

"Did they already interview the Head? What did the cops say about the phone calls?" Josh and I are nuking cups of tea in the ancient microwave he keeps on one of the bookshelves. I never come here without remembering this is where we first met. I'd appeared, without an appointment, searching for answers in what turned out to be a ruthless and deadly insider-trading scheme. I'd expected "Professor Gelston" to be a Mr. Chips geezer, wheezy and old-fashioned. Instead, I went weak-kneed, faced with my teen heartthrob Atticus Finch come to life.

"They're pissed. I don't mind telling you." Josh hands me a ceramic mug, tea-bag tag hanging over the side.

He looks at me, perplexed. "Are you cold?"

"A little," I fib. I can't take off this parka. "Anyway, why'd the Head decide to spill it? And when?"

"Tonight. Before the EMTs got here. The Head was frantic. Panicked over the school's reputation. As well as his own reputation, naturally. Harrison Ebling was there, as well. He was all bent out of shape about his fundraising plans. Thinks the publicity will 'kill the take.' What an idiot."

"He must get a cut." I dunk my tea bag, calculating.

Josh shrugs. "The bursar is worried parents will yank their kids. And then, goodbye tuition money. You see the pattern."

"And so?"

"But finally I told them, forget about the money, it'll be worse if we cover it up. What if it came out we'd all known about this? That we didn't say anything? What if the students are in danger? Avoiding a problem is never the answer."

I take a tentative sip of not-quite-hot-enough tea, proud of myself for successfully resisting the urge to say I told you so. Anyway, there's something more important I need to tell him.

"Speaking of which," I begin. "I got a call this morning."

A sharp rap on the door. Without waiting for an answer, it's pushed open by a uniformed Brookline police officer. He consults a spiral notebook. "Professor Gelston? I'm

Officer Jeff Petrucelly. Will you come with me?"

Josh puts down his mug.

I can't stand it. I hafta know. I take a chance, relying on my unlikely outfit for cover. "Officer? Could you tell me —"

Josh frowns. "I'm sorry, Officer. My fiancée."

"Yes," I continue, hurrying to pick up my sentence. "Professor Gelston's fiancée. I just came to keep him company. But I just wondered, is there any news on Miss Espinosa's condition? Did she say anything? About what happened to her? And were there any other footprints on the steps?"

"We're still working this case, ma'am." Officer Petrucelly flips his notebook closed and tucks it inside his jacket pocket. Then he looks at me, assessing. "Miss Espinosa is in critical condition. However, Miss *McNally,* any further information will have to come from our public-affairs officer."

"Nothing. I'm just tired. And my tooth hurts." I wince, not in pain, of course, but at my awkward attempts to reinforce my escalating deception. Problem is, if I tell Franklin what I was doing last night, I'll unquestionably have to tell him everything about what's happening at Bexter. I do trust

Franklin to keep secrets. But these I promised not to tell.

"Sorry to hear that." Franklin raises an eyebrow, not sounding that sorry. He turns back to his computer, leaning toward the screen, telegraphing his focus. I see my lists of VIN numbers on half the split screen and the NHTSA Web site on the other.

"Did I tell you Annie Vilardi got a new car?" I turn my desk chair toward him, trying to fill the uncomfortable silence, plowing through the tension. Hoping to lure Franklin back to normal. Maybe it's only guilty me who's uncomfortable. Maybe Franklin is just working. "Well, it's new to her, at least. I guess her parents bought it from —"

"What's the VIN? I assume you got it."

"Yes indeedy. You bet I did. Girl reporter, always on the job. Do I get a big gold star?" I cross my legs, movie star, pretending to pat my hair into place. This is throwing Franklin an irresistible softball. When he teases me back, all will be well.

"Tell me the number. I'll search the databases. You haven't done that, I assume."

Thud.

Franklin doesn't even look up. Guilt washes over me again. I should have searched it myself. I forgot.

"I wrote it down here," I say, putting my notebook on Franklin's desk and pointing to the string of letters and numbers. He taps them into the computer, no comment.

Fine. I can be professional, too. I'm not required to share everything with my producer. I'm allowed to have a personal life. A private life. And if Franklin's going to be so huffy and unpleasant, maybe I don't feel so guilty about not warning him of Kevin's New York offer. Maybe I'll just go down to Kevin's office now. Tell him yes, I'll go to New York. Then Franklin can be dismissive to the new reporter.

"You got the number wrong." Franklin swivels. He looks at me, his voice almost accusing. He points to the screen.

That's weird. And unlikely.

"No, I didn't," I finally reply.

At least, I hope I didn't. That's just what I don't need this morning. There's no "wrong" in TV. I scoot my chair toward Franklin's desk, squinting for a closer look at the monitor and get an uncomfortable thought. Because I was in a hurry, on the way to the Head's party, I didn't actually see the VIN. "I mean, I suppose Annie could have read it to me wrong."

"Yes, well, whatever. This can't be the VIN of Annie's white Ombra."

"Okay, fine, it's not the VIN of Annie's white Ombra." If I'm wrong, which I suppose I could be, I might as well take the hit. Who cares, anyway? I can always go back and get the number again. But I'm curious. "How do you know it isn't?"

Franklin begins to sort through the brown cardboard box of tape cassettes parked next to our television monitor. "Do you have the logs from the Rental Car King? Let me show you something on the video."

"Can't you just tell me, without making a big drama of the whole thing?"

Franklin ignores me. "The logs?"

I hand him the stapled sheets of paper, lists of numbers and descriptions typed by our current college-student intern. Ashley's watched our undercover video, keeping track of what pictures correspond to the time codes electronically burned into the tape. Unlike counter numbers, which can be reset to zero-zero-zero with the push of a button, a tape's time codes are always the same. That makes things easy to find.

Franklin slides the cassette into the viewer, then consults the log. "Zero one, fifteen, zero eight," he mutters, twisting the fast-forward dial to find one hour, fifteen minutes and eight seconds.

The pictures speed by until Franklin

163

whaps the yellow Pause button. The counter shows 01:15:00. He twists the machine's fat black dial to click the seconds forward. At 01:15:06, the camera lens flares with a hit of sunshine, then auto-irises down. The hood of a white car wobbles into view. The camera lurches as Franklin walks closer to the vehicle. At 01:15:07, the lurching stops and the video settles into focus. At :08, it shows a white Ombra.

Franklin looks at me, gesturing dramatically at the picture. "Here's the proof you're wrong. This car, in the RCK rental lot, has the same VIN number you gave me. So you must have written down Annie's VIN incorrectly."

He pushes the red eject button. The tape pops from the machine. Franklin leaves it, half in, half out, as if it's sticking out its tongue at me.

"Unless Annie's new old car can be two places at once. Which it obviously can't be." He crosses his arms across his starched yellow oxford shirt. Waiting for my answer.

With one quick motion, I lean over and push the tape back into place. The motor whirs as the tape threads into position. I push Play, then Pause. Stare at the screen. A white Ombra. With the same VIN as Annie's. Impossible. Impossible for a car to be two places at one time.

But actually, I know it is possible. And I know exactly how.

"Franko, listen. I mean, look." I twist my chair around, and scoot back to my own computer. I punch up Google, and type in three words.

As soon as we find Annie's car, we'll know.

"There it is, on the end. By the yellow lines. See it?" Annie's parked her Ombra in Bexter's tree-lined student lot. Seniors go back a week earlier than the other kids. Which, today, is lucky for me and Franklin.

"I see it," Franklin replies. He steers his Passat past a row of cars, each labeled with the elaborate gothic *B* of the Bexter parking stickers.

Garrison Hall is in the distance, which makes me wonder about Alethia. No word from Josh yet this morning about her. Last night's police interview had been short, the cops divulging nothing. Afterward, we'd dumped the sweater and scarf mélange from my bed and collapsed together, exhausted, without even getting under the covers. We're both going on about four hours' sleep. But my Google search has given me quite an energy boost. I can be tired later.

Franklin pulls up beside Annie's Ombra.

He leaves the engine running, and we hop out into the cold afternoon, our words puffing white in the January chill.

"There's no dealer sticker that I can see. And no dealer name tag around the license plate," Franklin says, going around to the rear of the car. "Do you know where Annie's parents purchased this?"

I tug lightly on the driver's-side door. Locked. That means I can't check the VIN on the metal plate attached inside. "Nope, no reason to ask. But let's just see what Annie's parents really got here. I'll read you the dashboard VIN, okay? I can read that through the windshield. Ready?

"One. Y, B, one . . ." I begin. Seventeen digits. A one-of-a-kind combination. Supposedly unique. Like a car's DNA.

But if my theory is right, and I bet a million dollars it is, at least two white Ombras have the same VIN. Because one of them is a fake. A copy. A clone. And it might be this one.

"Yup, the number's the same," Franklin confirms. "Weird."

I lean against the hood of Franklin's idling Passat, grateful for the engine's heat coming through my winter coat. Branches rustle around us, a late-afternoon wind kicks up. Towering gray clouds invade the once-sunny sky. More snow coming.

"Not weird. Auto identity theft." The three words I searched on Google.

"Auto identity theft?"

"Yup. One of the fastest-growing crimes in the country. Let's say someone swipes a car, say, a white Ombra. All the crooks have to do is find another white Ombra. They copy its VIN number, make new VIN plates and replace the ones on the stolen car."

I make a gesture like a magician with a wand. "Prestochango. The stolen car disappears. And if cops are looking for a stolen vehicle with a certain VIN, well, that VIN doesn't exist anymore. The bad guys can easily sell the clone because the stolen VIN comes back as clear. Pure profit."

Franklin leans into Annie's windshield, peering at the VIN, then shakes his head. "You're right. It'd be so easy. VINs are just numbers on metal plates. A snap to reproduce, a snap to put into place. Man."

He opens the Passat door, slides into the driver's seat and buzzes down the window. "Now what?"

I take a last look at Annie's mystery car. Then I pull out my cell phone and click a camera shot of the VIN. And then a wide shot of the car. Good enough for now.

"Now what? Well, curiouser and curiouser," I mutter to myself, considering. I knock the snow off my boots, one against the other, before I'm guilty of trailing deadly slush into Franklin's always-pristine interior. Yanking on my seat belt, I turn to face him.

"Here's 'now what.' Seems like someone has a cloned Ombra. It could be Annie. If her parents were sold a stolen car."

"And if that's true, she's got a problem. You'll tell her parents, right?"

"Of course. But there's another possibility. Besides the unrepaired recalls and the missing air bags, it could be the Rental Car King — whether he knows it or not — is also renting stolen cars. I think it's time to give him a call."

I pull out my cell again.

"Either way, it's blockbuster." Franklin reaches a flattened palm in my direction.

I return his high five with a flourish and a smile. We're back.

"Either way," I say. And I punch in the phone number.

CHAPTER TEN

Trying to channel Mike Wallace, I step onto the journalism tightrope. Here's where I'm balancing our quest for a good story with my guilt-ridden reluctance to throw a Bexter bigwig under the bus. The result? I'm afraid the Rental Car King may end up with tread marks.

Holding up my mirrored compact between me and Randall Kindell, I pretend to check my lipstick so I don't have to chitchat with him. Small talk, especially right before a potentially contentious interview, is impossible. You can't be nice, because you're about to nail someone. You can't be aggressive, because the interviewee might walk out before you get the good stuff. The old "checking my makeup" stall always works. Men never interrupt it.

Franklin is adjusting the tiny lavalier microphone on Kindell's pin-striped jacket, tucking the thin black cord behind his lapel.

J.T. clicks a cassette tape into his camera and twists his molded earpiece tighter into place. He's ready.

We've rigged up a portable tape player on a round walnut side table next to me. Someone familiar with television interviews would get the instant message there was trouble ahead. If someone's going to show you video and have a photographer tape your reactions, you probably will not be happy with what's on the screen. Kindell, however, seems unfazed.

Kindell had surprised us by instantly and amicably agreeing to our request this afternoon for an on-camera interview at the Rental Car King office. I used my best "it's a consumer-education story and it will help the public" pitch. Within an hour, J.T., Franklin and I had packed up our portable tape player, our pile of video logs, our biggest light kit and all our story ammunition, piled into the car and arrived at RCK. Ready for battle.

Kelsey Kindell, in a lacquered updo and op art fingernails, greeted us from behind her counter. At least, she greeted J.T. Franklin and I were apparently invisible.

She led us down a narrow fluorescent-lighted hallway and unlocked a gray metal door. A brass nameplate on it announced

President. She gestured us inside with her clanking ring of keys.

"I didn't know you were from TV before." She checked out J.T. more brazenly than Emily Post would approve of, settling a hand on one cocked hip. "Do you guys ever need, like, interns?"

"In here?" I had interrupted the impromptu job interview, gesturing J.T. and Franklin inside to save them from having to answer. Then I stopped myself from judging a book by its cover.

"Sure," I told her. "But only for college credit."

She shrugged. End of job interview. "My uncle says he'll be with you in five."

The Rental Car King's throne room pays homage to his own good-guy credentials. Curliqued "Man of the Year" plaques from several local chambers of commerce, gilt trophies flanked with generic winged goddesses, chunks of crystal perched on ebony holders. A sleek model of a flashy convertible emblazoned RCK — 20 Years of YES. Silver-plated frames display the stubby, broad-shouldered Kindell in smiling foursomes; golf outfits, tennis outfits, dinner jackets. Kindell, the curls of his almost comb-over hidden by a baseball cap, surrounded by grinning kids with bats and balls.

I'm about to throw him a curve.

He thinks — because that's what I told him — this is an interview about the importance of repairing recalled cars. He thinks — because that's what I told him — that we're interviewing him because of his stature in the car-rental field. But after I pitch him those puffballs, we're going to hit him with our video. Show him Annie's car and then the one in his own lot with the same VIN. If he's truly surprised, he should try to help us with our investigation. That would be good.

If he's angry and defensive, that means he might be involved. That would be good.

He might even throw us out. That would be even better. We'll have the whole thing on video.

Ambush interviews like this are not my favorite. But they're effective. Revealing. And always great television.

I close my compact, tuck it under my thigh in case I need it later and turn to J.T.

"Ready?" I ask.

"Rolling," J.T. replies.

"You're one hundred percent certain these numbers are correct? Beyond a shadow of a doubt?" Kindell leans back in his chair, staring at the still-frame of video on the monitor. It's a close-up of Annie's VIN. We transferred my very successful cell phone snapshots to tape so we could display RCK's white Ombra and Annie's white Ombra side by side. It's irrefutable.

"We checked the numbers again this morning," I reply. J.T. is still rolling, of course, and we got the perfect images of Kindell's face as I showed our evidence ten minutes into the interview. First he was baffled. Then calculating. Of course, I'm not revealing Annie's name. "We confirmed the private car. And the one in your parking lot. It's still there, in fact. You can check for yourself."

I glance at Franklin, who's sitting off to the side, out of Kindell's view. He makes a surreptitious motion, slam dunk.

"So, Mr. Kindell? What's your reaction to that?" I ask. "And to the unrepaired recalls we found in your cars? And to the missing air bags?"

I wait while Kindell mulls my tricky-to-answer questions, deepening the already-etched lines across his forehead and along his boxer's nose. I'm patient.

Kindell holds up a hand. "Let's turn off the camera."

But two can play this game.

"No, I'm sorry, Mr. Kindell. I'd like to get your reaction on camera." If he doesn't want to talk, what he doesn't want to say is exactly what I want to hear. I've got the power of videotape and I'm not giving it up. "These are critical questions. And we need your answers."

Kindell smiles. He nods, acquiescing. "I understand. The question again?"

That's the boldest move I've seen in a while. He's taking me on?

Franklin raises his eyebrows. I feel J.T. shift position.

"Rolling on a two shot," he murmurs from behind me, letting me know I'm also in his picture. Okay, rental-car king. You're up.

"What's your reaction to the missing air bags and unrepaired recalls?" I ask again.

The silence is so profound, I can almost hear Kindell thinking. He crosses one leg over the other. One black wingtip taps, gently.

Suddenly, he sits up straight, planting his feet on the floor. He points to me.

"Miss McNally, you're right. I've got a problem. Thank you for bringing it to my attention. Be assured, I'm going to take care of it."

I'd been expecting Mr. Defensive. Big

bluster, sputtering derision and instant dismissal. What I'm getting is "good guy"?

"That's great, Mr. Kindell. How will you —"

"First," he interrupts me, holding up one index finger. "First, I'm instantly requiring my employees to check all our cars to make sure there are no unrepaired recalls. We do our best to follow up when we get notifications from the manufacturers, but sometimes things fall through the cracks. Be assured, by this time day after tomorrow, not one car on my lot will have an open recall. You have my word on that."

I hear the zoom of J.T.'s camera motor. He's going in for a close-up. J.T.'s skeptical of instant capitulation. I am, too. It's an old trick designed to get reporters to go away and forget to follow up. Not gonna happen here. I'm not going to "be assured" of anything just yet.

"In addition, I'm going to contact my colleagues in the business. Inform them of the recall situation and urge them to do the necessary repairs of their inventories. If it's happening here, it's happening elsewhere."

He pauses, clearing his throat.

"Finally, I run a clean business. There's no VIN cloning or air bag swiping around here. I'd know it."

175

A knock at the door. It half opens. Kelsey's head appears around the edge.

"Oh, sorry," she says. "Uncle Randall? You wanted me to remind you when it was five o'clock."

"Thank you, Kelsey. We're fine." Kindell waves her away, then shrugs at me. "Just a precaution. However. As I said, no VIN cloning. No air bag stealing. If my cars have been harmed? I'm a victim, too. I'll do whatever it takes to find the culprits."

He stops, jaw set, his eyes locked on mine. As if daring me to question his sincerity.

"That answer your questions?" he says.

He's certainly persuasive. And seems sincere. And I'm surprised to realize that I'm, tentatively at least, won over. If he's guilty, why would he be this helpful? Our investigation won't stop here, that's for sure. Time to test the limits of his helpfulness. And I know how to do it.

"Terrific," I say. I'll buy his version of the truth. For now, at least. "And we'll certainly include that in our story. But there is one additional way you can help. Can you give us all the past year's rental agreements for the white Ombra? And also for the car J.T. and I rented?"

"Not a problem," he says. "We done with the interview?"

■ ■ ■ ■

"What is it you want me to see?" I ask. As J.T. packs up his gear and Franklin heads off with a foot-dragging Kelsey to copy rental agreements, Randall Kindell said he "wanted to show me something" in the company garage. After I agreed, I followed him out the back door and into a separate building in the rear. He buzzed open double-wide doors, flicked on a series of long fluorescent lights and gestured me into the concrete-walled space. Two cars are up on lifts, two others parked side by side in a bay, but the place is deserted. Chilly. Unlike the impeccably organized Power House, the RCK mechanic shop is layered with oil and gas and dirt and grease. Tall stacks of tires form towering rubber columns in every corner. Toolboxes, lids left open, reveal expanding drawers full of bolts and screws and fuses.

Kindell hasn't said a word. J.T. and Franklin will be waiting, so if Kindell is setting me up for a deadly attack, he's not going to get away with it. Although justice for the bad guy won't matter if I'm conked to death with a lug wrench or something.

"Mr. Kindell? Again, what is it you want

to show me? Franklin and J.T. are going to be looking for me."

"There's nothing to see. I just needed a private word with you." Kindell, wearing just his suit, no overcoat, is barely as tall as I am, but now I decide he's almost handsome in a craggy, aging-athlete sort of way. He leans against one of the parked cars, looking across at me. "I helped you. Now you help me."

I lean against the other car, drawing my coat closer around me. The ceiling lights buzz and crackle, gradually whirring into a blue-white glow, one tube at a time. One flickers, knifing Kindell's face into moving shadows.

"Help you? Help you — what?"

"I got a phone call. At home. Yesterday. From someone who mentioned my daughter, Nancy. He — or she —" Kindell stops, then looks down at the oil-spotted concrete floor. "Forget it. It's probably nothing."

He looks up. He's made a decision. He stands up straight. "Never mind."

No way.

"Does Nancy go to Bexter Academy?" I ask.

"Yes."

"And did the caller indicate there's some sort of scandal at Bexter? Drugs?"

Kindell's expression morphs from shock, to relief, to anger. He hesitates, then plunges in. "Yes. Exactly. Listen. I went to Bexter, got a scholarship, years and years ago. Bexter is the best there is. That's why my wife and I sent Nancy there. Least I could do is give back, so I try to donate what I can. But aren't they watching the kids? Now some stranger tells me there are drugs at Bexter? Nancy's fourteen!"

"Have you told the police?" I'm all too certain what his answer will be. But maybe someone has some sense.

"No."

Of course. I wish I could ask if Nancy Kindell knows Lexie and Talbott Dulles. And the timing of this means the black-mailer couldn't possibly be Dorothy Wirt.

"The caller said if I didn't —" He stops.

"Pay? Send a money order to a post-office box?"

"How do you know that?" Kindell is frowning, looking at me through squinted eyes. "The voice said I had a week."

"Forgive me, Mr. Kindell. And I know you'll understand why I can't tell you all I know. I've been asked to keep it confidential. And perhaps this will reassure you, too. About my ability to keep secrets. But extortion, blackmail, drugs at Bexter? It's a matter for the police, it really is. And I can't say any more about this, but I'm telling you . . ."

I pause, making sure he understands I'm trying to say something without actually saying it. "I'm telling you, if you did call the police? They'd understand why. And honestly, I'm so sorry. But there's nothing I can do."

Kindell blinks, considering. His gold wedding band glints as he runs a hand across the sleek hood of the car. Then does it again.

"I hear you," he finally says. "But the police are going to have to figure out this thing without my help. I'm keeping Nancy — and my wife — out of it."

"Drugs? At Bexter?" Josh rolls over, propping up his head on one hand. "Of course. It's a school. No place is immune. But some huge scandal?"

Josh shrugs. The blanket slides away, revealing bare chest and the drawstring of his plaid flannel pants. We're in bed earlier than usual. And it's not just the result of last night's late-night Bexter catastrophe. Penny's sleeping over at Annie's and we're alone. Botox is curled up, a calico puff at the end of the bed. She's pretending we're not here.

I turn over, facing Josh. It's all I can do

not to reach out one hand and postpone the conversation. Maybe give a little tug at that drawstring. Resolute, I yank the pale blue blanket up to my chin. He yanks it down. I yank it back up.

"Don't try to distract me," I instruct. Although it's too late. I'm already wavering. "First, Wen and Fiona Dulles. And now Randall Kindell. You still promise not to tell, right? I said I'd keep their calls secret. And now I'm feeling guilty even telling you. But demanding money? That's new, isn't it? Did Dorothy say anything about a blackmail demand?"

Josh rolls his eyes, then reaches to yank down the blanket again. I pull it up. Determined to stay on track. "The police are investigating. Let's let them investigate."

"Or Alethia?" I'm ignoring him. I just had a thought. "Did her caller say anything about money? It could be the police don't even know about the extortion. Hey. Speaking of Alethia. Is there news? Has Alethia been able to tell the police anything about her fall?"

"Nope. She's sedated. Sleeping. I hear they think she'll come out of it. But, honey? Nothing is going to happen between now and tomorrow. So, I say we . . ."

He creeps his hand toward the blanket. I

smack it to a halt.

"So do you know Lexie and Tal Dulles? And Nancy Kindell? Do you think there's a drug thing going on? Have you heard anything? Would you?"

"Honey, as I said. Drugs in school? I wouldn't be shocked. Still, Nancy Kindell? The Dulles kids? I wouldn't have thought so. Tal's a top senior, plays football. Would I know if kids were smoking dope behind the athletics shed? Probably not. Are kids falling asleep in class? Strung out like crystal-meth users? Not that I know of, at least."

With a sigh, I flop down on my back. "I wish they'd all just tell the police, you know? I'm tired of keeping secrets. I can barely remember who knows what."

"I know something secret," Josh says. He reaches out for the blanket again, and begins to pull it, inch by inch, away from me. "I know how to be two places at once."

The phone rings. Jangling. Botox leaps from her spot on the bed. Josh pulls the entire blanket off the bed and tosses it over the phone. It rings again, muffled.

"Hey!" I yelp, grabbing the blue-striped sheet. I scramble after the blanket, naked, laughing, pawing for the phone. "It might be Penny, you know? Hello?"

Listening to the voice on the other end, I

slowly wrap the sheet around me, tucking in a corner to keep the fabric in place.

"I'll let you tell Josh," I say. I hand him the phone. "It's the Head. About Alethia."

The room stills as Josh puts the receiver to his ear. I know he's hearing what Byron Forrestal just told me. Alethia's in a coma. She's not coming out of it. She's dying. Her family is bringing in her priest. It's over.

I watch Josh's face go solemn. He's murmuring into the phone.

Sitting on the side of the bed, I tuck the sheet more tightly around me. Maybe the cops are buying the accident theory. But I'm not. Not about Alethia. And not about Dorothy.

CHAPTER ELEVEN

This may be a huge wild-goose chase. We're headed for the Longmore Hotel. More specifically, the parking lot of the Longmore Hotel. This could be dynamite. Or it could be a big fat goose egg. Nothing.

Franklin and I spent the morning plowing through RCK rental agreements. We're following up with every person who rented the car with Annie's VIN and every person who rented the same car I did, the black Vallero, the one without air bags. There are dozens of agreements, each printed onto a pink piece of paper with the hint of blur that comes with a toner-challenged copy. First we put them in chronological order, then, using the tried-and-true phone survey routine, we called each person who rented the car. We're looking for clues, patterns, anything that will give us some idea of where and when the bad guys might have the opportunity to clone VINs and swipe air bags. We're thinking: parking lots.

Phone surveys often result in a big time-sucking nothing. But I love digging for journalism gold. About an hour into the car-renter pursuit, after some dead ends and hang-ups, I'd hit possible pay dirt.

"Check it out, Franklin," I said, holding up a rental agreement. "I just talked to this guy in Maine. He rented a car for the holidays. The same car I rented. Stayed at his parents' in Boston, he ever so willingly told me. Guess where they had a celebration dinner?"

"Just tell me, Charlotte."

"Spoilsport. Okay, they had dinner at Bistro Zelda. And, ta dah, they used valet parking there. Just like —"

"Michael Borum."

"Exactamundo."

"Wait a second." Franklin shuffled through his paperwork. "I had a valet parker, too. In the RCK car that has the same VIN as Annie's. Not at Bistro Zelda, though."

He held out the rental agreement. His notes, in Franklin's precise, square handwriting, were attached on top with a red plastic paper clip.

"Longmore Hotel," I read out loud. I

shrugged. "Maybe they're doing it there, too?"

"Easy enough to check," Franklin said.

"You're reading my mind. As usual." I had stacked up the documents into a neat pile, no creases, no folds, to keep them pristine for the camera, and slid them into a protective folder. "Longmore Hotel, here we come. Time to see if we're on the right track."

Now we're turning the corner onto Milk Street, winding through the impossible one-way streets and prohibited left turns.

When we pull to a stop in the semicircular driveway of the Longmore, a skinny kid in a too-big black nylon jacket positions himself at Franklin's window. "Valet parking? How long will you be?"

The words give me goose bumps. We are so on the right track. I'm just not sure where the track goes from here.

Franklin hands over the keys, a gesture I've seen a million times. Suddenly it seems like such a stupid thing to do. The kid takes them, a gesture I've seen a million times. Suddenly it seems sinister.

I hop out of the passenger side, getting myself a good view before the valet gets in the driver's seat. I have just enough time to see the name on the back of his jacket.

Beacon Valet.

Once we enter the lobby, I leave another voice-mail message for the elusive Michael Borum. Franklin's across the room, texting again. We told the valet we're picking up the car in twenty minutes. Not long enough for any dirty tricks. If there are any. Today we're just scoping out the system.

Borum's parting words to me were to threaten a lawsuit. I'm not sure whether that makes a callback more or less likely.

"Anyway," I continue my message, "we've got a bit more information about what might have happened the night of the accident. I'd like to share it with you. You had said you used valet parking? At Bistro Zelda? And I wanted to confirm . . ."

"Hello? Hello? This is Michael Borum."

"Oh, thanks for picking up, Mr. —"

"Do I take it you've been doing your homework?"

I can't gauge his hostility level, so I go for a cease-fire. Put a smile in my voice. "Well, in a manner of speaking. You said you used valet parking at Zelda that night?"

"Yes, I did use valet parking at Zelda that night. I didn't just 'say' I did."

"I understand. Now, I know this sounds off the wall. But was there any trouble with the valet service? Maybe . . ." I pause. I

187

don't want to lead a witness, but this ain't court. And my suspicions are not yet fully formed. "Maybe it took longer than it should have? A delay of some kind?"

Silence. I let him think.

"In fact, Miss McNally . . ." His words come out slowly. "In fact, thinking back, there was a 'delay,' like you say. I guess you could call it a delay. We were supposed to be there for drinks and dinner, but one of my friends wasn't feeling too hot, and had to leave. Before the apps arrived, if I remember right."

Oh. *Bingo.* I knock on the polished wood of the Longmore's carved end table. Don't want to jinx it.

"So," I say, fingers crossed. "Then what?"

"Then, nothing. It took a wicked long time for the valet to bring back our car. We had to send Jeff home in a cab. We were pissed as hell."

My fingers are crossed so tightly they hurt. "Was it Beacon Valet? How did they explain why it took so long?"

"Who the hell remembers what they told me," Borum says. "And who the hell cares. It would have been a lie, anyway. It's a Mustang. They were probably out joyr—"

He stops.

"Ah," he says.

Silence. We're both letting this sink in. At this point, I'm not going to mention the possibility that someone swiped his car's VIN. Or the air bags. I'm just nailing down the timing.

"Would you be able to identify the valet? The one who took your car?" I try to get Franklin's attention, bring him into this conversation, but he doesn't look up from his phone. Probably texting again. Maybe love notes to Stephen. "Do you think you could point him out?"

"Listen, Charlie . . ."

Borum's suddenly calling me Charlie now, I note. The Borum versus McNally lawsuit is probably in our rearview.

". . . this is bull. You say you have a photo of my car blowing through the Fast Lane tollbooth? I couldn't have been driving it. I didn't even have the damn keys at the time. And I'm gonna get nailed for some hit-and-run? I don't think so. I'm going to head for Zelda myself. Talk to the valet-parking manager."

Oh. No. This is the worst thing that could possibly happen: the victim decides to take matters into his own hands. When victim turns vigilante, the story slips out of the reporter's control. It's a touchy situation because what I'm really asking him to do is

189

put aside what could help him, personally, for what could help me, professionally. Plus, he doesn't even know about the possible cloning. If he rats us out to Zelda, our story is blown. The bad guys might stop cloning cars and ripping out air bags, which of course would not be a bad thing in real life. But this is television. The bad guys are only supposed to be thwarted after we expose them on the air. I can't allow us to be scooped by our own witness.

I have to stop him.

I have just one card to play, a card Mr. Borum has played himself at one point. And I'll use the patented McNally reverse psychology. Which also gives me deniability. Stuff they don't teach you in journalism school.

"Mr. Borum? Absolutely. Do that. If that's what you feel is proper." I pause. "But you know, we only have suspicions. It might be, you know, just a bit premature, and perhaps even legally risky, for you to go accusing a corporation of criminal wrongdoing, based on what a reporter told you. You know? Lawsuit?"

I pause again. Letting the L word sink in.

"And, of course, I can't give you the photograph of your car," I say. Especially because we don't actually have it. That I don't say.

Silence. I go in for the clincher.

"We'll continue to investigate and keep you updated at every turn. Remember, we don't want people to start shredding documents and fabricating stories."

I hear Borum puff out a breath.

"Fine. You win," he says. "But listen, you let me know what you find."

"Of course." Now. Here's where I should just let well enough alone. Say goodbye, tear Franklin away from his messaging, retrieve the car, get some lunch, go back to the station, check on Maysie and Maddee, then see how we can clinch our story. But my conscience is bugging me. I grit my teeth.

"Mr. Borum, one more thing. If you have a chance, could you take your car to a mechanic and have them check to make sure all your air bags are still there?"

I hold the phone away from my ear. Borum's response is an indecipherable bellow of sentence fragments.

"Are you honestly saying — and you don't want me to — and I could be —"

Reluctantly, I explain our suspicions. They're only suspicions, but how can I leave him in such potential jeopardy?

"Check with a mechanic and then let me know, okay?" I fire the last salvo of a desperate reporter. "Remember, it may be for the greater good."

"Miss McNally, you amaze me. You have two days. Before I go to the valet people myself. T-W-O."

"Oh, that's —"

"But here's what you'd better know by then. Who the hell was driving my car on the Mass Pike? And why?"

"We should check police reports. See if a blue Mustang is reported stolen," Franklin says. I've just finished replaying my conversation with Michael Borum. We're back in the car, which the smiling valets instantly provided, and on the way to Channel 3. "If they've copied his VIN number, they're going to slap it on a stolen car that's just like his. That's a possible lead," Franklin adds.

I look at him. My expression must show I'm distracted.

"What?" he says. "Your tooth hurting again?"

"My — ? Oh, no. I just had a thought."

I pull my cell phone out of my new maroon tote bag.

"Hang on," I say. I punch a few buttons and get connected to the number I need. When someone picks up, I put on a cheery voice. "Hello, we're coming for dinner tonight? You have valet parking, right? Which company is that, again?" I pause. "Beacon Valet? Oh, that's right. Thank you!"

"And voila," I say. "Beacon Valet. At Zelda and the Longmore. The game's afoot, kiddo."

We're almost back at the station. "Stop," I say.

"Huh?" Franklin looks confused. "Stop what?"

"Stop the car. Or, better, turn. I had another thought."

Franklin rolls his eyes. "Lunch?"

"Great idea. But no, listen. I know where I saw a blue sports car. And it might have been a blue Mustang. The light was horrible and I could be wrong because the car was high on a lift with the hood and trunk up. But it was in the garage at Rental Car King. Let's pay another visit there. See what we can see. Maybe get the scoop on what Randall Kindell is really doing."

Franklin checks his mirror, then turns on the right blinker, carefully turning away from the station. "If it was a blue Mustang, that could have been a stolen car. And someone at RCK may have been attaching Michael Borum's VIN to it."

I stare, unseeing, at the toes of my black leather boots. "But if Randall Kindell is in on the scam, why would he give us those rental agreements? I mean they led right to the same valet service Michael Borum used. Though he couldn't have predicted we'd put those pieces together."

"True. If they are pieces."

The afternoon traffic swirls around us, drivers honking and jockeying for position. Why is there rush hour on a Wednesday midafternoon? It's Boston. It's always rush hour. The snowplowed piles of crusting snow encroaching on both sides of the street don't help.

What puzzle pieces are we certain we have?

If we hadn't checked Annie's car for recalls and then confronted Kindell with his car's duplicate VIN, we could never have connected the dots in this potential valet scheme. Poor Annie may have a stolen car. And because of Michael Borum's visit to valet parking, someone's blue Mustang may be in the bad guys' sights. Kindell's in the middle of it, that's for sure. But as victim? Or mastermind?

"What were you two doing in the RCK garage anyway?" Franklin asks. "You never told me. What did he want?"

I hesitate. That's a piece of information I can't reveal. Time for a diversion.

"Here's another thought, Franklin. Can you find out who owns Beacon Valet? See where else they handle the parking?"

"Before or after we waste time at RCK looking for a theoretical blue Mustang?"

"You're right," I say. Truth be told, I don't want to face Randall Kindell right now. "It was a bad idea. And I don't have Michael Borum's VIN with me, so we couldn't check it, even if we had the opportunity. Let's head back to the station. You can track down the Beacon Valet info while I call more renters. That may be more important at this point. And we can get lunch."

Franklin, with an affected sigh, flicks on the left turn signal. Mr. Drama.

"You've gotta stop trying to be two places at once," he says.

"I'm in Kevin's office. On speakerphone. Can you come down?" J.T. and I have a great idea. But I don't want to float it to the news director without Franklin there.

"On my way," Franklin's voice buzzes through the receiver.

I can't wait. But I have to. And it really proves what a team player J.T. is.

"Hey, all," Franklin says. It's taken him about thirty seconds to arrive at Kevin's doorway. Franklin shoots me a questioning look. I smile back from across the room, trying to communicate "it's a good thing."

"Hello, Franklin," Kevin says. He gestures to a place on the couch, next to J.T. Franklin sits on the edge, as far away from J.T. as he can.

"Charlie just told me all about your VIN-cloning story," Kevin continues. "Great job. Sounds like a winner. Now she says she and J.T. have an idea. But they wouldn't explain it until you were here."

J.T. points to me. "Showtime, McNally." I get up from my chair, rebutton my gray flannel blazer over my chunky black turtleneck dress and take center stage.

"Okay, the plan. It was really J.T.'s idea, to give credit where credit is due, but he wanted me to pitch it. I had told him about what we found out today, and he suggested — well, listen. What if we were to rig up two, maybe three hidden cameras inside J.T.'s Audi? It's a cool car, very desirable, Audis are number eight on Boston's most-stolen list. J.T. will drive it to the Longmore. He'll turn on the cameras, then hand the car over to the valets."

"It's a complicated camera setup," J.T. says. He leans forward on the couch, propping his elbows on the knees of his dark-wash jeans. "But at the network, we did it all the time. Caught a bunch of mechanics faking repairs, that type of deal. And it'll work."

"Then we leave it at the place, pick it up in the morning. Make it clear we're staying overnight," I continue. "We can say we're having a big celebration, late night, couldn't possibly drive home. Letting them know, see, that we're not going to come get that car."

I check Kevin's face to see how he likes the idea. Unreadable. I plow ahead.

"And when we get the car back, we'll have all the video. A complete record of what happened and who did it. We'll take it to a mechanic, the Power House or someplace, and confirm the air bags are gone."

"Here's the rest of it," J.T. adds. "The three of us will be in an unmarked car outside. Staking out the place. We'll follow wherever they take the car. And get video of that, too."

"Right. And of course, then we'll know where their headquarters is. Or at least, what garage they're using to do the work. And who's doing it. Perfect, huh?"

"Cool, huh? Very network."

Kevin looks as if he's trying to hide a smile. "Franklin, what do you think about that plan? I gather this is the first you've

197

heard of it."

Franklin takes off his glasses and holds the lenses up to the light. He puts them back on. And looks only at Kevin. "I must say it sounds like J.T.'s quite the team player. I wouldn't hand over my Passat to such an enterprise."

"My point exactly." Kevin's eyes twinkle as he looks between me and J.T. "J.T., you want the bad guys to rip out your air bags? Who, might I ask, were you planning on getting to pay to replace them? Just put it on your expense account? I'm afraid Gigi in accounting would steamroll right through my door if that happened. Not to mention the station lawyers."

J.T. and I exchange glances. We don't really want to use J.T.'s car, of course. Now we'll see if Kevin has taken our bait.

Kevin stands up, hands planted on his wide desk. His tie, complicated rows of giraffes today, hits a pile of yellow pads in front of him. "But I must say, I admire your dedication. And the video would be beyond compelling. So let's do this."

He smoothes his giraffes, then comes around and leans against the side of his desk. "Let's use a station car. One of the new Explorers."

I look at J.T. with a secret smile. Our plan

worked.

"The registration is in the station adminis-trator's name, so it won't come back to Channel 3. Insurance should cover the dam-age. If there is any damage, of course."

Kevin winks at me. And I get it. If the story works, it'll be his triumphant swan song at Channel 3. If it's a bust, he won't take the heat. Because either way, he's outta here, headed for New York and the network. And I bet he thinks I'm going with him. But Franklin and J.T. don't know any of that.

"I'll check with the lawyers," Kevin says. "But let's get this show on the road. Can you rig it up for tomorrow night, J.T.?"

"You got it, boss."

"And, Charlie, you and Franklin work a late shift tomorrow. Come in late. You could be on stakeout overnight. Don't want to overwork my investigative team. Too much."

Franklin nods, still looking only at Kevin. "Of course."

"Sure," I say. I can't stop smiling. "Thanks, Kevin. This'll work. Thanks, J.T."

"Then we have a plan," Kevin says. He lifts a wrist and points to his watch, then gestures us to the door. "Sorry, guys, my nightside producers' meeting."

"So do you love it?" I say to Franklin.

We're walking through the newsroom, out of Kevin's earshot. I wave a happy goodbye to J.T., who's heading downstairs to the engineering department. "It's going to be fantastic. J.T.'s the brain behind this one. Terrific, huh?"

"Terrific?" Franklin says. "Making you present a harebrained scheme to rip out his own air bags? No news director would ever have agreed to that."

"Oh, piffle." I wave him off. "Like you said. He's just trying to be part of the team. And listen, of course we wouldn't use J.T.'s car. It was all part of the plan to bring Kevin in. Make him think he's participating. The whole point was to get Kevin to offer us a car from the station. You know? Psychology. And it all worked perfectly. Beyond perfectly."

Franklin stops, middle of the newsroom. He picks up a yellow pencil from someone's desk, suddenly fascinated by it. Then he looks at me.

"Part of the team, huh? Part of the plan? What if I had left you out of something big, Charlotte? If J.T. and I cut you out of the loop and went straight to Kevin with some — psychology? How teamy would that be?"

"But, I —"

Franklin puts up both palms, shaking his

head. Then he turns on his heel and walks away. I've never seen Franklin this angry. And I didn't mean to leave him out. Still, being a team doesn't mean you have to do everything together.

Does it?

Chapter Twelve

"Chocolate chip cookies for breakfast? You totally rock, Charlie Mac." Penny, today in an Annie-clone outfit of knee-length heather-blue sweater, black leggings and bright orange plastic clogs, plops herself onto a kitchen stool and props her elbows on the counter. Botox follows her into the room. The cat has, somehow, been won over. Even sleeps in Penny's room sometimes. I suspect Penny is sneaking her tuna. "It smells yum."

"The chocolate cookies are *not* for breakfast, my darling child," I say, closing the oven door. I set the timer for five more minutes. I turn to her, smiling. "I'm taking them to someone later this morning, but I'll save some for you. What time is Annie coming? You two got big plans? Cheerios or Special K?"

"Coo-kie. Coo-kie," Penny pounds both fists on the counter, making the Monster face, and performing a perfect *Sesame Street* voice. "How come you're not in TV clothes, anyway? You have a day off?"

"Chocolate chip cookies for breakfast?" Josh sniffs the air, then tucks a quick kiss behind my ear.

I shiver, every nerve ending on high, and can still feel his touch even after he takes his place next to Penny.

"Hey, baby girl. Charlie Mac's making cookies. And she's wearing an apron. Think she's been taken over by aliens?"

Today's Bexter tie is navy blue. On anyone else I'd think his wardrobe was a bit over-prepped. But on Josh? Pinstripes and tweed, oxford and corduroy, bring it on. Also, take it off.

Penny points to the trash can. "They're refrigerator things. The kind where you cut the dough. See the plastic wrapper?"

I cross my arms, pretending annoyance. "Hey, gang. Easy on the new kid, huh? Guess that means you don't care if I take all the cookies with me. If they're the gross refrigerator things. Speaking of the trash can, Penno, what's the deal with all the cans of tuna?"

"Cookie, cookie," Penny begins her chant again, and Josh joins in. Botox sits by the trash can, wrapping her tail around herself.

I place three boxes of cereal on the counter, then yank open a bag of dry cat food for Toxie. She sneers at me. And flounces out of the room. "I'm working the late shift today, remember, guys? So I'll be home really, really late tonight. You okay for dinner?"

Home, I called it. And I'm making sure Josh and Penny are set for dinner. Huh.

"Pizza!" Penny crows. "And Annie's coming. And school is almost here. And Annie says I'll love it. And Annie says the seniors are going to rock the prank this year."

I glance at Josh. I know we're thinking the same thing. Seems like Annie knows about the senior prank. Was Alethia somehow a victim? Is the prank phone calls?

Josh shrugs, telegraphing "go ahead." He pours cereal into red ceramic bowls, one for him and one for Penny, and adds milk.

"The prank?" I ask. I feign innocence to see if I can lure Penny to tell me more. Then I almost laugh. I'm using my reporter techniques on a nine-year-old.

"Yes," Penny pronounces. She chews a spoonful of cereal, then sits up very straight, honoring the significance of her knowledge. She points to me with her spoon. "You know the prank, Charlie Mac. Every year the seniors do it. It rocks. It's just a thing to freak the teachers out. And Annie says this year it's going to be the best. Annie says it's going to be —"

She stops. Claps a hand over her mouth. Then she puts both fists on her waist, her spoon dripping milk onto the tile floor. "No way. I can't tell you. It's a big fat secret. And I promised to keep it."

"Good for you," I say. I check the cookies, then Josh, then turn back to Penny. "Of course, you know it's not good to keep a bad thing secret, right? We've talked about that."

"Puh-leeze," Penny says.

"I remember one year, someone put a baby pig in the cafeteria." Josh puts his bowl in the sink. "Just tell me one thing. Does this year's prank include farm animals?"

"Oh, Daddo, that's gross," Penny says. "I guess it's okay to tell you. It won't have animals."

"So, the prank hasn't already started?" I ask. This is what we really want to know.

"No way." Penny shows me her now-empty cereal bowl. "One little cookie?"

The chocolate chip cookies are arranged on a white china plate and covered with a delicate white cloth napkin, embroidered and pristine. I'm hoping my Martha Stewart presentation gets me some points. I'd asked Millie Wirt if I might come over, sort of half indicating it was Professor Gelston's fiancée paying a condolence call after her sister Dorothy's "accident." And Millie said yes. Now I'm standing on the brick front steps of Dorothy and Millie's tiny white colonial house on Tindall Street. Waiting for a bereaved sister to answer the doorbell. I wonder if Millie gets to keep the whole house now.

The door to the garage where Alethia discovered Dorothy in her car is closed now and there are no remnants of the yellow crime-scene tape. It's been eight days since Dorothy's death. Everyone knows Alethia will not survive. I'm suspicious that two best friends will die within days of each other. I'm suspicious that people insist it's a co-incidence.

I feel a tiny rush of guilt over using someone's grief to get answers. I reassure myself it's for the greater good. Just what I said to convince Michael Borum. I hope he believed it. I guess I do.

The door opens. I hold out my cookies like a peace offering.

"Miss McNally. How kind of you."

Millie Wirt, cropped steel-gray hair, elegant but delicate with a touch of blush and palest of lipstick, accepts the plate with a gentle nod. A gold-linked bracelet dangles from one slender wrist. I know Dorothy's younger sister is some sort of business consultant, travels constantly. I can tell she's sad, yet she's chic and confident, a perfect exemplar that sixty-five is the new fifty-five.

"Please." Millie's voice drifts a bit as she waves me into the hallway. Several arrangements of fading flowers line a narrow table set in front of a tall gilt-framed mirror. A brass-and-glass light glows above. The Wirts' home smells a bit of lilac. Or lavender. Something gracious. Something refined.

In the living room, all chintz and needlepoint, I see a silver tray, flowered china teapot and two cups. But brown cardboard book boxes are flaps-open in front of floor-to-ceiling bookcases. Behind the couch, a door is open to a little office. I see a desk crowded with picture frames. More books. More boxes. And through an archway into the dining room, even more sturdy brown packing boxes marked Can-Do Movers line the floor.

"Forgive me," Millie says, taking my coat and gesturing me to the couch. She puts the plate of cookies on the coffee table next to the tea tray. "I'm packing, of course."

I perch on the edge of the couch, not quite

sure about my next move. How do you ask someone if they think their sister was murdered, and if so, why? But if she's packing, that means she's leaving. And everything she may know will soon be out of reach.

"I'm so sorry," I begin.

"Yes, it's Bexter property, of course," Millie misunderstands my regrets. "Bexter provided housing for Dottie for all those years. She invited me to live here with her, so much easier, my work and all. And she was getting on, even though she did love her job. We were the only ones left of the Wirts. It was lovely to be together. But of course, now . . ." Millie takes a breath, and pours a cup of pale green tea. "Well, I'll be moving, and Bexter will move someone else into the Tindall house. That's what we've always called it, the Tindall house."

"Is there anything I can do?" I try again, accepting my teacup. She seems grateful for someone to talk to. Fine. Talk to me.

Millie pours another cup. "The Bexter people have been lovely. The Head. Harrison Ebling. Bursar Pratt. You saw the flowers. And the students, of course, poor things. Dorothy knew every single one of them. And all about them. They were her family, you know. She'd been at Bexter for thirty-some years, poor thing. And now with Alethia, of course."

Millie places her spoon on a square linen napkin.

"And that's why you're here, am I right?" She smiles ruefully before I can respond to her very surprising question. "I know you're a reporter, Miss McNally —"

"Charlie."

"Charlie. I'm Millie. And I would have called you, very soon, had you not contacted me. I've seen you on television. I know what you do. Thank you for the cookies." She pauses, staring at her tea. "What I'm really looking for is information."

Wait. Isn't that my line?

"Information?"

"Yes. Information. Do you think I believe Dorothy fell asleep by mistake in her car? Boozed up on brandy from the Head's affair?" She shakes her head. "And Alethia just fell? I simply refuse to believe that. No matter what that medical examiner says."

She sighs. "Of course, there's nothing I can do about it. Police say the case is closed. But I'm just so . . ." She purses her lips, considering. "I'm just so . . . Charlie. I know Dottie told your Josh about the phone calls. Did he tell you?"

Uh-oh. I rewind through the promises I've

made, what I told people I would and wouldn't tell. What the police know and what they could have told me.

"I gather from your silence he did." Millie smiles. "And probably had you promise not to tell. Good for you. Let's go from there. Let's say I just told you about them, shall we? The anonymous telephone calls she received, disturbing and threatening, asking if she knew where the children were? Absurd. Nothing ever happened. But she was terrified. She was too involved in everyone's lives for her own good. I always told her that."

"So was she afraid? After the calls?"

"She couldn't sleep. And that was unusual. Dottie never had trouble sleeping. She came home one day with sleeping pills and started taking them religiously. Spent a lot of time in her study."

I take a sip of tea, considering. "Would she have made any notes, maybe? Kept records? Did she have a diary? A journal? Anything like that?"

Millie waves toward the little office. "I just don't know. A Bexter custodian delivered all her things. All her papers in those boxes in her study. I'll throw it all away, I suppose." Her voice catches.

She attempts a smile. "Forgive me. I just

can't bear to go through them right now, and the movers will be here in the next few days. I'm still a bit off center. With it all."

It's still before noon. I don't have to meet Franklin and J.T. for hours. "Millie? If, maybe, there is something in her papers. Would you like me to look?"

Millie nods, and I follow her into the study. But my search turns up nothing. No diary. No ledger. No file of incriminating letters. So much for my revealing investigation of Dorothy Wirt's secret life. If this is all there is, her life was an open book, centered on everything connected to Bexter. Letters from the bursar to the Head, asking to be in charge of the current push for money. Letters from a board member, somebody named Joan Covino, recommending "successful" consultant Harrison Ebling to lead the donation drive. Memos announcing Ebling. Memos outlining the fundraising campaign. The dean of boys demanding a bigger office. I write it all down in my notebook, names and dates. Boring, boring, Bexter inside baseball. You'd think there'd be more about education and less about money. All I've gotten from this search, so far, is a nasty paper cut.

Sitting at her desk in a needlepoint swivel chair, I try to make myself be bad Dorothy.

What would I do if I had incriminating information? Where would I put it? If I were embezzling from Bexter bank accounts? Where would I keep the records? Extorting hush money from worried parents? With Alethia as accomplice? Where would we keep track of our victims?

Much as it would make a great story to cast Dorothy as the bitter and vengeful Joan Crawford-y schemer, I just can't make it fit. Dorothy was a beloved member of the Bexter community. Her desk is crowded with photographs of her with students and parents and babies. Silver-framed graduation ceremonies. What looks like a Christmas pageant. A tiny infant swaddled in a flowered blanket. Dorothy, smiling, holding a bouquet of daisies, surrounded by students. Bexter was her family. Why would she decide to rip them off?

"How are you doing, Charlie?" Millie now has a pale blue smock covering her gray sweater and pants, and a scarf tied over her hair. "Forgive me, I'm packing up a bit. Any luck?"

"Nothing, so far at least. It's just run-of-the-mill paperwork. Nothing appears to be out of the ordinary. The photos are lovely, though. She was obviously very devoted. And everyone seemed to love her."

I hold up my right forefinger. "May I use your restroom, though? Before I finish up? I've got a little paper cut I want to wash."

Millie frowns. "Oh, dear. The powder room down here is cleared out, I'm afraid. Do you mind going upstairs? I apologize for the clutter."

The carpeted stairway is stacked with more boxes. I can see the rectangular discolorations in the paint where someone has taken down pictures or photographs. The upstairs hall is emptying, too. It smells of dust and bleach and change.

The cheery bathroom, blue-sprigged white wallpaper, yellow towels, seems almost sad. I stare into the medicine-cabinet mirror. *Tell me something, Dorothy.*

Silence. My finger throbs, reminding me I wish I had a Band-Aid. I look at the medicine cabinet again. Why not?

I swing open the mirror. I stare at the jars of pills. Do I dare? Millie asked me to help. And Dorothy is dead. I reach out a hand and swivel the bottles so I can read the labels. Patient's name: Dorothy Wirt. Temazepam, 10 mg. Take once daily for insomnia. Patient's name: Dorothy Wirt. Nifedipine. 5 mg. One each day for high blood pressure.

According to the date on the label, the

sleeping stuff, thirty pills, was dispensed . . .
I calculate on my fingers. About fifteen days
ago. Dorothy died . . . I calculate again.
Exactly a week ago. So there should be more
than twenty pills here, even if she took one
every day she was alive. Gingerly, I pick up
the amber plastic container. The label covers the whole thing, so I can't see inside.
No refills, it says. I slowly turn it upside
down, listening. *Click. Click. Click.* This
bottle is nowhere near full.

Maybe she took too many by mistake. But
when? Maybe she took too many on pur-
pose. Maybe she did kill herself. But why?

Millie will be wondering where I am. And
suddenly I realize I'm an idiot. I touched
the pill bottle. Should I wipe my fingerprints
off?

"Charlie? Are you all right?" It's Millie.
Her voice, inquiring, rises up the stairs.

I have to go.

Using the back of my hand, I push the
medicine cabinet closed.

Millie meets me at the bottom of the
stairs. Her once-composed face is blotched
and red. Her eyes are teary.

"I'm so sorry, Charlie. I started looking at
Dorothy's things, packing." She sighs, pulling herself together. Gives me a wan attempt at a smile. "I think I might just take a

short nap. Put my feet up. Before I tackle the rest of the boxes. I have a whole week, so they tell me. So no rush, I suppose."

A week. And she'll pack up the bathroom last. I may have some time, so I'll wait and see what happens. And if the pills prove Dorothy killed herself, accidentally or not, maybe better that her sister never knows.

"Of course," I say. "My coat?"

"Is in Dorothy's study. And please, Charlie. Do finish going through Dorothy's things, if you like. You may find something. And besides, then I won't have to face those boxes again. I would be forever grateful."

"Of course," I say. "I'll call you if I find something."

Millie starts up the stairs, her blue-veined hand holding on to the polished wooden banister. Suddenly she seems like the old sixty-five. "Just let yourself out, dear."

The only box left is marked "5 of 5." Helpful. I slit open the packing tape with a letter opener. Inside, wrapped in newspapers, what feels like a vase. Under that, a desk blotter. Under that, a couple of *Boston Globes.* Whoever packed this must have just thrown in everything in sight. I put the already yellowing newspapers aside. Under that, a ream box of paper, all blank. And next to that, the last thing in the box is a pamphlet with glossy covers, legal size, stapled on the spine. The title is in bold-faced embossed gold. Bexter Fundraising Report. On the cover, three noticeably diverse Bexter students stride cheerfully across the tulip-filled Bexter yard.

I page through it, half concentrating, and then flip back to the front cover, ready to put the booklet back in the box. The cover is dated March. But it's not March yet.

Odd? I lean back in Dorothy's chair, musing. Or not so odd. Maybe this was just printed and they were getting ready to send it out. Donations lists. Which reminds me. Wen and Fee Dulles made a big deal of how much they'd contributed. Randall Kindell, too. Might as well find out just how much. Or if it's even true. I open it again, searching.

And, I see, someone else has apparently done exactly the same thing. Fiona Rooseveldt Dulles. I find her listed on page 22 under Patrons. She's easy to find because her name is circled.

Circled? Why?

On page 24, in Benefactors, I find Randall Cross Kindell. Circled in pencil. Faint, but unmistakable. Wenholm Dulles. Circled. And then I see a few more. Names I don't recognize. Most names aren't circled.

Why did Dorothy mark these names? As targets? As suspects? As allies? Or enemies?

After carefully writing the names in my notebook, in order and by category, I close the pamphlet, and put it back into the cardboard box. Nothing more to look at. I'm done. I shrug on my coat, tying its woolen belt and flipping up the collar against the chilly afternoon. I pick up my tote bag. Done.

The little study is quiet. Millie is probably deep into her nap. A tiny shaft of sunlight struggles through the gauzy curtains, glinting briefly on the picture frames lining Dorothy's desk.

What if there's something I missed? What if something is marked or checked or underlined, and I didn't see it? What if that's the key to the whole thing — whatever it is?

I can't stand it.

I take the fundraising report and slide it inside my bag. Who will even know it's gone?

Chapter Thirteen

"Thanks for joining us on *Drive Time* all you car lovers out there. It's Tyler and Taylor on Wixie, here to . . ." The booming radio voice pauses. "Drive. You." Two voices talking now. "Car-razy!"

A souped-up version of the Beatles' "Drive My Car" fills my Jeep as I head back to my Beacon Hill apartment. I'm verging on late. I've got just enough time to get home, grab some food, change clothes and then go meet J.T. and Franklin for our valet-parking stakeout. I wonder if Franko is still upset about the Kevin meeting. I shake my head, tuning out the radio chatter. I wasn't trying to cut him out of the process. He'll have to get over it.

As for Kevin, I have about two weeks now to make my New York decision. My current vote is yes. This morning at home it was no. How can something that once seemed so irresistibly compelling fade into "maybe"?

Every television journalist dreams of going to the network. Do we outgrow our dreams? Am I afraid? Afraid of New York? Or of making the wrong decision? Over the past week or so, I've changed my mind about fifty thousand times.

"And here's Morris from Milton," Taylor's or Tyler's voice grates through the speakers. Maysie's next show is tomorrow, but she's insisting now that she's home, she can do it herself, over the phone. So much for my short-lived and low-paying radio career. But at least I don't have to listen to these guys hawking used cars.

". . . my wife and I are leaving Beantown," the caller is saying. "Yup, got a job down south, so we're getting out of Dodge."

"Good one," Taylor or Tyler retorts. "Dodge, huh? But it's not a Dodge you're selling today, right?"

This is appallingly stupid. I reach to change the station, but have to hit the horn instead. I glare at some teenager who's paying more attention to his cell phone than his driving.

". . . it's hot, it's cool, it's the Mustang you've always wanted," the voice says. "Metallic blue, perfect condition, and we're so pumped to sell, we're ready to deal."

"Sounds like a deal! And whoo hoo, listeners, you heard it here first. So let's give your phone number . . ."

A blue Mustang. They're selling a blue Mustang. Is someone moving stolen cars over the radio? Pretty smart. And pretty safe. The person on the phone is just a voice. An anonymous voice. Could be calling from anywhere.

Is the blue Mustang a clone of Michael Borum's car? I have Borum's VIN. All I have to do is see it, check the VIN, and I could prove it's stolen. And that means I could prove the seller is part of the — whatever it is. Bet Franklin can't stay angry through that.

Keeping my eye on the road and driving one-handed, I scramble in my Jeep's center console for some paper. Nothing. A pen. I could write the phone number on my hand or somewhere. I finally grab one.

The phone number is Boston's area code, 617 — I try to ink the numbers onto my palm. Nothing. The pen is dry. All I'm getting is red indentations.

I've got to remember the number. I flip off the radio and being singing it out loud, to the tune of an old Marvelettes song from the sixties. Still singing, I use one finger to write the number on the car window. The temperature outside is plummeting. The weather guy predicted it'll go below freezing. Maybe when I get home and puff my warm breath on the window, the number will appear. Just like in *The Lady Vanishes.*

Almost home. Five-five-five, zero-one-nine-three. I sing it, over and over. Pull into my parking place.

I yank open the building's front door. Race up the steps, still singing under my breath. *Five-five-five.* Up two flights of stairs, whirling myself around the newel post of the second landing. *Zero-one-nine-three.* Dig out my keys. Open the door. Run for the kitchen phone. And the pad and pencil I always keep there.

Five-five-five . . .

And there's the pencil and paper. Zero-one-nine-three. And the number goes safely onto the pad. I raise a triumphant fist. I win.

Grabbing the kitchen phone receiver, I punch in the numbers, my plan forming as I dial. I'll be the dumb-blonde car buyer, I'll take a hidden camera and go see the car, okay, in some kind of disguise, and nail the bad guys.

I hold the phone way from my ear, incensed, hearing the most irritating sounds ever created. Is there anything more ear-harassing than the rising scale doo-doo-DOO of "the number you have reached is not in service"?

Did I dial wrong? I punch in the numbers again. Doo-doo-DOO. I slam down the phone. Stupid short-term memory.

I stand there, fists clenched, seething. Staring at the phone number as if I can learn something. My stupid phone-number song is still going through my head. I'll probably never forget it. And it will take the place of something I really need to remember.

My fists unclench. I'll just call Wixie tomorrow. Get Saskia to tell me the number. Or I could call her now. I reach for the phone, then stop halfway. Why am I going to tell her I need the number? I suddenly want to buy a Mustang?

Plan B. I'll use the whole situation to make Franklin happy. I'll tell him about it tonight during the stakeout and he can call the radio station tomorrow. He can pose as the buyer, go undercover with the camera and get all the glory.

Another life disaster successfully averted.

"He's not coming? Are you kidding me? Why didn't he call me?" I lean out the window of my Jeep, motor running and headlights on. It's getting ready to snow again, tiny flakes spitting onto the windshield. I have two huge coffees in the cup holders, one for me and one for Franklin. Now, to my surprise, it sounds like they're both for me. "Is he sick?"

J.T.'s in the station's fiery-red Explorer, his window open, his headlights facing the opposite direction in the alleyway outside Channel 3. He buzzes down his window so it's open wider and leans out to reply. "Nope. He just said he's feeling like a third wheel. Something like that. Said we didn't need him."

I don't know whether to be angry. Or upset. Or hurt. Or guilty. I'm a little of each.

"Yeah, okay, fine. I guess." I shrug, trying to evaluate. And to think I'd been eager to share the WWXI blue Mustang lead. Still, eyes on tonight's prize, the stakeout will work. Even though part of the fun is doing the story together. "You drop off the Explorer in valet parking. I'll be waiting across the street. Are the cameras operating like we planned?"

"Yup. I did a few test runs. All worked great. We rented both cameras for two weeks, so we're set. There's, like, three, four hours of tape time. After that, we're done. No matter what happens. It'll go to black."

"We'll get what we get." I twist my head around, looking up at the sky. A big snowflake plops onto one eye. "You think this'll be a problem? The snow?"

"It's winter." J.T. shifts his car into Drive. "Valet parking could be even more crowded, you know? People don't want to walk? Drop off their cars instead?"

"We'll at least be able to see if the taping system works." I yank my gearshift into D. "Let's do it."

It's snowing hard as we arrive at the Longmore. It's 9:00 p.m. I stay back, sneaking the Jeep into a bus stop half a block down the street from the hotel. The city's glowing streetlights let me watch J.T. pull into the Longmore's curved driveway, and see the nylon jacket of the valet parker come out. They chat. J.T. should be telling him the "staying late, maybe overnight" story. And then, just as we planned, the valet slides into J.T.'s place in the driver's seat. J.T. pushes through the revolving doors and into the hotel. Inside the Explorer, three cameras are rolling tape. Just as we planned. We hope.

The Explorer, valet at the wheel, eases out into the street. Pulls to the curb. Double-parks next to a hotel van. Terrific. He can't leave it there for long. I'm transfixed. I can't take my eyes off the car.

There's a bang outside my passenger-side

door. I leap so high my head almost hits the roof. I whirl, eyes wide, terrified. It's J.T., trying to get in. I click open the lock, he slides into the passenger seat.

"I came out the side door," he says. "Worked without a hitch. One of these coffees for me?"

We keep vigil in our parking spot just down the street from the Longmore.

"You know, you don't really need to clamp the viewfinder to your eye the whole time," I say to J.T. "As soon as someone gets into the car, you can roll tape. Nothing's happening. You've been like that for almost an hour."

J.T. doesn't move the camera from its ready position.

"Soon as I put the camera down, something will happen. Never fails," he says.

I can't see his face, since the camera is between us.

"No question," I agree. "Can you believe the Explorer's been double-parked this long? All we've got is video of snow. And a couple valet parkers who used the front seat to get warm or something."

"Here comes someone." J.T. sits up straighter. One hand is on the lens, ready to focus on whatever happens.

My heart begins to race. This could be it.

I click the gearshift back into D. "Ready. Cross your fingers for the hidden cameras."

A man in a valet jacket, head bent against the increasing snow, opens the door to the Explorer. I see the rear lights go on.

"Here we go," I say. I realize I'm holding my breath. Stakeouts. Hours of boring surveillance. Followed by instant and heart-churning adrenaline.

The minutes tick by. One. Two. Five. And then the lights go off. The valet gets out. And he trots back into the hotel.

"Are you kidding me?" I say. My mouth drops open.

"Are you friggin' kidding me?" J.T. says.

"It's eleven o'clock. Do you know where your car is?" J.T.'s got his elbow braced on the passenger-side window ledge. He hasn't budged in the last two hours. And neither has our car. It's still double-parked in front of the hotel.

I throw him a look, creeped out a bit by the "do you know where your car is" line. But of course, he can't know about the Bexter phone calls. And it's a such TV cliché, everyone uses it. I quickly go back to watching the Explorer. I can't afford to miss anything that might happen.

"You're truly a good sport," I say, still facing forward. Despite what Maysie feared, this guy is the genuine article. Clearly not an ax murderer. And I may have judged him too harshly about the network stuff. He's sitting in the car, not complaining. "I really appreciate it, J.T. No matter what happens tonight."

"Not a prob," he says. His eye is still locked to the viewfinder. A few cars hiss by in the increasing snow, headlights briefly glaring through our front seat, then leaving us in the semidarkness. We've chatted off and on, passing the time, about nothing. Our coffees are long gone.

"You were with the network, huh? You like it?" Might as well let him talk about it, if he loves it so much. Television is relentlessly nomadic. Everyone always on the prowl for the next big job. Everyone with a where-I-came-from and a where-I-want-to-go-next story. And everyone loves to tell theirs. Which reminds me, again, of New York. I push the thought away. "Where'd you start in TV?"

"I left college right after graduation," he says. "Went overseas, you know, big adventure. See the world. Did some work as a stringer for Reuters, got some lucky breaks, got hired by CNN International. Israel. Syria, for a few weeks. Afghanistan. Then got nailed by the economy. Boom. Laid off. Everyone's closing their overseas bureaus. Jerks. But Boston isn't a bad gig. You?"

"Boring. Predictable. Lucky. J-school after college. Interned back home in Chicago, got a good résumé tape. They needed to hire a woman in Boston — equal-opportunity laws, thank you so much. So I got there at the right time and I got the job. That's the lucky part. Then it was weekends and nights. You know the drill. For a couple years."

I shrug, still facing forward. Still watching the car. "Seemed to work. Eventually I was assigned the investigative unit."

" 'Seemed' to work? How many Emmys you got now?"

"Not enough," I say. The car is silent for a moment.

"Your family must be happy you're back in the States." I try another probably safe conversational topic.

"Who knows."

Even though it's muffled by the camera, I can tell J.T.'s voice has changed. I wish I could look at him to gauge what's wrong, or different, but I can't risk it. More head-lights flash by, both directions.

"Who knows?" I repeat, wondering what he means. This could be precarious territory. But he seems to be asking for another question. "Are they — ?"

"Who knows," J.T. says again. "I was raised in foster families. Never found my birth parents. When I was eighteen, I decided to ask. They told me the adoption was sealed. I stopped looking. Now it doesn't matter. They must have had their reasons for giving me up."

"The Shaws?"

"Who knows. Shaw is the name of the hospital where I was born. My birth certificate just says — Tommy. Last name unknown. And that's where J.T. came from. Just Tommy."

We sit in silence for a moment. I know it's late, and I've had too much coffee. But it's so profoundly revealing. Maybe about both of us. I've been impatient with him, dismissed him as an egotistical know-it-all. He doesn't even know his own real name.

"J.T.," I whisper. Adrenaline time. "Roll."

I see the dashboard clock in my peripheral vision: 11:28. If we're lucky, and we often are, we'll have plenty of tape to record whatever is about to happen. I cross my fingers. And I watch.

The valet gets into the front seat. The rear lights, red then white, flicker on.

I look at J.T. "Are you — ?"

229

"Don't worry," he says. His eye is pressed to the viewfinder. The red light is on. He's rolling.

A puff of exhaust plumes from the back of the Explorer.

I click the gearshift into D.

The Explorer pulls out, slowly, onto Water Street.

I check my rearview. Coast is clear behind me. I turn the wheel, just enough, ready to hit the accelerator and follow wherever the Explorer takes us.

The Explorer stops. It backs into a parking space. The headlights go dark. The valet gets out, slams the door and walks away.

I let out a puff of air. "Bummer," I whisper.

So much for the stakeout. The car is clearly staying put. I leave my gearshift in Drive. We're done. And we're out of here.

"Tomorrow night?" I say. Like I'm asking for a date. Stakeouts don't always work. You've got to expect that and embrace it. You have to hear no before you hear yes. And tomorrow we'll be more experienced. I know all the rationalizations, chant them like some journalism mantra. "Same time, same place?"

"You're on," J.T. replies. He gets it. "Take two."

■ ■ ■ ■

"Are you already awake? How late did you get in? How'd it go? Did you get any sleep at all?" Josh, bleary-eyed and half-groggy, turns over to face me. "You're reading?"

I've got my back against the headboard, one leg crossed over my knee, wearing Josh's socks and a too-big Bexter sleep-shirt. I close the Bexter fundraising report, holding my place with one finger, and lean over to give Josh a good-morning kiss. It's almost eight, but my brain is too buzzy to sleep any more. Too much to think about.

"Yeah, I'm looking at the — Tell you later. Too complicated," I say. "Stakeout was a bust. We're trying again tonight. I have to go in late, again, sweets. I'm sorry."

"Hmm." Josh plucks the pamphlet from my hand and tosses it onto the floor beside the bed. He slides one hand, slowly, slowly, underneath my Bexter shirt. "What can you do to make it up to me, I wonder?"

Finally. A question that's not difficult to answer.

A tiny terracotta pot of white chrysanthemums, tied with a thin white ribbon, is in the middle of my desk. And next to the flowers, a steaming latte.

"My bad," Franklin says. He's standing by his desk. Looking sheepish. "I heard about the stakeout last night. I'm sorry it was a no-go. And, Charlotte . . ."

He blinks a few times, watching me hang my coat and staticky muffler on the hook. It's late afternoon, and since we're working overnight again, I'm just arriving. I had a very lovely morning.

I decide to let Franklin say what he wants to say.

"Charlotte, I'm truly sorry about standing y'all up last night. It was, well, it won't happen again." Franklin's southern accent only slips out when he's upset or nervous.

"These are from you?" I hold up the pot of flowers, sweetly pristine, a peace offering I instantly accept. "Is everything okay, Franko?"

Franklin nods.

We've worked together for almost three years and I really can't remember another time when there's been any animosity. Sure, we've disagreed over story ideas, and planning, and strategy. But that's typical reporter-producer. If you didn't disagree and discuss and debate, no good ideas would ever emerge. But what happened last night? He didn't show up. That's a new one.

And I wonder what's going on.

"Is it Stephen?" I venture a guess. "Your family? You know, you can tell me anything. Work isn't the most important thing, Franko. If there's something going on in your life, you can tell me. Or, you know, don't, if you feel more comfortable that way. We managed last night."

I take two steps and give Franklin a one-armed hug, still holding my flowers. "But it wasn't the same without you. You'll be there tonight, right?"

"I've already rewound the tapes so we can use them again," he replies. "No need to keep three hours of nothing. At least we know the setup works. Sorry you had to be alone with Mr. Network."

I swivel into my chair and make a spot for the flowers on top of my little TV monitor. Franklin's avoiding my questions. So I'll let him off the hook. Talk about our story. "You know, Franko, J.T.'s not half-bad, once you get to — What?"

Franklin's leaning into his monitor. He's clicking his mouse. He's typing. And he's completely not listening to me.

"What?" I repeat.

"Come with me downstairs," he says. "To ENG Receive."

ENG is television shorthand for electronic

news gathering. "Receive" is the control room where satellite, microwave and KU-band transmissions from around the country and the world are fed into Channel 3. The walls in Receive are covered with monitors, each one showing nonstop pictures. It all has to come through ENG receive before it gets on the air.

ENG Joe, a lumbering old-timer in plaid flannel and jeans, has watched over ENG since before I can remember. He's still got a cigarette tucked behind one ear, and it's probably the same one he parked there years ago when the suits made the whole station nonsmoking.

These days, when TV is all breaking news, all the time, Joe juggles hundreds of feeds a day, each one flickering on a different monitor. Each monitor has a number taped above it. Each monitor is attached to a tape machine so Joe can record the ones the producer requests.

"We are receiving Sat 6 on L-4." Joe pushes a button, and talks to a producer through a microphone snaking metallically out of the wall. Shaky pictures of what looks like a small plane crash sputter into view, then settle down. "We have audio. The window's open till 4:00 p.m."

"And I have Van Alpha on 2. I'm loading

tape. Ready to record. Standby, Van 2."
ENG Joanna, whose real name no one knows, was assigned to Receive a couple of years ago, ostensibly to learn the ropes. Everyone predicted they were moving Joe out, replacing him, like they do everyone else, with someone younger and sexier.

But Joe stayed and so did Joanna. Now they're a team. Yogi Bear and Betty Boop. As long as the feeds come in as planned and the video is solid, ENG Receive is their domain. The room has no windows. The only view of the outside world is through the dozens of 19-inch screens.

"Franklin?" I can't figure out why he brought me down here.

"One second . . ." Franklin holds up a hand at me, and turns to Joanna. "Joanna. Hey. I read the 'incoming' bulletin on the producer e-mail. Where's the video?"

"Bravo's putting up their mast now. They should be radiating in two from Eastie. It's a bounce from Chopper 3. Taking it in on monitor 14."

In two minutes, Microwave van B will be transmitting video via our helicopter from someplace in East Boston. Got it. But video of what?

I stage-whisper, "Pssst. Franklin. What?"

Franklin, wordless, points to monitor 14.

It's a high-and-wide aerial view, our helicopter banking over what looks like a parking lot. The aerial camera zooms down closer. Smoky flames. Flashing blue lights. Flashing red lights. The chopper hovers. The camera zooms to a close-up. Out of focus. The photographer is struggling to get the shot.

I step closer to the monitor, squinting as if I can get it into focus myself. Then the video snaps into perfect clarity.

A blue Mustang is melting down into a pile of twisted rubble.

I only get the frustrating beep from the voice-mail system. I'd called Michael Borum immediately. And immediately got nothing.

"Borum never answers the phone, we know that," Franklin mutters, pacing. Three steps across our office, three steps back. "Charlotte, there are more than three hundred blue Mustangs in Massachusetts."

"Remind me to tell you what I found out about another one," I say, hitting Redial again. I still haven't told Franklin about Taylor and Tyler, and my theories about their blue Mustang. I can't focus until we get an answer from Michael Borum. One toe of my boot is tapping on the mottled gray carpet. I stop it. It starts again.

Voice mail again.

"I'm leaving a message this time." I lean over to get closer to the speaker. Maybe Borum will pick up. He did before.

"Hey, team." J.T. appears at our door. He has the hidden camera in one hand, the lens to the hidden camera in the other. He's holding both pieces of equipment as if they were contagious. "I have good news and bad news," he begins.

I wave both hands to stop him, then point to the speakerphone.

"She's leaving a message," Franklin explains, his voice muted as if he's calling a golf match.

J.T. leans against the doorjamb, waiting. His eyes register increasing understanding as I speak. "Mr. Borum? It's Charlie Mc-Nally. Are you home? Just checking to see if you're there. If you're there, pick up, would you? It's important."

The sound of nothing fills the room. We wait.

"Mr. Borum?" I try again. I give my office number once more, my cell, my home. "Call me as soon as you can, okay?"

I turn off the speaker and send a silent prayer.

"Guess you can't say, hey, we're checking

to see if you got incinerated in a flaming
—"

"Shush." I frown at J.T. "It's not funny."

Then I cock my head at him, quizzical.
"Wait. How'd you know why we were calling?"

"ENG Joanna," J.T. says. "Anyway. We're
screwed for tonight. The undercover cams
are trashed. The health people. I don't know
how they broke them. The good news,
they're fixable. Engineering says it'll be
tomorrow, at least, before they're up again.
Maybe Sunday."

"Fine with me if we do it tomorrow or
Sunday," Franklin says. "I'm in, anytime."

"Me, too," I say. "There are no —"

"Weekends in TV," Franklin and I finish
the sentence together.

CHAPTER FOURTEEN

I'm trying to keep the grease on the red-printed brown paper bags of Chinese food away from my new camel coat as I dig for my keys to open the front door. Impossible. I bang on the door with my shoulder, but only produce a muffled thud.

"Hello? It's me. Come to the door, okay? I'm home early, didn't have to work late."

I try to ring the tiny doorbell with my woolen elbow. Failure. If I put the bags down on our front steps, they'll get wet from the snow and disintegrate before I get to the kitchen.

"Hel-lo?"

Botox responds from inside, meowing miserably as if she's been abandoned forever. Which means — no one's home?

I prop one stapled bag on the porch railing, and holding it with my chin, extract my keys and open the door. I push it open with one foot and one shoulder and, finally, step inside. Botox curls through my legs, insistent for attention. It's probably more my shrimp than me.

"Anyone? Guys?"

The light in the living room is off. I flip it on. The dining room is dark, too. I flip it on. We always leave a light on in the kitchen to fool the burglars. Nothing is out of place, so it seems to have worked.

I deposit my fragrant, oil-spotted parcels on the kitchen counter. Maybe Josh and Penny are at a movie, like a normal family on a Friday night. Or out to dinner. I thought my coming home early would be a fun surprise. Now they're out having the fun. And the surprise is that it's only me with hot-and-sour soup for three.

I should have called first. Which reminds me.

I find my cell phone and check for messages, hoping for word from Borum. Nothing.

Dumping my work clothes into the dry-cleaning pile on the shelf in Josh's closet, I steal a pair of his black sweatpants and my favorite Nantucket sweatshirt. Josh's socks. I see Penny's crayon drawing of us, pouffy-dressed bride and top-hatted groom, taped to Josh's mirror. Our mirror. And there on the bedroom floor, where Josh tossed it this morning, is the Bexter fundraising report.

Suddenly solitude is a good thing. I grab the pamphlet, head downstairs to the kitchen and pry the lid from a plastic container of still-hot soup. Pulling up a stool to the counter, I open the report and look again at the circled names on the donations lists. Five names.

Fiona Rooseveldt Dulles on one page. Randall Cross Kindell on another. At least I know where to find those people.

Alice Hogarth is circled. Brooks Fryeburg. Lesley Claughton. Never heard of them.

Each one is a Bexter donor. Did they go to Bexter? Do they have children at Bexter? Why are they circled?

"Chinese food!" Penny's voice echoes through the front door.

That girl has a terrific sense of smell.

"Sweets, are you home?" Josh's voice.

The two arrive at the kitchen door. Each is carrying a red-printed brown paper bag.

By the time we stash my white containers of moo shu shrimp and egg rolls into the refrigerator, and put Josh and Penny's containers of exactly the same items into the microwave, I've explained to Josh about my visit to Millie, and her suspicions, and the names on the fund-raising report.

"You just took it?" Josh says.

"Millie wanted me to look into things. You're missing the point," I say, giving him a chopsticks poke in the ribs. At least he's not annoyed I went to her house. "The more important question is, do you know any kids with the last name Hogarth?"

Josh shakes his head.

"Or Fryeburg? Claughton?"

"No, and no."

"Rats," I say, gingerly taking the cartons of now-steaming food out of the microwave. "How am I supposed to — Oh."

I stop, hot food in midair. I'm a genius. "Does Bexter have a yearbook? Like, an archive of yearbooks?"

Josh takes the boxes from me. "Get with the private-school program, honey. The last thing Bexter wants is photos of their students easily accessible to nosy-reporter types like you. Bexter has the BEX."

"Sounds like some kind of disease."

"They take a group photo of each class, starting in first grade, at the awards ceremony in the spring," Josh continues, ignoring my crack. "Then they put the photo into the BEX. Which, Miss Know-it-all, is a big leather photo album. It's kept in the Head's office. Are we eating in here or the dining room?"

"Perfect," I say, pointing him to the dining room. "Then I definitely need to have a look at this BEX. Darn. Tomorrow's Saturday. And the Head won't be in till Monday, right? Why are journalists the only ones who work weekends?"

"Wrong again," Josh says. "In fact, he'll be at our faculty meeting tomorrow afternoon. Penny! Dinner!"

"So I'll come to the meeting with you. Dutiful fiancée. I'll smile and be enthusiastic, bat my eyelashes and say, golly, I'd love to know more about Bexter history. Maybe see who's in Penny's class."

"Who's in my class at Bexter, you mean?" Penny flops sideways into her dining room chair, her flannel shirt predictably inside out, tucking one bare foot underneath her. "I can tell you that. Annie says fourth grade rocks. There's Tenley, and Sigrid, and Eve . . ."

The rest of the names get smothered by egg-roll chewing. Penny recently expanded her acceptable eating options from "white food only" to include anything fried or crunchy. Annie's influence, apparently.

Josh looks at me, peering over his chopsticks. "I suppose it can't hurt. But keep in mind that . . ." He pauses. Flickers a glance at the carb-occupied Penny. " 'He' doesn't know that I told you about the 'things.' And he doesn't know about the other things."

I nod. The Head doesn't know Josh told me about the phone calls. And he doesn't know about the extortion demands to the Dulleses and the Kindells.

"I'll think of something by tomorrow," I say.

"I hate to watch our newscast." I'm obsessed with TV news, can't live without it, but too often I cringe when I actually see it. Leaning back into the couch cushions, I wave one socked toe at the screen. "Can't anyone write? Why is everything alliteration? And look at that outfit. What's Tia thinking, wearing that jacket? There's no cleavage in journalism."

Josh props his legs on the coffee table, scooting the fortune-cookie wrappers out of the way. He puts one arm around me and draws me nearer, snuggling, burying my face into his sweater. I feel a kiss on the top of my head.

"We're having a 'Friday-night couch date,' as you always put it," Josh says into my hair. "Penny's upstairs. How about you try to relax. Instead of watching the eleven o'clock news, we'll put in a movie. And then you can fall asleep in the middle of it, as usual, and forget about the —"

"Give me the clicker." I wrest myself away from him and hold out my hand, eyes glued to the screen. "Really. I missed what they said. I have to play it again."

"No, you don't," Josh says, holding the remote above my head and out of reach. "I promise, whatever you missed will be in the paper tomorrow morning."

"Josh." I can hear the tension in my voice. Josh apparently can hear it, too. He hands me the remote.

I push Rewind — thank goodness for TiVo — and our otherwise reasonably dressed anchor starts from the beginning again. Tia's on camera, reading the prompter. I'd only heard part of what she said, but even that was enough to rev my fear level into high. Even though the video is going backward, I can read the garish black-and-red animated graphic behind her: Carjacking: Cause for Alarm.

I push Play.

"Police are asking for witnesses in an apparent carjacking and murder in the South End this afternoon," Tia intones. The graphic changes to a live shot of a sleekly serious African-American woman, bundled against the cold in a red hooded parka with our 3-in-a-circle logo embroidered on the front. I can't tell where she is — it's pitch-dark outside, and the one blasting spotlight illuminates only her. She could be anywhere. "Our reporter Elizabeth Whittemore is live now at Boston police headquarters with the latest. Liz?"

Liz nods, all business, as her image comes full screen. "Well, I can tell you, Tia, right now police are working two shocking crime scenes. And sources tell me they suspect those two events will turn out to be one deadly crime. Let me show you now, this is video you saw breaking first on Channel 3 . . ."

The screen switches to the same aerial pictures Franklin and I saw come into ENG Receive.

". . . a car fire burns out of control in an East Boston parking lot. Police this afternoon are baffled because they find no victim in the fiery conflagration."

"What's this about, honey?" Josh asks. "You look like you've seen a ghost."

I push Pause, freezing the flames into place and stopping Liz in midsentence. I turn to Josh. "I haven't told you about this yet, I was going to, but anyway, this video is from this afternoon. That's a blue Mustang on fire. And Michael Borum didn't answer the phone this afternoon, and —" I shake my head. "I'll tell you the rest in a minute. I need to see this."

I push Play. The camera is back on Liz.

"Now, some hours later, we're told, police get a call from a worried South End resident. They report a body in the bushes behind a South End brownstone. Now, I can tell you, this area is known to police for its high crime stats. Two shootings in the same block within the past two weeks. Those, sources tell me, were drug related. Let's show you the video we shot moments ago of the scene where police say the victim was found."

Nighttime. Streetlights illuminate some narrow apartment-lined street, the camera swaying as the photographer walks toward a barrier of cops and crime-scene tape. The front of the brownstone flashes into view as the camera light blasts on. And I've been there before.

"Damn," I whisper.

"What?" Josh says.

"One more sec," I say, never taking my eyes from the screen.

"Police are not allowing us into the parking lot behind this building, that's where they suspect person or persons still unknown apparently shot and, what we understand, killed the victim. Crime-scene techs are still examining the area. The victim's name is being withheld pending notification of next of kin, but I can tell you, residents here are saying he is the owner of that fiery blue Mustang we showed you earlier. Bottom line, this investigation is still a wide-open —"

The camera comes back to Liz, who suddenly looks distracted, then triumphant. "Stand by, Tia. I see Deputy Police Superintendent Frances Rivera arriving here at headquarters. If you'll bear with me for one moment. Deputy? Liz Whittemore from Channel 3? We're on live now and . . ."

"Fran Rivera's coming in, this time of night?" I say. "This must be huge."

"Why?"

"One more second."

Liz walks out of the light. A fraction of a second later, she's back in the frame. Next to her is a Valkyrie in a Boston cop's uniform. Behind her back, cops call Frances Rivera "the Goddess." To her face, if they know what's good for them, they call her "ma'am." Deputy Rivera towers over Liz. She adjusts her patent-billed hat, which on her somehow looks chic, then looks at her watch. She murmurs something into the radio Velcroed to her shoulder.

Liz is unclipping the tiny microphone from her Channel 3 parka.

"Go Liz," I say. I stop, remembering why I'm watching. Michael Borum may be dead. Someone who owned a blue Mustang certainly is.

"Deputy Rivera, thanks for joining us. What can you tell us about this situation?" Liz moves the mic toward the officer, waiting for her reply.

"At approximately 1830 hours, Area B officers responded to an anonymous call of a body found in the vicinity of Welkin and Ott Streets. Upon arriving at that address, a Boston police officer discovered one apparent victim. Male. That's the extent of what we can release at this time."

"We know the medical examiner was on the scene at the brownstone. Can you confirm the victim is dead?" Liz persists. "Do you have a cause of death?"

"We are not releasing any more information at this time, Liz." Rivera, her posture rigid and her voice tough and final, obviously thinks this interview is over. She takes one step, putting her face half in darkness.

But Liz, well trained in the tactics of local news and unwilling to let an exclusive interview end so soon, holds on to Rivera's arm and draws her back into the light. "Can you confirm, though, that the incident in the South End is connected with this afternoon's car fire in that East Boston parking lot? Did the victim own that car? Is this a carjacking gone wrong?"

"No comment," Rivera says. Her tone is chillier than the January night.

Liz lets go. Rivera disappears into the darkness.

"And there you have it." Liz is wrapping up her live shot with a final recap. But I don't wait to hear the rest. I click off the television and stare at the blank screen.

Liz had a good news night. She scored a big exclusive. She can go home happy.

Me, on the other hand? Not such good news. Has our search for a big story somehow resulted in Michael Borum's death?

I instantly call Franklin. Even over the phone, I can tell he's concerned. We're both trying to stay calm.

I'm failing. Josh heads upstairs, officially ending our couch date.

"Are you kidding me?" I say, my voice rising. "One blue Mustang, demolished. One blue Mustang owner, dead. One plus one equals murder. Even I can do that math."

Franklin sighs. "Yes, I suppose you're right. I even tried calling him again. Still no answer. But let's say it is Michael Borum, his car. What we don't have —"

"I know," I interrupt. "We don't have a

connection between what happened today and the valet parking thing."

"I can hear the cops now," Franklin says. "They'll say, 'It's a Mustang.' They'll remind everyone Borum lived near the projects. That's their 'one plus one.' Shiny car plus urban gang thugs equals carjacking. They'll figure when the jackers heard Borum was dead, they ditched the car and torched it so they couldn't be connected. Actually, the cops might have a point."

I stare across the living room, seeing nothing, trying to sort out the whys and what-ifs. Franklin must be doing the same thing at his place. For a few moments, there's only the hum of our phone connection. Music from upstairs. Running water. Everyone's getting ready for bed. Except me.

"Declan Ross," I say.

"He didn't do it," Franklin says. "Not even possible. He doesn't even know Michael Borum's car was the one that ran him off the road." He pauses. "I mean, did he? What if he found out about the car? Like we did. And decided to do something about it."

"I suppose." I play out the scene in my head, closing my eyes to envision a scenario where Declan Ross turns from victim to murderer. "But hunting down and killing someone over a car accident in a rental car? Killing someone to get car insurance money? Seems, well, counterproductive. To say the least."

"Maybe the killing part was an accident," Franklin says. "He was awfully angry in that interview, remember, Charlotte? Said someone should 'hunt that guy down,' or something along those lines. Remember, we don't really know anything about Declan Ross."

Declan Ross rented a car from the Rental Car King. If our theory is correct, he was forced off the road by someone driving Michael Borum's car. And it couldn't have been Michael Borum. Was someone trying to kill Declan Ross? Frame Borum for the "accident"?

"I'm trying to figure out where Borum fits," I say slowly. "Let's go back to square one. Say he's completely innocent. He just happened to park his car in the wrong valet parking lot. The bad guys take his car and don't get back in time. He's angry, but doesn't suspect anything. So later, if the bad guys killed him, swiped his car and set it on fire . . . why? They could easily find him, of course. All they'd have to do was copy his personal info, from his registration and insurance stuff, when they took the VIN. But why kill him? Why Borum?"

"To cover up," Franklin says.

"But why him?" This is the puzzle piece I can't click into place. "Our theory is that they're swiping VINs —"

"And air bags."

"And air bags, from desirable cars that come into valet parking. It's quiet, quick and untraceable. The whole point, the whole key that makes their scheme work, is that they don't call attention to themselves."

"So you're thinking — it *was* a carjacking? And Borum was once again in the wrong place at the wrong time?"

"I don't know, Franko. And I don't know how to find out. And what do we do about Declan Ross?"

Silence again.

"You know what I think?" I have an idea. "We need to find something that connects Michael Borum and his car to the VIN scheme. I think we've got to find that blue Mustang they're selling on the radio. See if it has Borum's VIN. Did you get that phone number from WWXI?"

"I called this afternoon, but it was after five. Story of our lives, I got an answering machine. Left a message, but I predict no one calls me back until Monday. No one works on weekends except —"

There's a click on the phone.

"Charlie?" Franklin says. "I think some-one's calling you."

The call-waiting click interrupts again.

We both pause. What if this is Michael Borum? Safely home, Mustang untouched, saying he'd been out of town, and just watched the news.

"I'll call you back," I say. "If it's him."

Whoever was calling hangs up before I can get there. No message. Of course, someone could have been calling Josh, since this is his house. Now, star 69 to the rescue.

"The number of your last incoming call was . . ." I'm too impatient to get up and get some paper, so my pencil is poised over a *New Yorker* I grabbed from the coffee table. The techno-voice begins to recite the phone number of the person who called. After I hear the area code, I put down the pencil and the magazine. I don't need to write anything. I already know this number by heart.

Mom.

I flop my head against the back of the couch, deflated. The air, and the hope, gone out of me. I guess I had really believed it was going to be Michael Borum.

A flare of worry. Why would Mom be call-ing me? It's past midnight. What can't wait until morning? What if —

I'm not even finished with my own thoughts as I punch in her phone number, curling myself up into a corner of the couch. I pluck the fringe on a plaid throw pillow. She has to die someday, I think, and if she has bad news of some kind, maybe she's waiting until now to tell me. Or maybe it's Ethan. Maybe something is wrong with her new husband.

"Mom?" I say, even before I hear the second syllable of her "hello." "It's me. What's wrong?"

"Well. Charlotte. Where have *you* been? And what have you been doing?" Mom, ignoring my question, sounds like she's interrogating fifteen-year-old me after some teenage transgression. I hardly ever transgressed, since there wasn't much transgression territory for geeks and bookworms. I still recognize the tone.

"Nowhere. And nothing." The time-honored teenage answer comes out before I can stop myself. I regroup, attempting to find a response befitting a forty-seven-year-old. "Is everything okay?"

"I've been leaving messages for you hour after hour," Mom says, ignoring my question again. "Miss Tolliver from the Paramount Hotel has called me several times, wondering why you're not contacting her about your wedding choices. I told her you were busy, but, Charlotte, it's somewhat embarrassing. She told me their desirable dates are already being booked. And now there are no openings available until next year. Unless there are cancellations, of course. Honestly. Most girls, in times like this, would —"

"Mom? It's after midnight. You're freaking me out a little here."

"Well, it's only a little after eleven here in Chicago, dear," she replies. "Why on earth didn't you call me back? I finally decided to call Josh to track down where you were. Now I know."

Forty-seven, I chant silently. I'm forty-seven and I can be anywhere I want. I go for a triple play: cease-fire, pacification and childhood nicknames.

"I'm so sorry, *Mamacita.* You're so right, I have been busy, and thank you for talking with Miss Tolliver. I promise I'll call her. But messages? Are you sure you called the right number? I've checked my cell, several times in fact, and there's no message from you."

"Your cell? I never called your cell phone," she interrupts. "I called your home, of course. Isn't that where you live?"

What's that line about trying to hold two

opposing thoughts in your head at the same time? I wonder after Mom and I promise to talk soon, and finally say good-night. Right now, I'm hoping there are more messages than Mom's on my home phone. At the same time, I'm hoping there aren't.

Another pitfall of trying to live in two places at one time. Out of habit, I gave Michael Borum my cell number, my office number and my home number. I never gave him Josh's number.

I can't punch the codes in fast enough. "You have five new messages," the flat computer voice reports.

Message from Mom. Delete. Another message from Mom. Delete.

"Message three. Received today at 7:00 a.m.," the voice drones.

From the first syllable, I know this one's not from my mother.

"Charlie, this is Michael Borum. It's Friday morning, early, I'm figuring you're home. Listen, I just got a registry citation in the mail. For blowing the tolls. It's bull. Those valet parkers are riding around in people's cars. I'm getting my air bags checked, then I'm telling those jerks I know exactly what they're doing. I'm not paying this ticket. They are. Good luck with your story."

And he hangs up. I sit, motionless, still holding the phone to my ear.

He just couldn't keep a secret.

CHAPTER FIFTEEN

My latte is too hot to drink, especially in a moving car, but some things I can't resist. The morning newspaper is propped on the dashboard. My cell phone is clamped to my ear. I'm reading the story on page two of the "Metro and Region" section out loud to Josh, since he can't read while he drives. Franklin's following along with the story from his house, silent on the other end of the line.

Carjacking Goes Wrong: Ends in Flames and Death, the headline says.

Underneath that, smaller print: South End Resident Murdered?

And there's a photo of Michael Borum.

Keeping the newspaper in place with my knee and elbow, I balance the plastic-topped coffee cup in one hand and my cell phone between my cheek and shoulder.

I risk a tentative sip of coffee, wince and continue reading out loud.

" 'Neighborhood residents, who did not wish to be identified, report they heard what could have been shots. Police report receiving one anonymous call that initially brought them to the scene. They also confirm the car in the East Boston parking-lot fire did belong to the victim.' "

It's just another murder to the *Boston Globe.* Not even front page. But to Franklin and me? It could be the linchpin of our story. I briefly wonder if they're running the valet scheme in New York. Maybe that could be my first blockbuster for Kevin's network. Millions of viewers. National attention. It would be hard work. Total commitment. But fame, and even fortune. If I take the job.

"So you think he confronted the valet people at Zelda?" Franklin is asking.

"Yes, I think he confronted the valet people at Zelda." I repeat what Franklin says so Josh doesn't feel left out of the conversation. "Remember, because of what I told him, he knew they were taking cars for joyrides."

"And maybe stealing air bags," Josh says.

"And maybe stealing air bags," I repeat for Franklin. "I never told him what we suspected about the VIN scheme. But then, he got that toll-violation ticket. So he goes in there and —"

"Lets them have it," Franklin interrupts.

"Lets them have it," I agree. "But once he says his name, he's in trouble. He doesn't know they know exactly who he is. And exactly where his car is."

We make the turn into the Bexter parking lot. Josh pulls his Volvo into the space marked Professor J. Gelston. The Head's car is already in his spot. There are also cars parked in the ones labeled Bursar Pratt and Dean of Boys. The Dev Consultant's space is empty. Alethia's space is empty. What used to be Dorothy's space is empty. Her nameplate has been taken down.

"They not only have to shut him up, they have to get rid of his car," I say. "Listen, Franko, we're here. See if you can get the police reports. On the murder, and on the car fire. See if you can get the Mustang info from Wixie. See if —"

"Do you think we should tell Kevin?" Franklin says.

"Don't you think you should tell the police?" Josh says.

One answer works for both of them. "Tell them what?" I reply. "That we're looking into a VIN scam at a valet-parking company, though we can't really prove it, and that one of the people whose car may have been involved, though we can't really prove it, may have been murdered, though we can't really prove that, either?"

Josh turns off the key. No one talks for a moment. There's not really a satisfactory answer. I open the door and start to tell Franklin goodbye, then think of another question.

"Franko?" I say, slowly opening my door as I speak. "Do you think Borum told the valet people about me?"

I hear Franklin take a breath. Josh looks at me from across the top of the car, and starts to say something. I point to the phone and hold up a palm, asking Josh to wait.

"I say no," Franklin finally replies. "He'd handle it by himself. Man to man. Plus, he got that ticket. That's why he went."

"Maybe," I say as the door clicks closed. "I hope you're right."

"Charlotte?" he says. "Still. Watch your back."

The phone goes dead. I scan the parking lot, making sure there's no one there I don't want to see.

Josh puts his arm across my shoulders, drawing me close. We tramp silently through the snow-spackled parking lot toward Main. Its stately stained-glass windows, in the very tops of the hexagonal towers, are glinting crimson and indigo jewels in the Saturday-morning sunshine.

"What did Franklin say?" Josh finally says. "About whether he thought Borum told about your visit?"

"He said — no."

We begin the climb up Main's steep granite steps. I can't help but think about poor Alethia. What went through her mind that night, standing on Garrison's ice-covered stairway, right before someone pushed her to her death? Did she know who it was? Did she know what was happening? Did she understand why?

What did Michael Borum see? And who? And is his death my fault?

"Raise your right hand and repeat after me," Josh says.

"What?"

"Do it."

I raise my hand, baffled. We're standing on the broad top step of Main, face-to-face, the massive inlaid-oak double doors twice as tall as we are.

"I, Charlie McNally, soon to be Charlotte Ann McNally Gelston, do solemnly swear on shooting stars and Shakespeare . . ."

Now I get it. I repeat his oath, smiling at our private joke. I first met him during an interview when I was trying to track a mysterious line from *The Tempest.* We'd first kissed, a week later, after seeing a shooting star.

"That I will allow the police to investigate the Borum case . . ." Josh says.

"That I will allow the police to investigate the Borum case . . ." I repeat. True enough. Because I'm not swearing I won't investigate, too. What happened to Michael Borum wasn't my fault. It was the toll violation that set him off. And I've decided Franklin's right. Borum didn't tell the valet people about me. He's too macho for that.

Was.

"And that I will never go anywhere alone until the case is closed," Josh continues.

"And that —"

One side of the oak door swings out between us, almost knocking into Josh's shoulder and pushing me back on the top step.

"Ah, there you are, Gelston," the Head says. He's got a blue-and-white-striped woolen muffler wrapped around his neck, and he's wearing a rumpled tan corduroy sports coat. The man is from central casting. "Are we ready for the meeting?"

I come out from behind the door.

A perplexed look crosses his patrician face, then it morphs quickly to polite. "And Miss McNally?" He flickers a glance at Josh.

Then back at me. "To what do we owe this lovely surprise?"

If Franklin could see me, he'd applaud. Maysie would hoot with derision. My mother would burst into tears of joy. Me, I'm trying not to laugh as the Head ushers me in and I see my preppie reflection in the massive gilt mirror that covers one whole wall of the lobby of Main Hall. I've taken off my coat and boots, revealing a black cardigan sweater that I have buttoned up the back, a tweed pencil skirt, a tiny patent belt, pearls and a silky scarf. Ladylike black pumps adorned with interlocked gold-ring logos, a not-so-subtle present from Mom, finally came out of my closet. I'd drawn my personal style line at wearing a headband, but other than that, I'm in the full Wellesley. The Bexter bigwigs are going to swoon.

Mata Charlie. Ready to scope out the secrets of the BEX.

"And so," I finish my pitch to the Head as we walk toward the conference room, "since Penny begins here this semester, I'd adore to take a look at the BEX. Josh has told me so much about it. It'll be a history lesson for me. Who knows, maybe it'll make some sort of wonderful feature story, the lions of industry and national leaders who have been so formative in the country's development, all of whom got their start right here at Bexter." Big smile. I can't believe I'm saying this stuff.

"Of course, Miss McNally. You're part of the Bexter family now. Stay right here. I'll bring you the BEX."

The Head waves me into the anteroom of his office. A sturdy cherry-wood desk is empty of personal belongings, its flawlessly glossy top covered with a pristine paper blotter tucked into a leather holder. Two pencils, perfectly sharpened, stiff in a cordovan-leather container. A letter opener with a matching cordovan handle.

The desk chair has a needlepoint seat pillow.

I look at Josh, my eyes questioning. He gives me a tiny nod.

This was Dorothy's desk.

The Head returns, his arms wrapped around what looks like an oversize scrapbook, bound in aging brown leather.

"The BEX," he says, handing it to me.

I can smell the leather. The BEX is much heavier than it looks, thick as a New York City phone book, trimmed in brass. The front is stamped with an embossed Bexter seal, tastefully discreet, and the school motto, *Bex et Lux.* The brass at the lower right corner is burnished at the tip, exactly where someone would turn the page.

"You can sit right at Doro— at this desk to look at it," the Head continues, waving me toward the chair. He looks at his watch, then back at me. "We'll be meeting for approximately an hour. I trust that's sufficient?"

"That will be lovely," I say.

Sitting at Dorothy's desk, in Dorothy's chair, I page through the book, trying to get a sense of it. It's expandable, held together with two metal posts with removable silver tabs on the back. I suppose that's how they add new pages every year. The pages aren't numbered, so it would be easy enough to remove a page. I tuck that thought away.

Each page has its own stiff black backing. Two class photos on each side of the page, the pictures covered in clear plastic. The students are arranged similarly, the class sitting on the front stairs of Main. Names, by row, are printed underneath each one. The first one, a fifth-grade class dated 1928, shows six students. By this year, there are maybe forty per class. There's no index.

I'm looking for Hogarth, Fryeburg, Claughton. They must still be alive, I suppose, since their names are on the donor lists. Only one way to find them.

I start at the back of the BEX. Class of 1928. The photo is sepia, the edges scalloped, tinged yellow on the edges. The girls are wearing essentially the same plaid skirts, white shirts and navy sweaters Josh and I just purchased for Penny. Only their carefully waved hair, white socks and chunky shoes mark them as of another time: 1928. That would make those kids about a hundred years old now. Probably not doing anything sinister.

I skip a few decades to the fifth graders who started Bexter in 1967. The girls' hair is teased and pouffed, and bangs have appeared. I count on my fingers. They'd be about fiftyish now. And would have graduated in 1974. Turning to that year, I find the senior class and run my fingers along the names. And there in the front row is Alice Hogarth. Class of '74. She's in a classic flip with a headband, a circle pin centered on her round oxford collar.

After writing her name and class in my notebook, I turn the glossy pages back through to the senior class of 1973. There's Brooks Fryeburg. A girl. Lesley Claughton, also a girl, is class of '72.

I flip ahead to the newest pages and work backward. I know this is a losing proposition, because if those girls had children at

Bexter now, their last names could be different. I'm right, I guess. I can't find anyone named Hogarth, Fryeburg or Claughton. But I do see teen heartthrob Talbott Dulles, Wen and Fee's son. That gives me an idea.

Counting on my fingers again, I wish for a huge calendar as I turn a few more pages. There's Loudon Fielder, the prosperous owner of WWXI, already taller and more elegant than his classmates, sitting by the teacher. I guess that explains why he was at Dorothy's service. The heavy pages creak as I keep searching. Doesn't seem like the BEX gets much viewing. I turn one more page.

And there she is. Fiona Rooseveldt, in the senior class of 1971. I start to count again, and consider making a time chart, but it's quicker to page through. I see a broad-shouldered Randall Kindell on the end of a top row. I don't see Wenholm Dulles. And there's Fiona again, with students who were freshmen in 1966.

Something is off. I turn back to her senior photo. Back to her freshman photo. Forward again. Back again.

None of her classmates are the same. I blink at the pictures and names. Maybe I counted wrong?

I look again, trying to memorize each class

photo, which is tough, because the kids are sitting in different places each year. But no. Fiona Rooseveldt graduated a year later than she should. Other students come and go, new kids arrive and some students leave. But no one else leaves and then comes back. I clamp my pencil between my teeth, staring at the photos.

"We all miss Dorothy very much."

My pencil clatters onto the desk and rolls across the blotter. Why do I feel so guilty? I have permission to be here.

The development consultant — is it Ebling? — coat draped over his arm and a Bexter standard-issue muffler twisted around his neck, stands in the doorway. Gray hair, wire-rimmed glasses. Do they hire only people who look like each other?

"Meeting is over. Your Josh will be out soon," he says. He tilts his head, assessing. "I see you're looking at the BEX. For one of your investigative stories?"

"Well, no, it's not that, of course, I . . ." I tuck my hair behind my ear, stalling. And then I realize, this guy, the big fundraiser, probably knows exactly where everyone is. I quickly duck under the desk and pull Dorothy's report from my bag. And from out of nowhere, I get a brilliant idea.

"Actually, I guess I can tell you I'm working on a special project. Kind of a surprise gift to the school. I was thinking of a 'where are they now' kind of thing? Interviewing former students to illustrate how Bexter has changed their lives?" I pause, checking his expression to see if he's buying this. I hold up the fundraising report.

"I circled a few names from this pamphlet," I say, all smiley and earnest. Yes, I remember now, his name is definitely Ebling. Harrison Ebling. "And, Mr. Ebling, I figured that was as good a way as any to come up with random names without asking any faculty members. You know, to keep it a surprise."

"Very resourceful of you, Miss McNally." Coat now on and buttoned, Ebling takes a pair of charcoal suede gloves from a pocket.

"Please call me Charlie," I say. I'm on the verge of fluttering my eyelashes, but restrain myself. "Especially since I'm about to ask you a favor."

"Ask a favor? Of me?" he says. He stops, one glove partly on.

"Yes," I plow ahead, coming around the desk to face him. I hold out the pamphlet, pointing to the names. "I've found their photos in the BEX, but now I'm wondering how to find them. To interview. To follow up my research. I could do a Google search, of course, but I was thinking, maybe you could give me their addresses? Since they're all donors, you certainly have them in your files. Right?"

Ebling pauses, sizing me up. Then he smiles as he pulls the glove onto his hand. "Well, I suppose it's all in the family. Let me consider it. And perhaps if we could agree you didn't tell them I told you?"

I nod, reassuring. "Of course. I always protect my sources."

"So. What. Did. They. Say?" I click up the car's heater a few notches. We're halfway home. This is the fourth time I've asked Josh for the scoop, and I still haven't gotten a satisfactory answer. He's relishing his tale about what he called his "undercover assignment" in the Bexter staff meeting.

This is what I get for being engaged to the drama coach. Drama.

"I'm telling you," he says, turning to me as we stop at a red light. "But you have to hear the whole thing."

I gesture the stage back to him, and wrap my cashmere scarf a little closer.

"Anyway. I waited through the entire meeting, as I said, for the right time to bring up a question about drug use. I waited through the latest on the fundraising report, and the rundown of the new semester's schedule, and the search for a new Dorothy. And then, the new policy about the senior prank. And then, since school starts Tuesday, the ever-popular assignment of counseling and detention duty."

"Sounds fascinating."

"But that was the opening I needed," he says, ignoring my sarcasm. "After the Head went on endlessly about our zero-tolerance drug policy, I eased into my question. Asked myself, what would Charlie do? So I said, do we have any information about drug use on campus? Even any rumors? Anyone get wind of anything, talking to students?"

"What did —" I begin again.

"So, there's a silence. Everyone looks at each other. The Head, Ebling, Bursar Pratt, the dean of boys. There's Alethia's empty chair, which was disturbing. Silence."

"Did you say where you'd heard . . . ?"

"Of course not. Anyway, they all looked bemused, I suppose is the word. All said they hadn't heard a thing. Nothing drug related, any more than the usual whispers, at least. No. No. No. All around the table." He takes one hand off the wheel to illustrate "all around," then turns the car onto Bexter Academy Drive.

"Do I get a gold star?" he says. "And what

did you find in the BEX?"

On the floor by my feet, my tote bag sings out the seventies' TV theme song from *Charlie's Angels.* Franklin programmed the ringtone into my phone as a surprise. It only rings that way when it's him calling.

"Your master's voice," Josh says.

"Hardly," I say. I flip open the phone. "Hey, Franko. Did Wixie call you back? Any news about the blue Mustang?"

"You have ESP, Charlotte? Yes, Saskia called. She's checking with Tyler and Taylor for the number. She says they're 'wack,' by the way, and she'll call me back when she tracks them down," he says. "But switch gears. I just got a call from engineering. The undercover cameras are fixed. We can go to the Longmore tonight. Stake it out. You up for it?"

Nothing. Zero. Nada. We got absolutely nothing.

Our story may be on life support. Breathing its last. If our story dies, I'm not far behind, journalism-wise. Maybe this New York thing is my lifeline.

We'd tried the valet scheme Saturday night. Nothing. Deciding the likelihood of the valets recognizing our car — or caring — was small, we'd tried again Sunday night.

Nothing.

It's Monday. We're doomed.

"Tick, tick," I say, stirring skim milk into my coffee-type beverage. After sitting almost all night in the front seat of the news car, my black pants are a mass of indelible wrinkles. My black turtleneck has tiny lint balls across the front after six hours of being chafed by a seat belt. My boots are toasting my feet into sweltering blobs and I forgot to bring backup shoes. I want to go home. J.T., Franklin and I are sick of stakeouts. We're wiped out. Frazzled. And bemoaning our fate around a wobbly plastic-topped table in the Rat.

The station's cafeteria is in the basement of Channel 3. It's more like a graveyard for ancient vending machines. Windowless, and with the constant faint odor of decaying fruit and rancid yogurt, it's the only place to get coffee without going outside into this afternoon's sleet. After tasting the vending-machine coffee a few years ago, someone dubbed this place the Dead Rat Café. Not surprisingly, the name stuck.

Franklin's morosely dunking a tea bag. J.T. has water. Much wiser.

"Monday. Two weeks until the February book. And we have zero," Franklin says.

"Zero," I repeat. I take a sip. Mistake.

"You think they put their valet scheme on hold? After Michael Borum confronted them?"

"Maybe they only do it on certain nights. Or when certain people are working there," Franklin says.

"Or aren't working there." J.T. tips back in his chair, precarious. He's wearing a khaki canvas vest with a million zippered pockets. His jeans are wrinkled, too. "Or maybe —"

"We're doomed," I say, interrupting him. I'm shredding a paper napkin into strips, punctuating my litany of impending disaster. "This was my idea. I blew off the fake-organic-food story. And I left us with nothing. Kevin will flip. I've never failed on my sweeps story. This is it. The time I've always dreaded. The time it all falls through. Sorry, guys. We're doomed."

And Kevin might rethink his New York offer. That, I don't say out loud. I look at Franklin, hoping he has an idea that will pull me out of my dead-story spiral.

"What if Kevin yanks the station car?" Franklin's making it worse instead. "And the overtime for J.T. is probably in the stratosphere."

J.T. tips his chair back into place with a metallic thunk. His bottle of water wobbles on the table. "Listen, McNally. I say, let's give it another go. Maybe two. The suits have spent this much on the project, they might as well spring to see it through. Who needs sleep, right? How about tonight?"

Of course we can't give up. Of course we should try again. But tomorrow is Tuesday. I can't be tired on Tuesday.

"How about tomorrow night instead?" I say. "Tuesday's Penny's first day at school. I'm taking her, and if we stay up all night tonight, I'll be a zombie."

J.T. punches Franklin in the arm. "Parrish, come on. You up for Tuesday night? I know you don't want to let this baby go."

Here we go. I stiffen, waiting for Franko to escalate. But Franklin shrugs. "Sure," he says. "You think the hidden cam setup is the best it can be? Seems like it is."

Well, well. Détente. Franklin's on board. J.T.'s turning out to be a quite the team player. And also a good stakeout buddy, which is a critical skill. It still haunts me that he doesn't even know his own real name. Just Tommy.

Just a minute.

The boys' conversation blurs into a buzz as I focus on what I should have realized before now.

Only one good reason Fiona Rooseveldt

left school for a year. I don't care what her family pretended back then. She disappeared to have a baby.

I begin to count on my fingers again. And I don't need to be a math whiz for this computation.

Does Fiona have another secret?

CHAPTER SIXTEEN

"I can't find my sock!" Penny's wail echoes across the stair landing. I creak my eyes open. Five a.m. It's Tuesday morning. I struggle to calculate. Penny has to be at Bexter at eight. Even in my bleary state, I can figure it's too early to be worrying about socks. But it's the first day of school. That happens once in a lifetime. And it's comforting to have a pal to share it. Even a stepmom-to-be.

I throw off the quilt, leaving Josh still zonked with one arm draped to the floor, and pad down the carpeted hall into Penny's room. She's perched on the side of her bed, also wearing one of Josh's Bexter T-shirts, but she's added pink ballet slippers. Her hair is pillow flat on one side, spiked on the other. Botox drapes on her lap. A battered stuffed giraffe named Diz, who used to be spotted but who is now a weathered generic gray, is in a serious necklock under one of

Penny's spindly arms. In the other hand, Penny's holding up one navy blue sock; stark evidence of impending disaster.

"Pen?" I slide into place beside her, lowering one arm across her shoulders. Botox arches her tail, and plants it across my lap. "How you doing, kiddo? It's pretty early."

"I know." A wail. "But I'm trying to get ready. Like you said to. And my other sock is gone. And I don't have another other sock. And I've got to wear socks."

Penny's Bexter uniform of plaid skirt, navy V-neck sweater and white shirt is displayed on the puffy pink-striped chair by her closet. I untangle myself from cat and nine-year-old, and pick up the skirt. Underneath, stuck by static to the woolen plaid, is one knee-length navy blue sock.

"It was hiding, I guess," I say, laying it across the arm of the chair. I take its mate from Penny, and put the pair back together. "And now you're all set. Want me to stay with you until the alarm goes off?"

Penny's head is already nestled on her pillow; her hands, palms together, tucked under her cheek. Her eyes are closed. I lean down and give her wayward hair the briefest of kisses. "It's going to be great," I whisper. I hope I'm right.

She doesn't even open her eyes. "I know,

Charlie Mac," she says.

I have Maysie on speed dial. Just in case. She's done this with Molly and Max, and in a few years, will be such an old hand that she'll probably ship baby Maddee off to her first day of school with a casual wave and an envelope of lunch money.

But as Penny and I walk through the oak front doors of Main, I'm as unsettled as I was on my first day at Public School 11, home of the Anthony Wayne Blue Devils. We middle-schoolers were the Baby Blues. P.S. 11 had grungy lockers along the walls, recalcitrant padlocks that I still dream about battling, yellowing linoleum and hallways full of people who were taller than I was. I hardly remember smiling. Though I could be wrong about this.

One thing haunting me more than my own past this morning. Bexter is hiding some secrets.

"Your dad says he'll see you at lunch, in the cafeteria," I remind Penny. I'm determined to keep this day normal. "He had to be in extra early to —"

"I know," Penny interrupts. "But I told him, no way. I mean, the other kids do know he's my dad, and they know he's a teacher. So it's cool if I catch him later. No biggie."

The lobby has the air of a small-town British train station at rush hour. Chilly. High ceilings. Identically dressed students, carefully diverse. A few hovering parents. There's the low-key buzz of hellos and goodbyes. Everyone bustling, everyone determined, everyone with a destination. And all keeping to schedule.

It all appears peaceful, probably as it's been every new semester since 1923. But I know how much has happened over winter vacation.

I see Dean Kent Bishop and the bursar, Aaron Pratt, standing in one corner, observing the morning chaos. The Head, arms crossed, watches regally, hovering outside his corner office. Harrison Ebling gives me a nod. I recognize a few of the teachers, stationed strategically. They might as well be plainclothes cops. And maybe they are.

I wonder who knows what and how much. I wonder if Talbott and Lexie Dulles are here. And Nancy Kindell. I wonder if Harrison Ebling has addresses for me.

But Penny comes first. I can't let anything ruin her first day.

"Your dad really wanted to come with you, you know." I hope Penny's not having some permanent life-trauma moment, where she'll someday tell some therapist how her mother deserted her, and then her father wasn't there on the first day of school, and how he sent some interloper as substitute parent.

We arrive under the two-story timbered archway that connects Main's lobby to the branching hallways lined with classrooms. I look down at Penny, checking for terror, and reach for her hand.

Penny stops. Looks up at me with that Penny face.

"Are you freaking out, Charlie Mac?" Then she actually winks at me and tucks her hand through the strap of her backpack instead.

"You're going to be my mom," she says, solemn. Pronouncing the rules. "I'm too old to hold hands." This time, she's wearing the headband, unnecessary to control her inch-long hair, but apparently required for preteen fashion. She'll hang her navy pea jacket in her new classroom. Underneath, her new uniform is starched and pleated and pristine. She has two socks. And she's smiling.

"Then you get that cute fanny to class," I say, giving her a pat. "No throwing chalk. No sticking your gum under the desk. No passing notes."

"Huh?" Penny says. "We text."

"Hey, Penny," two Penny clones speak in unison as they arrive, in identical uniforms, lugging books. I wonder again how their backpacks don't tip the little girls heels over head.

They all perform some elaborate handshake thing that seems to include elbows and forefingers. They look up at me, register my bafflement, then remember their Bexter manners.

"I'm Tenley Eisenberg. And this is Eve Nillsen. We met Penny at orientation." Tenley moves her bangs out of her eyes, then holds out a hand. Then she stops. Hand in midair. And looks at Penny. "Is this — ?"

"Told you," Eve says, cocking her head knowingly. "The one on —"

"The news." Tenley finishes the sentence. Reverent.

"She's Charlie McNally," Penny says. Her nose tips up the slightest bit and an unmistakable note of pride tinges her voice. "She's going to be my new stepmother, and I'm going to be her junior bridesmaid. In the wedding. She's already brought her cat to our house. And Charlie Mac's going to live there, too. With me and my dad."

"Cool."

"Totally."

"So nice to meet you both," I say, reaching out to shake hands. "How lovely of you to —"

Penny holds up her tiny wrist, interrupting. It's weighted down by the pink-and-black plastic watch Josh presented her last night. "Time for class," Penny announces. "See you at home, Charlie Mac. You guys ready?"

The plaid-and-backpacked trio sashays down the center hallway, hunter-green pleats swinging under their matching jackets, heads close together. Penny already has friends. Parents are forgotten. Is this how mothers feel? About a hundred years old? And happy to be so?

"Take care," I whisper to their backs. "See you at home, Penneroo."

Home. New York is a million miles away. And maybe? Should stay that way.

I know I should get right back to the station. Franklin may have heard more from Saskia about the blue Mustang offered for sale on the *Drive Time* show. He may have dug up the info about who owns Beacon Valet. And right after the noon news, we're scheduled to meet with Kevin and regroup about tonight's stakeout. We've decided not to start tonight until ten or so, theorizing cars that could be at the Longmore Hotel overnight are more likely to be taken. It could be a pivotal evening.

I'd watched Penny until she was out of sight. I'd traipsed back to my car. Even turned on the engine.

Then I couldn't resist. Grabbing my phone, I leave Franklin a vague voice mail explaining that I'll be there soon but have to do one little errand. I turn off the car, slam the door, head to Landman Hall and down the corridor to Josh's classroom. I have several more-than-reasonable excuses if anyone stops me. I'm engaged to the teacher and I'm a parent. But the main door to the building is not yet locked. The halls are empty all the way to room 418. Not such great security, but it's making my goal very easy. I want to see Josh in action.

If the amount of e-mail he gets and the sign-up sheet for his office hours are any indication, the kids adore him. And I've always been curious how he handles his students in class. How they react to him. His expression. His posture. His demeanor. I'll be undercover tonight at the Longmore. Might as well be undercover this morning, too.

At this time of morning, classes in full swing, the hallway is empty. No kids clutching late passes, no bustling administrators carrying clipboards. The lacquered oak door to 418 is closed, like all the other doors down the hardwood corridor. A brass plaque, at eye level, is engraved "Professor Gelston. English Literature." A four-paned window, beveled glass with brass edging, is positioned just high enough to be out of reach. Tiptoe height.

Tiptoe it is. I put down my purse and make myself as tall as possible. And I get a surprise. I know this is Josh's room, but I don't see him. I stand on my toes as long as I can, calves straining and balancing with two fingers on the doorjamb. I don't see him. I peer through the frustratingly small window, ready to duck out of sight if anyone looks up.

I don't see him.

The navy-sweatered students are seated in ladder-back chairs at wooden double desks, facing away from me. At the front of the classroom is a curly-haired woman, playing down her obvious attractiveness and dressing for respect in a careful dark blue shirtwaist, camel cardigan tied around her shoulders. I purse my lips, flipping through my mental Rolodex. Did I see her at the Head's party? Some sort of intern? Teaching assistant? Substitute? Josh never mentioned having anyone like that in his classes.

She's pointing, one at a time, to some names written carefully in white chalk on a floor-to-ceiling blackboard. Leontes. Perdita. Hermoine. Whoever this is gestures to one student, and then to a pile of books on the teacher's desk. Josh's desk. The student gives one book to each of her classmates, then takes a seat.

Someone's at the front of Josh's classroom, and she's teaching Shakespeare. *The Winter's Tale.* Who is it? And where is Josh?

By the time I get to Josh's office, I've given up pretending to be casual. I've tried his cell phone. No answer. Now I'm calling his office phone. I hear it ringing in my ear and on his desk as I walk up to the door. No answer. I pause, click my cell phone closed and give a quick rap with my knuckles under his brass nameplate. I wait. No answer.

Hesitating ever so briefly, I put my hand on the old-fashioned wooden doorknob, and click open the door. Pause again. Nothing. I push the door wide open. Josh's office is empty.

I flip my phone open again, checking for a voice mail. Josh probably was leaving a message for me while I was calling Franklin. No. No new messages. With a click of the lock, I close Josh's office door. I need to find some answers.

Penny. Is she where she's supposed to be? The nasty phone calls to Dorothy and the Dulleses and the Kindells flash unpleasantly through my mind. "Do you know where your children are?" Can I be sure Penny's in her class? Josh sure isn't in his.

By the time I get to the Head's office, my own head is churning. Maybe Josh is simply taking over someone else's class this hour. Maybe he's in a meeting. Maybe he's conferring with some parents. Maybe he was really in the back of the classroom this whole time and I've now panicked myself into believing a dark — and wholly fictional — tale of disaster.

There's no one at the secretary's desk. Of course. They still haven't hired a new Dorothy. The Head's office door is closed. Reluctant to knock, I stand in the empty anteroom, staring blindly at the glowing green glass of the brass lamp on Dorothy's desk, trying to decide what to do. If anything.

"Miss McNally? May I help you with something?"

I whirl at the voice behind me.

Harrison Ebling is frowning. The development consultant's pursed lips push up toward his nose, and his eyes narrow behind his wire-rimmed glasses. He looks like someone who's caught a wayward student sneaking into the Head's office without a hall pass or a reasonable excuse.

"Oh, Mr. Ebling," I say. Finally someone who may know what's going on. If anything is. "I'm wondering if you could tell me —"

"I'm afraid I can't," he says. He takes off his glasses, folds them deliberately, then tucks them into the breast pocket of his corduroy jacket. His ears are beginning to turn red. "And the Head is, well, out."

"Can't what?" I'm not asking him about the donor addresses he promised to find for me. "I'm wondering about Josh. I went to his classroom and he's not there."

Ebling makes that pursed-lip move again. "I know that, Miss McNally."

He adjusts his tie, pushing it up even closer around his neck, then makes a raspy sound in his throat.

"We're all very concerned. I'm sure it's just procedure. However, the officers instructed us not to discuss it."

"Officers? What officers?" I search his face, then clench his corduroy arm, insistent, my hand, knuckles white, gripping hard. My engagement ring sparkles against the thick brown fabric. All the blood rushes from my brain, then rushes back in again. I'm sweltering. I'm freezing.

"Mr. Ebling. Where. Is. Josh?" I try to remember to breathe. "And where is Penny?"

Ebling doesn't answer. He backs away from me, disengaging his arm, and glances around the room. His office door, the Head's door, out the entryway.

"Mr. Ebling. I don't care who told you what to say. Or what not to say." My voice is icy, honed to a demanding whisper. I take two steps closer to him, locking eyes. Giving him my death stare. "Where are Josh and Penny? Tell me. Right now."

Ebling can't meet my gaze. "Come with me," he says, turning away. He waves toward the open door of his office. "We can have some privacy."

I close my eyes for a fraction of a second as I follow him. I'm desperate to stay calm. If they were hurt, or dead, someone would have called me. No one has called me.

Ebling waves me to a high-backed wing chair, overstuffed and oversize, upholstered with muted tonal blue stripes. Its twin is positioned conversationally beside it. A round mahogany table, a bouquet of yellow chrysanthemums and two Bexter catalogs placed artfully on top, sits between them. The fundraiser's lair.

I perch on the edge of the one chair, digging in my bag for my phone. I'm ready to run. Or call for help. Or both.

"Mr. Ebling? Please."

Ebling is at the door. I hear it click closed. He crosses the room and goes to sit behind his desk. He has about one more second or I am going to kill him.

"Miss McNally," he says. "I'm so sorry to tell you . . ."

My heart drops.

"Josh is downtown. In Boston. At the district attorney's office."

"At the — ?" My heart is beating again. But my brain is struggling to understand. "Is he all right?"

"He's being questioned in the deaths of Dorothy Wirt and Alethia Espinosa."

"What?" My voice pierces high C. The entire contents of my tote bag spill to the floor as I leap from my chair, glaring at Ebling. He's fidgeting like a scared ferret. "What on earth are you talking about? Questioned? When did he go? Who took him? Where?"

I crouch to my knees, still wearing my coat, half looking at Ebling while I frantically scoop up pens, pencils, lipstick, change, my phone and my checkbook, scraping my fingernails across the tight weave of the Oriental rug. "Is he charged with something? Why didn't anyone call me? And you, you knew this?"

I hear Ebling punching buttons on his phone. He leans forward, elbows on his desk, resting his head on two fingers as he apparently waits for someone to answer. He's put his glasses back on and the receiver is clamped to his ear so hard it's pushing them cockeyed.

"Miss McNally," he manages to say, adjusting the glasses back into place on his nose, "in a moment or two, I certainly can determine whether he'll be back here soon."

I don't feel like waiting a moment or two.

"Where's Penny? Is she in class? She's supposed to meet her father at lunchtime. What if Josh wasn't back by then?"

"Miss McNally, please. I'm attempting to help you here." He looks as if he's on the verge of tears. Wimp.

If I hadn't come back to peek into Josh's classroom, I wouldn't know anything about this. Whatever this is. Why didn't Josh call me?

Ebling is murmuring into the receiver, his end of the conversation monosyllabic. I make out "Gelston" and "McNally" and "Soroff." Jeremiah Soroff is the new district attorney. His predecessor, Oscar Ortega, resigned in ignominy after Franklin and I proved he was in up to his flashy bow ties in evidence tampering and fixing cases. I'd hoped his replacement would be one of the good guys.

I plop back onto the chair and yank the zipper on my bag, closing everything but my phone and car keys inside. The theme from *Charlie's Angels* makes Ebling look up, expectant, from his call.

"Is that Josh?" he asks. He puts his hand over the mouthpiece.

"No," I reply. "It is not Josh. I'm still waiting for you to tell me exactly where Josh is, since you clearly know. And you are clearly refusing to tell me."

"Yes, she is," Ebling says. Into the phone.

He nods at me, pointing to the receiver and holding up an index finger, attempting a charade I'm apparently supposed to translate as "I'm hearing something encouraging."

"Immediately," he says. "Yes, my office."

My phone warbles again, the perky theme music yanking me back to my parallel reality.

Franklin. I look at the tall grandfather clock beside the stolid redbrick fireplace, its pendulum relentlessly ticking away my options. It's almost noon. I'm supposed to be at the station. We're supposed to be meeting with Kevin about tonight's stakeout. A conversation with myself, a blur of words, volleys through my head in a fraction of an instant.

I have to take care of Josh. Franklin and J.T. will have to go on the stakeout alone.

What if they hit pay dirt, catch the valet parkers in the act, find where they're taking the cars, and I'm not there?

What if Josh is in trouble?

What if I miss the story? J.T. and Franklin can't confront the bad guys. I'm the reporter. I have to be there. It's my job.

Josh is my life. Penny is my life.

I can't be two places at one time.

I flip open my phone to tell Franklin I might be late.

"Miss McNally?"

Bursar Aaron Pratt appears at the door. I know from the BEX he's a Bexter graduate. I've seen his fifth-grade photo, a pudgy Humpty perched on the front row, and a few pages later, his charismatic image in the graduating class, suddenly with shoulders, class-president hair and tall enough to be in the back with the other hunks. That was almost thirty years ago. He's still got the shoulders and most of the hair. And the charisma.

"Procedure, procedure, procedure," he

says, shaking his head in what I'm apparently supposed to recognize as sympathy. His outstretched hand precedes him into the room.

Now I'll get some answers. I clack my phone closed and stand. I'll have to call Franklin back.

"What procedure?" I ask. I shake his hand so he'll get the show on the road. "Mr. Ebling told me that the district attorney —"

"Please sit," he says, settling himself in the wing chair opposite mine.

I'll do anything to get these people to stop stalling. I plop into the chair, once again, and look between the two. I can't decide which of them is acting more uncomfortable, the ferret or the movie star.

The movie star seems to be in charge. "Miss McNally, I'm so sorry you were concerned, there's simply no need," Pratt begins, leaning forward and putting his elbows on his knees. "It all happened so quickly there simply wasn't time."

"There's time now," I say, getting to my feet. "Right now."

Pratt waves me back to the chair, acknowledging my impatience. "District Attorney Soroff's office called us, just as the students were beginning class this morning. He explained he was sending several plainclothes detectives here to Bexter as the school opened, and that they would wait in Main until the classes began. To prevent anyone from being alarmed. After classes begin, he said he would need to ask several of our employees to come in for questioning. All voluntary, he said."

I open my mouth, but Pratt continues. "Be assured, we checked with our attorneys. They called Soroff. It's all quite legal."

Pratt runs a hand through that hair, then leans even closer to me. "Apparently our two — unfortunate incidents, with Dorothy and Alethia, have piqued the curiosity of someone in authority. Now they're looking for additional information. According to our attorneys, the D.A.'s office is rechecking the blood tests performed on poor Dorothy after her death."

"The tox screen," I say. Interesting. We had been told it showed nothing unusual. High level of carbon monoxide, exactly what would be expected. My mind goes back to those pills in Dorothy and Millie's medicine cabinet. And to the fingerprints I left on the container.

"The tox screen. Exactly. In conjunction with this renewed investigation, if that's what it is, they've called in several people to discuss their whereabouts the nights of the accidents. The Head. The dean of boys. And . . ." Pratt pauses, then narrows his eyes at Ebling. "You?"

"No," Ebling says. He gives his phone an edgy glance, as if his summons might be imminent.

"And Josh," Pratt continues. "I'm sure it's nothing. But I'm sure you're upset."

Duh.

"Let me drive you to the district attorney's office," he offers.

"Let me drive her," Ebling pipes up. He stands, leaning forward, and places both palms on his desk. "The Head left you in charge here. Perhaps it's best if you don't leave. It would be no trouble, Miss McNally. My car is right outside."

"That won't be necessary." Pratt's voice, curt, doesn't match his smile. "And Ebling, you check on Penny. I'm sure her father will return before the end of today's classes. If not, please keep her in your office. I'll drive Miss McNally downtown."

"Thank you, both, but I'm driving myself." I stand, hoisting my tote bag to my shoulder. Holding up my cell phone, I look between the two of them as I back toward the door. "Do I need to call a lawyer for Josh? Is your firm handling this? Who is at the D.A.'s office advising him?"

Pratt and Ebling, now side by side in front of the desk, wear matching frowns. And then, one after the other, they switch on nervous smiles.

"I'm sure everything will be fine," Ebling says.

"I'll take care of Penny, don't worry," Pratt adds. "We don't want to disrupt her first day at Bexter."

CHAPTER SEVENTEEN

"I'm not press. I'm family." I'm facing an expanse of government-issue wood and metal, the front desk in the foyer of the district attorney's office. And I've suddenly hit the wall.

The wall in this case is the flame-haired, lip-liner-addicted, fashion-challenged receptionist of the D.A.'s office. Her green plastic nameplate says Monica Beales. Her demeanor says go away.

Monica flips the tiny microphone on her Time-Life operator contraption up over her head. Looks at me through disdaining eyes.

"You're Charlie McNally, Channel 3. Correct? I remember you from before." The Gorgon taps an acrylic nail on the laminated press pass I've placed in front of her. "Unless you quit your job since your last story about our office? And you're somehow hanging on to your credentials?"

"No, I still work at Channel 3, of course.

But you can understand this is a different situation. It's personal," I say, making my eyes plead, which isn't that difficult since I'm verging on frantic. Attempting to elicit some sisterly empathy, I hold up my engagement ring, fluttering my fingers in the time-honored notice-my-diamond gesture. "Like I said, my fiancé, Professor Joshua Gelston, hasn't answered his cell phone. I've been calling and calling. And I know he's here. And I need to know if he's okay. What's happening. If he needs a lawyer."

"You're a reporter. You're press. Press is press," Monica says. Reciting the gospel according to bureaucrats. "Family is family. But you're not family. You're press."

"I understand, I really do. And I know you're doing your job." Gag. "But in this case —"

She's not going to let me finish my sentence. One imperious finger points me to the yellowing arrangement of earth-toned seventies-era chairs and pockmarked coffee table in to one side of the foyer. The wall is covered with a time-travel array of former district attorneys. Their photographs evolve from sepia-toned scions with pince-nez glasses and high white collars to power-suited pinstripes and designer ties. All men, I can't help but notice. The recently impris-

oned Oscar Ortega's photo has been re-
placed, as if the disgraced ex-DA never
existed, by a stern-faced Jeremiah Soroff.

Although her previous boss Oscar Ortega
was ousted, Monica remains at her post.
And apparently she blames me for Ortega's
demise. Hey, I didn't corrupt the justice
system. I just reported on the guy who did.
That hardly makes it my bad.

"Take a seat," she commands. "I'll notify
the press secretary you're here."

"But I don't want the press secretary. I'm
not working on a news story. Listen, Monica, I'm only wondering if —"

"Or you can call her later, for an update,"
she says. She flips her microphone thing
back into place. Lights on the phone console
begin blinking green. "I'm on duty till five."

I've lost this round. But I'm not defeated.

"I'm staying here. Until Josh is finished.
Do you know how long it'll be? He'll have
to come out this way, right?" I'm edging
toward the tired-looking couch, proving I'm
being obedient, but still digging for information.

"Sorry." She aims a finger at one of the
green lights, and punches down the button.
I'm dismissed.

At least Franklin had good news. After

unsuccessfully trying Josh again, Franklin was the second call I'd made from the makeshift office I've set up on the D.A.'s sprung-cushioned couch. Coat thrown across one corner. Tote bag open. Laptop humming on the scarred coffee table. Notebook and pencil out. Cell phone to my ear. From time to time, harried-looking people wearing clacking necklaces of laminated badges scurry by. With practiced I-don't-want-to-get-involved attitudes, they entirely ignore the worried woman in black pants, black sweater and plaid muffler who's spread out in their waiting room. Fine. Today I'd rather not be recognized.

Josh is still not answering his cell. I just hope he's not in one.

According to Franklin, Kevin's staying with the program. Franklin, J.T. and I are set to hit the Longmore Hotel valet parkers again tonight. Franklin is playing phone tag with Saskia about the blue Mustang and he's tracking down the owner of the valet-parking company. He says Beacon Valet is apparently set up as some sort of elaborate trust designed to obscure the actual owner's name. Or names. The trust designers might say it's to "protect" the actual owners' names. I would disagree. But Franklin will figure it out.

I try Josh again. No answer. Next, Toni DuShane, the station's lawyer. I land in voice mail, story of my life. I punch out a text message. CHARLIE MC. CALL ASAP. Seconds later, my phone rings. It's not the *Charlie's Angels* ring. It's Toni.

"Hey, sister. What's happening?"

Sistah, she says. Toni's Harvard Law, out of Roxbury High, by way of a stint as a fashion model, her career capped by an award-winning cover on *Essence.* Now, her street-corner accent is long gone, except when she resurrects it to charm her pals or win over jurors. She's what they call a "green-light" lawyer because she works to get our stories on TV, not keep them off. We bonded many years ago over the First Amendment and scotch on the rocks. The hard stuff is a little more risky as we both now push fifty. We're both still as devoted to the First Amendment. She and Maysie are shopping for wedding outfits.

In the briefest possible way, trying to avoid commentary about Bexter's patrician hierarchy and leaving out the Dulles and Kindell phone calls completely, I tell Toni what I know. I keep my voice low to keep Monica from eavesdropping as I give Toni the bullet points.

"And doesn't that seem odd?" I finish my

recitation with an all-encompassing question. To me, the whole idea that Josh is being questioned is odd.

I hear a dismissive snort from Toni's end of the line. "Well, not only odd. It's absurd. To send your own employees into the unholy maw of the shiny new district attorney's office? Without a lawyer?" She pauses, and I hear someone's phone ringing in the background. "No one should ever, ever talk to the police without a lawyer. I mean, it's not only in the movies that you see innocent people being framed. Or getting so nervous they say something they shouldn't. Or saying something that makes them a prime suspect. Rule one, sister. If there's a murder investigation? Shut the heck up."

"I know, I know," I say, looking at my watch. "He's been in there for hours. That's why I'm calling you, of course. Can you get over here? Call them, or something?"

"Oh, kiddo, I'm so sorry. I'm in court. The clerk's calling our case. Listen. I have two minutes. Let me ask you something. Go with me, here, okay?"

"Sure."

"Do they think Josh is guilty? Why?"

Exactly what I've been wondering. Obviously Josh is not a murderer. So why is he now being kept behind closed doors in the highest law enforcement office in the county? I glance at Monica. She's stolidly ignoring me.

"Why do they think he's — well, they don't. As far as I know." I'm fully whispering now, hiding my mouth behind my hand. Maybe Monica is only pretending to ignore me. "They're just, what was it Pratt said? Checking everyone's whereabouts the night of the, um, deaths."

"Precisely," Toni says. "It's all about alibis. So? Does Josh have one?"

I turn my back to receptionist Monica, my shoulders hunched and head down, facing the lint-filled inside corner of the mustardy couch. My two minutes with Toni are almost up.

"Well, yeah. Listen. No. I guess he, really, doesn't have an alibi. Because see, on the night that —"

"Charlie, hon, I'm so sorry," Toni breaks in. "They're calling me. Listen, quickly, I'm walking down the hall. But if Josh comes out, you have him call me. Okay?"

"*If* he comes out?"

"When he comes out," Toni says.

And she's gone.

I lower the cell phone from my ear, slowly, and stare at the photograph displayed on its tiny screen. It's Josh, in a baggy bathing suit and Red Sox cap, a citrus-striped beach towel over one shoulder, standing on an expanse of white sand, the turquoise Caribbean twinkling behind him. The sun glares from his dark-lensed sunglasses. If you look closely in the reflection, you can make out a wavy Charlie, towel wrapped around my waist and camera raised, snapping the photo. Every time I see it, I can almost smell the coconut sunscreen.

We'd been engaged for exactly one day when I took that snapshot.

I lean back into the couch, propping my boots up on the coffee table before I remember that's probably pushing it with old Monica. I hold my cell phone in one hand, my lifeline, so I can answer instantly if it rings. When it rings. With a sigh, I put my elbows on my knees and stare at the unfortunate rug.

I can hear the buzz of the ancient fluorescent lights above me. My computer screen, keys untouched, clicks to black. Somewhere, behind closed doors and unreachable, is the man I'm going to marry. What if he gets arrested for murder?

Forget about it. I put my boots on the table, and clonk my head on the back of the couch. This is script fodder for some made-for-TV movie. Penny and I, hand in hand, going to court every day while Josh sits at the defendant's table. While he takes the stand. Manipulative police officers, one after the other, spout a parade of lies. Jeremiah Soroff gloating. Cameras rolling. Josh's career in shambles. I'd have to quit my job at Channel 3, take a leave of absence or something, in order to stand by him. Maybe I could even work on his case. We could hire the best of lawyers, someone like our pal Will Easterly, or the media-savvy Oliver Rankin. The jury would —

My phone rings. *Charlie's Angels* jars me out of my melodrama. I shake off my absurd scenario. Josh has done nothing wrong. Nothing any district attorney or cop tries to say can possibly change that.

"Hey, Franko. What up?"

"News?" he asks.

"Nothing," I say. "You?"

"Well, yeah. I talked to Saskia, at the radio station. Got the phone number. Called it."

"Fantastic. I guess I wrote it down wrong, right?"

"Wrong. You got it right. It's just not a phone number."

"Not a — ?" I can't help but sing it to myself. I'll be able to sing it forever: 555-0193.

"Not a phone number. There's no such number. There's no prefix 555. It's only used for movies and stuff."

"Could it be a cell phone? One of those prepaid phone things?"

"Oh, darn, Charlotte. Y'all are so awfully smart. I jes' forgot to ask the phone company that." Franklin pauses, making sure his sarcasm sinks in. "Yes, of course I checked on that. And no, it's neither of those. Trust me, it's not a phone number. It's a dead end."

"Hssst."

I twist around, trying to gauge where the hissing sound is coming from. It's Monica.

"Hang on, Franko." I look at Monica, questioning.

The receptionist cocks her head backward, toward the closed doors behind her. She holds up five fingers. Then, with a dramatic twist of her head, turns back to her blinking phone console.

"Gotta go, Franko. I'll call you." I click the phone closed before Franklin has a chance to answer. I close my computer and return it to my tote bag. Flap my notebook shut, click my pen closed and stash both of them in the side pocket. I grab my coat, but the sleeves are somehow hopelessly tangled, refusing to let me put my hands through as

I struggle to put it on. I adjust my muffler around my neck and stand, staring at the doors.

Five minutes until what?

Until Josh comes out, in handcuffs, being led away to the lockup?

Until Josh comes out, smiling and free, and we can go home?

I look at my watch. Two more minutes. I look up. Monica is no longer at her desk.

Monica slides through the opaque double doors and into the back rooms of the D.A.'s office. Franklin and I have been here countless times, and I know it's nothing but zigzags of fabric-covered movable walls, a checkerboard of cubicles. Behind that, a row of actual offices, with actual walls, and with windows overlooking the gold dome of the state Capitol.

The doors open. There's Josh. His back, at least. He's wearing his coat, which I hope is a good sign. He turns halfway, looking back toward the hallway and offices, talking to someone else I can't see. Josh gestures, a swift chop of one hand I've seen hundreds of times. He's not wearing handcuffs.

I have to press my lips together to keep myself from crying. Then I see another man's hand on one of the double doors, keeping it open. Who? Why? Pale long fingers, a wedding ring. Then a pin-striped arm comes through. A broad shoulder.

My own shoulders drop in relief. It's Will Easterly. When we first met about a year ago, he was a lanky pale whisper of a man, gray hair a bit too long, cheekbones a bit too high, suit a bit too off the rack. Back then, he was crusading to get an innocent woman out of prison. Now he's happily married to her. Now he's much better dressed and clearly found a barber. But he's still crusading. He's one of the best defense lawyers in Boston.

Josh turns and sees me.

And the doors close behind them. Josh is out.

I'm at Josh's side in an instant. Burying my face in his shoulder, I lock both my arms through the crook of his, inhaling his scent, still close to tears.

"Why? How? Who? When? What?" I say, my voice muffled by navy blue wool. "Are you okay? Why didn't you call me?"

"Charlie, darling, how did you find out I was here?" Josh is talking at the same time. "I didn't want to worry you. I had my phone off. I'm fine."

"Hey, Charlie," Will says. "Long time no see."

■ ■ ■ ■

The coffee is disgusting. Inside the lobby of the Saltonstall Office Building it's as dank and chilly as it is outside. Still, I have never been so happy to be anywhere, drinking anything. Josh is out. And if Will's lawyer-magic worked, Josh is not going back in.

Toni DuShane was right. It was all about the alibi.

"They kept asking me where I was when Dorothy died. Where I was when Alethia fell. But I knew you would have killed me if I hadn't called a lawyer, sweetheart." Josh is leaning against a dingy mottled wall, propping his coffee cup on the marble pedestal of a statue of Leverett Saltonstall himself, the fifty-seventh governor of Massachusetts. "Will was good enough to hurry over from court."

"And Josh was wise enough not to say a word to the cops on the way," Will says. He pats Josh on the shoulder. "Those pompous-ass assistant D.A.'s — Soroff has them convinced their ends justify their means. That it's more important to catch bad guys than to respect the Constitution. The idea that they'd try to strong-arm Josh into confessing. Appalling."

"But he's —" My voice rises, my interruption almost a squeak.

"Yes, of course he's innocent, if that's what you were going to say, Charlie."

I nod. I haven't let go of my death grip on Josh's arm. Except to put about five sugars into my coffee. Which didn't help it.

"But they're devoted to their 'mission,' " Will continues. "Their law, and their order. Anytime they can steam-roll some poor sucker, the Fifth and Sixth Amendments go out the window. Our tax dollars at work."

"But what happened?" I look at Josh. "Ebling and Pratt told me the plainclothes police were swarming around Bexter this morning."

"Right. I got buzzed to come to the Head's office. He told me they had sent a teacher's aide to my class. I've never seen him look so flummoxed. Anyway, the assistant D.A., this Ross Monahan, was standing there like Joe Friday. He asked me to come downtown and help with their investigation. 'Look at some photos,' he said. Told me it was 'voluntary.' So, fine. I have nothing to hide. And what the hell, I want to find out what happened as much as anyone."

Josh shrugs one shoulder, remembering. "But once we were in their car, headed

313

down the Pike toward their office, it turned into a parody of a cop show. Monahan was driving, some state trooper next to him in the front seat. I was in the back. We're chatting about nothing, when the trooper turns around, drapes one arm casually over the seat and asks me how I had heard about the threatening phone calls Dorothy Wirt received. I said, from Dorothy. And then he says, 'Where were you on the night of Dorothy's death?' "

"Did they read you your rights?" I ask. I glance at Will, fearful. I also, briefly, wonder where the Head was all this time. Pratt said the D.A.'s investigators had called him in, too. But I have to hear about Josh first.

"No," Josh says. "But that question certainly pushed our 'interview' into another realm entirely. So much for their charade that I was 'helping in the investigation.' At that point, I told them I'd prefer to have a lawyer present."

"Wise decision," Will puts in.

"I know," I say.

"They were not happy, that's for sure. The trooper actually asked me, 'Why do you need a lawyer if you have nothing to hide?' Asshole. I didn't say another word until we got to the D.A.'s office. They put me in some bleak conference room where I called

Will. He was in court, all the way in Leominster. So I waited, staring out the window, fuming, until he arrived. They stationed another statie at the door. Young enough to be one of my students."

"That's pitiful," I say. I look down at my murky coffee, imagining Josh in solitary, worrying. Wondering about his future. "But, Will, then what? Shouldn't Josh have been able to leave if he wanted to?"

"Yes, but of course they rarely inform you of that. It's all about intimidation. When I arrived, I notified the district attorney's office I was representing Mr. Gelston. Josh and I conferred. Subsequently, I informed Mr. Soroff and his state-police lackeys that if they were not prepared to charge Josh with something —"

"What?" I say. My voice comes out a squeak. That seems risky.

Will holds up a hand, smiling. "If they were not prepared to charge Josh with something, we were out of there. Of course, they have, as we say in the legal world, zippo evidence against Josh. So we left. Case closed."

We stand in silence for a moment. Me wrapped around Josh. Josh staring into nowhere. Will scoots his cordovan briefcase closer to the wall, its metal feet sliding across the scuffed tiles.

"Watch this, will you?" he says. "I'm getting more coffee for the road. You two?"

We both shake our heads as Will heads back to the remarkably decrepit excuse for a coffee shop in the corner of the lobby. The same frizzle-headed guy has doled out miserable coffee and weak tea and little bags of chips and packets of stale red licorice for the past thirty years. He must have photographs of someone important.

"Well. I'm glad that's over," Josh says. "That sucked."

I almost burst out laughing, even though I know Josh has been through hell and nothing about it is funny. Josh never says *sucked.* Instead of laughing, I snuggle a little closer. But then, because Josh is fine and Will isn't worried, I can't resist asking one question.

I pull back, still not letting go completely, and look up at Josh.

"Honey? Did they ask where you were when Dorothy was 'murdered'? I mean, did they say the word *murder?* For Dorothy or Alethia? And did they say anything about Dorothy's tox screen?"

Josh blinks, considering. "No. No, they didn't. They did talk about Alethia's fall, though. All the time I was keeping my mouth shut, they were yapping, one after the other, trying to goad me into responding. Seems like it was Alethia's fall that's got them concerned. One of them said it turned out, her briefcase and purse were still in her office. So I suppose they were wondering why she was outside."

I nod. "Good question, actually. Though how would *you* know?"

"Problem is, as I told Will. I don't have alibis for the nights of either death. Remember? I took you home then went back to campus the night of the Head's party. I was working late the night of Alethia's fall. You can see how that makes me a prime suspect."

"But we know that's absurd," I say. "And they do, too. They let you go. You have no motive whatsoever. Besides, dozens of people were at the school the nights of the murders. Some we know. Clearly, some we don't. And that's who killed them."

Josh raises an eyebrow.

"Yes," I say. "Killed them. That's what I think. Hey. You should call Penny. Leave her a message, in case she comes to your office when classes are over." I zip open my purse, digging for my cell. It's disappeared, somewhere down into the black hole. I pull out a file folder that's blocking my search. "Hold this."

"How you ever find anything in that suitcase —" Josh begins. He looks inside the folder. "What's this?"

"That's the fundraising list, the one I told you about. From Dorothy's study," I say, my face half-buried in the tote bag. "You know. With the circled names."

Josh is silent.

I look up from my search. "What?"

"Well, this report." Josh flips through the pages. "It's not distributed yet. We received several boxes of them from the printer. But until they're mailed out, the Head's storing them all. Some in his office, some in Ebling's. So from his point of view, there's no way you could have gotten a copy. Ebling didn't mention that?"

"No, but as Penny would say, no biggie, right? Are the boxes all sealed or something? I mean, lots of administrative types must have the report. Maybe Ebling thinks I got it from you. Or the bursar. Or the Head. Here's the phone. Call Penny. Tell her you had a meeting."

Josh hands me the report, shrugging, as he takes my phone. He flips it open, and smiles as he sees himself in the St. Bart's photo. "No, the boxes aren't sealed. Anyone at Bexter could have them. I suppose you're right."

"As always," I say. Which reminds me. I look across the room as Josh begins to leave his message. Will is in deep discussion with the coffee guy. Both are waving their arms, making gestures that look like football passes.

"Sweetheart?" I say. "After Will leaves? We should talk."

"It's a crosswalk, moron!" I point an accusing gloved finger of the hand that's not intertwined with Josh's as we almost get nailed by a driver who's actually texting as he careens onto Cambridge Street. The moron almost takes out both of us. And just as I was getting to the crucial part of my speech. Once across the street and though the tree-lined pigeon haven called Cardinal Medeiros Park, we'll be at the front door of Channel 3. I better get to the point.

We dash across the painted white lines and arrive at the circle of snow-covered benches surrounding a snow-covered mound of earth in the center. Three months from now there'll be daffodils, and workers eating brown-bag lunches in the sun. Now the circle of grass and bricks is bleak, white and empty.

"And so," I continue, stepping carefully down the three steps to a curving stone pathway, "Kevin's offer is a tempting one. And basically a dream come true."

"If you want to go," Josh says, smiling quietly, and taking my other hand, too, "I can deal. We can deal."

"But wait. Here's the deal I'd like to offer," I say. "How about, I put my condo on the market. Can you make enough closet space for me on Bexter Drive? And then, let's go back and taste the wedding cakes again."

I feel, absurdly, as if I should be going down on one knee. Like Josh did in St. Bart's.

"There's no dream come true that's more important than being with you," I say. "When you were in that office, when I knew the stupid D.A.'s cops had actually taken you away, and then stupid Monica would not let me see you and I didn't know if you had a lawyer, and no one would . . ."

My eyes fill with tears of anxiety and leftover worry. I might have lost Josh forever. Not only because he might have been accused of murder, which is ridiculous, but because I might have chosen to turn my back on a real once-in-a-lifetime offer. Josh's offer. Of high-level battles over breakfast cereal and calamities of missing socks. Of sharing closets and sharing secrets.

I'm a reporter. I'm devoted to my career. I can't imagine giving it up. But I can't be two places at one time. And I only want to be here. With Josh. From now on.

"Sweets?" Josh says. He puts an arm across my shoulder and pulls my plaid scarf away from my face. His leather-gloved finger tilts my chin to look up at him. "It's fine, honey. I'm not in jail. I'm not accused of anything. It's all over. Over. Why are you crying?"

"Because you *might* have been. What if I had been in New York? What if you had been in trouble? What if Penny had been left alone?" My voice rises, high-pitched, and a couple of steel-gray pigeons skitter away at the sound.

"It's over, honey. Nothing's going to happen." Josh pulls me close, our heavy wool coats and gloves and mufflers keeping us uncharacteristically far apart.

His words puff into clouds of winter white, then dissipate as we stand silently. I'm having a daytime nightmare about what might have been. And how we escaped it. A siren screams by and horns blare from the intersection. I tuck myself in as close as I can to Josh's warmth. He's right. It's over.

When I look up into Josh's hazel eyes, I see something new. It's the road ahead. I know this will turn out to be a moment we remember. An illustration of how the worst of days can become the best of days.

One tear makes its way down my wind-chilled face. At this very second, part of my life is over. And a new part is beginning. I have no doubts about what I'm about to say. I take one step back from Josh so I can look at him full-on. Then I head into our future.

"Kevin can find another reporter in New York. It's you and me, sweetheart." I pause, suddenly shy, plucking at the twisty fringe on my muffler. "If that's still okay with you."

After a few moments my mouth actually hurts from our kisses. And luckily Cardinal Medeiros Park stayed deserted as we almost venture into private personal areas that are not really for public view. And activities the good cardinal almost certainly would not have approved of. Probably a good thing it's so cold.

"So we're picking a date? And you're staying home?" Josh whispers into my hair as we walk the last hundred yards toward the station. "Is that what you really want?"

Our arms are tangled together so tightly, we must look like one person. And that's exactly how I feel.

"I do," I reply. Franklin and I are a team

at work, but Josh and I are a team for life. And I won't allow anything to change that.

CHAPTER EIGHTEEN

"This is what they don't teach you in journalism school, Franko," I say. Channel 3's basement garage is deserted this time of night. All the news cars are out on assignment for the eleven o'clock show. Franklin will be driving the camera-wired Explorer and dropping it into the Longmore's valet parking. His job is to stay in the hotel bar until he gets a call from J.T. and me that the game's afoot. "You're getting paid to hang out at Fizz, with drinks, TV and a bathroom. Of course, we'll be in the lookout car, cramped, freezing and bored."

"Well, if they decide to swipe our car, they may check to see where I am," Franklin says, ignoring the dig. "They'll want to make sure I'm not getting ready to leave. And let's hope you're not bored. Kevin's possibly going to pull the plug if tonight's stakeout goes down the tubes."

"Cross that bridge when we come to it,"

J.T. says. His head is deep into the rear of the Explorer, tweaking the hidden-camera setup. He ducks out from under the hatchback and slams it shut. "Each video chip has a four-hour run time. You should stop a block from the Longmore and push the record button on each tape deck. Then we've gotta hope it all happens fast enough so the video time doesn't run out."

"Given that that something *does* happen," Franklin says.

Franklin looks as if he's ready for a night on the town in a black leather sport coat, a black turtleneck with a polo pony on the front and black corduroy jeans.

J.T. and I dressed for comfort in jeans and turtlenecks (without ponies) and black coats. We look like some pretend SWAT team. Which we kind of are. But instead of tear gas, we're using cameras to smoke out the bad guys. We hope.

"It'll happen," I say. I look around for some wood to touch, but have to settle for the fake stuff on the dashboard.

I put a plastic bag of stakeout provisions on the floor of the front seat. We've got J.T.'s camera in the backseat. Full batteries and extra tapes.

"Bar's got to close at two," I say. "If it's going to happen, it'll happen before then."

We caravan out the rackety mechanical garage door and out into the narrow alley behind the station. Still following Franklin in the Explorer, J.T. and I wind through the twisty downtown streets toward the Longmore Hotel. The festive blue-and-yellow lights of the Custom House Tower say 10:30. Twenty-six stories up, on top of the old Hancock Building, the four weather lights are showing "steady blue," meaning forecasters predict the night will be clear. I stare out the car window, wondering what the night will hold. Josh is home with Penny. She knows nothing about what happened. She had a great first day of school. She's the only one in our family who did.

"And welcome back tonight to Maysie Green, the sports machine!"

I jump in surprise as a hearty announcer voice booms from the speakers. J.T.'s turned on the radio while I was in Josh world. "Coming up next, *Drive Time*! But now, heeeere's Maysie!"

"Good evening and hey to all of you out in Celtics land." Maysie's familiar lilt buzzes through the car. I can't help but smile. I know she's doing the show via phone from her living room couch. I can picture her, cuddling baby Maddee in one arm, and holding the receiver between her shoulder and chin. She's talking sports to ten thousand listeners and taking care of one tiny newborn at the same time. Talk about having it all.

"And a big shout-out to investigative reporter Charlie McNally, who took over my slot while I was otherwise occupied. And now to your favorite green team, the number-one-ranked Boston Celtics," she says.

"How'd you like doing radio?" J.T. asks. He turns down the volume, happily agreeing we don't need to hear about basketball.

"It's a paycheck," I say, shrugging. "Though not a big one. Apparently Wixie is doing some budget-driven belt tightening. Doesn't matter, I did it for Mays, not for money. And on radio, you don't have to worry about getting hidden-camera video, of course. But I'm more interested in what's happening at Beacon Valet, you know?"

I just thought of something.

"Hang on," I say. I paw into my purse for my cell phone and punch Franklin's speed dial. He has hands free, of course.

"Franko. Did you ever find out who owns Beacon Valet? I mean, who's behind the trust?"

"Yes and no," he replies. As if the question didn't come out of nowhere. Actually, it didn't. "I've got a pal in the Secretary of State's office trying to untangle it. Some smart lawyer did a good job creating the trust, Marjorie tells me. She says it's one of the best she's seen."

"Best for hiding something," I reply. I realize where we are and point a finger. "Hey, J.T. The gods of journalism are smiling. There's a perfect parking place. Right where we were before. Franko, you set?"

"Yes, indeed," Franklin says. "You pulling up and parking now? I'm a block away. Cameras are all in place. And I'm pushing the record buttons."

Arriving at the Longmore, we quickly switch places, so I'm driving and J.T.'s in the passenger seat. He pulls out his camera and pushes the blue standby button, ready to shoot whatever happens. We turn the car radio off so we don't get extraneous audio. The car is idling so we don't have to turn the ignition when the time comes. Plus, we need the heat to stay warm. We crack the window so our breath doesn't steam up the glass.

In the light from the street lamps and the glaringly bright marquee of the hotel, J.T. rolls tape on Franklin dropping off the car. Handing over the keys. We get shots of him talking to a Beacon Valet–jacketed man, one I hadn't seen before. He's wearing a baseball cap, but I can't read what's printed on it. Even though we're not recording audio, I know Franklin is feeding him our story, explaining that he's meeting someone in the bar, and would definitely be there for a few hours, until closing. Franklin gives the valet some folded dollar bills, then goes inside. We cross our fingers that the hidden cameras installed in the Explorer are recording. And that tonight is the night. We have four hours.

The valet pulls the Explorer just two parking spaces up, then double-parks with the headlights still on. But this time, instead of getting out of the car, he stays inside.

I reach down for the bag of almonds I've brought, ready to settle in for a night of waiting.

"Yo. Charlie. Check it out," J.T. says. He's got his camera up on his shoulder, eye to the viewfinder.

One hand still in the plastic bag, I peer up through the windshield. And then I forget the almonds.

Another man, also in a Beacon Valet jacket but without a hat, trots out of the hotel, and leans into the driver's window of the Explorer. Thin gray plumes of exhaust puff sporadically from the car. That means the engine is still running.

I sit up and click my gearshift into drive, though I keep my foot on the brake. Have to be instantly ready to follow the Explorer when it pulls away. If it pulls away.

"You rolling?" I say. I'm not taking my eyes off what's happening.

"You need to ask?" From behind the camera.

A car drives up, headlights glaring. The car pauses outside the hotel, blasting light through our windshield.

Flinching, I hold up a hand to shield my eyes. "Ow."

"Damn," J.T. hisses. "Lens can't handle that. Can't see a thing."

"It's okay," I reassure him, still squinting. "They're leaving now. And nothing's happening with the Explorer."

The three of us haven't really discussed it, but my "steal-the-car-for-a-brief-time-swipe-the-VIN-and-the-air-bag-and-return-the-car-before-the-owner-knows-it" hypothesis is only a theory. An assumption based on guesses and conjecture and a few juicy facts. It may be proven false. If it is, we won't have a story and my speculation will thereby doom three perfectly hardworking journalists to ratings-book hell. Investigative reporting isn't easy. That's what makes it fun.

I stare out the windshield, flexing my fingers on the steering wheel. Trying to remember that this is fun.

The driver's-side door of the Explorer opens.

"J.T.," I whisper.

"Yup. I see it."

The first valet, who I've been calling "Hat Guy," gets out. The other valet, "No-Hat," gets in. As Hat Guy heads back toward the hotel, he taps the back window of the Explorer with the flat of one palm. *Tap-tap-tap.*

He doesn't look back as he pushes through the Longmore's revolving doors.

"Charlie." J.T.'s tone is sharp.

I yank my eyes back to the Explorer. Damn. Never should have looked away. At least J.T.'s on it.

A blast of gray now puffs from the Explorer's exhaust. I sneak a glance in my rearview, checking to see if any cars are behind me, in case I have to pull out. One slushes by slowly, then another one. Not many people are out this late. The good news and the bad news. No one will be in our way as we pull out. And the first moments are critical.

But it may make it tougher to follow this guy without being noticed. I've done this many times, carefully keeping at least two car lengths away. Making sure there's at least one other car between me and my quarry. Sometimes, I even pull ahead. So far, I've never gotten caught. Nighttime makes it easier in some ways. Harder in others.

"We'll have the hidden-camera stuff, at least, if we lose him on the road," I say, reassuring myself as much as J.T.

"If he actually goes anywhere," J.T. mutters.

"Ye of little faith," I say, keeping my eyes on the Explorer. Although I was thinking the same thing. And I have no plan B.

The Explorer's brake lights flicker on, then go off. And then the car starts to move.

"Check it out," I breathe.

The car eases forward and into the street. No-Hat's arm comes out of the window. With a quick gesture, a gloved hand adjusts the side mirror. And then almost before I realize it, No-Hat hits the gas.

The Explorer powers up Water Street, taillights disappearing into the Boston night.

"Go!" J.T. yells.

But I've already hit the accelerator.

"He's getting onto the Pike," I say, eyes

glued on the Explorer.

We turn left down the ramp to the west-bound side of the eight-lane highway. No-Hat is driving like a sixteen-year-old taking the Registry of Motor Vehicles's licensing exam. He stopped at every red light between the Longmore Hotel and the entrance to the Massachusetts Turnpike, stayed within the speed limit, and used his turn signals.

"Probably doesn't want to get pulled over by the cops," I say to J.T. "Smart for him. But he sure is making it a breeze for us."

"That's not what the guy did for Declan Ross, though," J.T. reminds me. "The guy in the blue Mustang? Was driving like a maniac."

I pull to the right and follow No-Hat, close but not too close, along the Pike and through the first set of automated toll-booths. J.T.'s rolling video on the whole trip, making sure we can document exactly what happens. It's a challenging shoot. All of our tiny hidden cameras are mounted in the decoy car, so J.T. has to use his full-size Sony. Including the bricklike battery pack; it weighs more than twenty pounds. J.T.'s steadying it with one elbow braced against the passenger door. And he still has to wear a seat belt.

"True," I say, remembering. I let a brown

sedan get ahead of us. Luckily, the Explorer has such a high wheelbase, it's easy to see even in the dark and with a few cars between us. "But remember, he probably got a call ordering him to bring the car the hell back. Remember? Michael Borum was waiting for it."

We're silent, briefly. I, for one, am thinking about what happened to Michael Borum.

As we move west through the alternating headlights and darkness on the Pike, it becomes easier and easier for me to blend us into the traffic. The Highway Department's erratically flashing lighted arrows help, too, by briefly forcing everyone into the left lane to avoid construction. When drivers are forced to change lanes and follow signs, there's less time for them to notice there's someone on their tail.

I hope.

I keep my attention balanced between monitoring the position of the Explorer and driving safely. But the night is clear, and the road is clear, and my view of the Explorer is clear. So far so good.

Plus, No-Hat has got to be focused on getting to wherever he's going, doing whatever they do there, and returning to the Longmore before Franklin asks for the car back.

He's not worrying whether there's a reporter in a unmarked news car trying to track his every turn.

I hope.

"You know what," I say. "No matter what's on the other end here, no matter where he's going. This guy's stolen our car. I mean, it's supposed to be in valet parking. You know? And instead, it's headed up the Mass Pike."

"And we're getting video of the whole thing," J.T. says. "Who knows how big this is. How far it goes. But you're right. We've got this guy nailed."

My mind briefly wanders to Franklin, missing everything, probably sipping club soda in Fizz and certainly wondering whether he'll still have a story in the morning. Maybe he called his adorable Stephen, inviting him to keep him company on his boring-but-important role in the stakeout. I should have suggested that. I will when I call him.

"Yo, McNally. I need to change tapes." J.T. interrupts my pangs of conscience. "We've only got half hours. And I have maybe five minutes left on this one. Change it now? Or later?"

"Do it now, no question," I say, pointing at him. "And make it fast." No tape means no pictures. And he who hesitates runs out.

J.T. lays the bulky camera flat on his lap, the first time it's been away from his eye for twenty-five minutes. I press my lips together, anxiously counting the seconds, as I hear the motorized buzzes and clicks that mean he's opened the side of the camera. I hear the whir as the yellow cassette pops out like a piece of toast.

"Got it? Put the tape in my bag," I say. I see J.T. holding the cassette. He looks like he's searching for something. "Don't bother with a case. And I'll label it later. Just bang in a new —"

"He's getting off the Pike!" J.T. yells. He's holding the camera with one hand, waving the other at the highway. "He's moving into the right lane. I bet he's taking 17, the Newton exit."

I turn to look at J.T. The camera is still in his lap. No cassette is inside it. Not good.

"Just put in a —"

"Watch it!" J.T.'s voice suddenly rises to a yelp.

With a blare of an air horn that almost blasts my heart from my chest, a massive big rig careens in front of us, swerving across two lanes. It's a double-wide silver-and-black cab, pulling an empty but lethal flatbed that threatens to jackknife right

336

through us. The pavement between me and the eighteen-wheeler disappears. This truck is at least ten tons of trouble, pointed toward Exit 17, and the driver doesn't care who's in the way.

I see the Explorer accelerate, powering off at Exit 17 as J.T. predicted. It's headed up the steep two-lane ramp and into a complicated intersection that leads at least four ways. To industrial Newtonville. Chic Newton Center. Working-class West Newton. Or he could make a U-turn back onto the Pike and toward Boston. If No-Hat gets a green light and makes his turn before we get there, we've certainly lost him.

To follow him, we've got to get in front of the truck. If we don't, we risk losing the Explorer altogether.

I glance into the rearview. Nobody behind us.

"Hang on," I say. My voice is low. Determined. "Going for it."

I yank our car hard to the right into the narrow breakdown lane. The wheels rumble, catching in the uneven, roughly paved strip that's supposed to be used only for emergencies. Fine. This is one.

I hit the accelerator, and have just enough room to pass the still-speeding truck on his right. If I go too far, I'll crash us into the highway's corrugated aluminum guardrails and we'll wind up like Declan Ross. Or much worse. Praying for the slightest bit more speed and hoping I have enough room, I swerve in front of him.

"Holy . . . !" J.T. yells. "Careful!" He's cradling the camera on his lap with both arms, protecting it, the seat belt holding him in place.

I am being careful. Much as I can. The length of the exit ramp is my only hope. If the Explorer hits a red light at the top of the hill, we can catch up. My hands clench on the steering wheel, my eyes narrow, focusing on the road ahead.

The hulking truck moves over, pulling into the left lane, giving up just enough room so we can both drive without the side of his flatbed slicing our car — and me — in half. I cling to the right, leaning into my turn, and try to slow down without slamming on brakes.

Several hundred feet in front of us, I see the intersection. And the glorious red light. Waiting in the front of the line, brake lights on, is the Explorer.

"Are you freaking kidding me?" J.T.'s voice comes from beside me, a mixture of terror and approval. "Are you nuts? Or lucky?"

"Are you rolling yet?" I reply. "We've got him."

And now we'll see where he's taking our car.

CHAPTER NINETEEN

"Tobacco Road," I say, counting my blessings as I squint past the steering wheel, out the windshield, through slashes of shadow and into the open double doors of the garage across the street. The moon is full, but mostly hidden behind thickly scudding pre-snow clouds. Inside the car, we're sitting in total darkness. Our heat is off. The engine is off. My feet and nose are freezing. "Or someplace out of the Dust Bowl. Skeevy buildings. Creepy houses. And look at the streetlights. Or what's left of them. Probably someone's target practice."

"The Dust Bowl wouldn't have snow," J.T. mutters. His tinted window is cracked open wide enough for the lens to fit through. His eye is still pressed to the viewfinder. We've switched off the red record light on the camera, in case someone looks our way. Don't want *us* to be target practice.

"Whatever," I say. Franklin's in a cozy bar,

probably watching ESPN. I'm sipping my now-tepid coffee, which somehow didn't spill in the truck-avoidance maneuver, and watching the ramshackle building across the street. Rantoul Avenue, a potholed two-way in a bleakly needy neighborhood of Newtonville, is pretty much deserted this time of night. That's bad news, because we're an unfamiliar car and right out in the open. With luck, No-Hat and his pals are under such a crushing time pressure they'll figure we're visiting one of the houses here. If they notice us as all. Our tinted windows are almost opaque at night. We can see fine from inside, but from outside, our car looks empty.

I hope.

J.T. is shooting everything that moves. And some stuff that doesn't. It's been a video bonanza.

We got the doors to the garage opening from inside as the Explorer drove in. The roll-away door on the left is wide open, providing an ideal view of the complete garage setup inside. Rows of bright lights studded across the ceiling illuminate the whole scene, bright as a movie set. No-Hat hops out of the driver's seat and disappears into the darker recesses of the garage. The hood of the Explorer pops up. Men in jeans swarm, one into each of the four doors. Another unlatches the hatchback. Another, lying on his back, scoots a wheeled dolly underneath the chassis.

A flash of worry. What if there's something incriminating in the car? Something that screams Channel 3. A mic flag. A press pass. It's too late to matter, though, I reassure myself. They've taken the car, which is illegal. And it's on tape. We win.

I shift in my seat, tucking one leg under me, trying to get a better view. It's driving me crazy that I can't make out what they're doing. But what I'm seeing is not what's important.

"You're getting this, right?" I whisper. Camera lenses can be touchy. I'm worried about the murky distance to the garage. Or if the light inside is too bright.

"Pretty sure," J.T. says, his voice low.

"We can always —" I stop talking, not wanting to ruin the audio. I know we really only need to select a few crucial shots from this to put on the air, the clear and revealing ones that confirm the crime beyond any question. My brain clicks into planning mode.

We'll eventually need to interview more victims, maybe another car-rental-agency owner, a cop, state and federal officials reacting to our story, and try to approach whoever the bad guys are. Besides the outside stuff we're shooting tonight, we also have the hidden-camera video from inside the car. Our on-air story can last maybe six minutes. One of the most difficult decisions in TV news is choosing what to leave out.

"Yo." J.T.'s voice is softer than a whisper.

Careful not to jounce the camera, I turn so both knees are on the seat, peering to get a clear view through the one tiny corner of open window that's not blocked by the lens.

A man in jeans and a dark sweatshirt with cutoff sleeves walks toward the passenger side of the car. Sweatshirt Man is holding some sort of tool — a flat lever? Like a very thin crowbar? — in both hands. As he leans into the front seat, my view is blocked. Worse, the camera view is blocked.

I close my eyes briefly. The audio won't be ruined by my puffed sigh of frustration.

"Hidden cams, remember," J.T. whispers.

In the Explorer. Which is good news, bad news. If our shot is blocked, the hidden cameras will get the video. One the other hand, if No-Hat's compadres are taking the car apart, they'll find them.

Nothing we can do about it now.

"Ah." The sound comes out of me like a prayer. I actually feel tears come to my eyes as Sweatshirt Man eases his way back into view. In one hand, his crowbar thing. In the other, what I instantly recognize as a section of leather and plastic he's apparently pried from the Explorer's dashboard. It's flat and rectangular. I know exactly where it came from. It's the cover of the passenger-side air bag.

I risk the audio, speaking close to J.T.'s ear, barely able to control my excitement. Franklin is going to flip. Kevin, too.

"You saw that, right? You got it?"

"No," he whispers.

He's kidding. My heart is racing. My feet are somehow no longer cold. Now there's something else in Sweatshirt's hands. I touch J.T. on the shoulder, the softest of taps.

"Keep it rolling, brotha," I say. I rise up, still on my knees, leaning toward him and straining to see out the window, as close as I can get without bumping the camera. "That's the first air bag."

The wail of the siren crashes me into J.T.'s back, clanking the camera lens against the window. I scramble to regain my balance. This time, the dregs of my coffee spill from the cup holder and onto the floor, the plastic cover of the paper cup popping off onto the rug down by my tote bag.

"We're screwed," J.T. says.

"Dammit, dammit, dammit," I hiss.

It's the cops. A dark two-toned sedan, headlights wigwagging and blue lights whirling on a bar across the roof, pulls up two car lengths behind us. I see a huge emblem painted across the hood, all eagles and flags. It says Newton Police.

"J.T. Right now. Put down your camera. Put it on the floor of the backseat. And close your window, except for just a crack."

"But —" J.T. begins. There's enough light for me to recognize the fear in J.T.'s eyes. And mine must certainly mirror his expression of alarm. Is it us they're after? Or something — or someone — else?

"Do it. The windows. The cops can't see us inside."

I yank my focus back to the garage as I feel J.T. lift the camera over the front seat and lay in on the floor. The rolling metal door is on the way down, almost closed. That's the end of getting video of whatever they're doing inside. I mentally cross my fingers for the hidden cameras. And for our story. And for J.T. and me. Although we're not the ones doing anything wrong.

The garage door hits bottom. Its metallic slam on the concrete below clangs across the street. No-Hat certainly knows the cops are here. Question is, does he know about us?

Not a move comes from the police car. The siren is now off, but the whirling blue lights blast unnatural indigo shadows through scrawny municipal trees and onto snow-spotted front yards. I see a light pop on in a house next door to the garage, a fragment of motion barely visible behind a gauzy curtain.

"What if they're coming to arrest the garage people? To take down No-Hat and his pals?" I whisper. "What if they're busting this whole operation, right in front of us?"

That would be a horrendous disaster. Except I suppose there might be one tiny silver lining. "I guess we'd have exclusive video of the raid, at least. Still, that would —"

"Suck," J.T. says.

I smile, despite my thudding heart, thinking for a fraction of a second about Josh. Safe at home.

"Exactly," I say.

Back to the cops. Nothing. Then a light flips on inside the car. Through the windshield, I can make out two uniformed officers in the front seat. One is talking into a radio. No other police cars arrive. Maybe it's not a raid?

Still, this is grim. And, if you like irony, I suppose it's kind of funny. Our surveillance of the bad guys is getting ruined by the good guys.

I untie the belt of my black coat, struggling out of the sleeves. Then twisting over the back of the seat, I cover the camera with the dark wool, like a blanket. Now it's invisible. Now we're a man and a woman sitting in a car on a public street. No biggie. Which reminds me, fleetingly, of Penny. Safe at home.

J.T. and I have to play this out. But I'm not quite sure how.

"We can't tell them what we're doing," J.T. begins. Then, eyes widening, he points out his window. One door of the police car opens, then slams. Then the other. "Uh-oh. What should we — ?"

J.T.'s question is interrupted by two beams of white light, crisscrossing in the murky darkness.

Flashlights. And behind them, the still-shadowy but obviously determined figures of two uniformed police officers. Cops on a mission. Their booted strides are confident as I watch their high beams play across sidewalks and front lawns and onto our car.

Through our windows. The good news? They're not headed for the garage. The bad news? They're coming for us.

"We're not doing anything wrong, remember that," I whisper, touching the arm of J.T.'s leather jacket. "Let me handle this."

Footsteps crunch on frozen grass. Coming closer. A beam of light glints on the hatchback. It crosses the roof of our car. And then, there's a sharp rap on J.T.'s window.

J.T. turns to me, his eyes questioning.

There's no time to explain it to him, but I think I have a plan. It's not a clever plan. Or a very original one.

"Roll down the window, *honey*," I say. Batting my eyelashes, I make a little kissing motion with pouted lips. J.T.'s expression almost makes me burst out laughing. But there's no time for that.

"Oh," J.T. whispers. "Gotcha."

The window buzzes down. The dark glass recedes. Revealing — nothing.

"Newton Police." A brusque voice comes out of the darkness. "Everything all right in there?"

I know they don't come up close to the window right away. In case you're planning to shoot them.

"You've been sitting here for a while now," the voice from behind us continues. "Neighbors were concerned."

Nailed by Neighborhood Watch. You're kidding me. Why don't those folks report the people who are really doing something wrong? I flash a look at the garage. Closed and dark. Damn.

What's making this even more complicated is the fact that No-Hat's got to get the Explorer back to the hotel before the bar closes. What if the cops' arrival has unwittingly trapped them inside?

Go *away.* I send the telepathic message to the police. Go *away.*

"Sure, no problem, Officer," I say. I try to make my voice sound completely innocent but somewhat embarrassed. As if we've been caught making out. Or whatever they call that these days. "We were just leaving."

One officer takes a step forward, possibly because we haven't a pulled a gun on them. He holds his flashlight high, aiming it so he can see inside. Now we can see him, too. His gold-and-black plastic name tag is embossed Ofcr. Solano. His fifty-something face is round as tonight's hide-and-seek moon. Every part of it — chin, hairline, eyebrows — is receding.

He points the flashlight directly at J.T. J.T. holds one hand up, shielding his eyes, instantly on the defense.

"We're only talking," J.T. says. Very man-to-man. "Me and my girlfriend. You know how it is."

The flashlight shines on me. "Ma'am?"

"Yes?" I say. I put my hand up to block the flare of light as well as cover my face a bit. Then I look down, going for demure. I hope he doesn't notice I don't have a coat on. Or maybe that'll play right into our love deception. "Are we doing something wrong? I'm so sorry."

Officer Solano is gesturing "come closer" to someone else. I hear more footsteps. Then he turns his attention — and his flashlight — back to us. "May I ask why you were taking pictures? Lady across the street saw your camera. Called 911."

Busted.

I lean back into the beam of light, defeated. Might as well get this over with, quick as possible. We can't draw attention to ourselves. It's bad enough that we've lost our view into the garage. But No-Hat and his crew are no doubt watching this shake-down. If they recognize me, or figure out we're TV, the whole cloning operation will shut down faster than you can say no comment.

"Officer? I'm —"

"Charlie McNally! Hey, I'm a big fan."

Cop number two is at our window, leaning his elbows on the door and grinning as if I'm the prize in a scavenger hunt. "I'm Hal Harker. Used to be in vice. Remember when we worked on the — hey, what are you guys really doing here? You're not makin' out. Hey. You working a big story? What are you guys really doing?"

Music comes from the floor by my feet.

It's the theme from *Charlie's Angels*.

Harker stops, midsentence. Then he grins, brandishing a thumbs-up as he recognizes the tune.

And finally, I get a really good idea.

"McNally," I say, almost before I flip the phone open. I know it's Franklin, but the cops don't. Smiling conspiratorially, I hold up one finger, signaling "wait." Franklin begins talking. I talk right over him.

"We're in the wrong place?" I say, feigning disappointment into the phone. "It's the other Rantoul Street? The one in Lawrence? That's ridiculous. You have got to be kidding."

"What in hell are you talking about, Charlotte?" "Hell" comes out southernized, like "hay-ull," which means Franklin's tired and cranky. My usually intuitive producer isn't understanding my strategy tonight. No reason why he should, I guess.

"Listen." I try to interrupt his escalating tirade.

"You listen. I don't know what's going on at your end, but it's last call here. They're closing the bar. Half an hour, and then I've got to get the Explorer. I thought I would hear from y'all by now."

"Well, isn't that what we needed to hear. You had it wrong," I say. Oozing sarcasm and talking over him again. I shake my head and shrug at the police officers, performing as many rueful-looking gestures as I can. "Now that means we'll have to come pick you up, I suppose. I'll call you in ten minutes, okay? And then we'll talk."

I snap the phone closed with a theatrical flourish. Franklin will be fuming, but not for long. And maybe this will get us out of here.

"Well, those idiots," I say, tsk-tsking. "You know how it is, right? Bigwigs sent us on a wild-goose chase. Bozos can't even keep their facts straight. Got the town wrong. Middle of the night, can you believe it? They're not the ones out here freezing, right?"

The officers are nodding at me through the open widow, making empathetic noises. "Scorn for the boss," a universal emotion, crosses all sectors of employment.

352

"With ya on that one, Charlie," Harker says. My new best friend.

"The suits strike again, huh?" Solano snaps off his flashlight and we're in semi-darkness again. Thank goodness.

"No story here," I say to J.T. with an exaggerated sigh. "We've been ordered to head back to the barn."

He nods. "Bummer."

Solano and Harker touch the brims of their hats. "Have a good one," Harker says. "We'll inform the neighbors you're clear. See you on TV."

"We've gotta go. Turn on the heat," I say. Our cop buddies have pulled away, actually waving in newfound solidarity. J.T. and I are regrouping. We need to move fast. I turn the key in the ignition and hope the engine noise doesn't freak out the neighbors again.

J.T.'s hoisted the camera back onto his lap. I've got my coat back on. Outside, the door to the garage is still closed. The lights are still off. I look at the clock on the dashboard. Quarter till two. I really-really-really want to get video of No-Hat driving back on the Turnpike and returning the car to the hotel. That would be the real clincher of the story, proving the car was driven into the garage with an air bag and driven out

353

without one. Chain of evidence. On the other hand, if we miss that, it'll still be recorded on the hidden cams. If they worked.

Should we wait here? Or try to catch up with them on the highway? If we leave right now, and the traffic is light and no state troopers nail me for speeding, there's a chance we could manage it. And arrive at the hotel the same time they do.

"The Explorer's got to be gone. Doesn't it?" I shift into Drive but don't pull out onto Rantoul Avenue. "They're going to assume Franklin will want the car back by closing. No-Hat's gotta know that."

"Who?" J.T. says. He looks at me, confused, as he clicks the heat to high.

"The driver. The valet. He wasn't wearing a hat. You know." I wave him off. "Anyway, the question is, is the Explorer still here? Is it in the garage, and they're waiting for the cops to leave? Or what if there's a back door? And they've already gone?"

"Your call. I'm set to roll if we need it." J.T. shrugs and adjusts something on the camera.

Stay? Or go? There's no way to know the answer to this.

"They've seen us, our car at least, and they know the cops came. I bet they wouldn't risk moving the car in front of them." My fingers are drumming on the steering wheel, but I'm staring at the still-closed garage door. At least I'm beginning to feel my toes again.

We're staying.

"I bet they're still here. They wouldn't connect this car with what they're doing in the garage." I shift back into park. "They have no idea we followed them. Probably. And they pushed the timing with Michael Borum's car, remember? They know people aren't suspicious if the car is a little late."

"Valets always take a long time returning your car," J.T. says. "I guess now we know why."

"Exactly. So it takes, what, fifteen minutes to get from here to the hotel?"

"With you or me driving?" J.T. says. He's staring at the garage door, too.

And it begins to open.

CHAPTER TWENTY

"The old camera-in-the-ceiling-light trick," J.T. says. "Works every time."

"I'm in love with it," I say, pointing. "Look at that."

"Slam dunk," Franklin says.

The three of us are crowded around the minuscule screen of our portable monitor, watching the video from the hidden cameras J.T. wired into the Explorer. At some point, ENG Joe and ENG Joanna will transfer them to normal-size cassettes so we can look at them on our regular playback machine. But we can't wait for that. We're exhausted and I'm starving, but we can't resist success. We need to see each one of the tapes now, even on this frustratingly tiny viewer. We're addicted to the moving images on the glowing screen. So far, our surveillance worked. Every tape. Every time. Every shot.

Lots of little pictures. One big story.

"There's the air bag," I say. "See? They've popped it right out. We got this exact moment on our camera, too. And I bet they're taking all the air bags, not just the ones in the front. That's why they have to go to the garage."

"Good thing I didn't get into an accident driving home," Franklin says. He steps back from the screen. "Oh. Charlotte. I almost forgot. Remind me to tell you about *Drive Time.*"

"Check it out," J.T. says. "They're stuffing — newspapers? Into the space in the dashboard where the air bag came from."

Franklin turns back to the screen. "Newspapers?"

"So the dashboard won't sound hollow if you tap on it. I've read about that," I say.

"This should be on the network," J.T. says. "Let's look at a different tape. Check another angle on the air-bag shot. And let's see if we got them writing down the VIN."

No one else is here to share our triumph. The bleach-and-lemony disinfectant smell means the cleaning people have come and gone. At three forty-five in the morning, the Special Projects office is deserted, littered desks empty, lights off.

"I wonder how long they've been doing this," I say. While J.T. selects the next tape,

I push a stack of notebooks out of the way and perch on the edge of my desk, imagining hundreds and hundreds of cars left in valet parking by trusting drivers.

"You go in, you hand over your keys, you have a nice dinner. You're thinking how convenient the whole valet system is. No parking hassles. And little do you know."

J.T. flips open the lid of a clear plastic cassette box and dumps the tape into his hand. "Yeah. Your car is going for a ride. Without you."

"Hand me that box. It needs a label," Franklin says. He's busily pressing narrow stick-on strips to each tape and cassette box. From my vantage point across the room, I can see they're somehow numbered and color coded. Only Franklin understands how. "Wish we could record audio."

"You know state law," I say. "No can do with a hidden camera. Doesn't matter though. A picture is worth —"

"Yup, usually," J.T. says. He pushes Play, then points to the little screen. "But look at this picture. This one's worth a million words. That's the VIN number, see? And there's a guy's hand, writing it down on a piece of paper. Man. That close-up lens above the dashboard rocks."

The piece of paper and the man's hand

358

leave the frame. And then we see nothing but the dashboard and a snippet of windshield. Doesn't matter. We got the money shot.

Suddenly the screen gets darker and darker. We see shadows moving, nothing we can recognize. The screen finally goes dead black.

"The garage door," I say. "This is when they closed it. This is when the cops arrived. There's not enough light for the camera now."

"It's rolling, though," J.T. says. "The counter's moving, so it's not broken or out of tape. But we won't be able to see any more till the lights come on again. So let's look at a cassette from my camera, okay? Check what we got from inside our car."

J.T. pops a tape into the player. He pushes Rewind. And when the tape clicks to a stop, he pushes Play. The tape whirs to a start. The video is grainy from the darkness. But perfect. This cassette, which Franklin has already labeled DT5, includes the trip back to the Longmore. We'd followed No-Hat and the Explorer out the garage door and down the highway, chronicling the entire return trip. Far as we can tell, he never had a clue.

"Check and mate," J.T. says. "The car's

back at the hotel. Like nothing ever happened. And we got the whole thing on camera."

"And there's you, Franko," I say. "Coming to get the car. Who's that with you? Must be waiting for his car, too. Bet he was annoyed. Still, you both look very hip for two in the morning."

"Two-twenty in the morning," he corrects me, holding up his watch and pointing to it. "I had to pretend I was angry that they took so long to return the car. The guy you've so cleverly named No-Hat told me they were 'busy' and that I should have asked for the car sooner. Like it was my fault." He's now lining up the cassettes in a corrugated-cardboard box which, in blocky and symmetrical black Magic Marker letters, he's labeled "Drive Time."

He holds it up. "See? All our tapes. Organized and ready to log. We can come in early tomorrow and do it, okay?"

"*Drive Time?*" I say. I don't even try to stifle my yawn. It's pushing four o'clock. The need for sleep is slowly and surely suffusing all my brain cells. And tomorrow is going to be an extremely gratifying day. Our story is a go. Kevin will be thrilled. Next step, we have to track down out who's running the scam. "T and T may not appreci-

360

ate you ripping off their —"

"Charlotte. I told you to remind me," Franklin interrupts. "And I was using that as a working title. It's supposed to be funny. Irony, you know? What I wanted to tell you, the replay of tonight's *Drive Time* was on the radio when I was driving back here."

I blink at him, then again, my weary brain trying to battle its way toward understanding.

"So?" Is the best I can do. Then the fog clears. "Oh. Is it the blue Mustang? Or are they already selling the clone of our Explorer?"

"Good call," Franklin says. "And we'll have to listen for the Explorer if we're right about this. But no, it was the Mustang."

"And?" J.T. says.

"And?" I say. I grab my coat and muffler from the rack. I've got to go home — to Josh, who's safely in bed and not in custody for murder — and get some sleep. Was that just this morning? No wonder I'm bleary. "Did you get the right number?"

"Well, apparently you remembered it correctly," Franklin replies. He pulls a scrap of paper from his jacket pocket and holds it up. "See? Isn't this it?"

"Five-five-five," I begin to sing. "Zero-one —"

Franklin holds up a hand, wincing. "Yes. But please don't sing. It's late."

"But that's . . ." I pause, trying to fathom exactly what it is. "That's ridiculous. Whoever's trying to sell a car isn't going to be terribly successful if there's no way for a potential buyer to reach them."

"Like I said, it's not a phone number." Franklin shrugs.

"Sure it's a phone number." J.T. waves him off. He zips up his jacket and pats the pockets for his gloves. "It's just the wrong phone number. A typo or something."

"Idiots," I say. My brain is about to give out. And I don't want to fall asleep on the drive home. "So much for that lead."

"Mmmff?"

"Fine, sweets," I whisper, translating. Hanging my terry robe over the closet door, I slide carefully between the striped yellow sheets, trying not to disturb a sleeping Josh. He has school tomorrow.

His eyes flicker, a valiant attempt to wake up and welcome me home, and he turns over, draping one bare arm around me, pulling me close. His body is sleep-warm, and melts, spooning, fitting comfortably into mine. "Missed you," he murmurs into my ear. "How did it . . . ?"

His voice, drowsy and pillow muffled, trails off into silence.

"Tell you in the morning," I say. "Go back to sleep, honey."

He already has. But I can't. Botox pads onto my stomach, then turns around twice, swiping her tail across my face each time. She finally nestles into place, purring.

"Comfy?" I whisper to her. I'm not. Everyone's asleep. But me.

I have crossed the line into exhaustion insomnia. My brain will not turn off. I squint at the glowing green numbers on the nightstand clock. Doomed.

In two hours, Penny will start her second day of school. I smile, a little sleep-deprivation humor. She has no idea of the panic and chaos her father and soon-to-be-stepmother endured on her first day. Penny had lunch with pals, didn't even notice her dad wasn't there. Annie had brought her home, Josh had made their dinner — or, purchased it, if the flat white boxes on the kitchen table are any indication — and all is now well at 6 Bexter Academy Drive.

But tomorrow, Penny has to go back to Bexter. Josh, too. Will the cops still be there? Why? What do they know? Who else will be brought in for questioning? Have there been any more phone calls?

The damn phone calls.

Dorothy got one. She's dead. And Alethia. And now she's dead. Randall Kindell got one. And Wen and Fiona Dulles.

I close my eyes, trying to think.

Kindell and Dulles. I picture all of the names circled on the donations list in Dorothy's pamphlet. Why did she circle them? Did she know them? She certainly knew their kids.

I rearrange my pillow, trying not to disturb Josh or the deadweight of calico cat on my chest. Maybe someone else circled them? Maybe Harrison Ebling because they were prime candidates to give even more money to Bexter? He and the bursar were certainly on the money hunt at the Head's party. I struggle to keep my eyes closed, hoping I can trick my mind into agreeing I need to get some sleep.

But if it was someone else's book, why was it on Dorothy's desk?

I'm wide-awake. I can't keep my eyes closed one more second. When I open them, Botox is staring at me.

"Why are the names circled? And who did it, Toxie?" I mouth the words as I stare back at her.

And then I realize. The cat's not the one I should be asking.

364

■ ■ ■ ■

"Have you ever seen this?" I take the fund-raising report out of my battered canvas briefcase and hold it up, showing the cover to Fiona Dulles. She's sitting beside me on a maple-leaf red damask love seat in her Wellesley living room. Two silk plaid throw pillows are tucked behind her, her posture ballerina perfect, her ankles properly crossed. Her charcoal trousers and muted gray cashmere twin-set cost at least twice as much as my own workaday sweater and skirt. And her pearls are real. Fee's balancing a white ceramic cup of tea on a flowered saucer. The expression on her composed face does not change as I hold up the pamphlet. She does not reach out to examine it.

"Why, no," Fee says. She takes a careful sip of tea, looking at me from under her lashes as she tilts her cup. A gold disk on her intricately linked charm bracelet clinks against the china. "Is that the new Bexter fundraising report? When you called, Miss McNally, I thought you wanted to talk about Tal and Lexie. I had hoped you might have some news."

I put the report in my lap, turning to a

certain page as I listen to her. It's true I had been a bit ambiguous when I called Fee this morning, asking to come for a short visit. She'd assumed it was about the threatening phone calls. And it is. In a way.

Apparently, we're alone in her Currier and Ives white clapboard suburban mini-mansion. No maids. No animals. No kids. I wonder who laid the fire in the flagstone fireplace. Fee had carried in her tea herself. I brought my own Dunkin' Donuts coffee, the paper cup out of place in the Dulleses' formal residence.

I'm running on empty, sleep-wise, but I'm consumed with getting some answers about the Bexter names. And this may be my last chance for a while. Franklin and J.T. are meeting me at the station this afternoon. We'll have the fun of telling Kevin about last night's success. Then we have to focus on tracking down the owner of Beacon Valet and getting our story on the air.

I'm spinning a lot of plates. And I'm trying to make sure they don't all come crashing down. But the phone calls are haunting me.

"Look at this list," I say, keeping my tone mild and unthreatening. I find the page I'm looking for and fold the report so it's showing on the front. "See how your name has a circle around it? You were Fiona Rooseveldt, isn't that right?"

Fee still makes no move to take the book. I shift my weight, inching a bit closer to her on the love seat. She backs up into her pillows ever so slightly, politely but distinctly keeping her distance.

I turn to another page, pretend not to notice.

"Let me show you this," I say. "On the benefactor page. Here's your husband's name. It's also circled. Randall Kindell, see? There's a pencil line around his name. And Alice Hogarth. See them? And these others?" I've studied the names so many times, I know them by heart.

Leaning forward, I invade her space a millimeter more.

"Do you know why that might be? Do you know these people? Why you might be connected to them?"

Fee moves a gold-embossed coaster into place on the varnished walnut coffee table, then carefully puts her cup and saucer on top of it. She stares at it for a moment. Then, slowly, looks back at me.

I'm still holding up the list. I'm not saying a word. Fee's deciding what to answer.

I can wait.

The fire crackles, an ember popping

against the ornate brass screen.

"I have no idea why the names are circled. I know Wen, of course." Fee offers a fleeting smile. "But I'm not acquainted with the others."

She pushes back the cabled sleeve of her sweater, making a show of looking at her thin-strapped watch. Then she reaches one manicured hand toward the cordless phone that's tucked under an arrangement of shaggy golden mums on a lacquered end table. Is she planning to call for help? Or expecting the phone to ring?

I'm not going to let her stall with any phone tricks. She's lying. And that changes everything. Now I'm not sure whether to be afraid for her — or afraid of her. Is she in danger? Or dangerous? And I have to handle this carefully. No one knows where I am, I remember.

I shake off my paranoia. I could take down the diminutive Fee Dulles with one whap of my purse. She has secrets, just as I suspected. And I bet they have to do with the missing year at Bexter.

"Fee?" I slide the pamphlet back into my briefcase. It's my only evidence of — of whatever it's evidence of. "Forgive me, but I know that's not true."

"Of course it's true. You're mistaken," Fee

replies. She takes her hand off the phone and holds out both palms, imploring. Her eyes are wide and direct, her expression innocent and earnest.

Like a child who's practiced lying.

"You were in the same class as Randall Kindell," I say.

"I was not." Her voice is clipped.

"I've seen the BEX, Mrs. Dulles." Keeping my voice calm. "This is a silly thing to lie about. It's so easy to check."

"I —"

"And if you're not telling the truth about that," I say, gently interrupting, "it makes me wonder about the phone call you told me you received. Whether you were telling me — and your husband — the truth about that."

"Of course I was telling the truth." Fee sits up even straighter, if that's possible, and lifts her chin. She looks away from me and reaches toward the phone again.

Time to play my full hand.

"You missed a year at Bexter," I say.

Her hand stops, and she turns back to me.

"And you have children there now," I continue. "What if Tal and Lexie are in danger? Whoever called you knows where they are. Every day. You don't want to put them in harm's way by lying about whatever is happening to you. Don't you care about protecting them?"

"I am protecting them," she says.

"Protecting them from what, Fee?" This is harsh, but she needs to know I'm serious.

Her haughty expression is unchanged. But her hands are clenched into fists.

"Why are you asking me this?" she says. "If you already know?"

"If I already know what?"

She doesn't answer. We sit, silent and face-to-face, in the glossy living room. Fiona Dulles's past is about to become part of her present. Best to let her tell me in her own way.

"I'm a bad mother," Fee Dulles finally says. She looks down at the plaid pillow now clenched in her arms. "But back then, I had no choice."

She looks up at me, tilting her head, her eyes pleading.

" 'Unwed mother.' An absurd label, isn't it? But that's what we were called so many years ago. A completely different world. Yes, I was fifteen. Yes, we were young and in love. Yes, I left Bexter. Yes, I had the baby. Yes, I gave her up for adoption. At the Services."

"And your parents?"

"Like nothing ever happened. They whisked me away. Told everyone I was 'trying a new school.' I came back the next year. Started over. Just like that." She flips a hand, like, *poof.* "My past was erased. And my daughter? Not a day goes by that I don't wonder about her. Worry. Regret."

She shakes her head again, drops her eyes, lays the pillow back beside her. "I'm a bad mother. I should never have listened to anything but my heart. I should have made my own decisions."

"You had no choice then," I say. I try to be reassuring. "And it was a long time ago."

"No one knows." Her voice lowers, but her eyes flare. "Not my husband, not my kids, not my friends. My husband would —" She crashes to silence, putting both hands over her face. I see her chest rise and fall in a body-wracking sigh.

"He doesn't know? Are you sure?" This must be so difficult for her. Keeping such a heartbreaking secret. And maybe it's unnecessary to keep it. "Maybe he'd be supportive. Grateful to hear the truth from you."

Fee holds a hand out, palm up, to stop me.

"No. Never. Ever. I can't bear to tell him. Or anyone else. Never. This is my secret. Mine. So how could someone call and threaten to do it for me?"

She stops, her face set in fear.

"So, that's what the phone call was actually about?" I get it now.

"Yes. Yes. Yes. The caller threatened to tell Wen about my baby. After she was born, I saw her for barely a moment. I kept my eyes shut, tight shut, so I wouldn't have to see her face. Or remember it. I don't know where she is now. The whole procedure was sealed. The birth. The adoption. Confidential. They promised. It's impossible to trace."

"Apparently not," I say. But I'm still not clear on the blackmail. "So what did the caller say?"

"He said, 'Do you know where your children are?' Then he — or she — laughed. Disgusting. And then went on to say I should tell my husband there was a drug scandal. Make up a story that Lexie and Tal could be involved. He said I had to insist so Wen would pay. And that was the only way I could keep my secret. It's terrible. Terrible. Wen would do anything to defend Tal. And I had nowhere to turn."

"Fee? You said you couldn't tell if it was a man or a woman on the phone. Do you think it's your daughter calling?" This seems like the obvious answer. Many adopted children search for reconciliation. Maybe this one wants revenge. "She'd be, what, in her thirties?"

"How could she know?" she asks. Her voice rises and I see tears come to her eyes. "Did the law change? Can confidential records be opened?"

"Let me ask you this," I say, trying to think it through. This is a pretty risky venture, depending completely on Fee's need for confidentiality. "Was Dorothy Wirt at the school at the time you left? Working at the office?"

"She was."

"Could she have known the reason you left?" I've suddenly realized one disturbing way this all might fit together. Could Fiona have killed Dorothy? Because she knew her secret? Or maybe Fiona made the calls to the school. To give credence to the blackmail story.

Fee blinks a few times, considering. I can't read her expression.

"I suppose she could have known," she answers. "But she's dead now."

And so is my theory. And my Fiona-as-murderer idea can't be true. Because if she's the bad guy, who called her? I don't think she's making that up.

"There's no one to help me." Fee's voice is brittle and trembling. "No one. And I know whoever's calling me will never stop. Wen will find out. My marriage will be over. My children will never forgive me. How could they? I can't even forgive myself."

She covers her face with her hands again.

"Could I get you some water?" I say. I stand, setting my briefcase on the floor. "I think I can find the kitchen."

She nods, not moving her hands from her face.

I'll give her some privacy. Although I'm not sure how long that can last.

By the time I return with a crystal glass with ice cubes and water from the stainless-steel fridge, I have a theory. A good one. Fee seems to have regained her composure. I hand her the chunky glass and perch on a chintz wing chair.

"Maybe it was the baby's father who called you. Maybe he knows you're well off now. Forgive me, but maybe he's angry and thinks he deserves some of your money." I gesture at the living room, assessing the antiques, the art, the silver. A museum-quality clock on the mantel reminds me how much time I don't have. I'm now incredibly late. I need to leave. And I need to wait for Fee's reply.

"It's not the father who's calling," Fee

whispers. She takes a tentative sip of the ice water.

"It could be," I persist, leaning forward. "And since you know who that is, maybe we could —"

Fee Dulles stands and takes a step or two toward the fireplace. The fire flickers, still crackling, flames licking the crisscrossed logs.

"It wasn't the baby's father who called." She turns to face me, hands on hips. "That's why I thought you were here. That's what I thought you knew. The baby's father is Randall Kindell."

I stand, slowly, attempting to take this in. All the puzzle pieces of the Bexter mystery shift and rearrange in my head, taunting me as I struggle to put them together into an accurate picture. Randall Kindell got a phone call, too. Does Fee know that? Does the caller know the Rental Car King is the father of an illegitimate daughter? Or not? Exasperatingly, I don't have time to figure this out. I pick up my coat from the love seat and grab my briefcase.

"Fee, I'm so sorry," I say. "This must be terribly difficult for you. But I urge you to go to the police. This is blackmail and cannot have anything but a tragic ending. And trust your husband, maybe? Tell him?"

"And if I don't tell, you will, Miss Mc-Nally?" Fee raises an eyebrow.

"No, of course not." I drop my bag on the love seat and slide my arms through my coat sleeves. "Making sure information stays confidential is part of my job as a journalist. Otherwise no one would trust me."

I pull on my gloves, pick up my briefcase and my purse, and head for the front door.

"I only came here to see if you knew any of the people circled in the fundraising pamphlet," I remind her of the reason for my visit. And myself. I'm late, but I need to ask one more question. Turns out, she actually did know Randall Kindell. Now that she's telling the truth, what can she tell me about the other names? I put my hand on the doorknob, then hesitate.

Taking my hand off the knob, I dig into my bag for the Bexter report.

It's not there.

I scramble, opening zippers and searching in side pockets. And again. It's not there.

I look in my purse. It's not there.

The back of my neck goes clammy. I feel the blood drain from my face. My brain searches for answers. Did I leave it in the living room?

I look at Fee Dulles. She's watching me, without a word.

"I'm so sorry, Miss McNally. I know you're trying to help. I don't know what the names mean. I don't know who marked them. Or why. I honestly don't. But my name is circled and so is Randall's. I can't let us be linked in any way."

I'm so tired. I'm so confused.

"The report," she says. "When you went to get my water, I burned it."

CHAPTER TWENTY-ONE

It doesn't matter. It doesn't matter. I repeat my desperate mantra as I drive back to Channel 3. Harrison Ebling has the names. I gave them to him to look up. He saw them in the book. Josh saw them in the book. It doesn't matter that Fiona Dulles is a certified wack —

I stop myself mid-tirade as I aim my automatic opener at Channel 3's garage door. I'm not really supposed to park in here, except when we're doing a story, but I'm late and no one will care if I sneak in for a little while. I'll move my Jeep after we talk with Kevin. But I can't miss this meeting.

The door hums upward as I reconsider Fiona Dulles. She's not so much a wack job as she is concerned about her future. And her past. As far as she knows, that pamphlet could sandbag her entire life. And maybe that's what it is. Someone's hit list.

The door is open, but I'm too caught up in my own theories to press the accelerator. If there's no drug scandal — which makes sense, because according to Josh at least, no one at Bexter has ever heard of such a thing — then it could be someone is concocting that story to cover up the real threat. Each person on the list has a secret. A secret the caller somehow knew about. A secret the caller knew they'd pay to keep quiet.

Who's making the calls?

A horn blaring behind me blasts away my thoughts. Someone else is waiting to get in. I look in my rearview to see the tape coordinator, ENG Joanna. She's smiling and waving at me with both hands. And in the driver's seat of the news car, J.T. Shaw. He must have driven her on some errand. To the transmitter or some technical chore. And now he's here for the meeting. Which means it hasn't started yet. Which means I'm not late.

I wave back, shift my Jeep into Drive and return to my theorizing. Kindell. And Fiona Dulles. Their secret past.

My stomach lurches as the parking-lot ramp takes the familiar sharp drop. I edge my way into the crowded garage, searching for a place to stash my car. And then, the answer hits me. I slam on the brakes.

"Hey!" J.T.'s shout from his open car window echoes through the garage and his brakes squeal at the same time. "You can't just stop, McNally!"

"Sorry!" I yell back. Though he can't hear me.

Kindell and Fiona. Together. Of course Kindell knows about the baby. What teenager wouldn't tell her boyfriend? And when busybody Dorothy — who probably suspected it when Fiona was yanked from school — found out about their tryst, and the reputation-ruining result, she knew she had a gold mine, especially when Fiona married the affluent Dulles. She called, threatening them with exposure. They had to get rid of her. Kindell and Fiona concocted "blackmail" calls to themselves to steer away suspicion. After all, as far as I know, they're the only parents who got the calls. Or should I say, who allege they got the calls.

And Alethia? They actually called her, then killed her, too. Dorothy's best friend. Who they might assume she confided in. Mystery solved. Kindell and Fiona. Yes. Definitely yes.

But as I hurry through the basement door and up the inside stairway toward Kevin's office, I reconsider. No. Definitely no. It's not Fee Dulles and Randall Kindell. If Fiona and Kindell killed Dorothy and Alethia, how'd they do it? They would have been noticed hanging around at Bexter the night of Alethia's "fall," certainly. And would it mean Wen Dulles was in on it, too? He and Fiona were together at the Head's party. He'd be Fiona's alibi for the night of Dorothy's murder.

I shake my head as I yank open the metal stairwell door to the my office floor. This theory is too complicated to be true.

It's all about the names on the list. The list I used to have.

"Harrison," I say out loud as I walk into the hallway and turn toward Kevin's office. "He's got to have those addresses for me."

"What addresses?" Franklin comes through the double glass doors of Special Projects, and into the hallway. He's in his usual perfect khakis. Today's crewneck sweater is pale blue. Both his arms are loaded. He's carrying a box of yellow videotapes with a sheaf of papers stacked on top.

"Hey, Franko," I say, changing the subject. "You get any sleep? Can I help carry something?"

"Welcome to work," he says, eyeing my overcoat and muffler. "These are the tapes from last night. And the logs. I came in early to transcribe them. Remember, we planned to do that together this morning? So we could be ready to cue up the appropriate video for Kevin?"

I look at him, feeling my mouth drop open in dismay.

"What, did you forget?"

He's right. I forgot. I completely forgot.

"How could you forget?" Franklin's face twists in concern. "Are you — okay? You haven't been yourself lately. Not connected to our story. This is big, Charlotte. And this is the first time I've seen you so distracted. You're always gone. Is there something you're not telling me?"

"No, of course not," I begin to defend myself. But he's right. And of course there's something I'm not telling him. A lot. At least I won't have to tell him I'm going to New York. I hold up my left hand, fluttering my fingers, choosing a believable fib. "Wedding jitters. And I am not always gone."

"Well then, how come —"

"Hey, Charlie . . . hey, Franklin." Liz Whittemore, the nightside reporter, strides down the hall toward the stairway. She's snapped into a TV-sleek red parka with the Channel 3 logo prominently displayed. Knowing they'll never show on the air, she's put on the world's ugliest snow boots. "How's it go —"

Franklin stops talking.

Liz pauses, looking between us. "Oh. Sorry to interrupt."

"No, it's nothing," Franklin says. Clearly he's lying. And Liz knows it.

"Great job with Fran Rivera the other night. Good story on the carjacking." I try to smooth the edges of the awkward moment, giving the young reporter a thumbs-up.

"Thanks, Charlie. Means a lot, coming from you."

Franklin raises a derisive eyebrow in my direction. Liz, looking at me, misses his unspoken commentary on her compliment.

"In fact, I'm on my way to another one," she continues.

"Another one?" I say.

"A carjacking?" Franklin says.

"Apparently. This time they took an Explorer," Liz says. "No one's hurt, though. Probably won't even make the six o'clock news."

Franklin and I look at each other, argument forgotten, as Liz runs off. This may change everything.

"We're right on time, and with a big breaking story," I say, peering through the glass door of Kevin's office. "And now Kevin's on the phone?"

Franklin and I are pretending the skirmish in the hallway never happened. The arrival of J.T. outside the news director's office made our cease-fire easier. And the idea that the bad guys have carjacked an Explorer has pumped all three of us full of story adrenaline. If it's fire-engine red, like ours, we may be in the money.

I can barely keep from rubbing my hands together in expectation.

"That Explorer is going to have our car's VIN number. It probably already does," I say. "It'll be a clone of ours. Now we've got to find that car."

"Which is, of course, the big mystery," Franklin says. "Where would they hide it?"

"Well, they have to attach the new VIN, right? So I say, not such a mystery. Those guys are definitely going to take their ill-gotten treasure to the Newtonville garage, slap on the swiped VIN and transform that stolen car into our not-stolen Explorer."

"Look at him," J.T. says, waving a disdainful hand toward Kevin's closed glass door. "He's, like, completely ignoring us. And we're out here with the story of the century."

We see Kevin, phone clamped to his ear,

elbows on his desk. He's oblivious to everything but his conversation.

"Maybe he's got a job offer," I say. Oops. That was supposed to be sarcastic. But it's not so funny, since it's actually true and I'm not supposed to mention it.

"So, you think it's hidden-camera time?" Franklin says. "Go back to Newtonville?"

Franklin doesn't seem to be picking up on my potential slip of the tongue. So I guess I'm fine.

"We go back out there — and I want to go with you two this time — and see what they're doing?" he continues. "See if they bring in a red Explorer?"

I lean on the edge of an empty desk and cross my arms, thinking. The newsroom is deserted. The noon news is just over. Almost everyone has bolted to get lunch.

"I suppose the hidden-camera thing could work," I say. "But problem is, even if we see an Explorer inside, we'd only be able to get wide shots of it. I mean, it's a garage. People expect cars to be there. People expect mechanics to be working on them. How would we prove they were changing the VIN?"

"Hey, Miss McNally."

I turn to see an intern pushing the battered mail-delivery cart toward Kevin's office. The cart is probably older than she is. The intern has on matchstick jeans that she's somehow rolled up in precisely the same thickness over each of her shiny leather boots. She apparently purchased her sweater from the too-small store.

"Hey," I say. I jump up, getting out of the way of the wobble-wheeled cart. For a million dollars, I have no idea of this person's name. She knows me, that's easy enough. I've been on television since before she was born. But who on earth could keep track of all the interns' names?

"Hi, Kaitlin," Franklin says.

"Hey, Kaitlin," J.T. says.

Show-offs.

"Oh, Miss McNally," she says, rummaging through rubber-banded stacks of padded manila mailers and narrow white envelopes. She pulls out a packet and hands it to me, smiling. "You've got mail."

"Job offers," I say to Franklin, making sure he knows all my job-offer references are teasing. "And certainly fan letters."

I take the mail, then change my mind. I don't want to carry it all into our meeting. And it looks as though Kevin may be wrapping up his call.

"Thanks, Kaitlin." Like I knew her name all the time. "But can you drop it upstairs, as usual?"

Then I glance at the envelopes. The top one is from WWXI. And it has a little see-through window. I slide the envelope from beneath the rubber band. "Oh, wait. This must be my paycheck from doing Maysie's show."

I hand back the rest of the mail, fold the Wixie envelope into thirds and — no pockets. I lift one edge of my skirt and slide the folded envelope down the inside of my left boot.

Kevin's door opens and he waves us inside. He reaches for his mail as we take our seats.

"Hey, Kaitlin," he says.

"This video is terrific. Blockbuster," Kevin says. Pulling the final cassette from his viewer, he hands it back to Franklin. "We'll get a whole 'Charlie Investigates' campaign in the works. You got the rental-car king to repair his fleet of cars. And now he's telling his pals to do the same. Public service. Excellent. And then the valet-parking scam? VIN cloning? Air-bag theft? Even more excellent. It hits our demos exactly, women and families. We'll assign you the first days of the ratings book. Promo will tease it big on Wednesday, then we'll run your stories

Thursday and Friday. We'll kill."

"That's great," I say. "But remember, we have to prove our Explorer is cloned. And somehow figure out where that cloned Explorer actually is."

"And we're still working on who owns Beacon Valet," Franklin puts in.

"And then we have to decide how to handle that," I say.

"Well, let me know what you figure out." Kevin comes out from behind his desk, signaling "meeting over."

"Too bad we can't call your stories *Drive Time*," he says. "That's the radio show, right? Well, I'll take care of the title. You take care of the story."

I hear the unmistakable sound of the old NBC network bells. J.T. jumps to his feet, unclicking the cell phone from his belt, and he heads out the door. "Sorry," he says over his shoulder. The door latches closed behind him.

The rest of us exchange inquiring looks, then shrug. Franklin and I both stand. We're done here. And we have a lot to accomplish in a very short time.

"Anyway, you guys never cease to amaze me," Kevin continues, shepherding us out. "And might as well exit on a high note, isn't that right, Franklin?"

I stop.

Exit? I take my hand off the doorknob and turn back to face them. Kevin is smiling. Franklin is not. In fact, Franklin's face is changing so quickly I can't even read the expressions as they go by.

Then I realize. Of course. It wasn't a complete secret. Kevin's told Franklin about his move to New York. How could I have thought he wouldn't?

"Well, of course," I say, nodding conspiratorially. I reach for the door again. "Glad we could make it happen. And we'll miss you. Right, Franko?"

"Charlotte," Franklin says.

"Charlie," Kevin says at the same time.

I don't move from the doorway. Franklin takes a step backward, deeper into Kevin's office, still clutching his pile of tapes and transcribed logs.

"I assumed you two told each other everything," Kevin says. His demeanor is uncharacteristically merry, like a salesman endeavoring to motivate a reluctant customer. "I told you to keep it confidential, Charlie, but you two have no secrets, right? Don't make a move without telling the other? The two musketeers?"

Franklin is silent.

I don't say a word.

"Well. Let me give you some privacy, then," Kevin says. He reaches behind me, opens the door. Then he turns. And actually winks. "The offer still stands for you, too, you know. There's still time to join us in the Big Apple. Love to have you."

And he disappears into the newsroom.

Franklin and I are alone. Together. Though it appears we won't be together for long. On the wall, five muted television screens flicker news and early-afternoon soap operas. I think the biggest soap opera may be happening right now. In real life. I only wish I'd been let in on the story. I'm not sure of my lines. And I don't know how this episode ends.

Franklin shifts the tapes piled in his arms, suddenly concerned with making sure they're all stacked just right. He pushes up his glasses with one finger, flustered. A few typed pages of transcripts escape, fluttering onto Kevin's desk.

"Need help with those?" I say. My words come out brittle. My back is stiffening and my insides are hollow. I'm — angry. And I'm enjoying it. "Or with anything else? Or, let's see now, would you like to handle it all on your own?"

"Let's just talk, all right, Charlotte?" Franklin sets the tapes and logs back onto

Kevin's desk, and turns to me. His eyes are wide behind his glasses, imploring. He slides his flat palms down the sides of his khakis, then stuffs his fists into his pockets.

"Talk?" I say. I still don't sound like me. "You must have already done a lot of talking."

Franklin drops his head, staring at the floor, then takes a deep breath.

"Charlotte, I wanted to discuss this with you. But you were never around."

"Oh, I get it," I reply. "It's my fault."

"Listen. Let me tell you the whole thing and then you can be angry. Whatever. You know Kevin is going to New York. He asked me to come with him, produce for the investigative team. He said he asked you, too. He told me not to tell you I knew about it."

"But, I —" I interrupt. I need to explain that I was going to turn the offer down.

"Let me finish." Franklin holds up a hand. "You've been distant. And distracted. You know you have. Wedding-planner meetings at fancy hotels. Taking Penny to school. The 'dentist'? *Please.* 'Forgetting' our plans? I must tell you, Charlotte, I was convinced you were out of here. You have to admit, it makes sense."

"But, I —"

He looks at me earnestly. "You're getting married. You'll have Josh, and Penny, and a whole new deal. I thought you were, you know, easing your way into that. And away from TV."

"But, I —" Now I need to explain I'm still learning to be two places at once, but I'll definitely be able to pull it off.

Franklin shakes his head, stopping me again.

"I'm almost finished. When Kevin offered me New York, the network, the job I'd always dreamed of, I had to consider it. As it happens, Stephen's office was thrilled to have him relocate there. I've been talking with the New York Bureau staff for two weeks now. I thought for sure you'd get suspicious of all my texting. And when I didn't show up for the first stakeout. I wasn't there because I had a meeting."

He gives a soft smile, remembering. "And when I kept clicking my computer monitor closed so you couldn't read our e-mails. The guy at the Longmore with me on stakeout night? He was from New York. The new exec producer. You didn't care."

"But, I —" I had noticed, I just hadn't pursued it. I was too busy with my own deceptions. Now I need to explain some other things. That a moment ago, I wasn't really angry, but terrified. And that now, my fear is dissolving into pure sorrow. That I understand change is necessary. And inevitable. And that change is the only thing that keeps our heads and our hearts alive.

"When you didn't say anything . . ." Franklin pauses. "It was proof for me that you had completely tuned out. You were leaving, too. You'd be Charlie the married lady. You wouldn't miss me. Or us. You'd be happy, Charlotte. As you deserve to be."

Now I'm unabashedly crying, tears streaming down my cheeks. I give a watery sniff and pat my pockets for a tissue. No pockets.

"It was hard to keep a secret from you," he says. "Like I said, Kevin told me he'd offered you a New York gig. He was sure you'd jump at it. But I know you. And I know you'll turn him down. Your life is changing, girlfriend."

He pauses. "And mine is, too."

We stare at each other in the flickering silence. Outside in the newsroom, the lunch bunch is returning. The newsroom is bustling back to life, exactly the way it was before lunch.

But for me, and for Franklin, things will never be the same.

"Congratulations, Franko," I say, taking a

deep breath. "Let's go out in style."

I throw one arm across Franklin's shoulders, giving him a brief, newsroom-appropriate hug.

"Get those tapes, Mr. New York producer. You've still got to knock 'em dead in Boston one last time. Let's do some good. Stop some bad guys. And we'll hope for one more Emmy while we're at it. You're the best, Franko."

"You're the best, Charlotte," Franklin says, scooping up the stack of cassettes. "You'll find a new producer."

"We'll see," I say.

I pull open the office door and the two of us step forward into our new reality.

Head down and almost running, J.T. crashes through the double doors into the newsroom, narrowly avoiding smashing into us. We all stop, regrouping. Franklin picks up the cassettes that tumbled onto the worn once-blue carpeting.

"Sorry, dudes," J.T. says. He eyes us. "Guess you talked about New York, huh?"

"You know about this?" My voice rises. Never a dull moment. "What, are you leaving, too?"

"Charlotte, he —"

"Listen, dudes, we can deal with that later. In Kevin's office? That was a call from ENG

Joanna. They were taking in a live feed from Liz Whittemore. Joanna said I might want to see it. And she was right."

"What was it?" Franklin asks.

"Another car fire?" My mind races. If another car has been destroyed, we're totally on the wrong track. Our Explorer is safely stowed in the station garage. No doubt about that. *Uh-oh.* "Was there another murder?"

"Nope. Nope. The feed was from downtown, from inside some parking garage," J.T. says. "The cops found it. They found the carjacked Explorer. It's red."

CHAPTER TWENTY-TWO

"You have to slow down. So you can take a ticket." Franklin points to the black-and-white ticket-dispensing machine, all that's standing between us and the cops. And, we hope, between us and a lovely close-up VIN view of the carjacked red Explorer. "Push the green button, Charlotte."

"I know how parking garages work, I'm going to take a darn ticket," I say. I am almost too impatient to wait for an automatic gate. I hit the brake grudgingly, lean out the window and punch the flashing green dome. It spits out a magnetic striped ticket and the long metal arm slowly, agonizingly slowly, lifts to allow us in.

The Garage at Fifty-Five Friend Street is a multi-storied, poorly lighted, perfect place to hide a car, because it's where all the other cars are. We could never have found the stolen Explorer. The cops did. According to the faxed news release from HQ that's now safely in my coat pocket, the license plates had been removed, but unfortunately for the bad guys, remnants of a telltale beach-access parking decal were still in place on the rear window.

"They're having a news conference, can you believe it?" I say. The car barely clears the gate as I drive through and go up the ramp to the fifth floor, where the police have notified the media they'll display their find.

"The cops are going to show off this car, trying to prove they're cracking down on the carjacking situation. But it's the key to our story. The solution to our where's-the-car dilemma. And it's right here, served up nicely by Boston's finest. You've got to love it."

"If it actually is the clone of our Explorer," Franklin says. He pauses, pulls a tiny spiral notebook from the side pocket of his suede jacket and starts flipping pages. "There are — let's see — 5,600 Explorers in Boston. Possibly fifteen percent of them are red. Plus, if No-Hat, as you've now indelibly dubbed him in my head, didn't get a chance to have his buddies transform the stolen car into a clone, it'll be a total bust. I mean, it'll be just another red Explorer."

"Eeyore," I say. "You're always Eeyore. How long can it take to slap on three VIN plates? So I'll distract the cops while you get a nice shot of No-Hat's nefarious handiwork with that lovely hidden camera you've got. We'll use the wide shots from Liz and her photog, since they're covering the news conference."

I sneak a quick look at Franklin as we hit the straightaway of the second floor.

"Cheer up, partner. We've done the hard part, getting video of them stealing our VIN. And now we're about to be presented a perfect view of the result. I'll bet you ten thousand dollars it's the clone of our car."

Franklin and I always bet ten thousand dollars. Sometimes one or the other of us is down a hundred thousand or so, but it always, eventually, evens out. I ease the car up around the corner, noticing a black-and-red sign indicating we're on Two Left. With a chill of sadness I realize there might not be time for any new big money bets to even out.

"Where'd they say it was again?" I ask. Changing the subject.

"Left side, space number one, according to the news release." Franklin says. "And I suppose it's in the best interest of the cloners to change the car's identity as quickly as possible. So, we'll see. All we have to do is get to the VIN number."

Third floor.

"And since the cops will impound this baby anyway," I say, "we won't have to worry about anyone messing with it. They're actually protecting it for us. Nice. We are having one big fat lucky day."

I look at Franklin as we head around the curves of the fourth floor, remembering. "Except that you've announced you're leaving me, of course."

The red Explorer is cordoned off with black-and-yellow plastic tape. Crime Scene, Do Not Cross, it announces in black letters, over and over. Although this is not technically the scene of the crime. There's no way for us to get close enough to see the VIN. Yet.

Between us and the car, I count six television crews arranged in a semicircle. Six reporters, creating a rainbow of multicolored parkas, hover next to six photographers. Six cameras with battery-powered lights mounted on top are at the ready on tripods. There's no power to plug in big portable lights, so the area stays dim, fluorescent tubes across the concrete ceiling struggling to make it approach daylight. The newspaper reporters keep to themselves in a pack to one side. Their parkas, aggressively rumpled, a dimmer rainbow of gray to tan, telegraph their disdain for their on-air competitors.

They're all waiting for the huddle of blue uniforms to come to a bank of microphones precariously rigged up with gaffer's tape and retractable metal stands.

Franklin and I stay behind them all. Waiting for our chance.

"Strange, though, that they'd carjack, you know? Why not just steal a car? This is so — out there."

"Stop fidgeting, Charlotte," Franklin whispers. "Here they come. They'll talk, the gang will ask questions, they'll all leave. Then we can try to get closer."

"We only need one shot," I say. I'm calculating the ways we could manage it.

All at once, the garage goes bright. In the instant heat and flare of six battery-powered spotlights, a parade of uniforms approaches the microphones.

"I'm Lieutenant Henry Zavala, Z-A-V-A-L-A, head of the Auto Theft Unit." A lanky forty-something with a bristling cop-issue mustache and matching eyebrows steps forward. The lights glint on his silver badge. "We are pleased to announce today we've recovered . . ."

"Yeah, yeah, you found the car, big deal," I mutter as Zavala continues. "So who took it? You know *that?* That'd be worth a news conference."

"Shush," Franklin says. "Maybe they do know."

The news conference sputters along, a series of self-congratulatory back-pats by the police officers, followed by solemn warnings to citizens to be watchful and keep their car doors locked, followed by fake-aggressive questions from reporters who have no idea they're on the edges of a real story.

No suspects, the cops finally admit. Victim barely saw the carjackers, can't describe them. The victims want to be anonymous. Won't do interviews. Fingerprinting to come. A cop had spied the car on a routine patrol. They confirmed it by the beach de-cal and a key the owners had hidden under the left front wheel well in a magnetic tin box.

"They haven't checked the VIN," I whisper. "Yay."

Franklin knows the stakes as well as I do. If this car is a clone, the cops could be on to the scam as soon as they try to confirm the VIN. As long as they don't, it's clear sailing for us.

I see Liz Whittemore's hand go up. She doesn't wait to be called on.

"Lieutenant? Is this carjacking related to the blue Mustang incident? Or do you think this one is a separate incident?"

I jab Franklin with an elbow. "Damn. That's the sixty-four-thousand-dollar question. I was going to ask it myself. But not in front of everyone during the news conference."

Zavala takes a step back from the microphones, confers behind his hand with a plainclothes colleague and comes back into the lights.

"That's under investigation," he says.

"Yay," I whisper. "They've got nothing."

"The perps carjack so they snag the keys, right?" A tough-guy *Globe* reporter points to the front with his pen, attempting to demonstrate his cop-speak cred. "But why would the skels dump the Ex in a garage?"

I see a few officers trying to hold back sneers.

"We don't know what's in the minds of the perpetrators," Zavala says.

"Hope not," I whisper.

"Shush," Franklin says.

There's a rustle of notebooks and clicking of ballpoints as reporters look at each other, wondering if someone else has thought of a question they should be asking.

"Anyone else?" Zavala surveys the pack in

front of him. No one speaks. A few photographers, knowing the end's in sight, unfasten their cameras from the tripods.

"If not," Zavala says, adjusting his cap, "we're done here. Thank you all for coming."

No one seems to care about any of it. Except Franklin and me.

"Okay, okay, let's do it." I can barely hold myself back. Some of the photographers roll off a few desultory shots of the recovered car, one go-getter even bothering to come up closer to the crime-scene tape. To them, this is as routine as it comes. There's no suspect, there's no excitement. It's just the police proving their Auto Theft Unit can find a stolen car from time to time, a public relations move to prove they're on the job.

Unless there's a body in the trunk, which there can't be because there's no trunk, this video will go straight to the newsroom "hold" stacks and only make it on the air if the cops eventually blow the lid off a huge and dangerous carjacking ring.

Which they won't. Because we're going to break an even bigger story. First.

Reporters and photographers toting their bags of gear click open their cars, electronic beeps from key rings echoing against the concrete walls. A few colleagues wave a hand in salute, off to their next assignment. Franklin makes his way oh-so-casually toward the crime-scene tape. I'm standing by. We're playing this by ear.

"How'd you draw the short straw on this piece of crap, McNally?" A familiar voice, speaking close to my ear. I hear one sentence, but a million memories return.

I turn, smiling, to greet an old pal.

"Is that cop talk for 'hello, great to see you'?" I haven't seen Joe Cipriani for more than a year. Detective Joe Cipriani, in his usual rough-knit fisherman's sweater and leather jacket, is the heartthrob of the Boston PD. I give him a quick peck on the cheek, appropriate for what we went through together a couple of stories ago, when he arrived just in time to rescue me from the gun-wielding sociopath I'd proved was mastermind of an insider-trading scheme. His curly hair has gone a little grayer, but he's still wearing that same cologne. This time, he hasn't arrived to save my life.

I smile as I pull away, changing my mind. Perhaps he has.

"Great to see you, too," I continue. "And I happened to be in the neighborhood. You know me, can't stay away from watching the good guys in blue win. What's your excuse, Detective? They bust you down to the auto squad?"

Over Joe's shoulder I see Franklin's now standing right next to the Explorer. A uniformed cop is pantomiming "this is as far as you get, buddy." He's not close enough for the camera to get a usable shot.

"Brass wanted a big show," Joe says. "You heard Henry Z. S'posed to remind the public to be vigilant, you know the drill. Plus, looks good they found the car. Driver wasn't hurt. Case closed."

I can barely keep from smiling. And I feel a bit guilty about what I'm about to attempt. But all's fair in TV, pretty much. And we can always get an authorized picture of the VIN later.

"Yup, that's a good outcome," I say. "And nice work about the wheel-well thing."

"Well, it's part hard work. And part luck."

Couldn't have put it better myself. And here comes a little of each. I pretend to be annoyed, even performing a little foot stamp with my boot. "Rats."

"What?" Joe says.

"Oh, Liz and her cameraman are gone," I gesture vaguely behind me, my voice laden with concern. "I never saw them get a close-up of that wheel well. The exec pro-

ducer is going to nail her for that. Could I
—"

I stop midsentence. Oh. Rats. And this
time I mean it. Franklin has a camera, but I
totally forgot it's the hidden camera. So I
can't ask if we can get a picture with it. Putting both hands on my knees, I pretend to
have a brief coughing fit, giving myself some
time to think.

"You okay?" Joe says.

I hold up a palm, standing back upright.
"Fine. All this car exhaust, I bet. Anyway, as
I was saying. Could I take of picture of the
wheel well for Liz? With my cell-phone camera?"

If he lets us get right up to the car, I'll
snap a photo of the wheel well with my cell
to distract the cops while Franklin gets the
VIN on his hidden camera.

Joe looks back at the car. The black-and-
yellow tape is being taken down. Franklin is
chatting earnestly about who-knows-what
with a crime-scene tech. I know Franko's
stalling. Or strategizing. Most of the other
uniforms have gone. A BPD flatbed tow
truck that had been parked to one side is
being waved into place. The Explorer won't
be here for long.

"Sure," Joe says. "For you? I can make
that happen."

"I'm driving. You know I can't look at the video," Franklin says. "But I got it, right? It's our VIN? Every number and letter shows up? The first few numbers are going to be the same on every Explorer of the same year."

"Duh." I've got the hidden camera on my lap, the flip-screen open, and I'm pressing Rewind. I watch the jaggedy video spin by, backward, once again. "Let me rewind again, check it, to be sure," I say. "But I think it's fine. Great job."

We're winding back down the twisting ramps of the parking garage, heading back to the station. If the VINs match, and I'm confident they do, our story is about to accelerate into high gear.

"I suppose," I say as the humming tape continues to rewind, "we could go on the air without knowing who's behind this, you know? Just show that cars are being hijacked and cloned, and that Michael Borum was a possible casualty of this potentially far-reaching, dangerous and —"

"And lucrative," Franklin puts in.

"And lucrative scheme," I finish. The camera clicks, signaling the tape is at the beginning again. "So let's check with Kevin. See if we can go with what we've got. I mean, let's say we do find the mastermind. What am I supposed to do, go confront him? Then say, hang on, sir, we're putting this all on TV next week?"

"Or ma'am," Franklin says, pulling up to the cashier's exit booth. "You have the ticket?"

"In the sun visor." I point to the flap. And then push Fast-Forward on the camera.

"I know I'm right," I continue, my eyes glued to the tiny screen. "We don't have to know who's behind it. We're not the cops. Let Jeremiah Soroff and his crew go after some real bad guys for once. Once they see our story, they'll —"

"Twenty-four dollars?" Franklin's voice, directed out his open window, is incredulous.

"We were barely here for an hour, hour and a half at most." I push Stop and lean across him, adding my two cents.

The attendant, who looks as if she has a supersize package of Dubble Bubble working, points to a glowing electronic readout that says $24.00, then to a hand-lettered and imaginatively spelled sign that reads "Attendant at Fifty-Five Friend cannot altar parking fees." The sign also offers a phone number to report problems or complaints. As if anyone's going to call some phone number.

I pause, staring at nothing, trying to retrieve an elusive thought.

"Fine, fine," Franklin says. He takes his wallet out of his inside jacket pocket, and with a show of annoyance, hands over a twenty and four ones. "Receipt, please."

"Gigi in accounting is going to flip," I say. What is it that I'm trying to remember?

We pull out of the lot, Franklin still grumbling, and turn onto Friend Street. It was light when we went in, but it's almost dark now, the weirdness of New England winter in daylight savings time. Franklin clicks on the headlights, then pulls the car to the curb. "Let's see the tape, at least. If the numbers are there, it's worth having Channel 3 bilked out of twenty-four bucks."

I hand over the camera, part of my mind yanking my attention somewhere else. And then I have it. Not fully formed. But enough. It's my song. My phone number song. I think I know what it means.

"Franko?" I say.

"What?" He's only half listening, his eyes focused on the screen.

"I'll be right back, okay? I'm going to check on something in the garage. I'll leave my stuff here," I say, pointing to my purse and tote bag. "I'll be right back."

CHAPTER TWENTY-THREE

I'm probably wrong about my idea. It's almost ridiculous. But what if I'm right? The parking attendant doesn't raise her eyes as I scoot around the entry arm and up the ramp into the garage. I suppose people walk in this way all the time, coming back from shopping or lunch or whatever normal people do.

Instead of trudging up five flights, I go for the elevator. The doors open. The car's empty. I get in and push the green button marked with a big black five.

The metal doors slide open as I arrive on five, but I don't get out. Holding the rubber edge of door open with one hand, I peer around the corner to space number one. The red Explorer is no longer there. That's no surprise, since the tow truck was obviously there to haul it to the police evidence lot. And I'm relieved that all the cops are gone. I don't want to have to explain why

I'm still hanging around the garage. It's not space number one I'm interested in.

The doors begin their automatic struggle to close, clanking softly and pushing against my gloved hand as I make sure the coast is clear. I step out into the empty garage. The doors swish shut behind me.

"Don't forget your floor. You are on Floor Five," a printed sign on a metal stand reminds those with short memories. Some genius has blacked out one letter so it says "Foor five." Hilarious. In about an hour, this place is going to be teeming with commuters ready to battle the inevitable rush hour traffic jam. But now, it's only me and rows and rows of cars. Hundreds and hundreds of cars, all in numbered spaces.

I'm looking for one particular space.

I trot down the rows of parked cars and vans and SUVs, the dim light dulling them to barely-varied shades of neutral. Twisting past the curving ramps and trying to follow the lighted signs and arrows, I hurry past the spaces in the thirties, past the forties, past the fifties. The signs are impossible. How can "no entrance" and "no exit" be in the same direction? At least the numbers are in order, stenciled, sprayed onto the water-stained concrete walls, blocky numerals with a black border, just at eye level.

Past the sixties. Then a wide exit ramp cuts another double-laned path through the numbering. A horn honks, twice. A navy minivan with two people in the front seat is coming right at me. Heart fluttering, I scoot to one side, getting out of the way behind a thick white-painted pillar. My heart beats even faster as I try, squinting, to recognize the driver or the passenger. Two women. Nothing sinister. They're just heading for the exit.

I'm heading for answers. And the closer I get, the more I convince myself I might be right.

The song in my head becomes a sound track for my search. It's all I can do not to sing it out loud. Five-five-five, zero-one-nine-three, my phone-number lyrics buzz through my brain, repeating and repeating like a broken record.

The lyrics are not a phone number. They're directions.

Fifty-five Friend Street. Fifth floor. Space one, like zero-1, is where the red Explorer was found. If I'm right, there'll be another carjacked auto waiting in space 93. 555-0193. Two cars, hidden in plain sight. One, in space 01, discovered by the cops. The other still waiting for the bad guys to come and retrieve it.

We've proved they first swipe a car from valet parking. Steal its identity. Then steal an identical-looking car. They do the presto-chango. Then they sell the stolen car.

But they don't put ads in the newspaper. Oh, no.

They send their for-sale notices to the *Drive Time* radio show, where each one sounds like just another advertisement for a used car. But it's really a free, widely broadcast and completely untraceable announcement to the rest of their team.

"We've got more clones," they're actually transmitting the news to their partners in crime. "Come and get them." And the "phone number" tells precisely where. In Boston, so it's area code 617. Fifty-five Friend Street. Fifth floor. And then, for the Explorer and the Mustang, 01 and 93.

Five-five-five isn't a real phone-number prefix. Franklin found that out. But it sure is a good headline. And if anyone out of the loop tries to call the number, they'll get the same irritating result I did. Doo doo DOO.

Who at Wixie is in on this? Possibly no one. The cloners are also hijacking the public airwaves. Maybe I'll call Saskia, casually, and see if someone's advertising an Explorer. Ten thousand dollars, I bet myself, the phone number is the same.

The stenciled numbers on the wall now say 90. Ninety-one. Ninety-two. And there's space 93.

Empty.

"What?" My astonished whisper hisses through the deserted garage. I cross my arms in front of me, staring at a six-by-ten area of concrete. It's marked parking space 93. Yellow stripes on each side. And in the middle? Nothing.

Nothing.

I trudge all the way back to the elevator. Bumming with every step. One hundred percent bummed. It was such a great idea. I jab the button with the black down arrow, preparing to tell Franklin I lost a glove or something. He's probably confirmed we got the video of the cloned VIN. Most likely he's so deep into texting, he won't even notice I've gone. A sigh escapes. For the last two weeks, I've assumed he was doing research, or checking with sources, or sharing love texts with Stephen. Turns out, he was plotting his career moves. In secret.

Why is this elevator taking so long? I punch the down button again, with a bit more force than necessary. "Don't forget your floor. You are on Floor Five," the sign reminds me again. I blink, staring back at the black words, white background. Floor

Five, it says. Not Foor Five.

Did someone fix it? Of course my brain instantly chooses the most unlikely alternative. Hands on hips, I stare at the sign. Only one answer. This is not the same elevator I came up in. And that means I'm in a different part of the garage than where I started. And in a different part of the garage than I should be. No wonder people can never find their cars. I turn, staring down the dusky rows of identical-looking car hoods and trunks and empty spaces. Seeing the confusion of twisting ramps and white pillars and neon arrows and ridiculous signs and double lanes.

Space number one, where the red Explorer was parked for the news conference, was empty when I checked. And I figured that's because they'd towed the car away. Which makes sense. But it may also be the space is empty because the car was never there.

Where did Franklin say the news conference was? Of course I don't have my phone, so I can't call and ask him. But. The news release is in my coat pocket.

"Ha!" I say it out loud. I unfold the white paper and see the solution. "Left side, space number one." I bet I'm on the right side. And by that, I mean the wrong side. Maybe I got turned around when I was dodging cars.

The elevator arrives. I hop on, jabbing the black button marked G over and over. The doors open on the ground floor. And there's Miss Bubble Gum in the ticket booth.

"Left side?" I say.

She lifts one bored finger and points. Across the garage. To the other bank of elevators.

I can barely see the bumper of our car through the array of lights outlining the garage entrance, but Franklin will be fine. I can get up, check out my theory and be back before he notices.

The elevator ride up is interminable. I drum my fingers on the waist-high brass railing encircling the elevator car. Maybe my theory is right after all. Nothing like a second chance. The elevator doors open on five left. I cross the fingers of both hands. And step out.

Space one, one-left, is empty here, too. Empty, except for a tiny scrap of black-and-yellow plastic curled in one corner.

I'm can't help myself. Now I'm almost running. Down the middle of the ramp, past more white pillars, past the lines of parked cars on each sides of the divided parking lot. Here the numbers have white borders, not black like the other side. Every few steps, I check the numbers. They're getting higher. The fifties. The sixties. The seventies.

Space 93.

I high-five the air. And I wish Franklin were here to see this.

This space is not empty. Blocky letters say 93. Two yellow lines along the sides. And in the middle? There's a blue Mustang.

I stare at it, mesmerized. If I'm right, this is the clone of Michael Borum's car. A car they stole. And the one they plan to sell. I take a step toward the shiny blue chassis, wondering if I can get close enough to it to check the VIN without setting off some kind of car alarm. Not that I know Borum's whole VIN by heart. But I could at least write it down.

I stop. Write it down with what? I left all my stuff in the car. I pat my coat pockets, pulling out the contents. The news release. A toothpick. A tan rubber band, covered with lint. A gum wrapper.

Fine. No problem. I'll run back to Franklin, get the car, drive back up here, copy down the VIN, get photos with the hidden camera, go back to the station, do our story, buy a dress for the Emmys and live happily ever after.

"Nice car, huh?"

Even without turning around, I can see him behind me. His body is reflected, distorted but distinct, in the Mustang's glossy blue paint job. My brain takes in the whole picture in a fraction of a second. Tall. Black parka. Sunglasses. Gloves.

Tamping down my fear — it's certainly just the car's owner — I turn with a friendly smile and a ready excuse. "Yes, I love Must—"

And then I stop. Now I see he's wearing sunglasses. Gloves. Levi's and grease-stained work boots. And no hat.

No Hat.

No-Hat is smiling, looking me up and down. There's not a flicker of recognition. He's either really good at acting or he has no idea who I am.

I wrench my expression back to normal, hoping he didn't notice my hesitation. All I can do is see where this goes. It's a public parking lot just before rush hour. He couldn't just shoot me. I put on a big smile. Because I have a little idea.

"I'm a big Mustang fan. Is this yours? Or are you just looking at it, too?" I use one hand to rake the bangs off my forehead, changing my hairstyle a bit, and also being the tiniest bit flirty. I pitch my voice a bit higher than natural. New England Valley girl. "I've really, really always wanted one. But I never found the right one. You know how it is."

I take a step or two toward the front of the Mustang. Toward the windshield. Maybe if I can keep him talking, I can get at least a glimpse of the VIN on the dashboard. But if he says this is his car, I'm going for more than that.

If he doesn't recognize me from TV — and he doesn't seem to — I might have a play here. After all, until now No-Hat and I have had a one-way-only relationship. I've seen him, plenty of times and in the most illegal of circumstances. I even have him on tape. I can easily find him at the Longmore Hotel. But he doesn't know that.

I hope.

No-Hat adjusts the collar of his waist-length parka, rolling his narrow shoulders.

"Yeah, it's mine," he says. He pushes his sunglasses to the top of his head, never taking his eyes off me. His black hair is so close cropped, it's a dark shadow. "You got a car here?"

Caw heah, he says. Southern? Not from Boston. Which may explain why he doesn't recognize me. Perfect.

"Oh, sure. But I'm a little lost? I think?" Then I go all little Red Riding Hood, pointing in the general direction of the elevator, but stepping even closer to the windshield. And closer to the VIN stamped on the dashboard. No-Hat is standing between me and freedom, but I have to see that VIN. If I leave, he'll move the car and we'll never find it again.

"And when I saw your car," I continue, "I had to stop and look. It's a real beauty. What year is it, anyway?"

No-Hat reaches into his pocket.

Uh-oh. Maybe he does recognize me. I imagine the gun that killed Michael Borum.

My heart lurches a beat. And lands in my stomach. I scan the garage behind him. Not one person. Not one moving car. Where are the pre–rush hour slackers when you need them?

And he pulls out a set of keys.

"It's last year's. And it's your lucky day. I'm selling it for way cheap," he says, dangling the keys at eye level. His eye level, which is higher than mine. "It's Windveil Blue. Aluminum wheels. Three hundred horsepower. V-8 engine. Five-speed. The whole nine yards. Zero to sixty in four seconds."

Huh? I look sincerely and suitably impressed.

"Cool," I say. "Is it really that fast?"

"Only one way to find out," No-Hat says. No. No. No way.

I laugh, a little throwaway ha-ha, and pretend I think he's joking. I'm pretty sure he doesn't recognize me from TV, and even if he did, it might not matter. But I have no desire to find the answer by driving away in a stolen Mustang with a possible murderer beside me.

"I'd love to maybe sit in the front seat, though," I say. This could be a dicey decision, but I won't close the car door. "Maybe I could turn on the engine?"

No-Hat pulls off one black wool glove, then the other, and stuffs them both into a jacket pocket. He takes the key ring, a narrow twist of silver, and turns one blue-plastic-topped key until it snaps free. Then he points a black electronic gizmo at the driver's-side door. And the door clicks open.

"There ya go, Miss . . ." He pauses. "I'm Doug. Doug . . . Skith."

Skith, I think. Clever. Because Smith sounds too made up.

"Jan," I reply. Because Jane sounds too made up. I take the key from Doug, who I still think of as No-Hat, and ease myself into the Mustang's creamy leather front bucket seat. I put one leg in the car, but leaving the car door open, I keep my other foot on the parking-lot pavement. In neutral territory.

Doug gets into the passenger seat. He swings both his legs inside. And he closes the door.

And I win. I can see the VIN number now, clear and precise, embossed on a metal plate inside the door frame. If we're right, that plate is a phony, printed with Michael Borum's VIN and attached by the No-Hat crew to this stolen car within the last few days. I memorize the last five numbers as I pretend to examine the fancy black-leather-covered dashboard. It's jazzy as a jet cockpit, covered with push buttons, red-numbered gauges and rows of tiny lights. The odometer says 21,203 miles.

"Go for it," Doug instructs, pointing both forefingers at me. "Get a feel for your new car."

Keeping my door open and one foot on safe ground, I turn the key. The engine whines, then roars, throbs, surprising me with its power. The seats vibrate. The seat belt alarm pings. Every light on the dashboard pulses red, then flashes to green. Music blares, speakers from all sides rattling the windows.

"Wow," I say, raising my voice over the thundering bass of sixties garage music. *Ra-*

dio. Drive Time. I can't let this car get away. It might be the proof of what happened to Michael Borum. What's more, a person almost certainly involved in Borum's murder might be sitting in the bucket seat beside me. I have about two minutes to think of something.

Doug flips the radio off, then waves a hand, gesturing me to close my door.

"Come on, Jan. Take a test-drive. You know you want to."

CHAPTER TWENTY-FOUR

"You know what?" I say. I twist the key off, pull it out of the ignition and hand it to Doug. "You should drive. It's too chancy. You know? For me to drive this."

Doug waves me off. "Hey. You want to buy it? You gotta drive it."

I plant both feet on the garage floor, extricating myself from the Mustang and, I can't help but think, from certain death. Semi-safely back on public property, I put both hands on the Windveil Blue roof and peer inside. Doug is still in the passenger seat, holding the ignition key.

"Too bad about the recall, huh?" I say. "You get the power steering fixed?"

This is pure fiction. But it might work. If it doesn't, I'm heading for the elevator. Zero to sixty in about one second.

"Recall?" Doug's brain is apparently sorting out possibilities of what this might mean. He finally gets it. "On this car?"

"Yeah, absolutely," I say, nodding sagely. "I did a bunch of research on these. Like I said, I'm in the market. And this one? At 21,000 miles? The power steering's gonna go."

If it could get my rented black Vallero recalled, I figure, it could do the same for a Mustang. A car's a car.

"I know how to check, though," I say. "Pop the hood."

It's a good thing this guy doesn't know me. If he did, this would be the moment he burst out laughing. I hope the hood lifts from the front and not the other way. I can't let him see what I hope to do. Thanks to Frick Jones at the Power House, I may be able to pull this off.

Doug, looking skeptical but curious, reaches across the stick shift and touches a square black button on the lower dashboard. There's a soft click. The hood pops open, just a fraction. And luckily, the latch is in the front. When I lift the hood completely, No-Hat Doug will not be able to see what I'm doing. But I should still keep him busy, just to make sure.

"Now, reach over and turn on the car," I say. "I have to see the engine idling."

I walk to the front of the car, briefly regretting the imminent demise of my black leather gloves to inevitable engine grease and wishing, madly, for a wrench. But ruined gloves are hardly life and death. The rest of this endeavor may be.

Attempting to channel Frick Jones, I lift up the hood and click the metal rod into place. And there's what I'm looking for. So far so good. I lean to the left, one hand still on the hood, checking on Doug. He's looking out the window, trying to see me.

"Perfect," I say. "Now, turn off the ignition. Then watch the steering wheel. Carefully. Keep an eye on it. See if it moves, even a little."

"Why?" he says.

"You just do it," I say, all twinkly and adorable. In our hidden-camera video, Doug is not actually taking part in the cloning or air-bag removal. And I'm hoping that's because he's only a valet parker, not a mechanic. If I'm lucky, maybe he's as clueless about car engines as I am.

"I told you I looked into this, right? I sure don't want to spend my hard-earned cash to buy a car with bum power steering."

The car is still vibrating under my hand. Under the already warm hood, I can see belts moving and a fan turning. Heat from the engine radiates onto my face. I feel flushed, and hot. Or maybe that's fear.

Then, everything stops. Belts, fan, heat, engine noise. He's cut the ignition. It's quiet. And now's my only chance.

"Watching the wheel?" I call out.

"Watching." Doug's muffled reply comes from inside the car.

Motor safely off and Doug, I hope, safely focused on the steering wheel, I tuck myself under the hood again. Doing the opposite of what Frick Jones demonstrated, I try to use my fingers to unscrew the nut connecting the thick black wire to the battery post.

It won't budge.

If this is going to work, I have just a few seconds.

I reach into my coat pocket and pull out that linty rubber band. Wrapping it around the nut for traction, like I do when the stubborn lid of a jar of spaghetti sauce won't open, I try to unscrew it again. I feel a tiny movement.

"Anything?" I call out to Doug.

"No," he calls back.

"Great," I reply. "One more minute. So far, looks like you're fine. Keep your eye on that wheel."

The nut moves. It turns. And it keeps turning. I lift the metal-connector thing from its stubby silver post, lay the black wire beside the battery and tuck the hexagonal nut in my coat pocket. Now, even if Doug knows how to fix it, he won't be able to. If I understood what Frick Jones was saying, this car ain't going anywhere. And, happily, I'll be long gone when Doug No-Hat "Skith" finds that out.

With a brief prayer to the journalism gods, I slam down the hood.

"Why are you so out of breath?" Franklin looks up from his texting as I slide into the front seat.

I ran the whole way to the car, terrified No-Hat was behind me. But no time to explain that now.

Franklin looks at his watch, then goes back to his BlackBerry, complaining while his two thumbs type at ultra-speed on the tiny keyboard. "And where the hell were you, Charlotte? Shopping?"

"Where's the little camera?" I say, ignoring him. My hands are shaking as I plow through my purse, digging for the notebook with Michael Borum's VIN. And I need my cell phone. My heart is pounding, my brain racing. I have to plan our next moves. And whether No-Hat is a savvy mechanic or not, this has all got to happen pretty darn fast.

"Why?" Franklin says.

He's still midtext, but at least he's looking at me.

"Really, Franko. Trust me on this, I'll tell you why on the way. Power up the camera. Give it to me and then we're going back into the garage. Fifth floor, left side. Same floor as the news conference. I'll show you where."

"But —"

"Franklin! Listen, just do it, please, okay?" I find the notebook. Yes. *Yes.* I think the VIN numbers are a match. We'll find out soon enough. I hit the green button on my cell, and punch three numbers. "Honest, I'll tell you everything in a second. But now we have to go. Go!"

"Y'all have lost it . . ." Franklin mutters as he pulls the minicamera from the console between us, flips out the screen and turns a silver wheel to lock it in record mode. Giving me a dubious look, he places the camera on my lap. He turns the key in the ignition, then looks back to me as I begin to speak. His face registers utter bafflement as I begin my phone performance.

"Is this 911? Yes, um, this is . . . well, anyway . . ." I make my voice high-pitched and whispery. Pretending I'm a frightened teenager. Or something like that. Anyone but me. "That blue Mustang that was just

430

stolen? That the cops are looking for? My boyfriend took it. And I know it's in the Garage at Fifty-Five Friend Street. Fifth floor left, space 93. He's wearing a black parka. But I think he's getting ready to leave. Don't tell him I told you."

I click the phone closed as we once again pull a parking-lot ticket from the automatic dispenser. Now we'll see if the cops arrive. And what happens after that.

Bubble-Gum Girl is oblivious as the metal arm rises to let us drive past. "Remember, fifth floor left, space 93. No, wait, go to the fifth floor. Then we'll decide what to do," I say, peering into the shadowy garage. Then I get an idea. "Let me have your hat."

"I'm not even going to ask," Franklin says. He pulls the black knit cap from his head and hands it to me.

We pull around the twisting ramps leading up onto the second floor. Flipping down the sun visor, I make sure all my hair is tucked under Franklin's cap. For as long as possible, I don't want Skith to recognize me. I wish I could wear my sunglasses to complete my semi-disguise, but I'll never be able to shoot video with them on.

By the time we hit floor three, I'm spinning out the story at light speed. I'm up to the part where I figure out the phone number indicates the address and the location of the stolen cars.

"It just hit me, you know? I guess it was when I saw the phone number on Bubble-Gum Girl's ticket booth."

"Who?" Franklin eases the car around another too-tight curve, avoiding a careening van full of teenagers. "I told you it wasn't a phone number."

No Windveil Blue Mustangs have passed us going the other way. And although this garage is an incomprehensible maze of curves, I'm pretty sure there's only one way out. Even if my scheme failed, Doug is still in the garage and on his way down. We could follow him. If my scheme worked, he's still in space 93. Trying to figure out why his car won't start.

"True, it wasn't a real phone number," I acknowledge. Franklin loves to be right as much as I do. I tell him about finally finding the Mustang and about the arrival of No-Hat. "He told me his name is Doug 'Skith,' can you believe it?"

"Because Smith sounds too made up?"

"That's what I thought, too." I look at my watch, frowning. "Do you hear sirens or anything?"

"Nope."

I tell Franklin the rest of the story, the

short version, as we drive, fast as we can, up the ramps. My tale ends with me assuring Doug his car is fine, giving him a fake e-mail address and letting him walk me to the elevator as if we had been on some blind date in bizarro-world. Thankfully, the elevator doors opened instantly for the first time in my life. I pushed the button for G with a vengeance, never so relieved to be headed for an exit.

"So, who knows what he did after that," I finish. "If my battery move was successful, he's probably pretty darn angry about now."

Finally I hear sirens.

"I guess we caught the same 911 call you did? Guy in a black parka, stolen Mustang?" I'm talking to Lieutenant Henry Zavala. The camera viewfinder is still up to my eye, no need to hide it, and I'm rolling on every bit of the cops' shakedown of an irate and fuming Doug Skith. Zavala, head of the Auto Theft Unit, is overseeing the operation.

"We were still in the neighborhood, so we got here pretty fast. So what's the skinny? This a stolen car? Or what? That guy under arrest? Seems like you all are having a big day at the parking lot."

"Could be," Zavala says, answering most of my questions at once. He shrugs his narrow shoulders, then adjusts his chunky black utility belt. Radio. Nightstick. Big gun sticking out of a snapped holster. "Guy told us this is not his car. We're holding him, under suspicion, while we run the plate."

I forgot to look at the Mustang's license plate. I wonder whose it really is.

"Thanks," I say, moving so I can get a better shot of the rear of the car. "Let me know."

Two black-and-white Boston police cruisers are blocking the Mustang into space 93. Sirens off, blue lights making glaring swirls on the shiny parked cars and flashes of shadow on the concrete walls. The arrival of the police has made it one-lane-only up and down the parking-lot ramp. A cadet cop in an orange cap officiously waves rubbernecking drivers past the scene.

Doug, legs spread, arms splayed and palms against the hood, is leaning up against a third police cruiser. Luckily, his face is planted in the roof of the car, so he hasn't seen me in my new role. So far. A blue-uniformed officer pats him down, checking his parka, his blue jeans, his work boots.

"No car keys," the officer calls out.

Another cop sits in the cruiser's front seat, typing on the keyboard of a computer affixed to the dashboard.

"Let me get a shot of you talking to the police," Franklin, standing behind me, whispers. "This'll be great in our story."

I hand Franklin the camera, still rolling.

"We may have a problem," I say.

"What problem?" Franklin's pointing the lens at Doug, who's still spread-eagle against the car.

The computer-clicking officer hauls himself out of the front seat, shaking his head. "Plates are clear. No reports of this car as stolen." He moves his hat with one hand, scratches underneath with the other, then looks at Zavala.

"That problem," I mutter. "They've certainly got this covered, they use plates from another matching car or something. This car's not gonna show up as stolen. That's part of the scam. It's why it works. It's a clone."

"Ya run the VIN?" Zavala asks.

"Doing it." The officer ducks back into the car.

"I see what you mean." Franklin's voice is low. "The VIN's not going to come back as stolen, either."

"I told you it wasn't my car," No-Hat yells into the police-car roof, slapping one of his flat palms against the white metal. "You have to let me go. I got rights."

One officer answers him, hand on his weapon, leaning close to his prisoner and saying something I can't hear. Apparently it was effective. Skith says no more.

"Right," I answer Franklin. I press my lips together, trying to think over the rising cacophony of blaring car horns, angry motorists annoyed at having their ride home delayed.

"They're not going to be able to arrest him," I say, my heart sinking with the realization that we're seeing, up close and on video, how diabolical this cloning scheme actually is. Even when police officers actually find a stolen car, they'll have no idea it's stolen. "When they run the VIN, they'll find — wait."

"What?" Franklin asks. "You figure out something?"

"Lieutenant Zavala," I say, raising my voice over the honking and giving Franklin a surreptitious thumbs-up. "Can we get a close-up shot? We need to see the VIN number."

"VIN's clear," the computer cop calls from his front seat. "Not on the stolen-car list."

"Let me go, you jerks." Skith is now performing in full wronged-innocent-citizen mode. "Police brutality. This is not my car.

436

I'm not stealing it. I didn't steal it. I was walking here. I was only looking at it. It's a free country. Whatever. Let me go!"

I take Franklin's arm, not waiting for Zavala's reply, and head both of us toward the VIN. Franklin moves closer to the car's windshield, camera pointing in the right direction. We've got to get shots of those numbers for our story. Plus, if the police let Skith go, our proof goes with him. He'll send some crony back to retrieve the not-stolen car. Game over.

"Loot?" the cop next to Skith calls out, waving him over. "We holding this guy as a suspect?"

"Lieutenant Zavala?" I call out, waving him toward me. "Please? First? Listen, quick question for you."

Zavala assesses the increasingly infuriated Doug, then looks back at me, then back at Doug. He holds up one finger to the officer by the cruiser, signaling.

"Stand by one, Hartwell," he says.

"Listen, Lieutenant," I say. He's giving me one minute, too. I dig into the purse that's slung over my shoulder, searching for the notebook that's inside. "I know this is off the wall. But remember the carjacking in the South End? The murder? The blue Mustang? The one where —"

"This is not that car, Miss McNally. That car was destroyed in a fire."

I swallow hard, nodding. Turning the pages in my spiral notebook. "I know. Exactly. But please, check this car's VIN again. Not against the stolen-car list. I'm telling you, it'll come back as the destroyed blue Mustang. And that guy?" I point my notebook toward Doug. "He's lying. He's part of the whole operation. And told me it was his car. He even let me inside. He's got the keys somewhere. He must."

Zavala looks me up and down, his face the picture of disbelief. "He let you inside this car? When?"

I hold up the notebook, pleading my case.

"See this number? It's the VIN of the destroyed Mustang. Take this. Compare this Mustang's VIN to the number I've written down."

"Lieutenant?" The officer calls out again. "Make it fast, sir. Mr. Skith is asking for a lawyer now."

CHAPTER TWENTY-FIVE

"He's stashed the keys somewhere. I'm sure of it." I touch Zavala's arm with one hand, drawing his attention back to me. "Can you have your officer look for them one more time?"

Franklin's shooting pictures of me talking with Zavala. Which means he's got enough of the VIN.

"We patted him down." Zavala says. "Suspect says it's not his car. We found no keys. Maybe he's telling the truth. Maybe the 911 call was bogus. Happens every day, Charlie."

This is bad. Switching to my first name, sympathetic and friendly, means he's about to end our conversation. Plus, of course, I know the 911 call was bogus. My time is running out.

"How about, maybe, look in the wheel well?" It's a last-ditch idea, but certainly the cloners heard how the cops identified the carjacked Explorer. And now it's in their heads, like it is in mine. Since Doug doesn't have the keys on him, he certainly knows where they are. Maybe he hid them, just in case, when he heard the sirens.

"You don't give up, do you?" Zavala shrugs, the beginnings of a smile appearing for the first time. He cocks his head toward the car. "I'll give you a shot, Charlie. Let's take a look."

"Franklin?" I say. I open my eyes extra wide, signaling potential success, and spiral my forefinger. *Roll tape.* We've got to get this on camera.

I briefly remember, with regret, I'm still wearing Franklin's stupid hat.

"Let's see that notebook now," Zavala says. He points me toward the windshield as I hand him my notes. "Now. You read me the VIN from the Mustang dashboard."

I get through all seventeen numbers before Zavala says a word.

"Hartwell?" Zavala looks toward the officer guarding Skith, calling out across the Mustang. "We'll need another moment here. You're sure he has no car keys? Check again, Officer."

I see Officer Hartwell begin another pat down. But since I'm right here anyway, I lean over and run my hand under the left-

440

front wheel well.

Nothing.

And then, something.

I stand, pulling out my empty hand. I look at Franklin, then at Zavala.

"I think you're both going to want to see this," I say.

Minutes later, Skith is in handcuffs.

I see Franklin is getting video of the whole arrest. I hope we're not running out of tape.

"So you found some car keys." Skith is spitting fire. "Who the frig says they belong to me?"

"Give it up, Skith," Lieutenant Zavala says. "We'll find your prints inside the car. Soon as we open it. Hartwell?"

The officer is now carrying a flat black plastic box, size of an anchorwoman's makeup kit. He puts the case on the garage floor and flips open two latches. The outside of the box is labeled PRINTS.

Another officer is unlocking the passenger-side door with the keys they retrieved from the wheel well.

"Plus, Miss McNally here says you tried to sell her this car." Zavala's voice is mocking, sardonic, as he gestures toward me. "And she tells me you let her get behind the wheel."

"Miss McWho?" Skith matches the sneer.

"I never saw her before."

I hold back the supreme temptation to whip off my cap and fluff out my hair like the heroine in some romance thriller. "Now do you recognize me?" I'd demand. It would be even more dramatically effective if I used some sort of exotic accent. But I restrain myself. And Skith, or whatever his name really is, already recognized me anyway. I watched his face change when he saw me with the camera. That reaction, even he couldn't keep secret.

"Your odometer says 21,203 miles," I say, keeping my voice calm.

"You could have seen that through the window," he retorts.

"Your radio's on Wixie," I say.

"Big deal, so's everyone's," he replies.

"And your car won't start." I can't help smiling.

"What?" Skith says, his voice rising. "How'd —" He stops. Clamps his mouth closed.

"What?" Zavala says.

"Yeah," I say, drawing out the word. "Try it."

"Hartwell." Zavala gestures to the officer who's sitting in the front seat and dusting for prints. "Turn on the engine."

"Huh?" the cop replies.

"Do it," Zavala says.

We hear the hiss as the exiting traffic behind us continues to leave the garage. We hear a few honks from annoyed drivers. We hear the sounds of a too-loud radio blaring through open car windows.

But when Officer Hartwell turns the key, we hear nothing.

Hartwell tries again.

Nothing.

"Pop the hood," I say. "You'll find one battery wire's disconnected."

I dig into my pocket. And then I bring out a little silver hexagonal nut, offering it in the outstretched palm of my gloved hand.

"You'll need this to fix it."

I trot after Lieutenant Zavala as he heads back to his cruiser, stationed in a yellow-striped no-parking corner of the garage. The engine's running, the blue wig-wags are flashing, there's a cadet at the wheel.

"Remember, Lieutenant, you wouldn't have this story without me. You'd have let him go, right? So the least you can do is hold off."

Zavala stops. Turns around. Crosses his arms. And looks at me.

"What?" I say. I stop, too. I can't read his expression.

"I'm sure you're aware, Miss McNally, that a fraudulent 911 call is a misdemeanor, punishable by a two-hundred-dollar fine."

I actually do know that. And I see where he might be going with this. It's not a good place. I stall. "So?"

"Anything you'd like to confess?"

"Heavens, no," I say, doing my best innocent look. My fake phone voice was pretty high-quality. Then I remember the best defense is a good offense. "All I'm saying is, there are no other reporters here. We're working on a big story. It'll be on — soon. Really soon. And if you'd keep this to yourself? For, like, a few days?"

Zavala's expression hasn't changed.

I slump my shoulders and stare at an oil spot on the garage floor, sensing imminent journalism disaster. Maybe I sacrificed our story to let the cops arrest Skith. But I couldn't just let him get away. My stupid conscience wouldn't let me ignore that catching the bad guy and potentially stopping a deadly scam is more important than our exclusive story. Even though we solved the case, not Boston's finest.

A car zooms toward us, the last of the rush hour, then cuts its speed in half at the flashing blue lights. I watch it go by, dejected. I solved this. I uncovered a major criminal enterprise, got photos of the entire operation, figured out a pretty clever code and tricked the bad guy into giving himself away. And now, the cops will get all the credit.

Zavala clears this throat. "Miss McNally?"

"What?" I try to keep the petulance from my voice. After all, Zavala is on the side of justice. And I guess that's what matters. Maybe they can get Doug to rat out the mastermind of this deal. Who that is, I admit, I still don't have a clue.

"Off the record?" He raises one eyebrow and doesn't wait for me to agree to the deal. "We'll need a few days to investigate this. And it would — perhaps — be beneficial to our case to keep the information about Mr. Skith under wraps from the press for, say, a week or so. Maybe more."

I see light at the end of the parking garage.

Zavala puts a hand to his forehead, shading his eyes, and pretends to look back and forth, as if he's scouting the area. "I don't see any of your cohorts around here. Do you? And, I suppose, it's not in the best interest of law enforcement for us to inform them of what transpired this afternoon."

I hold out my arms, so delighted my impulse is to hug him. Then I instantly drop them. There's no hugging in journalism.

"Thanks, Lieutenant," I say. "I owe you."

"Nope," he replies. "We owe you."

"So then Zavala promised he'd hold off," I say to Kevin. The last of the Doug Skith arrest video has rolled by on the playback monitor in the news director's office. I reach across him, push Eject and retrieve our prized cassette. "Great, huh? We have a week. Which is totally doable."

"We still have to move fast," Franklin says. "We'll bang out a draft script tomorrow."

"We can do it," I add. "Of course, we still don't know who's behind the cloning conspiracy, but —"

" 'Cloning Conspiracy.' That's a possible title," Kevin interrupts. He pauses, looking between me and Franklin, apparently trying to read our expressions. He holds up both palms, admitting defeat. "Okay, fine. Maybe not."

"I'll dub the minicam video to a regular tape tonight," J.T. says, holding out his hand for the videotape. "Gimme that puppy."

I hand him the little yellow cassette, then plop down on Kevin's tweed couch, my boots stretched out in front of me. I'm wiped. Josh and Penny will be waiting dinner. My feet hurt. And my brain hurts. I link my fingers on top of my head, thinking.

"The blue Mustang and the red Explorer

are both in police custody. So they're not going anywhere." I try to organize the elements of our story. "But, you know? There's one more missing piece. Besides who's in charge of it all."

The room is silent for a beat.

"Oh. You're right," Franklin finally says.

"As usual," I say without looking at him.

"What?" Kevin says.

"Well, we know the original red Explorer belongs to us. We also know that's safely downstairs in the station garage. But someone's missing a blue Mustang. Right? That car the cops impounded today at Fifty-Five Friend? The clone of Michael Borum's car? It's a stolen car. It belongs to someone. Where did it come from?"

"Listen, Charlotte . . ." Franklin gets up from his chair and motions toward the door. "Let's go back upstairs. I'll see if I can get my cop source to check out the stolen-car reports. I think she'll do it for me. And she's on the late shift."

"And we need to find the owners of Beacon Trust," I say. "Any news on that?"

Kevin's phone rings, interrupting Franklin's response. He checks his watch. "Got to take this, team," he says, picking up the receiver and swiveling his chair away from us. "Keep me posted."

"New York, I bet," I whisper to Franklin. We push open the glass office door. And then I remember what happened this morning. And what else is going to happen soon.

"Creep. Quitter. Short-timer." I poke Franklin in the back as I follow him upstairs to our office.

"You could come, too," Franklin says over his shoulder.

"Right."

Even from down the hall, I can see the red message light on my phone is blinking. Probably Josh, wondering where the heck I am. Happily, I'll be able to tell him I'll be home in half an hour. And I'll be able to share the blazingly good news about our story.

Franklin clicks onto his computer, pulling up his enviable compilation of alphabetically indexed phone numbers and e-mails.

I'll also be able to share the blazingly bad news about Franklin. I sit in my own desk chair, one ankle propped on my knee, staring at Franklin's back. Wondering who'll take his place. Some burned-out hotshot from the network, ready to rest on his laurels in local TV? Or a twentysomething up-and-comer, all ego and self-importance, burbling about Edward R. Murrow but clueless about the real world? I pick at the zipper of my boot, yanking it aimlessly up and down. I'm doomed.

I stare at my leg. A white thing is sticking out of my left boot.

Oh. Right. My paycheck from WWXI. I pull the now almost-damp folded white envelope from inside my boot. It's been there for the last four hours or so and it's somewhat the worse for wear. The edges of the little clear window are beginning to fray. But I guess the bank will still cash the check inside.

"Hey. Charlotte." Franklin swivels around, his eyes shining. "Listen to this."

"What?" I say, peeling back the envelope's flap. It sticks, so I get just a corner. Yanking open my desk drawer, I search through the salt-and-pepper packets, pennies and dimes, and loose Advils for a letter opener. Do I even have a letter opener?

"Here," Franklin says. He hands me a thin silver point set into a leather handle.

Of course. "Thanks."

"But wait, before you open that. Look here. It's major." He points to his monitor. He's got an e-mail open. "My guy at the AG's office is tracking down the real owner of Beacon Trust. He tells me all the legal documents are carefully set up to hide who it is. But for grins, he decides to look up

449

what else the trust owns besides the valet company. Check it out, my little Emmy winner."

He points to the screen. "See? Beacon Trust also owns . . . ?"

I squint at the screen, scooting my chair closer. Then my eyes widen. I turn to Franklin. The blue-and-white e-mail is reflected in his glasses. His smile is unending.

"The Garage at Fifty-Five Friend Street?" I say. "Whoa."

"Yup," he says. "They own the valet company. They own the garage."

"Fantastic." I nod. "Two for two. And that's no coincidence, Franko. That's a link in the chain."

"They swipe the cars through the valet service. They clone them in the Newtonville garage," he says. "And then they stash 'em in their own parking lot while they wait to sell them."

"No pesky traceable tickets from Bubble-Gum Girl's machine, no parking fees, just stolen cars hidden in plain sight." I think back over what I discovered today, the phone numbers as directions.

"And giving that fake phone number on the radio," Franklin adds, reading my mind. "Everything they did was boring, ordinary and mundane."

"Until they got sloppy. And got nailed by a leftover parking pass."

"Poetic justice," Franklin says, nodding.

"Karma." I smile at my lame joke. "You know, with a *C*. Bad car-ma."

I slide the point of the letter opener under a little gap in the WWXI envelope. With a flourish, I slit open my paycheck and wave the pale blue paper in Franklin's direction. "At least we know our last story will be a memorable one. You can come back for the Emmys. And hey, this paycheck from Wixie will buy your farewell dinner."

"You rich?" Franklin asks. "Lots of money in radio? We finally going to splurge at Rialto?"

"Not the way Maysie tells it," I say. "This'll probably be enough for Burger City."

I look at the little box with the dollar amount. And then I stare at the check.

"That bad?" Franklin says. "I'm going to have to buy the burgers myself?"

But it's not the amount that's got me speechless. It's the imprint on the check.

WWXI Radio, it says in the upper left corner.

And beneath that, the name of the station's parent company.

I turn the check toward Franklin, pointing

at the corner.

And now Franklin's speechless, too.

I turn the check back to me. "Beacon Trust. Owns the valet company. And the garage. And, according to this, it also owns Wixie radio."

"Wow," Franklin says. "The trifecta."

"Better," I say. Although I have no idea what's better than whatever a trifecta is. I do have an idea who the person is who owns WWXI radio, and who, as a result, must be a kingpin in Beacon Trust. In fact, I know it perfectly well.

Loudon Fielder. Bexter bigwig Loudon Fielder.

CHAPTER TWENTY-SIX

The blinking red message light on my phone might as well be my conscience. I know it's Josh. He and Penny will be waiting for me. He'll be wondering where I am. But problem is, no way I'm going home in half an hour. I've got to track down Loudon Fielder.

"You think Fielder knows Beacon Trust has turned into a triple-threat rip-off machine?" I reach for the receiver, my engagement ring taking over the conscience role. The receiver doesn't quite make it to my ear as I see Franklin clicking off his computer.

"Hey, Franko, what's with the log-off?" I point the phone at him. "Don't we have to track down the mastermind? See what the elegant Mr. Fielder has to say for himself? I say we head out to his house and —"

"Tomorrow, maybe," Franklin says, shaking his head. "Nothing gained by doing it now. You're tired. I'm tired. A lot happened today."

Now who's tuned out? I don't say that out loud.

The phone makes a *bee-bah* noise, reminding me I haven't retrieved my message from Josh. I hold down the hang-up button with one finger. I stare at Franklin, waiting.

Franklin looks at the floor. Then at his watch.

"I've got to meet with the New York people," he says.

"Oh, ho. Now the truth comes out." I can't resist teasing him. But I have to admit, even though I'm eager to take down Loudon Fielder, nailing our big scoop really can wait until tomorrow. And I should let him be excited about his new job. Dear Franklin deserves his success. Tough as it is to lose him, I'm proud of him.

"See you tomorrow, Big Apple Man," I say, turning back to the phone. I punch in my message-retrieval code. In twenty minutes, it'll be me, Josh, Penny, Botox, wine, a fire and carryout sushi. I can look at the wedding magazines Mom sent. Check on baby Maddee. Start my own new life, which is just as exciting. The message begins.

It's not from Josh.

After I hear the message, I hit the code to

454

replay it yet again. Maybe this time I'll understand it.

"This is Carter, the temp secretary at Headmaster Byron Forrestal's office?"

Okay, that's the easy part. I guess they hired a new Dorothy. A midwestern-sounding, youngish-sounding man.

"The Headmaster would like to chat with you, Ms. McNally? Perhaps this evening at his home?"

The first time through, this part sent me into a panic. I'd grabbed my cell, ready to call Josh and make sure nothing was wrong with him. Or Penny. But I put the phone away by the end of the next sentence.

"He's heard about your 'where are they now' project? And he'd like to discuss it with you."

Damn. I'm summoned to the principal's office. I'm forty-seven years old, and being summoned to the principal's office. Because he found out I was lying. Why did I ever think telling Harrison Ebling I was doing a feature story was such a brilliant idea? I've talked myself into a very awkward corner. And I hope I haven't put Josh into an embarrassing or job-threatening situation. All I need.

"Say, eight-thirty tonight? At the cottage? He'll expect you."

I push the code for save, even though the stupid message is now imprinted in my brain, and slowly hang up the phone. Did Ebling rat me out? To get me in trouble? Or was he chitchatting with the Head and happened to mention my so-called project?

Or maybe. Maybe he was warning the Head about something he might want to keep covered up.

I lean back in my chair, lifting one boot, then the other, onto the top of my desk.

I'm an idiot.

I close my eyes, remembering the Head's elaborately furnished cottage, the dimly soft sconce lighting, the hazy glow of flickering candles. The museum-quality antiques. The expensive heirlooms. A modestly paid school administrator, after all, living in a "cottage" full of treasures? He knew exactly which students left Bexter. And when. And, maybe, why. Maybe he's been extorting the students' families for years. That's how he bankrolls his patrician lifestyle. It would be a snap for him to make threatening calls. Just close the door of his sumptuous office and pick up the phone.

He killed Dorothy when she somehow found out. She died the night of his party. He probably drugged her. Maybe with his own brandy and those sleeping pills.

The Head killed Alethia, too. Pushed her down the stairs. He was at Bexter that night, as well.

And now. He's luring me to his house.

I open my eyes.

He's luring me to his house?

I clunk my boots down the to the floor and grab my coat. Absurd. The Head can't hurt me. My car will be in his driveway. I'll call Josh and tell him where I am. I slam one arm through my coat sleeve and shrug the coat into place. I'll call Franklin and leave a message. I'll call Maysie. Detective Joe Cipriani. J.T. Shaw. There's a whole list of names I could call.

List of names. The names.

What if the others circled on Dorothy's list had the same secret as Fiona and Randall?

I wrap my long knitted scarf around my neck, then loop it again, thinking.

Where did Fiona say she gave up her daughter? The — Center?

The Services. I loosen my scarf and, coat still on, sit back down at my desk, telepathically communicating with my computer to hurry up and get me Google.

"Adoption services Boston." I say it out loud as I type. My search takes .38 seconds. And first on the list is "The Services," Edgemere Street, Boston. Another click shows me a quietly dignified Web site, dark blue and soft green, all twisty vines and scrolled leaves and muted graphics. A simple logo that looks like a swaddled baby encircled by loving arms. There's a boldface quote across the top: "For 75 years, we've served those in need. Confidential. Caring. And Compassionate," says Executive Director Joan Covino.

I almost fall off the chair, digging into my purse for my notebook. I nearly tear the pages, searching for my notes from Dorothy's files. I need to see the name, but I don't really need to confirm it. I remember the Bexter board member who recommended Harrison Ebling for the job. Whose letter indicated he's done a "successful" long-term project for the Services.

Joan Covino is on the Bexter board. She's the executive director of The Services. Sure, Harrison Ebling did a wonderfully successful job on their fundraising. What a windfall when the Bexter job appeared. All he had to do was scour The Services' confidential adoption files, then cook up a little extra fundraising on the side. For himself.

He manipulated frightened victims into telling their spouses a concocted story about a nonexistent drug scandal, knowing they'd pay anything to protect their children. Their real goal was to keep their past a secret.

Dorothy discovered his circled list of targets. She took it. And she confronted him with it. First he made the phone calls to frighten her. And then he killed her.

He killed Alethia, too. Maybe he knew Dorothy had told her his secret. Maybe she showed Alethia his circled names. She was the next to get a phone call. She was the next to die.

Still wearing my winter coat and wrapped in my scarf, I stare at my computer screen. I stare so long that the screen goes black. I stare into the darkness as a particularly menacing picture begins to take shape in my imagination.

I'm the next one who saw the list. And what did I do? I showed it to Harrison Ebling. And sinking deeper into my own quicksand, I told him I'd circled the names myself. He's the only person left in the world who instantly knew that was not true.

No wonder Ebling never called me back with the information. And then Josh asked about the drug scandal. Which, of course, was Ebling's own fabrication. He must suspect I'm on the trail. And so is Josh.

I have to tell the Head.

Even in my coat, I'm suddenly chilly. I

draw my woolly scarf closer. Why isn't there an undo key in real life?

"Hey, gang, where is everyone? Josh? Penny? Annie? Whoever gets this, call me on my cell, okay?" I'm holding my cell phone between my ear and my scarf while navigating the treacherous reverse curves of Storrow Drive. Rows of balconied brownstones, blocks of Back Bay mansions on elegant side streets speed by as I dodge belligerent Boston motorists who don't want to let me merge into their too-narrow lanes. Across the shimmering Charles River, a constellation of lights forms a twinkling outline around the historic buildings of MIT. It's all a blur. All I care about is finding a real person and not an answering machine.

No one answers at home. Josh is not answering his cell. Penny's not answering hers. Not even Annie is picking up.

It's past eight o'clock. Where is everyone?

I need to tell Josh to stay away from Harrison Ebling. He's already killed two people who got in his way. What if Josh is next in line? What if they're together now? What if Josh is Ebling's next target? My insistence on investigating what happened at Bexter has put my darling Josh in danger. And he has no idea. Undo. Undo.

"Moron!" I yell, in frustration and fear, at some idiot in a white Ombra. He swerves around me, pulling ahead of my Jeep with inches to spare. My brain swerves, too. That Ombra is like Annie's. Where are Penny and Annie?

Driving with one hand and punching in speed dial, I try every number again. Home. Josh. Penny. Annie. Nothing. No answer. No one.

"Call me," I say over and over. "Call me. I'm going to the Head's."

I'm going to tell him all I know. I hope I'm right.

"Come in, it's open."

I lift the ornate lion's head, the brass knocker on the Head's lacquered front door, and tap it twice. Byron Forrestal's distinctive accent filters through the heavy door. Within moments, I'm inside. With a turn of a knob and a soft click, the door closes behind me.

"Mr. Forrestal?" Standing, tentative, in the soft light of the foyer, I'm not sure whether I'm supposed to wait or follow the Head's voice into the house. The cottage smells of cinnamon, and the woodsy burn of a newly lit fire.

"In the living room, Miss McNally." An

461

instruction, not an invitation.

Three or four steps down the hallway, my boots muffled by the muted Oriental rug, the fragrance of the fire is more pungent. As I reach the elaborately filigreed archway leading to the living room, I remember it all. Sconces. Candles. A comfortably elegant couch, two burnished leather club chairs opposite. A decanter of brandy and a silver tray of biscuits on the mahogany coffee table. Crouching in front of the fireplace, his back to me, the Head is using a poker to stir the logs that are stacked, snapping with blue-orange flames, in the oversize redbrick fireplace. He's in his usual herringbone blazer.

"Mr. Forrestal?" Standing on the edge of the room, I'm not quite sure what to do. The "where are they now" story I oh-so-cleverly fabricated is about to disintegrate into the lie it always was. But the Head will forget about that once I warn him about Ebling's treachery.

The Head rises from his crouch and turns, fireplace poker in hand.

But it's not the Head. It's Harrison Ebling.

A smiling, supercilious gray-haired killer with a hot poker in his hand.

In the Head's living room?

Of course. He and the Head are in it together. One had the idea, the other had the access to information. One had the plan, the other had the opportunity. One needed a job, the other needed the money. And if any outsider began to suspect one of them, the other could instantly cover it up.

They're a deadly double team. And now I'm their biggest threat.

"Hey, Harrison," I say. I attempt an expression that's somewhere between polite and curious, all the while scouting to see if I should make a dash out the front door. I glance down the hall to see if the Head is creeping up behind me with some sort of deadly weapon. As if a guy with a hefty cast-iron poker isn't threatening enough. I consider my personal weaponry. I could clonk him with my purse. Stab him with a lip liner. Spray him with hair spray. Pitiful.

"I was supposed to meet the Head here," I say, backing away. The front door is looking pretty tempting. My only real weapon is deception. "But if he's not here, I can always come back tomorrow. I told Josh I'd only be here for a little while, so . . ."

Ebling surprises me. He replaces the poker in a brass and wrought-iron holder in front of the crackling fire, then waves me toward the couch, the picture of a pleasant and gracious host. It's difficult to imagine this rabbity middle-aged pencil pusher as desperate extortionist and murderer.

"Oh, please, Miss McNally," he says. "Hope you didn't mind my little joke. Byron always gets a kick out of my impersonations. The Head is upstairs. I'm to offer you biscuits and brandy. You know Byron. That's his tradition."

Byron? That seems off. Maybe I'm wrong.

"Now, take off your coat and sit, please. I was just going, but Byron didn't want me to leave you alone. As it happens, I have that list of names and addresses from the fundraising report for you," he continues.

He pats the breast pocket of his jacket, then pulls out a piece of white paper, folded in thirds. He flips open the paper, holding it up so I can see it. It does look like typed names and addresses.

Am I wrong about Ebling? I take a tentative step or two toward the couch, slowly unwinding my scarf and placing my coat and purse on the upholstered cushions. If he's actually going to give me the list — is he? — he's not the blackmailer. But if it's not Harrison Ebling, or Harrison and the Head, then who made the phone calls? Who killed Dorothy and Alethia?

"See if this is what you need." Ebling hands me the paper, then fills two crystal snifters with overly generous portions of the amber-colored brandy. He sets the cut-crystal decanter back onto an ornate silver tray.

"Oh, no brandy for me," I say, perching on the edge of the couch. There are only two names and addresses on the list. Fiona Dulles. And Randall Kindell. The people I've already talked to. This is no co-incidence. Is it? My cell phone is in my purse. I could look at my watch and pretend I had to make a phone call. I could use the phone on the end table. Then get the heck out of here.

"Don't be silly," Harrison says. He's holding one snifter toward me. The other is cupped in his hand.

If the Head is on his way down, why are there only two glasses? Ebling said he was about to leave. So why did he pour himself a megashot of brandy? Or maybe that's for the Head.

I give the decanter a dubious look. I take the glass he's offering me and put it on the table. No chance I'm drinking one bit of this stuff.

"To your 'where are they now' project." Ebling lifts his snifter toward me, toasting.

So that glass isn't for the Head. Where is he?

Ebling takes a sip of brandy. I don't. The only sound is the hissing crackle of the fire. If the Head is now tiptoeing downstairs with a gun or something, I'm outnumbered, outmaneuvered and potentially out of luck. And farther away from the front door than I was just minutes ago.

Or I may just have a way-too-vivid imagination. From working in TV news too long.

Be that as it may. It's not my imagination that two people are dead. I don't want to be next. I reach across the couch for my purse. I'm heading for the door.

"You may be wondering about the rest of the names," Ebling says. Smiling, he sits down on the couch, between me and my purse, and pats his pocket again. This time, he pats a different pocket. "We have those, too."

We? What if the Head is waiting by the front door? To — somehow — stop me from leaving? If I run I could be in even more trouble.

Ebling's so close I can smell the fragrant brandy he's swirling his glass. See the gray stubble on his cheeks and chin. See a few tiny reddish-brown spots on his yellow tie. I place my glass on the coffee table and stand, moving toward the fire.

"Chilly," I say, edging away from him. This is not good.

"True," he replies. He stands up, coming elbow to elbow with me in front of the fireplace.

He's too close. The fire is too hot. I loosen the scarf around my neck. *Call me. Call. Me.* I send ESP messages to Josh, to Penny, to Annie, to everyone I called. All my dear ones who I'm beginning to fear I may never see again. My eyes well, and it's not the heat.

"I suppose you're wondering about Byron," he says. He takes another sip of brandy.

"As a matter of fact, I was." I'm trying to back up but I'm trapped between the couch, the coffee table, the fire and a mousy accountant who seems to be developing into another kind of animal altogether. A scary one.

"Truth is," Ebling says, "he is indeed upstairs. However. He will not be coming down. Our Byron was so despondent that you discovered his secret little financial stratagem that he killed himself. It's very sad," Ebling says, as if he's relating the plot of a movie, "because he could never have regained his reputation, let alone abide for the rest of his life in prison for three murders. He went upstairs to his room. And used his little antique pistol. Such a tragedy."

He pauses. With a flourish, he hands me my brandy glass, urging it on me like a gracious host from hell.

"So I fear you won't be having your meeting about your little project."

I instantly recognize his voice as "Carter the temp." And Ebling did a perfect imitation of the Head. I guess he's right. He's good at voices.

Oh. Which allowed him to hide his identity when he made the phone calls. And he said "three" murders.

Three. Did he and the Head kill Josh?

Am I next? I'm next. My throat closes. My brain spins, racing to get ahead of whatever is about to happen. Do I run for the door? Couch, coffee table, fire, Ebling.

"But now," Ebling continues, sounding like himself again, "the least I can do is show you that list of names you wanted so much."

He gestures at the snifter I'm holding.

"Byron did have one last glass of his very nice brandy," he says. He steps toward me. "Which you may also want to do."

He reaches inside his pocket again.

Of course there's no list. There's a gun. Pointing at me.

CHAPTER TWENTY-SEVEN

Couch, coffee table, fire, Ebling.

I've only got one idea.

The fire.

"No!" I yell. I crash the crystal snifter, hard as I can, into the crackling fire. With a hot whoosh of heat, the alcohol-fueled flames flare from the fireplace. Harrison leaps back, jumping away to escape the licking orange.

I grab the heavy decanter from the coffee table. With a cry of something that even I can't translate, I smash the crystal toward him, hitting his neck and lower jaw. Sticky, pungent brandy spills from the bottle, dousing my hands and Ebling's clothing and the rug beneath us. Ebling wails, outraged, and I hop in pain and surprise, frantically patting away spitting flames from the brandy spatters on his clothing.

I throw my scarf around his neck, pulling, pulling, pulling with every ounce of my strength. The soft loop of knitted fabric tightens, yanking Ebling off balance. Before he can untangle himself, I wrench the scarf, fabric straining and murderer howling, down toward the floor.

The heat from the fire is more intense than ever. It seems closer. Hotter.

The crack of Ebling's head against the coffee table, a thunk of skull against solid mahogany, is as shockingly loud as the silence that follows.

The gun drops from his open hand. I kick it out of the way with a sweep of my boot. It spins across the rug and slides under the couch, just the barrel showing. Keeping my eyes on the motionless Ebling, I move to try to pick it up.

And then I see I have another problem.

The fire.

Rivulets of flame travel across the Oriental rug, devouring the tight weave and turning the elaborate maroon and emerald designs into monochrome crusting black. Some alcohol-fueled flames are licking at the pleated skirt of the upholstered couch. The camel fabric begins to streak with smoke. The air is a suffocating, thickening gray, sweet with the brandy fragrance, acrid with burning fabric. I stomp my boots at the flames, grabbing for the phone on the round end table.

"One Bexter Academy Drive. Emergency." I say to the 911 operator. I struggle to keep my voice calm so she can understand me. "A fire. A big fire. And we need an ambulance. Someone's hurt."

I glance at the still-motionless Ebling. Can I drag him out of here? And what about the Head? Who's still upstairs? And maybe still alive?

"Operator?"

"One Bexter Drive. I understand, ma'am. Help is on the way. Now listen to me, ma'am. Are you listening?"

"Maybe we need two ambulances," I say, ignoring her. "And the police, send the police!"

I can't help it anymore, my voice sounds thin and frantic and terrified. I'm moving toward the front door. Through the increasing smoke, I see Ebling's head lift from the floor. His eyes open, then close again. And his head drops back down.

Should I try to get him out? What about the Head? The cordless phone is still clamped to my ear, my hand clenched in a death grip around it. The dispatcher, urgent-voiced, is trying to tell me something. I know. I know the firefighters are coming. But what if it's too late for the Head? I'm through the living room arch and into the front hallway. The stairway to the second floor is right here. I could race up, outrun the fire. Get to the Head. And when the fire-fighters get here, they'll —

"Ma'am? Get out of the house. Now. Right now." The dispatcher's voice goes harsh, commanding, demanding. "Get everyone out. Now. Go."

A piercing wail suddenly comes from every corner of the darkening living room. I freeze, baffled. Until I realize it's the Head's alarm system. The one guarding his treasures.

If he's dead, the fancy alarm system won't matter. Do I go upstairs?

And then I hear the sirens. Sirens from outside. Louder and louder and louder.

"He's, he's . . . it's, it's . . ." I jab a finger toward the living room, trying to explain everything at once, not able to compete a sentence, but the four black-suited firefight-ers, one carrying a huge silver cylinder, the others hefty axes and picks, don't care about a coughing and babbling woman standing in the doorway. I flatten myself against the wall to get out of the way as heavy boots clomp down the hallway. Radio static cuts through the wail of the sirens. The four instantly take control of the fire, the living room, the now-motionless Ebling and me.

In an instant, a mist of glittering water hisses from the black hose connected to one firefighter's triple-size extinguisher. The flames sizzle in protest. The gray smoke hisses into white. Through the fire and water and smoke and steam and the sounds of the sirens and the still-howling alarm, I watch one firefighter shoulder through the chaos toward Ebling.

"He's, he's — dangerous!" I yell. I step back into the house, heading for the living room. If they can be inside, I can be inside. I need to warn them about Ebling, and show them where I kicked the gun. "And there's a gun in the —"

"You need to be outside, ma'am." A black-suited monolith in a white helmet, with breathing tank strapped to shoulders, doesn't wait for me to follow directions. He picks me up, clamping two huge gloved hands around my arms, and moves me toward the open front door in about one second.

"There's a gun in the —" I'm in midair. The phone clatters to the floor. My feet are not touching the ground. I'm still talking. There's stuff they need to know. "A gun in the living room. And there's someone upstairs. Listen! They could be in trouble. You should —"

He deposits me on the front step.

"Move away from the house, ma'am," the firefighter instructs me, pointing one gloved finger in my face. "The fire's already out. I'll check upstairs."

More sirens. More red lights. An ambulance screams up in front of 1 Bexter, a Brookline police car right behind it. Doors slam. Radios squawk. The front windows of the cottage fly open. Every motion is hyperspeed. Two EMTs, ninja-tough in black jackets stenciled Brookline EMS across the back, hoist an aluminum stretcher up the front steps, then wheel it through the open door.

"Upstairs," I call after them. "I could show you —"

But they're gone.

"Charlie McNally?" Officer Jeff Petrucelly, followed by another blue-uniformed Brookline police officer, trots up the walkway to the front porch. Last time I saw him he was interrogating Bexter faculty about the death of Alethia Espinosa. "What's going on here?"

"The Head, from Bexter," I say, grateful that someone already knows who I'm talking about and actually wants to talk to me.

I know I sound on the verge of tears. And I guess I am.

"I think the guy in the living room shot him. He's upstairs. I don't know. He might be dead. There's a gun in the living room. I kicked it under the —"

But Petrucelly and his partner, no longer listening, are already sprinting inside.

"Don't leave," Petrucelly commands over one shoulder. "Do not leave."

Suddenly, my knees are weak. I can barely stand up. I may have escaped. But Josh. Penny. Where are they? My purse, cell phone inside, is probably a pile of ashes right now.

Hanging on to the wrought-iron railing with both hands, I lower myself to sit on the bottom step of the front porch. The Head is probably dead. And Ebling is in bad shape. Were they in it together? It's terrifying, and sad, and so tragic, that a beloved pillar of the Bexter community could be twisted and corrupted by greed and desire and, I don't know, envy. Byron Forrestal is dead. Killed by a money-hungry loser who had no remorse about tormenting people over secrets from their past. And who finally turned on his own partner in crime.

I lower my head into my hands, staring in dread at the concrete walkway. What if the

Head and Ebling got to Josh and Penny? I have to go home. I have to check on them. I start to get up. But I'm trapped. The police ordered me not to leave. My locked car, parked in the driveway, is blocked in by the ambulance.

The tips of my fingers are white with cold, my rear is freezing on the concrete, and I'm grateful for my thick sweater. I pull the turtleneck collar high over my chin, then push my bare hands up under the sleeves. It's dark. Frigid. And I've never felt so alone. Or powerless. Or afraid. When I look up, I'm shocked to see stars, every constellation glittering, arrayed across the winter sky. Like nothing happened.

"Miss McNally? You said someone was upstairs?"

The voice behind me is a firefighter, wet droplets glistening on his uniform, a deputy's white helmet strapped into place. He smells of fire and smoke and water. A smear of soot crosses one ruddy cheek.

"Yes, yes, upstairs," I say. Turning, I jump to my feet, straining to the left, then to the right, trying to see what's going on behind him inside the house. The smoke is almost gone and the way is clear, but the firefighter is blocking my view.

"The Headmaster, Byron Forrestal," I say,

pointing. "He's upstairs."

The firefighter is shaking his head. No.

"No what? No, he isn't there? He has to be. I mean, he might be hurt. Maybe you didn't look . . ."

"We checked everywhere, ma'am." The deputy's voice is dryly confident, puffing into the cold. "I know Headmaster Forrestal, of course. And he's not —"

Then I see his face change. With raised eyebrows, he points a gloved hand, one canvas-covered finger directing me to turn around.

The Head. Is trotting up the front walkway.

Framed in hat and coat and scarf, his face is the picture of fear and confusion.

"What on earth? How did this start?" He looks at his house, then the firefighter, then me, then this house. His face goes bleak. Sagging with terror. "My collection?"

"It's all fine, sir, nothing badly damaged," the deputy says. "We got here in time. You'll have to replace a rug, and your living room couch and a chair. It's smoky, but nothing some ventilation won't cure. We got the vent fans going now. The EMTs are still working on Mr. Ebling, but he'll make it."

"Ebling? Why was —" The Head steps toward the front door, pointing. "I need to go inside."

"Miss McNally?" The firefighter faces me briefly, holding up a palm to stop the Head. "We saved your purse, but your coat's a goner. Sir? You can come inside in a minute or so. After the EMTs leave."

The deputy turns on his heel, saying something into his squawking shoulder radio, and heads back into the house.

I couldn't be more confused.

"Ebling told me you were upstairs." I ping-pong my gaze between the Head and the house, reconciling actual reality with Ebling's concocted version. The third murder — was me. He was going to try to frame the Head for my death. But how?

Suddenly, I get it. When the Head got home, I'd already be shot dead on the rug, killed with the Head's pistol. Ebling would kill the Head, then pretend to find us both. He'd say I'd uncovered the Head's scheme and confronted him. He'd killed me, and then himself. It could have worked.

But the Head doesn't know about that part yet.

"Ebling? Told you?" The Head is answering me, shaking his head. "Preposterous. Of course I wasn't here. It's Bexter board meeting night. I was at the school. Your Josh was there, didn't you know? Ebling knew that. You can't be two places at once, you know."

Josh is okay. I begin to breathe again.

"Do you know where Penny is? Don't those board meetings usually last until midnight or so?" The words tumble out. "Why are you home now?"

"Senior prank," the Head replies. "We all had to leave the building. Seems the seniors spread mashed-potato flakes across the floor of Main lobby. They hid and waited until Mr. Parker tried to mop them up. Your Penny was there, too. Watching with Annie Vilardi as the lobby turned to potato soup."

He takes a few steps toward his front door, then turns back to me.

"You and Josh might want to have a little chat with her about it. After they finish helping with the cleanup. It's pretty unpleasant."

I'm speechless. And on the verge of laughing. Until I think about the body in front of the fireplace. The one who might have been me.

I hit the snooze button, curling up against my pillow, getting ready to savor the next eight sweetly stolen minutes before today's chaos begins. Botox purrs and cuddles up closer. I smile and sigh with my eyes closed, going over the whole thing once again, a long, confusing, frightening night ending with Ebling in jail and Penny in the doghouse. I think Josh grounded her for the next twenty-five years. Ebling's sentence is probably going to be longer.

I flip over, ousting a protesting Botox from her nest behind my knees, and mentally chew over the one journalistically annoying element in all this. I can't do the Bexter extortion and murder story for Channel 3, since the same person can't be a witness to a crime and the reporter on the same story. So Liz Whittemore, who showed up at the Head's house as the emergency crews were all wrapping up, gets a big break. Courtesy of me.

I'll help her, of course. And I guess I'll be interviewed today about it. Weird to be on the other end of the microphone. And weirder to watch it on TV.

Eyes still closed, I reach out a hand to touch Josh. He's not here. Probably in the bathroom. I have about four more minutes. I nestle in again, holding on to peace. I'll go to the office, help Liz with the Bexter story.

Then Franklin and I will figure out how to approach Loudon Fielder.

"Sweets? You awake?"

I feel Josh standing by the bed, his presence altering the darkness behind my closed eyelids.

"Yes," I say, because it's true. And there's only three minutes until the alarm rings. My eyes struggle to open and through my still-fuzzy vision, I see Josh holding a cup of what I hope is coffee in one hand and a newspaper in the other. Caffeine and news. Makes it much easier to wake up after a rough night of almost getting murdered.

I ease upright, scooting my rear against the pillows and reaching out to Josh. He hands me the ceramic mug, and kisses me on the top of my head. He sits on the edge of the bed, still holding the newspaper, as I take my first delicious sip.

"Mmm," I say. "This is perfect. A good day to be alive."

"Sweets?" Josh says. "You might want to look at the paper."

"The — ?"

He takes my mug and hands me the folded *Boston Globe.* I open to the front page.

The story is on the left, one column, below the fold.

Radio Mogul Dead.

I look at Josh. My brain races to makes sense of it. "How — ?"

"Read it. Apparently the police . . ."

But I'm not listening to him anymore. I'm reading. Fast as I can.

The story is certainly surprising and definitely big news. But our story, even bigger, is safe. The *Globe* doesn't have anything about car cloning, or air-bag theft, or valet parking, or the radio show. Even so, the paper's last paragraph is a shocker.

"A massive stroke when the cops went to question him," I say to Franklin, waving the paper at him as I walk into our office. I called him this morning at the same moment he called me. Of course.

"I called Zavala, of course," I continue, taking off my coat and tossing it on my chair. "He told me No-Hat — whose name really is Doug Skith, astonishingly — ratted Fielder out in about thirty seconds. He gave up Taylor and Tyler, too. Now Zavala says the talk-show morons and No-Hat are battling it out with the district attorney to see who can turn state's evidence faster."

"Police came to Fielder's door? And he just confessed?" Franklin asks.

"Well, no. He kept demanding a lawyer. Upset. Yelling at the cops," I reply. "According to Zavala. He found out the rest from Skith and the *Drive Time* boys. Apparently Fielder was out of money. Radio station revenues tanking, fewer people using valet parking. So he decided to reorganize his resources. Took cars from one of his businesses, cloned them at another —"

"The Beacon Trust owned the Newtonville garage, too?"

"Yup. According to Zavala." I nod. "He sold the air bags on the black market. Big bucks. And then sold the stolen cloned cars via the radio show. Even bigger bucks. Oh, and guess what? The stolen blue Mustang? The one No-Hat tried to sell me? No-Hat told them it was stolen from Randall Kindell's rental lot. It was the car I saw on the lift."

"So Fielder's implicated to the hilt." Franklin's multi-tasking, of course, sorting his mail as we talk. He tosses a manila envelope into the wastebasket and places another envelope in a growing stack on his desk. He picks up his letter opener.

"Yup. Zavala told me it was No-Hat Doug Skith and his thug buddies who ruined the operation. Crashing the Mustang into Declan Ross, that's one thing. But killing Borum? Carjackings? Fielder never authorized anything like that. Still, it was his setup. As they handcuffed him to take him to the police station, he collapsed."

I tap my pen on the *Boston Globe,* now

spread out on my desk. "But all the paper has, thanks to my beloved Lieutenant Zavala, is Fielder questioned about some undisclosed financial scheme, dies of a stroke, his wife mourns the tragedy."

And there's the shocker. I read, for the millionth time, the last lines of the brief *Boston Globe* article.

The radio mogul's wife, Alice Hogarth Fielder, told a reporter she was bewildered by the developments. According to sources, she is now in seclusion.

I don't need the now-burned Bexter report to confirm that Harrison Ebling had also circled Alice Hogarth's name. That means she was probably being blackmailed, too. Did she give up a baby? Did she ever tell her husband? Did she pay extortion money? Did he?

Out of the corner of my ear I hear paper ripping. And then unfolding. And then I hear Franklin catch his breath.

"What?" I say. Fleetingly, a selfishly unworthy thought flickers through my mind. Maybe the New York deal is off.

"In a plain envelope," he says, holding up a white piece of paper. It looks like a photocopy of a photo. "It's a picture of Michael —"

"Borum's blue Mustang." I finish the sentence. "David Chernin at the Mass Turnpike offices must have sent it to us."

"Not that it matters now." Franklin folds the photo back into the envelope. "That car's a crispy critter."

I think back about Michael Borum, an everyday guy who did an everyday thing. Tossed the keys to his car to a valet parker and expected it to be returned after dinner. But Michael Borum gave his car to the wrong valet at the wrong time. And got killed for it.

"No, it's still important," I say. "Because this photo proves his car was not where it was supposed to be. Can you believe it? After all that, turns out Michael Borum is helping us."

CHAPTER TWENTY-EIGHT

I push the black button that connects me, electronically, with Liz Whittemore. I'm surrounded by flashing monitors and muttering technicians in the bustle and squawk of ENG Receive. Liz is across town, outside on the snowy common in front of Main Hall, ready to front her first live shot about the Bexter murder and extortion. J.T.'s with her, shooting it all, since there's no reason for him not to be part of it. Suddenly, someone flips on the portable light in front of her. Liz's red Channel 3 parka pops against the white snow and the lofty evergreens. I lean closer to the silver microphone.

"Congratulations, girl," I tell her. "Just give me credit when you pick up your Emmy."

I see Liz put a gloved hand to her ear, holding in her earpiece as she listens to me. She smiles, though she can't see me, and gives a thumbs-up to the camera.

"Your story's on next week, Charlie," she says into her microphone. "It'll blow this one out of the water."

Secretly, I hope she's right. But that I don't say.

"Private School, Private Lives." The too-sensational-for-my-taste black-and-red graphic suddenly appears in several monitors as the bright green numbers of the digital clocks tick toward the six o'clock news. The thumping drive of the electronic news theme fills the room.

ENG Joanna nudges me out of the way and leans into the mic.

"Fifteen seconds, Liz," she says.

Liz nods, her lips pressed together. She's nervous. My own heart races in reporter empathy, remembering the feeling. Being the new kid. The pressure of a first big story. A career maker. Or breaker. The anchor has begun the introduction to the story, but there's still time for me to give Liz one more bit of encouragement. I reach for the mic button. And then I see Liz change. Her head comes up, her eyes sparkle, she radiates confidence. She doesn't need me.

"Go for it," I whisper.

Even though I know the story much better than Liz does, it's still a blockbuster.

"Police say Harrison Ebling, now in custody, murdered two prominent and beloved faculty members at Brookline's privileged and respected Bexter Academy because they discovered his blackmail-and-extortion scheme. Officials are charging he killed Dorothy Wirt with her own sleeping pills and carbon monoxide, attempting to make it look like an accident. They say he killed Alethia Espinosa by pushing her down a steep set of ice-covered stairs."

I know the rest. I barely listen as Liz voices over the mug shot of Ebling, BEX photos of Dorothy and Alethia, and exteriors of the Bexter campus, carefully selected so they don't reveal the faces of any students. I know police found at least some of Ebling's stash. Now safely protected evidence, the D.A.'s office confiscated the confidential files he copied and stole from The Services. Channel 3 lawyers, panicked by potential lawsuits and fearing expensive liability, absolutely refused to let Liz mention any of the victims' names on television.

The journalist in me is outraged. It's the public's right to know exactly what happened. The other part of me is relieved. It won't help anyone to know about Alice Hogarth or Fiona Dulles or Randall Kindell. Their secret past can remain a secret.

I smile, thinking about the rental-car king. After checking his entire fleet for recalls and missing air bags, he began spearheading a national campaign to clean up his industry. What's more, police finally confirmed Annie's car had indeed been stolen. And Kindell, grateful that I'd kept his secret, gave her an Ombra from his fleet to replace it. He also called Declan Ross's insurance company, wiped the incident off his policy and got his money refunded.

"There's you!" ENG Joanna pokes me in the ribs, jabbing me out of my reverie. "You look hot, sister."

I almost missed my part of Liz Whittemore's story. I know it says — because I wrote it — "Channel 3's Charlie McNally broke this case wide open, confronting and outwitting the alleged killer as he threatened to make her his next victim."

Now I'm seeing myself, in high definition, wearing my crimson blazer, black turtleneck and trademark red lipstick, and showing almost no grayish-brown roots. The lighting works. I catch just the tail end of my sound bite.

"Bexter officials have assured me they are replacing all the money frightened parents paid to the disgraced Harrison Ebling. What's more, Liz, The Services executive director, Joan Covino, told me she's certain no other information was taken from her organization's files."

I burst out laughing.

"What?" Joanna says. "You're great."

"Private joke," I say, waving her off. I've just realized. I'm talking on television. And standing here in ENG Receive. I'm officially in two places at one time.

"Franklin, come on. Smile. You, too, Charlie," Maysie calls out. Her face is hidden behind her camera viewfinder, but her voice sounds upbeat.

Franklin and I are standing arm in arm, posing for photos, unintentionally dressed alike in black down vests, big turtlenecks and striped scarves. My scarf is new, the old one having met its fiery, alcohol-soaked demise a few weeks ago in the Head's living room. We're on the front steps of Josh's house. Our house. The movers are still packing up my condo. What used to be my condo. According to the closing documents, starting tomorrow it will belong to ENG Joanna and J. T. Shaw. Who, we all finally discovered, had some secrets of their own.

It's not the best time to take a picture of Franklin and me. My eyes are puffy from crying. Franklin's eyes are red, too, though he insists it's from too much champagne. But it's the last time we'll all be together like this.

"Come on, say cheese. Or say something. You guys look like you're losing your best friends." Maysie takes the camera down from in front of her face. I can see she's on the verge of tears, too. "I guess that's the problem, huh? You really are."

"Cheese," Franklin says. His voice is quiet. And glum. And almost a whisper.

"Cheese," I say at exactly the same time. My "cheese" comes out sounding like good-bye.

Baby Maddee, swaddled in a thick yellow blanket and cradled in Penny's arms, chooses that very instant to burst into a howling wail.

Which makes all the rest of us — except for a bewildered Penny — explode into laughter.

"Got it!" Maysie says as the camera flashes.

"Come on, you all," Josh says. "This is not the end. It's a beginning, right?"

Franklin and I look at each other. Uncertain and unhappy.

"Drive time to New York is what, maybe four hours?" Josh steps behind us, throwing his arms around our shoulders. "You two will see each other all the time. And Franklin will be back for the wedding, of course."

Maysie's camera flashes again.

"Good one!" Maysie calls out. "Now, Penny, you and Maddee get in the picture."

Penny's almost-too-big pink plaid boots clunk up the two steps. She stands in front of us. Maddee is snuffling, but her crying has stopped.

"I suppose Josh is right," I say reluctantly. I'm still looking at the camera. Which is easier than looking at my dear Franklin. Stephen will be here any minute to pick him up. Then he'll be off to the rest of his life. And so will I. Just the way it's supposed to work.

"Smile!" Maysie commands. And the camera flashes.

"We'll be doing the 'open recalls in rental cars' story together for the network, right?" Franklin says. His arm goes tighter across my shoulders. I can't tell if he's looking at me, because I still can't face him.

"Now one of Charlie and Franklin," Maysie yells. "Josh, Penny, stand over by the car."

"Kevin says since you broke it, you should be our Boston correspondent," Franklin continues. "So we'll still be a team, Charlotte."

493

That does it.

"No one else —" I can barely get the words out, and I bury my face in Franklin's black nylon shoulder. "No one else . . . calls me Charlotte. And now you're leaving."

Franklin's arms go around me, tight. I realize he's never really hugged me before. I can feel my tears arrive, unstoppable, and I let them come. We've conquered broken equipment and absurd deadlines, pursued obstinate sources and impossible stories. We've read each other's minds. We've changed laws and changed lives. And both of us almost got killed doing it.

We've learned to trust each other. We've learned to love each other. And now, it's come to an end.

"Honey?" I feel Josh touch me on the shoulder. "Stephen's here. Franklin has to go."

I wipe my eyes, blotching my red leather gloves, and reluctantly pull away.

"I'll miss you, Franko," I say. I blink, feeling the tears clinging to my eyelashes, and try for a watery smile. "Can I have your Rolodex?"

Josh holds out a hand to Franklin, then changes his mind. He wraps Franklin in a bear hug, just for a second.

"Thanks for taking care of her," he says.

"She took care of me," Franklin says.

"Smile!" Maysie says.

And as we all turn toward her, the camera flashes one final time.

"That's the last box, ma'am." A jumpsuited Hercules, one of the Dan's Vans burly, bulked-up moving crew, waves a muscled arm toward Josh's front door.

Our front door, I correct myself again. I've spent the last three hours directing traffic, watching brown corrugated boxes filled with my life's accumulations carried out of a silver moving van and into my new life. Franklin left yesterday. Now, stationed on Josh's front porch — our front porch — it seems the last of my transformation to suburban bride-to-be is almost complete.

"It's all inside? Nothing left in the truck?"

"Yes, ma'am. No, ma'am. We put the boxes where you marked 'em." He looks me up and down, taking in the ripped knees of my jeans and the cutoff sleeves of my fraying Bexter sweatshirt.

"The closet and bedroom are pretty full. You're gonna have to get rid of some of those clothes boxes before you can get in the room. I'll get the guys. And we're out of here."

He dusts his hands on the rear of his

jumpsuit, then heads back inside.

"So that's that," I say out loud.

"What's what?" Josh, smiling, comes through the open door. "You talking to yourself again?"

"Get used to it," I say. "One of my many deep secrets you have not yet learned."

Josh stands behind me, his body pressed against mine, his chin resting on the top of my head. "I know all I need to know about you," he whispers.

We're silent for a moment, looking through the open door. Penny scampers by, then Botox, tail held high, pretending she's not following her.

"The movers are done," I say, leaning into Josh. I can feel his heart beating, his breath in my hair. "I'm all yours, Professor Gelston. There's nothing else to lug inside."

"That's where you're wrong," Josh says.

I turn to face him. "Wrong?"

"Absolutely wrong," he says. "There's definitely one more thing that needs to go inside."

I feel my feet leave the ground as I'm scooped into his arms.

"You," he says. And we step across the threshold.

EPILOGUE

"There she is. Middle of the back row. She's gotten so tall!"

I point to Penny, who's jockeying with her classmates for position on the steep steps of Main Hall. The Bexter photographer has finally arranged the fourth graders in some semblance of order. After a few false starts resulting from two-fingered rabbit ears, funny faces and a whole row of tongues sticking out, Penny's first BEX photo is on the verge of taking its place in Bexter history.

"She did so well this year," Josh says. "I wasn't quite sure how she would handle it. A new school in the middle of the year. You. Being away from her mother for the first time. But look at her. She's a happy girl."

Penny's laughing, then whispering something behind her hand, into the ear of the little girl next to her. In one motion, they both throw a kiss, big drama, then dissolve into giggles.

"I'm happy, too," I say.

The photographer comes out from behind her camera, long blond ponytail swinging, hands on hips. "Listen. No kissing. No funny faces. This is the BEX. You can deal with me. Or I'm going for the Head."

The fourth graders go silent. The photographer goes back to her camera.

Awards Day at Bexter. Josh and I are arm in arm, in Bexter sweatshirts and blue jeans and Red Sox caps, standing in a crowd of parents all watching the rambunctious students and reveling in the April sunshine.

"Charlie?"

I feel a tap on my shoulder. There are Wen and Fiona Dulles. Holding hands.

"We're waiting for Tal's and Lexie's photos," Wen says, gesturing toward the steps. "But we wanted to tell you —"

He stops, and looks down at his wife. "Go ahead, honey," he says.

I almost can picture them thirty years younger. In love and with the whole world ahead of them.

"I told Wen about my daughter," Fee says. She puts one hand on my arm, clutching hard. "And now, Joan Covino is helping us contact her. We're thinking, we'll let her know we'd like to meet her. Let her decide what she wants. If she wants. You know? Thank you, Charlie. For giving me back my heart."

"I — well, that's lovely," I say. "But I'm not sure it was me who —"

"Thanks, Charlie," Wen interrupts. His voice is still gruff, but his eyes are soft. "You certainly know how to keep a secret."

"He's right," Josh whispers as the couple walks away. "But no more secrets, right?"

The daffodils are already in full golden bloom. The legendary Bexter tulips, hundreds of them, are beginning to reveal their colors. In a few weeks, the campus gardens will be bursting and glorious. The birds are back, noisily, and the trees are green again. It was a scary winter. And now all that is over.

I've promised myself I won't spend one moment of this day worrying about my sweeps story for May. The newly hired news director assures me she's "green-light-go" for my investigation into Boston's burgeoning movie industry. But I'm not so sure. And my new producer, Franklin's replacement, finally arrives next week. I okayed the hire. But I'm not so sure. Still, I'm not going to spend one moment of this Saturday worrying about that.

Or about the wedding. Or about the dress

photos and invitation designs Mom keeps sending. Miss Tolliver is now on my speed dial.

"Charlie Mac!" Penny's trotting toward us, plaid skirt swinging, carrying something in both hands. A present? A small flat box, white, and tied with a thin white ribbon. She hands it to me. "I'm supposed to give this to you. It's from that lady." Penny turns, pointing.

"What lady? A Bexter lady?" I say, following Penny's finger. "I don't see anyone."

"She's gone, I guess," Penny says. Unconcerned. She grabs Josh's hand, tugging. "Come on, Daddo. Time for the teachers' picture. You need to get in the front."

"Be right back," Josh says, following his daughter. Our daughter. "Duty calls."

I pull one end of the white ribbon, then lift the lid from the box. I look around again, wondering what "lady" gave it to Penny. And why. But there's no one.

Inside, a fold of white tissue paper. On top of that, a tiny white enclosure card. I lift the stiff paper, reading the message, written in careful script and in black ink.

Thank you for what you've done for Bexter, and for Dorothy. I trust she'd want you to understand. Because you know how to keep a secret. Look in the back. With gratitude, Mildred Wirt.

Look in the back? I turn the card over, but the back is blank.

I lift one side of the tissue paper, then the other. Inside is a photograph in a sterling-silver frame. I lift the photograph from the box. It's an infant, a tiny baby, wrapped in some kind of blanket, face almost covered.

I know this baby. This looks like a copy of one of the photographs I saw on Dorothy's desk, in her study, the day I found the fund-raising report.

Look in the back?

Putting the box on the grass, I turn the photo over, and slide the frayed velvet backing from the frame. Underneath is a folded piece of paper.

I look up again, searching for Millie. But there's only throngs of kids and masses of daffodils and Bexter's historic campus.

I unfold the paper. It's also a copy, lined with creases, and the lettering is fading. It's a birth certificate, typed on an old typewriter. The heading says "The Services."

The date is 1950.

Mother's name: Dorothy Wirt. Father's name: Not given. Child's name: TBA.

I stare at the paper. The puzzle pieces of

501

three lives, no, many more than three, re-arrange and shuffle and settle into tragedy. Love and mistakes, loss and revenge. And secrets.

Standing in the sun, possibly in the same blossoming garden young Dorothy might have enjoyed so many years ago, I slowly refold the paper. I tuck it in against the photo. And slide the velvet backing back into place.

I hold the photo close. Like a baby.

"I'll keep your secret, Dorothy," I whisper. "I know you'd want me to."

ACKNOWLEDGMENTS

Unending gratitude to:

Ann Leslie Tuttle, my brilliant, wise and gracious editor; Charles Griemsman, patient and droll, king of deadlines. To the remarkable team at MIRA, Tara Gavin, Margaret O'Neill Marbury and Valerie Gray. The inspirational Donna Hayes. Your unerring judgment and unfailing support make this an extraordinary experience.

Kristin Nelson, the most remarkable agent and friend.

Francesca Coltrera, my astonishingly skilled independent editor, who lets me believe all the good ideas are mine.

The artistry and savvy of Madeira James, Charlie Anctil, Judy Spagnola, Patrick O'Malley, Jeanne Devlin and Nancy Berland.

The firefighters at the Newton Fire Department. The savvy mechanics, including Howard Tarnower, at the Pretty Good Garage. The experts at Carfax. The expertise, guidance and friendship of Dr. D. P. Lyle and Lee Lofland.

The inspiration of David Morrell, Mary Jane Clark, Jim Huang, Marianne Mancusi, Suzanne Brockmann, Carla Neggers, Gayle Lynds, Liz Berry and Sue Grafton.

The posse at Sisters in Crime and Mystery Writers of America.

My amazing blog sisters. At Jungle Red Writers: Jan Brogan, Hallie Ephron, Roberta Isleib, Rosemary Harris and Rhys Bowen. At Femmes Fatales: Charlaine Harris, Dana Cameron, Kris Neri, Mary Saums, Toni Kelner and Donna Andrews.

My dear friends Amy Isaac, Mary Schwager and Katherine Hall Page; and my darling sister Nancy Landman.

Mom — Mrs. McNally is not you, except for the wonderful parts. Dad — who loves every moment of this.

And of course Jonathan, who never complained about all the pizza.

http://www.hankphillippiryan.com
http://www.jungleredwriters.com
http://www.femmesfatales.typepad.com

ABOUT THE AUTHOR

Award-winning investigative reporter **Hank Phillippi Ryan** is on the air at Boston's NBC affiliate. Her work has resulted in new laws, people sent to prison, homes removed from foreclosure and millions of dollars in restitution. Along with her 26 Emmys and 10 Edward R. Murrow Awards, Hank has won dozens of other regional, national and international journalism honors for her hard-hitting investigations. Hank began her television career reporting and anchoring the news in Indianapolis and Atlanta. She's also worked as a proofreader, a radio reporter and a legislative aide in the United States Senate, and in a two-year stint as editorial assistant at *Rolling Stone* magazine, helped organize presidential campaign coverage for Hunter S. Thompson. Her debut novel, *Prime Time,* won the prestigious Agatha Award. She and her husband live just outside Boston.

www.HankPhillippiRyan.com

The employees of Thorndike Press hope you have enjoyed this Large Print book. All our Thorndike, Wheeler, and Kennebec Large Print titles are designed for easy reading, and all our books are made to last. Other Thorndike Press Large Print books are available at your library, through selected bookstores, or directly from us.

For information about titles, please call:
  (800) 223-1244

or visit our Web site at:
  http://gale.cengage.com/thorndike

To share your comments, please write:
  Publisher
  Thorndike Press
  295 Kennedy Memorial Drive
  Waterville, ME 04901